CRYING BLOOD

The Cuban Project

Enjoy!

Rube Wardell
Oct 2005

Copyright 2005 Donald R. Waddell

All rights reserved. No part of this publication may be reproduced, stored in a retrieval system, or transmitted in any form or by any means, electronic, mechanical, recording, or otherwise without prior written consent of the author.

ISBN 0-9772048-1-2

Library of Congress Control Number. 2005907594

This book is a work of fiction. Names, characters, places and events are either the product of the author's imagination or are used fictitiously. Any resemblance to actual persons living or dead, business establishments, events, locales is entirely coincidental

Printed in the United States of America.

Lexis Publishers 2005

Cover design: Ron Johnson of Value Print, Inc.

CRYING BLOOD

The Cuban Project

Donald R. Waddell, Col. USAF Ret

OTHER BOOKS BY AUTHOR

"Forget Me! Not!"

"Twisted Justice"

FOREWORD

Operation Homecoming brought back into U.S. Custody 591 men. A majority of those spent in excess of six years in the POW camps in Hanoi. The tales they brought to light on their return made us all weep at the horror some endured. In addition to that total, another 113 men were captured who subsequently died in captivity. To this day 44 of those captured who died in captivity, have not been accounted for nor have their remains been returned to their loved ones. A Cuban Project was identified and blamed for some these deaths.

Interrogators from Cuba were sent to North Vietnam as trainers for the Peoples Army of North Vietnam. These trainers were to display their methods of gathering information and re-educating imprisoned dissidents in the new Post Revolutionary Cuba. Three of these trainer/interrogators from Cuba were instrumental in the deaths of American Prisoners of War.

Repatriated POWs upon their return declared their extreme hatred for these three Cuban Nationals. To this day none of the three have been positively identified by the U.S. Government. The DIA, the CIA, and the FBI joined forces to make this proper identification but to no avail.

This book, *Crying Blood*, is a work of fiction, exploring the possibilities as to how these three Cubans might have been found. These acts of torture, mayhem, and physical disfigurations inflicted by three Cubans were truly War Crimes that have never been pursued. The names *Fidel* and *The Bug* were taken from official documents, books, and articles. Using those names seemed appropriate. All other names are fictional.

I was a pilot with The United States Air Force and went through Escape and Evasion, Survival Training, and lectures on the Code of Conduct. Nothing would have prepared me for what those 591 returnees faced during their incarceration. It is doubtful in my mind that I could have survived with such honor and dignity.

Many times we challenge ourselves to see just how strong our character might be. After reading and truly absorbing the contents of the book, *Honor Bound*, by Stuart I. Rochester and Frederick Kiley, I still wonder if I am made of the right stuff those men possessed.

There is a quote I have remembered for a long time and I am uncertain of its origin or of its true wording. The essence is this; "A hero is an ordinary person who, when faced with an extraordinary situation requiring extraordinary measures and extraordinary sacrifice, directly accepts the challenge with personal sacrifice and honor". This quote well describes those 591 men who returned during *Operation Homecoming* and the 113 others who gave the ultimate sacrifice.

By Donald 'Rube' Waddell

AUTHOR'S NOTES

This work is a novel. Any similarity to actual persons or events is purely coincidental. What isn't coincidental is the use of the names *Fidel* and *The Bug*.

I have done a vast amount of reading about our POWs languishing away in prison camps in North Vietnam. Camps with names like Plantation, The Zoo, The Hilton, Little Vegas, Briarpatch, Dirty Bird, Alcatraz and numerous others. I was struck by the proclivity of the American fighting man to make something acceptable and even humorous out of the worst possible conditions. That spirit was most evident in the book, *Honor Bound*, by Stuart I. Rochester and Frederick Kiley. I was compelled to use the names of *Fidel* and *The Bug* which I found in nearly every reference document. I wanted to locate someone in some document who might have originally coined these names and attribute the names to them. If that person is out there, let me apologize for using those names without attribution. Those two names were critical to this novel and were used throughout the work. It made the work come to life and for that I am grateful.

I interviewed four individuals with knowledge of past and present day Cuba. Two of the individuals were Cuban born and two were visiting tourists. I hope I have fairly displayed their comments and visions. Names and locations in Cuba were used freely to provide authenticity to this work.

CHAPTER I

"Penny, are you awake"? He spoke softly, gazing down into the night through the upstairs bedroom window. The amber security light on a utility pole in the garage area lit up his face.

"Penny...Penny." He raised his voice as he turned toward the bed. "Penny, are you awake"? His voice louder, more determined to get an answer.

"Well, I am now." She spoke with disdain at being forced out of a perfect sleep. Her body, immobile from a paralytic sleep, began to move slowly under the sheets. Her sluggish fingers found the right temple and she subconsciously scratched at her hairline, bringing life back into her sleep filled body. It was never easy for Penny to awaken; being pulled from a sound sleep made it even more difficult.

"I need to talk." Jay spoke quietly, trying not to further injure his wife's wakening moments. Most of the window was filled with his 6-foot frame and broad shoulders shutting out the light from the security pole.

Penny raised herself with an elbow digging into the plush mattress. With half opened eyes she squinted toward Jay. Her body was awake but her mind was yet to absorb the moment. Resting on one elbow, she looked toward Jay who remained in a fixed stare out the darkened window. Penny peered at him for a moment, then turned toward the clock on the nightstand. Glaring in digital red letters was the time, 2:35 a.m. Her squint became more pronounced. Her head dropped as if to say 'what now'? She pushed soft blond tresses away from her face. The astonishment on her face became more dramatic.

She pouted a complaining thought, "What is it?"

"I'm going to Cuba."

"You're what?" She didn't comprehend, her thoughts still muddled.

"I am going to Cuba!"

Now Jay had her full attention. Penny sat up, placed both hands over her eyes and after a gentle rubbing, responded, "What are you talking about? Why are you going to Cuba?" After having her sleep invaded, she needed a good answer. Her brow wrinkled automatically as she squinted through half opened eyes.

"I am going to find my father's killer." He spoke with conviction.

"You're what?" Penny recoiled upward. She reached toward the nightstand, fumbling for the lamp switch. She flinched against the sudden glare. Turning back toward Jay, she searched his face for explanations. This was unbelievable!

She spoke in disbelief, "You've got to be kidding! She stared through him. "You are going to Cuba to do what?" She imagined a misstatement from her husband of four years. She sat straight up in bed. Pulling both legs to her chest, she encircled them with her arms and leaned forward. Penny, with soft blond naturally curly hair, buttermilk white skin, and pinkish cheeks, was a wife Jay was proud to call his. His family joke was to refer to her as his 'trophy wife'.

"I don't know what!" He shrugged his shoulders. It was obvious he hadn't thought this through. "I feel compelled to find my father's killer. Since my mother and I returned from our trip to Washington, I've been obsessed with the thought that a Cuban national killed my father in North Vietnam."

"Did they tell you that in Washington?" She threw the question. "That a Cuban killed your father?"

He reluctantly offered, "No!" Penny's questioning was expected. Jay just wanted to talk to someone who might understand. Talking this over with his mother was out of the question. It would upset her and she would be negative about the entire thinking. He walked away from the window toward the bed, and sat beside Penny. The bed sagged under his 210 lb. weight. His mind, wrestling with disturbing thoughts had kept him awake all night. He had to talk.

"Then I don't understand." She looked deep into his eyes, penetrating straight into his brain. "I know you haven't slept well since you returned and you've been forgetful. You don't talk to me. We sit through our meals like we are strangers." She used both hands to push her hair behind her ears. "This thing you have, what brought it about? I knew when you returned something was wrong. You weren't yourself. You were too quiet. I knew something was bugging you. I asked you several times what was on your mind and you merely shrugged your shoulders."

"It wasn't just the trip, although the trip certainly had the most to do with it." He paused before continuing, "It's a culmination of things...the retracing of past events...the suspected cover-up...the idea that my own government tried to keep information from my mother and me about my father...this whole thing is growing into a nightmare all over again, much more than it ever was in the past." Jay looked for understanding in Penny's eyes, hoping for acceptance. He knew beyond all doubt she would be confused and shocked. He needed for her to understand. He tried desperately to read some acceptance in her eyes.

Penny was overwhelmingly blank; she was dumbfounded, not comprehending his thoughts. Still held hostage to midsleep arousal, all she could do was question his thinking.

She offered a solution. "If you'll wait just a little, I need to use the bathroom. After that why don't we go downstairs to the kitchen, put on some coffee and finish this conversation?"

Jay found her remarks to be right on target. He wanted nothing more than to talk. He needed feedback. It was important to know if Penny thought he was crazy. He had to tell her everything before he could respect her verdict. He raised himself slowly from the bed. His harried expression spoke louder than words, he was disturbed and in mental anguish.

Jay's father had been thoughtfully responsible for making certain arrangements before leaving on his tour in South East Asia. When he first received notification for training into the F-105F with subsequent duty in Thailand, he immediately made permanent plans for his family. He went to Tulsa to sell the mineral rights to his family's 320-acre homestead, 30 miles north of Claremore, Oklahoma. He negotiated for a price that allowed a per barrel royalty on all future production. He used the money to build a home for his wife Marcie and their two children, Jay Jr. and Melanie. Marcie had made it into a perfect home. A brick and stone structure with two floors. The upper floor had three bedrooms and three separate baths while the lower floor housed the living quarters, the master bedroom, bath and a huge kitchen. Since they lived thirty miles from the nearest grocery, he knew a big kitchen with lots of storage space was needed. The kitchen area should have had more warmth built in. It was all white tile and stainless steel giving it an institutional look. Functionally complete but missing the hominess; a chef would have thought it was ideal. A wife would only accept its functionality. Otherwise, the home was well planned.

He chose a building site about half way up a five hundred foot hill in the western Ozarks overlooking the Tallaha Creek. There were duplicate surrounding porches at both levels with access doors from all bedrooms. The same as most plantation homes of the 1800s. Jay's father completed the house before he left to make certain his family had a home if something happened.

Since going into the Air Force immediately after college, Jay's family had never owned a home. Now they did! Jay's sister Melanie, married early and moved away with her husband. Jay Jr. dutifully stayed with his Mom after college. When he married Penny, it was understood they would move in with his mother. Jay's Mom lived downstairs and the upstairs became Penny's and Jay's domain. One upstairs bedroom was converted into an all purpose room to complete their apartment. It included a small sink, a microwave unit, a small under the counter refrigerator and countertops for utility. This home had all the assets his father dreamed of having for his family.

Jay's father had said many times in the past that the physical body and the body spirit were separate. The body spirit needed nourishment just as the body needed food. The view from the upper porch was added with this in mind. The view of the sights and sounds of nature and the falling waters of the creek were food for the spirit. On his final leave before departing for South East Asia, Jay's Dad sat in one of the many green painted rockers on the upper porch and drank in the serenity. He remarked that looking down at the Tallaha Creek coursing gently under the oak trees toward Lake Oolagah, caressed the mind and soul.

In the years of the Nixon administration, there was a cry for oil exploration to increase supply and the Cobbs were the beneficiaries of those efforts. Jay's Dad had sold the mineral rights to the land in the 1960's. It wasn't until 1974 that oil exploration on their property took place. Since then the Cobb family had benefited from the thirty-barrel's a day oil production from each of four wells sunk on their three hundred and twenty acres. They were very comfortable for the future. The home they built was typical of oil field wealth throughout Oklahoma.

As Penny returned from the bathroom, both Penny and Jay collected themselves, donned their robes and went quietly downstairs to the kitchen trying not to awaken Jay's Mom. No words were spoken. Penny mentally preparing questions, and Jay preparing answers. The coffee maker, prepared the night before was switched on. Both sat opposite each other at the table, each waiting for the other to break the silence.

Penny seized the moment. "Is this about what went on in Washington?" She waited for an answer. Jay nodded his head. "Is this why you've been wearing that medal around your neck, since you came back?" Jay again nodded his head.

He thought the better of his silent response. "Well...Yes it is...in a way." His mind was churning. "It does have something to do with Washington, ...and yes, it does have something to do with why I am wearing this medal." He pulled the necklace out of his nightshirt. It was a pewter image of the Indian Thunderbird. He began to finger it thoughtfully. Oklahoman Indian soldiers of the Second World War wore the same symbol as their shoulder patch, a golden Thunderbird on a field of red. His Grandfather Matthew Jayhawk Cobb fought with the Forty-Fifth Infantry Division in the Italian campaign and wore the patch proudly. The Golden Thunderbird was a highly respected Indian symbol of tradition and heritage. Jay's Father, E.J. Cobb, always wore the Thunderbird around his neck for 'Good Luck', especially when the going got tough. When his father arrived in Thailand, he had two identical pewter Thunderbird medals custom made with their initials engraved on the back. He sent one home for his son.

Jay continued to finger the pewter image as he spoke and would occasionally rub it against his lower chin area fondly. He was deep in thought about his father. This small one inch size image symbolized their Indian heritage and reminded him of his father. It helped him to be closer.

"So tell me, what's going on. I've known something was bugging you. Since returning from Washington your mind has been somewhere else. "So!" She made a long pause and smiled as she spoke. "Tell me what's been taking you away from me. I want you back."

Jay was reluctant to speak. He wanted to tell her everything; he just didn't know. His thoughts went back to when he was seven years old when he and his father had all the good times he remembered the most. He knew bringing her into the picture was going to be difficult. They had been married for only four years and hadn't talked much about his past. He wasn't certain she would even begin to understand.

Jay's family was true descendants of the Cherokee Indians. As he matured, he began to feel more of his heritage than he had shown in the past. Penny was from white Irish descendants and well accepted in the Country Club Society in Claremore. Jay had always tried to fit into her life rather than hers into his. He knew this was going to be difficult to explain. His anguish caused him to bury his face in his hands and then massage his head vigorously, looking for just the right starting point. He couldn't find one because of his confusion. His thoughts ran deep into the past and of the trail of tears.

Jay had a print of the famous "Trail of Tears" painting by Robert Lindneux given to him by his Grandfather which was hanging in the hallway. Viewing the painting was always a religious experience to Jay. He could stand in front of the painting for long periods of time mentally losing himself to the past. His reverie would bring mental pictures of long lines of his forefathers walking the lengthy, lonely trail to Oklahoma. How disease, hunger and pure exhaustion caused many deaths. How the forced removal from their ancestral homeland was placed on them by an uncaring government. How the Indian became a non-person and was destined to become a vanishing breed. The "Trail of Tears" started this demise. He couldn't quite put his finger on it but somewhere in the dark recesses of his mind, his family's past was confusing the present. There was a haunting premonition lurking in his mind telling him he was reliving that trail of tears. Amidst his jumbled thoughts, this prophetic reflection seemed appropriate.

Jay well remembered trying to find an appropriate place to hang his painting. Penny and his Mom had, right from the start, chosen to find fault with the placement of the painting saying it didn't fit the décor. Jay had taken their comments to mean the painting was inappropriate and needed to be hung in a less conspicuous place. Placing it in the back of the hallway was all he could get to keep it displayed. This concession made him feel lesser a man than he wanted to be. It was a compromise. He frightfully knew the conversation could again lead to compromise. The path that tacitly said, 'let's not bring up the Indian heritage thing again'. Penny was a pretty, alabaster skinned society woman and deep down he always felt a little below her standing. He was reluctant to speak.

Jay's Great Grandfather Luke Jayhawk Cobb was their family's last full blood line as Cherokees. Luke Jayhawk's real name was Hunting Bear, and he married a Cherokee woman. Jay's grandfather married a white woman, as did his father and now he also. The Indian heritage was strong in his background. He had been raised listening to all the folklore passed on by his forefathers. Jay's father had religiously passed them to him. He felt the heritage deep in his body, mind and soul. Jay was certain his wife Penny, wouldn't understand what he was going to tell her. Telling her Indian stories in the middle of the night was certain to bring derision. He thought long and hard before speaking.

"We have been treated, I'm talking about the Cherokees in particular and the Indian in general, like second class citizens. We have too often been treated as if we didn't matter, as if we didn't exist. It didn't matter what we said, we were not taken seriously and always placated with words to make us shut up. That is exactly how Mom and I were treated in Washington. I got that same old feeling again. We went there believing we could help in doing something for all the families with a loved one lost in Vietnam. We were only placated.

"My father was shot down in North Vietnam in January of 1968. He was an F-105F pilot. His mission, as I understand it, was to kill surface to air missile sites in North Vietnam, to protect the strike aircraft which would follow. My father and William O. Sutton were in the same aircraft as a crew when they were shot down. My father was imprisoned in Hanoi in a place called The Zoo as a prisoner of war. His backseater, William Sutton was also imprisoned in the same place. We were ultimately notified by the Air Force that my father had been captured and was a POW." Jay watched Penny to see how she was taking the information. He could see dispassionate thoughts in her eyes.

She spoke, "I've heard this before, it isn't new." Her voice was calm and showed no emotions.

"I know, but please let me explain as best I can. I'm trying." He stopped to gather more complete thoughts. He twisted a spoon between his fingers and watched with intensity as the spoon circled.

"I was seven years old when the Air Force called my mother to tell her about my Dad being shot down and taken as a prisoner of war. Five years later, when I was twelve, all the POWs were released by the North Vietnamese. All the wives and families were notified their husbands would be home soon. We weren't notified! My father wasn't on the roster of returnees. Mom was devastated! She immediately called the Air Force to find out why. They gave her no information other than he was still listed as a POW. To add to her worry, they erroneously listed him in a Defense Intelligence Agency document as missing in action. My mother tried to find out where Major Bill Sutton was. He came back but my Dad didn't. The Air Force gave Mom his address. She found him in the Orlando area in Florida, called him, and they talked for about two hours. I was on the extension phone listening to the conversation. The discussion started to get too graphic, like how my father had been treated and even tortured. Mom told me to get off the phone. After the conversation was over, my mother explained to me and my sister what happened. Sutton told her that a Cuban interrogator by the name of *Fidel* had unmercifully beaten my father to death. He didn't say he was dead. He just said that after three days of non-stop torture, they never heard of him again and assumed he was dead. When Mom told me that, I cried and couldn't stop crying. It lasted for days. My stomach felt hollow. It felt just like being homesick. I felt terrible. I couldn't get over such bad news. My Mom cried with me. Anytime she cried, I cried. Any time I cried, she cried also. Neither of us could get out from under this black cloud of despair. It was like being homesick forever. All the crying and all the tears made me think of the trail of tears. Mom and I were reliving a modern day disaster like trail of tears.

"My Dad and I were real close. He taught me about the Indian ways and folklore attributed to Indian customs. Anytime my Mom would tell me, 'you are the spittin image of your father' I would feel proud. I wanted to be just like him. He and I would play catch baseball all the time. His favorite heroes were Will Rogers and Jim Thorpe. My Dad was proud of his Indian heritage. He wore a medal just like the one I have on. He sent it to me from Thailand where he had it made. He told me he had one just like it and would wear it all the time until he came back home." Jay's voice broke. Emotions were encroaching into his speech. He chose to stop. He waited. Penny allowed his moment of passion to recede.

He started again, "Well, it wasn't until 1979 that my father was declared as DIC (Died in Captivity). My Mom was never notified of this. Some of her POW/MIA acquaintances had seen a report listing Emanuel J. Cobb as DIC and called to offer her support and condolences. Needless to say my Mom was devastated. To receive information in that manner was less than she had expected from the Air Force. She immediately requested detailed information under the Freedom of Information Act. She FOIA'ed them to death trying to gain confirmation of his death. They obviously had none or surely they would have replied. Finally she received a CIA document listing my Dad as DIC. But there was nothing in the document that confirmed his death. No evidence what so ever. Most of that document was deleted by being blacked over or cut out. What they call redacted. Since then, she has lambasted all the military and the administration about their handling of the situation. Mom was always faithful to the Air Force. She knew there were risks and the possibility of harm coming to the pilots, that didn't bother her. It was accepted as a risk. What she did mind was not only the fact that the war was unnecessary and a total disgrace, but that she was being handled like a dim-witted housewife. They treated her as an overwrought spouse, completely off her rocker and overzealous in her efforts. Appease her and she'll go away. I can't stop thinking that it was just like they treated our people in the 1800's. Again our President sent our people off to a slaughter. And now the politicians continue this charade. They were using us for their own gain. Mom got real mad. She was outraged. As I understood more, I became angry too." Jay paused to catch his breath. His heart was pounding and he could feel the pressure at his temples. "Some of this, I know you have heard before," Penny broke in before he continued.

"Hold your breath for a minute, I'll get us some coffee." She busied herself going through the typical motions of pouring two cups both with dainty saucers. She put two spoons full of sugar in Jay's along with a bountiful amount of cream. Then served them with stealth like silence, trying not to break the mood. She wanted Jay to get it all out of his system, while secretly hoping it would then go away. As she sat down, she picked up her cup and held it in the palms of her hands to sniff the flavor. She waited for Jay to continue.

"In 1988, nine years later, my Mom was asked to go to Washington to testify before a Senate Select Committee and a House Congressional Committee about the POW/MIA problems. We went and nothing ever happened. We are still waiting for answers. We had been back for three weeks when Mom got a letter of thanks from our Senator and our Congressman, but no further word about my father and his fate. Three months ago we went through that same exercise all over again.

"Next year 1996, it will be twenty-eight years since my father was shot down and we still have nothing official. All we have is what Bill Sutton told my mother when he returned. He said my father most likely died at the hands of a Cuban interrogator." Jay paused to take a sip of his coffee for the first time. He made his normal sucking sound as he sipped his coffee. Penny wanted to grin at the sound. She had always made derisive comments about his noisy coffee drinking. This time she didn't.

"After the last meeting, Mom and I went up to the dais to talk to our Senator. While she was talking, I was looking over the shoulders of some of the staffers who were busy collecting all the papers on the dais. I saw something and asked to review one of the papers. I was handed two pages, pages 28 and 29 of a fifty-six page document. On the first page there was a cut-out, probably a name, followed by an identifier, WPP05061980, with an asterisk. Beside the asterisk at the bottom of the page was a name, Benitez Aguillar. The name was Benitez Aguillar or Aguillar Benitez. I couldn't tell whether there was a comma between the two names or not, so I don't know which one is the right sir name.

"What grabbed my attention were two words penciled in the left margin, 'Cuban/Miami'. Jay took a sip of coffee to maintain his cool before starting again. "On the next page was the name Mr. Guillermo, followed by the same identifier,

WPP05061980, again an asterisk, and again at the bottom of this page by the asterisk was the name Benitez Aguillar. Beside the name were the same two words again penciled in 'Cuban/Miami'. I asked to make a copy of those two pages. There was a bank of copiers in the foyer for our use. I have those two pages in my brief case. I surmised those two names were two of the three Cuban interrogators." Jay reached for the pewter image of the Indian Thunderbird held by a silver chain around his neck. He rubbed it gently to his lips while his brain churned away at other thoughts. "I almost have to think, the man Benitez Aguillar is in Miami!"

Jay was beside himself. Blood was rushing to his head, his faced flushed red and he held his stirring spoon tightly in his fist. He was becoming very animated. "How can anyone torture somebody until they die, and why a Cuban? What in the hell were Cubans doing in Hanoi anyway? Why has our own government been so secretive about this whole POW/MIA problem? Why have they withheld information? Why do they still not come clean about that entire war? Why were we there anyway? I get so fed up with the way things are! The Cherokee custom passed down to me from my father says 'we should live in peace and harmony with the things The Great Spirit has given us'. Am I wrong? Right now I want to kill somebody! I want to kill that Cuban son of a bitch! No one in politics is worth their weight in rat shit!" Jay shook his head in disgust. He pounded a clinched fist lightly on the table, but just enough to rattle the cups in their saucers. "And what really pisses me off, is that next year, 1996, is another Presidential election year. It is also an election year for many Senators and Congressmen. The only reason we were summoned to Washington was for those self serving Senators and Congressmen to get their faces on television. Those political ass holes only wanted to help themselves not us, not the families, just themselves and unknowingly we played right into their hands." Jay was seething with animosity.

Penny dutifully waited for a break. She began to feel his pain and as she looked into his eyes, recognized his turmoil. Her eyes moistened. She reached out for his hand and felt an unseen quiver.

Attempting to lighten the conversation, she said, "When your mother talked to this Mr. Sutton, did you hear him say that the Cuban killed your father?"

"No, I was off the phone by her directions, she told me that later."

"Well, then I think what you should do first, is to call Mr. Sutton and ask him all these questions about your father's death. And don't be too quick to draw some conclusions. This thing will eat you up inside if you let it." She paused to show more concern by rubbing his hand in hers. "That kind of hatred, if kept bottled up, will destroy who you truly are. The real you will disappear. I love the real you. The kind, loving, happy man I married. I don't want that to change. I want you happy again."

Jay seemed to calm slightly. "My father had a true Indian spirit and if he were here would invoke the 'crying blood' philosophy of the Cherokee. He would be hell bent to straighten out the wrong that has been laid at my mother's feet. I feel compelled to act on his behalf. I would like to get my mother closure and it will not come from our own government, so I have to find out what happened and set it right. There has to be evidence somewhere giving the true story about my father. He could have been killed in captivity. If they were to show me a document that proves he is dead. Then send us his remains. Nothing the government says can be believed. I even question myself about what is right and what is wrong. I've got to straighten this out in my own mind. I've got to find out what truly happened.

"I thought about starting with Bill Sutton too. Tomorrow I'll try to locate and telephone him; maybe set up an appointment. Then I'll fly to wherever he is and talk to him face to face. He can be believed. He may even have the answers I'm looking for."

Penny was unable to speak. Not because she was dumbfounded or astonished, but because she didn't know how to respond. She was uncertain if this was just a lark or was for real. Did Jay truly intend to do what he said, take this search all the way to Cuba or was he just blowing off steam. She placed the coffee cup up to her mouth and let the heat warm her breath. Being lost in thought was new to her. Normally she was outspoken about anything and everything but now silence seemed wise. The quietness permeated the room, a mystic spell that demanded no action. After minutes of unbroken silence Jay looked at her as if questioning what she might be thinking.

Jay spoke, "My father and I were very close." As he spoke a smile formed and a radiance appeared to lighten his face. "Dad used to call me his sidekick, and when we were horsing around he called me 'Little Beaver'. I liked that. He and I didn't have that much time together but the times I remember were all good times. Did you ever wonder why we never remember the bad times?" Jay closed his eyes to better remember the past, a grin molding his face. Jay raised his right hand and formed a fist. Then he stuck out his little finger, then the thumb making a huge 'Y' including his arm. Jay then slapped his chest with the 'Y' symbol. "My father used to do that to me when he wanted us to do something together. He explained, the little finger was me, the thumb was him and the arm was us together. When he touched his chest, that meant 'strength together'." Jay felt a warmth course through his body. He smiled. "I don't know whether it was an Indian symbol or not. But I always took it to be so.

"My Dad was 35 years old when he was shot down, the same age I am now." Jay continued to reminisce. "He was a big man about 6' 2". He had thick and course jet-black hair, much like mine but he had no body hair. The only hair he had was on his face and head. His eyebrows were full and black. When he stood up, his back was straight as a board. His shoulders stood squarely and straight out from his body. His skin didn't look dark. He looked like he had a good tan. But his nose was unmistakably Indian. There was a slight bump at the bridge of his nose hinting of a hawk-like bill and wide at the nostrils." Penny could tell that Jay was envisioning his father just as he remembered him and loving the remembrance. "You would have liked my Dad. He had a very strong character; he was more headstrong than I am. He always gave in to my Mom if there was anything she wanted. To everyone else he stood tall in his convictions and you couldn't change his mind. Mom called it country stubbornness and would typically say that he had a burr under his blanket when he tried to straighten something out.

"I think of my Mom and Dad as a true couple. They met while in college at Oklahoma State. Dad went there to study Geology and she was going to be a teacher. Mom tells it like it was love at first sight. They were both inseparable from the time they met. After college, Dad went to pilot training as a commissioned 2nd Lieutenant out of the ROTC program and he did well. Mom was proud of him. She called him E. J. but when she got mad, she called him Emanuel, knowing that would irritate him." Jay stopped to contemplate the past. Penny let him recall and enjoy the moment.

Jay's thoughts continued. "In Indian lore, there is a tale about prairie dogs. The tale is a metaphor about marriage. Prairie dogs have only one mate. When they mate it is for a life time. As they get older they care for each other. One will forage for food when the other is lame. When one dies, the other falls into depression weeping for the other. It too dies within a week or two. My Mom has been robbed of the opportunity to live out her partnership. The destiny we all face is old age. We want and need a partner to make that journey easier, to provide love, friendship, and care for each other. When I seriously think about that, I know I married you for life. Strangely, I look forward to growing old with you. Like the prairie dog, you are my chosen mate for life. When the end comes I know I'll be there for you and that you'll be there for me. My Mom has had that opportunity taken away; taken away by others who don't care about life and about growing old." Jay twisted the soft cloth belt of his robe subconsciously in deep thought.

"Did I ever tell you how the name Jayhawk came about?" Penny shook her head.

"My great, great Grandfather's real name was Yelling Bear. This was at a time before the civil war. The Jayhawkers from Kansas came here to buy horses, strong, plains mustangs. These horses could go forever. Jim Montgomery, a leader of the Jayhawkers had a sidekick named Cobb. My great, great Grandfather called him Jayhawker Cobb. Then later when they tried to take a census of all the Indians, they needed a Christian name; my great, great Grandfather gave the census taker the name of Jayhawk Cobb as his name. Since then our family name has been Cobb and the name Jayhawk was also handed down. I tried to go back and look at the census, but Oklahoma didn't become a state until 1907. The Indians were not required, nor recognized, as being a part of census taking until 1890. The name Jayhawk Cobb had to be handed down from our forefathers. I could only go back as far as the 1920 census and that was the first time I saw our family name in writing as an official person. It seems the Indians were considered as non-persons. One thing I read told me they had trouble deciding who was an Indian. How much Indian blood made an Indian? I thought that was strange. Something else I thought strange, was that the U.S. Government gave more consideration to the blacks than they did to the Indians. They call us Native Americans but they have never truly recognized us unless we married into whites. Only then were we recognized as real persons. My Dad told me often that I was a real American. I liked that!"

For the first time Jay was getting into areas he and Penny had never discussed. She was quietly listening to everything he had to say and absorbing it all. Usually in the past, when Jay wanted to talk about his heritage she would change the subject. He was so aware of it that he seldom mentioned the word Indian around her. Now he was freely talking about his heritage and she was listening intently. Her attitude made him feel more comfortable. Pride began to show as he talked about the past.

Both heard the shuffling of slippers in the hallway and knew they had awakened Jay's Mom. They looked toward the doorway waiting for her to appear. Jay's Mom walked through the door still adjusting her robe. She too had been awake all night and easily heard the two talking in the kitchen. Her hair was uncombed, her eyes were encircled by puffy pouches admitting sleepless tossing and her feet moved as if weighted by lead. Jay's Mom, a typical farm woman, sturdy, strong, and healthy, wiped her mouth with the back of her hand in a most unladylike gesture. Her 66 years of age could not have been guessed by anyone. Her nearly six foot tall frame was well tanned from her outside chores.

Marcie spoke softly and offered a faint smile, "What's going on?" Moving toward the cabinets she took out her favorite cup to pour her own wake-up elixir. The first sip was critical and couldn't happen soon enough. It was the potion that brought her to life each morning. Not getting a response, she spoke again. "Why are you two sitting here at 2:30 in the morning?" Raising her eyebrows and tilting her head toward the two was her signal for them to answer.

Jay was the first to speak. "We're just discussing things." He looked at Penny as if announcing we are not going to tell her the truth.

His Mom showed a faked grin of annoyance. "Come on now, I'm your mother. What's going on?" Her instincts were always on target. "Tell me now." She settled into a chair beside Penny and leaned over to touch shoulders with her in a gesture of togetherness. She brought warmth into the large institutional style kitchen.

Penny spoke. "Jay has this thing about your trip three months ago to Washington. He believes you two are getting the run around, and wants to do something about it."

"Can't say I disagree with that. What does he want to do about it?"

"He wants to go to Cuba to find his father's killer." Penny was ridiculing Jay.

Jay, slightly perplexed spoke out. "Now let's not get this thing blown out of proportion." Jay tried to keep his mother away from the real conversation.

Penny wouldn't let go. She knew she had Jay trapped and was ready to let his Mom stop this ridiculous scheme. "He told me he was going to Cuba!" She looked at Jay. "Is that not what you said?"

Jay was reluctant to speak. He nodded in the affirmative.

His Mom wrinkled her brow in questioning his nod. "What in the name of heaven has gotten into you boy?" Both waited for a response from Jay.

Jay was on the spot. He felt trapped. He felt some repugnance toward Penny for her treasonous acclaim. He thoughtfully formed his return volley.

"Mom," Jay paused before continuing to search for thoughts. "How did you feel when they notified us that Dad was a POW?" Jay continued without waiting for an answer. "How did you feel when Dad wasn't on the list of returnees? And how did you feel when we were told he had Died In Captivity? And when you spoke to Bill Sutton, how did you feel when he told you that Dad had been beaten and tortured to his death? And how did you feel when they provided us with no evidence of his death?" Jay stopped short knowing he was bringing back the death monster that had plagued him and his Mom for twenty-eight years. "Do we really know he is dead?" Jay was getting his dander up again. He looked at his Mom for a response.

"Jay!" His mother addressed him sternly and directly. "You and your sister are comfortable because of your father. He planned everything before he left. Those royalties from the oil have made us what we are. Thanks to your father. He knew going to South East Asia was going to be risky. He made every arrangement he could to see that we were taken care of if he didn't come back. When we were notified of his shoot down, I was devastated. I knew I had lost my best friend and the best husband in the world. I mourned his loss. Then months later we were notified that he was a POW. I rejoiced and thanked God daily for his deliverance.

"During that period of only five months, I had been at both ends of the emotional spectrum. When he didn't come back with the other prisoners, I dropped back into that black hole. But then we were again told that he was MIA. The ax was to fall once again when we talked with Bill Sutton. I believed what he told me. I didn't want to believe it, but I did. Then years later, we were told by some friends, that E. J. had been listed as Died-In-Captivity. When we checked, we found out that it was official." She paused to let her mind rest a moment. "I'm afraid going to Washington was a mistake. It started that up and down roller coaster ride all over. We shouldn't have gone." She looked straight at Jay, making distinct eye contact.

"When we talked about those Cubans, Mr. Guillermo or Benitez Aguillar, as possibly being the *Fidel* character that caused your Dad's death I had hatred running through every vein in my body. I had hatred for the U.S. Government, for all politicians. I was on the verge of mental collapse. I had truly had enough. Going into a hole and hiding deep in darkness seemed enticing. But the one thing that pulled me through was you and your sister. Your Dad and I both talked often about the future and what we both wanted. Do you know what he wanted more than anything else in this whole wide world? He wanted grandchildren. He wanted the Cobb name and his heritage to be remembered. We both wanted grandchildren. Now Melanie is married and you and Penny are married. It is time for me to have grandchildren.

"That has kept me going since we left Washington. Forget the politicians. They are in a different world, their own misguided world. Let's get on with our lives. Your Dad told me many times, we should live at peace and harmony with the things The Great Spirit in the Sky has given us. I believe in that too. Let's, as a family, have peace." She looked down, staring through the table into infinity. She knew she had given some balance to the conversation. She looked at Penny. "So when am I going to have some grandkids?" She grinned as she spoke.

Jay was quiet. His mother's input had placed him out of step. He wanted to retreat and fight the battle at a better time and place. His stubbornness overcame his timorous attitude. He was compelled to speak, but wanted to soothe his mother's mind.

He spoke quietly. "Mom, when Dad was here on leave before he went to Thailand, he took me aside and told me that I had to be strong, that I had to be a man and take care of you. I have tried to do just that. I want nothing more than for us to be a quiet, peaceful family. In our conversation Dad spoke of the Cherokee ideology, or way of life. He told me this story. He said just like you said to live in peace and harmony but there was an exception when warring was necessary to the Indian. And that was when family blood was spilled. That was the Crying Blood. When that happened, it was then O.K. to fight back. I feel that Crying Blood has been spilled and I need to fight back. I need to avenge his death. It is my duty to do this. I need to find his killer and seek revenge."

"Whoa!" His mother blurted out in horror. "Whoa! Rein yourself in cowboy! You can't do that! You can't do anything but accept life as it is. Don't be stupid!" His mom wrinkled her brow and her light green eyes became flushed with red veins. The arteries at her neckline bulged under the adrenalin forced pressure.

"Do you know how crazy that sounds. You can't take someone else's life. An eye for an eye ain't going to enter this picture!" His mom let that thought sink in before continuing. "It's utter nonsense to take an outmoded custom from the past and apply it into the present. That Crying Blood thing is no longer valid. You get off that horse right now!" His Mom was very adamant. She intended for this matter to stop right at this very moment. She grabbed for his hand and Penny's at the same time. Holding them both in hers, she talked with strength in her voice. "Promise me, promise me right now this is the end of it." She held their hands tightly waiting for an answer. "Promise me!"

Penny readily nodded her approval displaying a tension relieving smile on her face. Marcie also grabbed Jay's hand as if to affirm the commitment. Jay was not ready to commit. Uncertainty engulfed his mind. He began to squirm in his chair as his hand reached for his Thunderbird necklace. He pushed his chair back away from the table. His head moved slowly from side to side, only hinting disapproval of censure. Penny stared at him with darts of fire in her eyes. He finally nodded, knowing it would comfort his Mom.

Jay's Mom, with an aura of matriarchal control and charm, spoke. "O.K. then...when can I expect some grandkids." All three smiled.

Hours passed, Jay found himself back in bed with the same dilemma invading his sleep. He stared at the ceiling as he made plans to continue. He had to know exactly how and why his father had died. He found nothing wrong with contacting Bill Sutton. And if necessary, he could find nothing wrong with going to Mr. Sutton and having a talk with him face to face. He rationalized each and every thought with positive results. The certainty of uncovering further information had completely driven his thoughts away from the half-hearted promise he made to his mother.

Jay had his own firm, Geological Surveyors Inc. It was a small but financially sound company. He and another geologist were partners in the company. With a receptionist, a draftsman, a physical land surveying crew and numerous ground penetrating electronic sonar devices, his company was complete and enjoyed success based on huge contracts with four major oil companies. He tried to think of anything and everything that might interfere with his plan. Nothing he could think of would stop him. It would be easy to take a few days off to find and meet with Bill Sutton.

His thoughts turned to the imperatives if Bill Sutton again confirmed his Dad's treatment and death at the hands of those Cubans. How would he find these men? Would he need to speak some Spanish? What were the passport and visa requirements? Maybe the U.S. Government didn't allow travel into Cuba. The more he thought about it, the more it seemed impossible. He began to realize how little he knew. In his mind, the challenge would be a secondary driving force. Staring at the ceiling gave him no answers just questions. Maybe his Mom and Penny were right. He might be crazy to think this was possible. Then his mind turned to the ultimate challenge, was he capable of killing anyone? This thought made him face himself. He again rationalized, no one knows this about themselves until faced with the moment of truth. He lay perfectly still in bed trying not to convey his mental struggles to Penny.

His next burst of thought was how to keep this away from Penny and his Mom. His closeness to both his Mom and Penny placed him in the vulnerable position of exposure if he wasn't extremely discrete. This was a worry he willingly accepted. His office was thirty miles away in Claremore. But Penny and his Mom often went to Claremore for shopping and for leisure time away from home. Escaping from the office would be easy, but relying on his receptionist for a cover up was tantamount to announcing it himself.

He looked across Penny out the window to view the first light of day. It was mid October and days were getting shorter; early morning light came later. A gentle breeze could be seen rustling in the trees in the hills behind the garage. Leaves were just beginning to turn in the cool autumn temperatures. Jay's thoughts momentarily turned away from his surreptitious foray and to the present. Autumn and spring were his most enjoyable times of the year. His family liked horseback riding, especially his Mom. This too was a legacy left by his father.

Away from the house in a small boxed pasture, a red clap board barn housed four quarter horses for each family member. Melanie still boarded her horse even though she seldom came to ride. His Mom was a leader when it came to horseback riding. Being sixty-six years old didn't slow her down. She owned a prize winning sorrel quarter horse which she loved. She was always first to suggest a ride. Especially in the spring when nature was fresh and there was an innate desire to be outdoors. Getting out into the fresh air after winter was exultingly welcomed. After a hot humid summer, the cool breeze announcing winter was equally received. The first touch of autumn held the same wonderful intrigue. Both seasons foretold new beginnings. Jay's thoughts brought similar emotions. This could be a new beginning. If he could find his father's murderer, a new beginning could close the past.

CHAPTER II

Bill Sutton was waiting in the doorway when Jay drove up. He watched as the tall, fine looking young man strolled forward to meet him. Bill, a much shorter man and only wearing socks on his feet, had to look upward as Jay came closer.

"So you're E..J.'s son! It's my pleasure to meet you."

"My pleasure also!" Jay smiled graciously. He couldn't help but observe how casual Bill Sutton appeared. Wearing shorts and a golfing shirt, he looked like an advertisement for Florida living.

"When you called on the phone and gave me your name as E. J. Cobb, I just about flipped out. My mind really was jumbled. That's why I said I thought you were dead." Sutton tried to ward off the uneasiness by being extra cordial. "Come on in." He ushered Jay through the door. "My wife is off to her Saturday morning bridge club meeting so we can have the entire morning to ourselves." Sutton kept walking through the living room toward a set of sliding glass doors leading onto a patio. "Why don't we sit out on the patio and watch the golfers as they go by." Jay nodded his approval.

The two settled into comfortably padded lawn chairs. Bill Sutton looked at Jay taking in every detail of the man. He had met Jay when he was six years old at McConnell AFB in Wichita, Kansas. The man sitting before him was now thirty-five and hardly a trace of the boy he met back then. Sutton drank in the sight and was pleased. Sutton would have been proud to have a son like Jay. He and his wife had no children. After returning from five years and ten months as a POW both Sutton and his wife figured they were too old to bring a child into the world. They felt their age would be against proper care and nurturing. Bill hated that thought and would liked to have had children but he went along with his wife's choices. She was four years older than Bill and honestly believed her time had passed to guarantee a healthy child.

"Tell me, what's on your mind? You said you wanted to talk about your Dad?" Bill Sutton tossed out the comment as a starter and continued to look directly into the eyes of E. J.'s son. "You sure do remind me of your Dad. You have the same eyebrows, the same hair and your shoulders stick straight out from your body just like your Dad's did. We used to kid him about his shoulders. We told him he looked like he was always wearing shoulder pads. Your Dad was a great jokester. His favorite response to any joke was 'you ought to be in show business'. He took everything handed his way just as if it was too trivial to worry over." Bill laughed to himself as he thought about it. "It was like he could turn you off. He had a strong mind. He was a stubborn guy. When he was right, he never gave in, no matter what." Sutton paused to let Jay do the talking.

Jay accepted the pause. "Mr. Sutton, first of all, my Mom doesn't know I am here. If she knew, she would be ready to kill me. I promised her I wouldn't do this. But I can't stand not knowing about my father. I want to know him better. Know more about what he was like. You have already started in the right direction. I want to know anything and everything about my father. When he left for Thailand, I was nearly seven years old. He and I didn't have that much time together. I would like to get to know him better. I thought you might help."

Sutton showed surprise and wrinkled his brow at the comment. He asked, "Hasn't your mother told you about your father and about his character, and how good a father and husband he was?" Bill stretched his arms upward above his head and brought them slowly down to the back of his head. Interlacing his fingers at the back of his head, he rested his head in his palms and watched Jay. Jay knew he was on stage being looked at, being assessed and being evaluated by his father's yardstick.

"Yes sir." Jay answered strongly. He knew he must stand up to the scrutiny. "My Mom has told me everything about my Dad. But that isn't the same as hearing it from someone else. I believe I knew my Dad better than anyone else, but I knew nothing of his life as a pilot." Jay leaned back deeply in his chair, crossed his legs and rested a moment. He searched his mind for the right question.

"I'm here to find out what happened during his last days as a POW. I've done a lot of reading about POWs. I've read lots of books and government documents written on the subject. I'm here because I want to hear it from you, first hand. The government hasn't been too direct with my Mom and me. They seem to be carrying on some agenda we don't know about. You have all the details. I'd just like to hear them, the shoot down, the bail out and the treatment you received." Jay viewed Bill for any signs of negative thoughts or anything indicating he should back away.

Bill accepted the comments and grinned slightly in approval. "You know that's going to be a lot of talking." Jay nodded in response. "Let me get us something to drink before we start. What would you like, coffee, coke, water... what?" Bill rose from his chair and stretched his back muscles. He waited for Jay's response.

"Coke would be fine." Out of respect Jay rose from his chair.

"Sit back down I'll get it, sit here and watch those Saturday morning duffers. I stay off the course on weekends. That's when all the working stiffs and all the old farts come out. I'm on the committee for course maintenance. We don't worry about them destroying the course 'cause they can't stay in the fairways, but our homes are very vulnerable to being hit on weekends."

Jay grinned openly at the comments. His thoughts were about Bill, an old fart himself, condemning the other old farts. It was an amusing comment.

"Before you leave, you'll see somebody bounce a ball off my patio screen. The best time to play is on Mondays. That's ladies day. After they run out of tee times then the men are allowed on the course, as long as we don't push them. So on

Mondays you can play very leisurely. You can even practice a little waiting for them to get off the greens." Bill walked through the sliding glass doors, laughing to himself. Jay smiled at his comments.

Bill returned, both hands clutching an ice filled glass of coke. He stepped down onto the patio. "How much do you know about what your Dad and I did?" Bill asked.

"I'm afraid, not very much." Jay shrugged his shoulders.

"Well let me start from the day we were shot down. Occasionally, I have a recurring nightmare about the shoot down but that was small potatoes against what was to come." Bill again settled into his chair as the two sipped reservedly on their cokes.

"Our call sign that day was Sturgeon 03. Our Wing, the 355th, always used the names of fish for squadron recognition. Our frag order called for a flight of four F-105Fs loaded with Shrike missiles to seek out and destroy Surface to Air Missiles around the port city of Vinh. Each aircraft had two Shrike missiles, a cluster bomb unit and 6,000 rounds of bullets for the Gatling gun in case we ran into some MIGs. We were to make contact with a Mig Cap of F-4s before crossing the border into North Vietnam." As an aside Bill chortled, "Other pilots referred to North Vietnam as Indian territory. I had to watch myself because your Dad took an affront to the comment since his home state of Oklahoma was the original Indian Territory."

He continued, "As soon as we started across the border, we started to get ringers. That's when our RHAW, radar homing and warning, gear started receiving radar impulses telling us we had been spotted. We had three ringers and all of them were from the right side of the aircraft. The Shrike missile had a killing range of only about seven miles. The SAM sites had a killing range of fifteen miles, so it was part of our job to know when we were within fifteen miles of the radar sites that were tracking us. Our intelligence grunts told us where the SAM sites were and we knew we had only about two minutes, at 520 knots, before being over target. The ideal was to stand off about seven to ten miles and fire. The problem was you never knew exactly what the range to target actually was. Vinh was a rail yard feeding supplies into the south. It was to become the most bombed target in North Vietnam. It was the start point of the Ho Chi Minh trail. The rail yard was to be the target for the strike aircraft. Our's was to hit all the SAM sites we could around Vinh and make a path for the strike aircraft. We were advised by intelligence that something big was going on. Recon flights over Vinh indicated it was loaded with supplies heading south.

"Tactics for killing a SAM site were primitive and still evolving. At the time we were making formulas for figuring out maneuvers and times to fire. The tactic we developed was the 'dip check' method. When we got a ringer, we would put the strongest ringer right on the nose and then dive toward the site. When it was loudest and strongest, we checked our altitude and dive angle. Through quick extrapolation using dive angle and altitude, we were supposed to know when we were within the seven to ten mile killing range of our missiles. At the right dive angle and altitude, we fired a Shrike; then we would climb up putting the ringer off on the wingtip. We would watch for a SAM being fired. The question was when to dodge the missile after it was fired. If you dodge too soon, it'll get you anyway. The rule of thumb jokingly, was to wait until you could read the writing on the side of the missile, then break. We fired one missile and started looking for any SAMs that might have been fired. This time we both saw one and watched as it rose toward us. God, that was like waiting for eternity. We had to do a break away at just the right moment. You didn't want to wait too long, nor did you want to break too soon. Both were deadly. I watched that thing get so big, I about shit in my pants. Your Dad broke at just the right moment and we watched as it went on by us and exploded out of range. We both howled like coyotes. Your Dad did this kinda gobbling sound." Bill looked at Jay. "Did he ever do that gobbling sound for you?"

Jay's eye lit up and a grin formed instantly. He immediately recognized what he was talking about and exclaimed. "Oh, Yeah!" Jay showed immediate excitement. "Yes sir, he sure did! My Dad loved Indian lore. The gobbling sound was the 'sound of death', a sound that announced death for the enemy and victory for the warrior. Warring nations would make the sound of death when attacking. When we visited his Dad, my Granddad Matthew, he would carry a .22 caliber western frame revolver with rat shot and we would hunt for rats in the barn. When he would see one, he would gobble and then shoot. I know the sound well. My Dad taught me how to do it. I don't do it very well but I know exactly what you are talking about."

"Well, that missile missed us. We lowered the right wing to look for other SAMs. We saw the site explode. We enjoyed the shot and waited longer than usual to pull off target. We were making a turn out bound to get away for another run. That's when we got hit. It wasn't a missile. But something like anti-aircraft fire. We got a slight bump in our engine. He asked me if I heard that. I said yes. We both checked instruments and looked back to see if we could see anything. Hell...you can't see anything from the back seat, nothing. We thought we were O.K. and continued to set up for another run. Then we got smoke in the cockpit and our wingman told us we were on fire. We immediately headed west for Laos, toward NKP, Nakhon Phanom, Thailand. We let our speed carry us up to about twenty thousand feet, then some one yelled over the radio, Sturgeon 03, bail out now! We waited for another transmission. Neither of us could believe we had to leave our comfortable cockpit for the outside world. The transmission came again, Sturgeon 03, bail out...God dammit bail out...now 03! Your Dad told me to eject. I did. Then the aircraft exploded. I didn't think your father made it out. But as I floated down, I noticed another chute not a mile away. I knew it was your father and I felt better. We were somewhere close to the Laotian border. I believed we were actually in Laos and a sense of relief came over me. I was glad to be alive." Bill stopped and waited for some questions. Jay had none but it was obvious he had absorbed every word.

Bill continued, "Our speed was slow when we bailed out and both of us came out O.K. I yelled toward your father but he didn't hear me. Our three flight aircraft and the F-4s came over us and stayed around as long as they could. Once on the ground I tried contacting them on our survival radio. I told them I was O.K. I listened as they talked to your father. He was down O.K. also. But he was too far away for us to join up. The flight gave me a vector of 295 degrees in case we wanted to try and find each other."

Sutton stood up to stretch and walked slowly to the patio screen. He watched as three golfers hit their next shot. Jay could tell he was reliving the shoot-down and hesitated to say anything.

Bill continued but was labored in speaking. "The area we came down in had mountains all around. From flight altitude you never think of the terrain as being mountainous. You can see hills and valleys but it's like looking at a vegetated relief map. Once on the ground these topographical differences become very real. The mountains around us were not as high as the ones in the distance, so I felt we were lucky in coming down where we did. I was at the base of a hill and landed in a washed out gulley that fed into a stream. I gathered in my chute and collected my thoughts. I guess I was on the ground about thirty minutes before things got quiet. I mean real quiet. There was a lot of comfort knowing there were aircraft overhead and having someone to talk to. But when they left it got too quiet. My thoughts focused on being rescued. I did all the things I was supposed to do. I hid my chute, checked my weapon and made an inventory of what I had with me. Then I sat down and waited. I was in a reasonably open area and felt that rescue choppers could easily find me. So I waited and waited. Things stayed quiet. Off in the distance I watched as other strike aircraft dropped their ordnance on Vinh. I drank some water from my canteen. Nervous, yes, I was plenty nervous. But I fully expected to be picked up by a chopper. We were briefed that search and rescue would be just off shore and could pick us up within a few minutes. I figured we couldn't have been more than seventy-five miles from shore. I searched the distant horizon to the east watching for rescue choppers."

Bill turned toward Jay and spoke. "Suddenly and without warning, four peasants appeared. Right out of nowhere. I mean they just appeared. One minute they weren't there, the next minute they were. All four smiled at me and offered some hand gestures that I didn't understand. All four were dressed in predominantly black clothing. I don't mean like the Viet Cong in their black pajamas, but in their own traditional native dress. The black fabric they wore was ornately interlaced with brilliant bands of red and orange. Their heads were wrapped in the same fabric, much like a turban. They wore open toed sandals. Each carried a hand carved walking stick similar to a hiking stick for mountain hiking. They smiled openly and appeared friendly. One guy in his teens or early twenties had a wide mouth of exceptionally white teeth. I knew these people were nomadic hill tribesmen with allegiance to no government or cause. This gave me a dilemma. Should I try to escape or not? While in The Zoo, I often wished I had bartered my way out of my predicament. I didn't even try. I will always regret not trying.

"Three of them had nearly no teeth, just black stubs protruding from the gums. I didn't know what to do. The four talked in rapid bursts of chatter, all four talking at once. All I could do was stand there. I didn't know whether to pull out my weapon or what. Looking back on it and the horror that was to await me for the next five years and ten months, I should have tried something instead of just standing there with my finger up my ass, but somehow I didn't feel threatened. They seemed friendly enough and I thought there was a good chance they could have been Laotians.

"My thoughts were toward getting rescued. If they didn't bother me, I would just wait. But those feelings didn't last long. All four came closer to me, they approached me as if I was waiting to jump them. They would take a step, then wait to see what I would do, then take another step and wait. They all four approached me in this manner. One man, more timid than the others, stayed directly behind one of the leaders. Coming forward only when they did. I gave some gestures using my hands like an airplane and pointing to the sky. I already had my blood chit out and my pointee-talkee pad. The blood chit was a cloth document you could give to indigenous people in exchange for help. They could give it to the Red Cross or friendly forces and get a reward for helping. I tried communicating. But all they understood was each other. When I would point to a word, they looked dumbfounded. They probably couldn't read, but then again, I was pointing to Vietnamese words. I thought maybe they weren't Vietnamese and I had a chance.

"After a few minutes of listening to their chatter, I heard search and rescue aircraft come up on my radio. This caused a big stir. The chatter tripled and got louder. They looked at me and looked at each other. I didn't know what was going on. I answered the call and stated my condition, who I was, and where I thought I was located. I also told them I was surrounded by four people. I was still making conversation on the radio, when one of the men came over and jerked the radio out of my hands. He threw it off into the woods. That was the first time I felt I was in real trouble. I sat down but they forced me back up. They took my weapon, my survival jacket and all the maps out of my pocket. One man jerked the pencil out of my flight suit and stuck it into the cloth bands around his head. At this point no one was smiling anymore; just chattering ninety-to-nothing. I got the feeling they were arguing about what to do with me. They hadn't harmed me yet; for that I was grateful. We had been shown pictures of captured POWs and there was the feeling they would immediately hurt you. These guys didn't. But that wasn't going to last long. We walked for four and a half hours before we came to a village. I still had my watch and knew the exact time. It was twelve noon. I wasn't aware a village was that close. I guess in the excitement of the bail out, I didn't pay close attention.

"Once in the village, things got worse, I mean much worse. The four hill tribesmen left immediately and headed back. An old man in a green military type uniform stepped out of the crowd and took charge. He wore no rank, no insignias and no weapon. He began to speak and all the spectators started getting excited, even angry. Soon there was a huge crowd. The uniformed man took a swipe at me with his bare hands. When he did the crowd of peasants yelled their pleasure. Soon another man in uniform came also. I was in the middle of this village. I know that because there was a water well in the middle of this roadway intersection.

Women were there pulling up water and pouring it into jugs. This had to be the center of town.

"A second uniformed guy, much younger, appeared and took charge. He began working the crowd. The first thing he did to me was put a blindfold over my eyes. I just stood there waiting, listening to the talking, the chattering and the cheers from the crowd. Since my hands weren't tied, I was sorely tempted to push it up, but I didn't. The next thing I felt was a stick in the middle of my back. It wasn't a strike or blow; it was thrust into my back like a spear. It hurt. From that point on, things went downhill. They pulled my arms backwards, put a stick between my back and my arms, and then tied both arms to the stick. At that point I was scared to death. Someone began hitting me over the head with a small baton of sorts. It could have been a short stick, anyway it was hard. The cheering crowd was getting a lecture about something. During the talking, I would receive a blow to the head from the baton and then the crowd would cheer."

Bill paused trying not to get too emotionally involved in his tale. He knew if he could keep himself aloof and outside his mind, he could be nothing more than a commentator and not relive this horrible memory. He could go on. But many times in the past, when telling the story, he found it impossible to keep himself at a distance away from reliving the event.

He started over by offering an aside that he expected would relieve his mind. "Let me throw something into this story. After I came back and retired from the military, I began to read about Vietnam, peruse maps of North Vietnam and to retrace my journey from the shoot down to Hanoi. There were some strange coincidences. The village where they took us was Kiem Lien Village. That was the birthplace of Ho Chi Minh." Bill relished in telling of his discovery. He had told this tale many times in the past. This one astonishing fact always elicited a reaction and caused his emotional ties to disappear. He used it every time he was forced to recount his experience.

"We weren't anywhere close to the Laotian border when we bailed out. We were northwest of Vinh about thirty miles.

This was Nghe An Province, the birthplace of the revolution. The first uprisings against the French started there." Bill sat his glass on the side table and took out his handkerchief to wipe the moisture off his hands from the frosted glass.

He started over. "At the time, I knew nothing about all this. I was more concerned about surviving than anything else. Standing there was scary. Let me tell you, I was so scared I about shit in my pants. With a blindfold over my eyes, I could not see a blow coming. I would get these sporadic hits and could only recoil after the fact. So I was standing there waiting for the next blow, scared to death. I have no idea of how long I stood there but it was a long time." Bill's hands articulated his excitement. He raised his eyebrows and opened his eyes wide.

"Suddenly the crowd started cheering again. I recoiled thinking I was about to get hit, but no blow came. I heard the onrush of the crowd and the shuffling of feet. I feared I was about to be rushed by the crowd. I didn't know what was happening. My right shoulder got bumped by someone else's shoulder. Like they were pushed into me. It caused me to stagger to get my footing." Bill paused with a delightful grin on his face. He looked straight at Jay.

"Then I heard your Dad's voice right next to me. He said to me, and I'll always remember this, he said, 'you think they greet all visitors this way'. He knew it was me, so I surmised he hadn't been blindfolded yet. His voice instantly lifted my spirits. You can be in a bucket of shit and if you have someone join you, that bucket don't smell as bad. We tried to carry on a conversation, but found out quickly, they were not going to allow it. We did get in a few words. Anytime we tried to speak, we would get a sharp blow to the head. He did ask if I were O.K. I said yeah. They must have blindfolded him also, as well as tying his hands behind his back. I kept hearing him grunt and could feel some movement."

Jay listened intently, focused on every word. He subconsciously reached to his neck and pulled out the small pewter image of the Indian Thunderbird which was identical to the one his father had. He rubbed it to his lips as if to be closer to his father.

Bill continued, "The talking to the crowd continued for about another thirty minutes then we were placed in the back of a vehicle and driven away. We both had to lie face down in the bed of a truck. The ride was bumpy and very uncomfortable. But at least we weren't getting hit about the head anymore. Both your Dad and I found by rubbing our heads against the floor we were able to adjust our blindfolds enough to see things. When we made eye contact for the first time, that was the most satisfying, most exhilarating moment for the both of us. He forced a wink at me and I had the comfort of feeling everything was going to be O.K. Your Dad was like that, when he was around you felt unafraid. We could see feet and the blades of machete like knives. We knew there was a man on both sides of us acting as guards. We started silent lip reading to communicate. We both agreed, we knew we were headed for Hanoi." Bill Sutton looked at his watch. An hour had passed and it seemed to Jay their conversation was just beginning. Bill asked if he should continue. Jay nodded his agreement.

"It took us three days of travel. We were never fed any food or water. That was a good thing, because they never allowed us to relieve ourselves. When we arrived at our destination, we heard the driver stop at a gate, say a few words, then enter into a compound. As we were pulled out the rear of the truck, our blindfolds were still up enough for us to see. This place was more like a villa. It had about ten buildings all within a walled compound. Your father intentionally stumbled into me and whispered, 'where do you think we are'? I quickly answered back, I don't know. I wasn't sure where we were. They put us in separate rooms. I thought they were rooms. Turned out they were our cells. We saw no one. There were no sounds around us. We had no idea where we were. We didn't even know this was a prison. When you think prison, you think high walls, bars, and locks. Our first glance out of the truck didn't give you that impression.

"I had been placed in a six by twelve foot room with high stucco walls and a concrete floor with nothing but a long, wide board for you to sleep on. There was a can at one end.

This was to be my make-shift toilet. We were stripped of all our clothing and given their skimpy underwear like pants and shirt. When they left, the heavy wooden doors were locked. As soon as I was alone, I felt a great sense of relief. This was my first peaceful moment in the last four days. I began to hear voices from other cells. I was asked my name, and rank, where from, and if I were O.K. I responded as well as I knew how, but almost instantly a guard showed up, rattled the door and said 'no talk'. Now I knew we were in prison and there were other prisoners around. I surmised that we were in downtown Hanoi. The interrogations started within a couple of hours. It was early morning when we arrived, after traveling all night. I would have guessed the time to be about 7:00 a.m."

Bill subconsciously looked at his watch. "I was taken to another room about forty feet away in a two story building. There was a table where three military guards were sitting at the front of the room. I was directed to sit on a stool in front of them. The leader started talking. He asked me my rank, serial number, home base, what aircraft I was flying, where I was shot down, was I being treated nicely and many other foolish questions. When I answered he would write down my answer. I knew I wasn't supposed to cooperate and I didn't. I only gave them my name, rank, and serial number. The interrogator showed anger when I wouldn't answer other questions and started telling me that things would be better if I answered his questions. I told him simply, the Code of Conduct didn't allow me to give certain answers.

"I was straight forward with them. I didn't get emotional, I didn't get mad, I just did what was allowed and nothing more. I know I made him angry. One time he hit the table with a stick, displaying his anger. Then he got right in my face, and yelled until he got red in the face. I responded rather stoically. I accepted his wrath calmly and that made him madder. It only took about an hour for me to get through this first interrogation. I was led back to my cell. Shortly I got some food for the first time in four days. I soon realized this was the 'new guy treatment'. Little did I know!

"I could watch out into the courtyard through tiny cracks in the boards of my door. I did this for a long time trying to figure this place out. Who was there, how many? What was the routine and any information I could get by watching. I saw them come get your Dad for his first taste of interrogation. They took him to the same room. If you listened closely you could hear their voices. I listened for about twenty minutes without hearing a word from your Dad. Then I heard the interrogator get mad, much the same as he had with me. Then I heard your Dad bark back. He called him a dirty, lousy son-of-a-bitch. I heard the stick hit the table, then a muffled thump. My eyes were glued to the crack in the door and my imagination went wild. I was scared for your Dad. After another thirty minutes your Dad was taken back to his cell. I noticed a long red welt across his right jaw and surmised he had been hit. One of the other inmates tried to talk with him after the interrogation, to tell him what he should do to survive these interrogations. Your Dad's response was, 'fuck 'em, I ain't telling 'em nothing'. I heard that statement myself. It sort of helped my spirit to hear your Dad's determination and the strength it showed.

"The next day we both went through the same maneuver but this time it lasted about three hours. The following day it lasted four hours, and the day after that it was an all day affair. I thought to myself 'so much for the new guy treatment'. They seemed to try getting to the newbies early. My attitude was changing. These guys were mean and they meant business. I had been placed on my knees on a concrete floor for four hours straight and asked the same questions over and over. They were relentless." Bill reached for his glass, and unconsciously fingered it deep in thought, then enjoying a long, cool swallow.

Jay took the opportunity to speak. He asked his long awaited question. "When did the Cuban interrogators come into the picture and why were they there at all?" Jay needed the answer to his question. He felt it was critical to know.

Bill almost welcomed this change of venue. He sipped on his coke formulating his answer while gazing at the golfers beyond the patio. "Tell me Jay, what do you know about Cuba?"

"I'm afraid nothing," was Jay's simple response.

"Then let me start by saying Fidel Castro hated the Americans and the Kennedy's, both JFK and Robert. I believe Castro was responsible for the death of both. I know the Warren Commission gave Castro a clean bill of health for JFK's death and blamed it all on Lee Harvey Oswald. I think it was all a cover up, a cover up at the highest level. The Bay of Pigs, The Cuban Missile Crisis, JFK's assassination, those events were all related. They were related because of Castro's hatred for the U.S.

"Castro stated, 'if the Kennedy's wanted to fight communism and prevent third worlds from going along communist lines, then why Vietnam? Why not Cuba? Cuba is right in the front door of the U.S. Why go all the way to Vietnam to stop world communism'? That was a well founded question. It's a question we should ask ourselves. The Cuban Missile Crisis wasn't about communism, but keeping Russian influence away from our front door. JFK was invoking The Monroe Doctrine with resolve and a show of force to back it up. After The Bay of Pigs fiasco in April 1961, Castro viewed JFK as a wimp and began to take overt action against U.S. interests. Castro's most promising effort was in North Vietnam. But he didn't stop there; he wanted to create other Vietnam's in all third world countries. He wanted to bring the U.S. to its knees by stretching its resources. Castro knew the U.S. held itself as the world's big brother, the world's peacekeeper. If he could start revolutions in all third world countries, he could debilitate the U.S. resources and undermine public sentiment.

"Castro even set up schools in Cuba to train Afro-Americans in terrorist tactics against their own country in hate groups and in organizing uprisings. As many as one thousand black Americans were trained in Cuba. This was all because Castro hated Americans and the Kennedy's. Castro was more anti-American than he was anti-capitalism. Then along comes LBJ, probably the most inept Commander-in-Chief we've ever had and suddenly we are thrust into a full blown war in Vietnam. I think we should make the rule that we have no more Presidents from Texas.

"Castro immediately sided with the North Vietnamese by sending aid. Russia tried to low key its efforts in North Vietnam. The SAM sites came from Russia and some pilots and planes. But for the most part Russia played a small role. In North Vietnam we faced Castro's thugs as well as the Viet Cong, the Viet Minh, and the North Vietnamese. So you ask why Cuba? The only answer is Castro's hatred for the U.S."

Jay asked quickly, "How do you know all this?" Jay was impressed by his knowledge.

"I've done a lot of reading on the subject since retiring."

"Why would our government want to cover up any assassination plot?"

"Because they didn't want a World War III! I was in Minot, North Dakota, in a B-52 Squadron during the missile crisis. We were airborne with nuclear weapons and assigned targets; ready to start or end World War III. I can't imagine or begin to understand what the administration was going through during those days. Kennedy stood tall. We won that bout. After the missile crisis, the entire staff, the Joint Chiefs of Staff, the whole administration was not about to go through that turmoil again. The feeling behind the cover up was that if the American people knew that Castro had plotted and killed Kennedy, there would be a tremendous out pouring of anger and national disgust. A demand that something be done. They would want Castro's ass on a platter. Russia would side with Castro and then we would have the same confrontation all over again. So the Justice Department took charge of everything and initiated a cover up. They got enough high-level people to go along. It was only a matter of controlling the evidence. We the people were duped again." Sutton shrugged his shoulders in disgust.

Jay wanted to get back on track and came back with a comment to redirect the conversation. "My Mom told me long ago, when she first contacted you, that a Cuban interrogator tortured my father to death. How did that happen?"

Sutton slowly and reluctantly responded. "You've got to remember one thing, being in prison is not easy. You live with loneliness, deprivation, hunger, torture, and some common rules. When we first arrived, I didn't know anything. Neither did your father. I found out the facts later. We were in Cu Loc Prison, a place we called The Zoo. The Zoo also had an annex just south of the compound. At the time, I believe there were approximately eighty guys in the Zoo. I was a captain and your father was a major. That's where my treatment and his treatment were different.

"Our interrogators always went after the higher ranking prisoners. The rank of major was high to them. Your father was in service longer than I was, so they figured he knew more. I was eventually moved down to the annex because I was a junior ranking officer. But we are talking about your father's treatment. He could have been the senior ranking officer. We will never know. He was immediately singled out for intense interrogation.

"The Vietnamese were meticulous record keepers. They particularly wanted a biography on everyone. There were three Cuban soldiers. This one Cuban fellow, the one who seemed to be in charge, we called him *Fidel*. He was there to help the Vietnamese get information. He was a big Caucasian, about the same size as your father. He was tall, with dark bushy hair and a Castro like beard. My guess was he was about the same age, around his mid thirties. He had big hands. The Vietnamese were dwarfed by him. They had to look up to him. His size to them made him a leader. They obviously respected him.

"This guy had two identifying features. He had a tattoo on the underside of his left arm just above the wrist. It wasn't an image of anything, just artwork, something like a pentagram. His other feature was strange. He had eyes of different colors. One was green and the other was dark brown. His skin color was light tan, honey colored, just like your father's. Our normal Vietnamese interrogators were persistent about filling out the biography for each prisoner. They tortured prisoners every day, trying to get data for their records. Sometimes I thought we could have made it easier on ourselves if we had just given it to them. But the common rules were not to give any information except name, rank, and serial number. It had to be this way. If they got anything, they wanted more. It would be never ending quizzing, followed by torture until you gave in. So it was better to stick to the rules than offer them help by giving them what they wanted.

"There was another interrogator we called *The Bug*. He was vicious, he spoke very little English and got mad when you didn't respond to his requests for information. He too was tall, maybe six foot, light skinned, nearly white skinned. But his attitude was bad. He didn't like any Americans and liked to hit anyone within reach whether he was interrogating or not. He even hit some of the North Vietnamese guards just to piss 'em off. Oddly, he was always neat. His neatness was a contrast to his character. He wore a green beret and looked like Che Guevera with his thin line mustache and a pointed goatee. He carried a riding crop which he used to his advantage.

"There was another Cuban whom they called Beanie. He was short and skinny, pleasantly quiet, always sucking his teeth. He wore a beret also, but it was always dirty, like it hadn't been washed, ever! He did what he was told. If *Fidel* said to lash our arms behind our backs, he was the one who did it. If he was told to put the manacles on us, he was the one who did it. If we got trussed up, hanging from the ceiling, he did it. Beanie was as bad as the others. He just didn't have enough rank to have any power.

"They had ways of making you talk. They used solitary confinement regularly for those not cooperating, sometimes for days and even weeks, and to some senior officers, months. They made you kneel while being interrogated. Kneeling for long periods on a concrete floor was terrible. Whipping you with an old fan belt was commonplace. Some times they would suspend you from the ceiling, hanging from your elbows, and leave you there until you broke. Starving was also lucrative for them. The understood rule was to take as much abuse as you could. When you were about to go into shock, then give in.

"At the time, your father and I were both new guys. We didn't know the rules. We didn't know what to expect or what was expected of us. We only knew the Code of Conduct and we stuck to it. We were already isolated from the other prisoners. We were very vulnerable to any treatment they dished out. I think they eventually targeted your father because he was new and because he was a senior ranking individual. They wanted him broken before he was assimilated into the prison regimen.

"*Fidel* was going to prove himself and display his techniques for extracting information. He was going to demonstrate to the Vietnamese how easy it was. When they came for your father, *Fidel* was in the courtyard waiting for him. Three Vietnamese were standing next to him. As your Dad walked toward the two-story building being led by a guard, *Fidel* shouted obscenities at him. He called him a mullafuck'n kike. I often wondered where he got that word. I knew he didn't understand the term. He had a better cursing vocabulary than any of us. He could curse like a sailor. And he used it with vengeance. He also carried a leather covered, wooden baton. It was similar to a small thin baseball bat with leather. I thought it was a riding crop until he hit me with it one day. It was a baseball bat! *Fidel* would stand very tall, like he was intentionally stretching his body to be taller and would strike his thigh with that baton making a loud snapping sound, the louder the better. Those who felt the strikes of his baton flinched each time they heard that sound. They held sympathy for any individual who was being interrogated and being thrashed with that bat.

"All morning long, I heard that bat ring out. Occasionally I heard it find its mark. Your father could be heard screaming under the pain. *Fidel* offered every curse word, every obscenity, every American expression possible. And he did it loud enough for us all to hear. I knew your father was being beaten and it lasted all day. I was terrorized by the sounds. I knew my turn was coming. I was afraid I couldn't survive the same treatment. My face was stuck to the crack in the door. I found eventually that I could lay face down and look under the door and see more area. I lay there all night, waiting to see your father return from interrogation. But he never came out. Turnkeys and guards would come and go, but your father stayed.

"The next morning it was the same thing. *Fidel* came out, wearing a fresh uniform, and stretched in the sun light. Used the bat on his thighs to get everyone's attention, then he walked into interrogation where your father was located. For the first thirty minutes or so, I didn't hear anything. Only an occasional curse word from *Fidel*. Then things got very bad, almost instantly. The noises we heard were frightening. Shouts from *Fidel*, then strikes of the bat. Heavy screams and then short periods of nothing. Then it was repeated all over again, shouts, blows to the body, screams, loud moans and then silence. This went on all day. I was nearly out of my mind from just listening. As I lay face down, I started praying for your father. I'm not a very religious man, but some higher power had to intervene. I heard your father loudly utter the words, 'you can go straight to hell'. That brought on a volley of strikes and more screams. *Fidel* finally took a lunch break and left for about an hour. I prayed that it would be over for the day. But no, after lunch it was resumed with vigor. God, it was bad!"

Jay tightened his lips and his worried brow wrinkled. He was beginning to feel the pain himself. He dropped his head, trying not to look at Bill Sutton, knowing he was also going through an emotional period.

Bill Sutton was visibly shaken and unable to continue. Recalling these visions were like living them over. Bills hands were shaking. He got up from his chair and placed his hands into his pockets to hide the tremors. He strolled toward the patio screen and looked silently through the view. He wasn't in the world. He was mentally transported back in time to 1968. No one could have survived what he witnessed.

"It hurts me deeply to say this, but your father would have been better off dead. I never had to take such punishment as was being dished out to him...the thoughts of being tortured put me in mental distress. I lay face down, looking under the door, the entire time your father was in interrogation. His treatment was mean, cruel, inhumane and unmerciful; totally against the Geneva Conventions. *Fidel* was a mean son-of-a-bitch. He had no sensibilities. He obviously got pleasure out of torturing people. He was a disgusting, repulsive, individual with a sadistic personality, a misanthrope of the highest order."

Jay listened to the words and readily agreed to such a nauseating characterization of a despicable man. His jaw muscles tightened as he gritted his teeth holding back his animosity.

"The rules we had to live by were well defined in The Code of Conduct. Surviving was different and indefinable. Somewhere between being resolutely headstrong without being a tough guy and being judiciously accommodating without divulging information was that indefinable area. That was a dilemma for each of us. It was most important not to be labeled a troublemaker. It was up to each senior ranking officer in the prison to establish certain rules and it was up to the rest of us to stay within the rules. Staying within these boundaries was the difference between surviving and dying. Each and everyone one of us faced that challenge each day. It was extremely tough. No one wanted to die and the majority desired to keep their honor and dignity. So you had to pick your own limits.

"I can't say how the interrogators picked out an individual as a target for collecting information. Being a senior officer was certainly against you. Sometimes, it was fate but in some instances it was attitude. Being a tough guy would get you trouble. It would get you earmarked as a troublemaker and when that happened you had to watch out. They had your number and you weren't going to escape their wrath.

"In your father's case, I think it was fate; like drawing a bad card in a poker hand. There was no way to win. Your father was a strong individual. I admired him and was glad to be crewed up with him.

"Cu Loc, the Zoo was a punishment camp, an exploitation prison. Your Dad was a major and his date of rank could have made him the senior ranking officer. We were placed in separate cells and I was interrogated just like your father. I took a lot of beating during my first interrogations. I found a niche in not fighting back. I took their blows without getting defensive. I yelled when it hurt, I cried when I thought I couldn't stand it any more and I prayed the rest of the time. But I never fought back. I was able to listen to your father's interrogations. They were pretty much, just like mine. He was beaten. It must have been difficult for your father to hold his tongue. Anytime he spoke out or showed any signs of an emotional outburst, the flailing intensified.

"After they brought him back to his cell, I communicated with him through the wall. He told me to hold on, not to let them get to me. He was the one getting beaten and he was telling me not to lose my determination. I couldn't believe it." Bill Sutton stopped talking. He picked up a golf ball from the ashtray and began to roll it around in his palm. He pensively stared at the opposite wall while blankly fondling the golf ball. His mind detached from the present and preoccupied with the past. Jay allowed his recollections to fill the silent moment.

Bill shook himself back to the present. "Well, anyway, they left us alone for twenty-two days. They resumed their daily interrogations with other prisoners. I watched under the door to see if I knew any of the people they took for interrogation. I didn't recognize anybody. That's when I found out just how many they housed in the Zoo. They paraded, by my count, forty-seven people into interrogation. I know there were others I didn't see that came from across the courtyard. This was a daily occurrence. Everybody, I could hear, each got the same miserable treatment. It was like an imperative, several prisoners had to be beaten each day. I wondered if they had a quota to meet.

"Then one day, about three weeks later, *Fidel* came again to interrogate us. He took your father first. I honestly think that was the luck of the draw again. And why I survived and your father didn't. This guy was brutal. I heard the first lashings, they were almost immediate. I don't know what was asked or what was said. But your father's yelling and the screams were blood chilling. Then I heard that gobbling sound your father would make and they beat him some more. They kept at it all day long. I prayed for your father, I knew he was going through hell. I stayed with my nose against the door, looking through the crack to make sure I didn't miss your father when he was returned to his cell. He never was returned to his cell. They left him there all night.

"The next day was a re-run of the same events, the screams, the torture, the lashes, the same brutal, unmerciful treatment. Your father took it all. They left him in there all night again. The third day was much shorter. Just before noon, they brought him out. Two men had to carry him back to his cell. He was bloody from head to toe. It was obvious his face and head had been beaten. There were welts on his face and blood draining from his scalp. As they passed I saw the back of his shirt. It was completely shredded and covered in blood. Your father's eyes were glazed over. They'd beaten him senseless. The expression on his face was horrible.

"He had the look of a dead man, eyes fixed, no sign of life. He couldn't hold his head up. It swung back and forth as if it were only attached by a string. He showed no control over himself. If he were unconscious, I would have felt better. But he wasn't, his eyes were open and his mouth was open. He was breathing heavily, but it was labored. I knew he was out of his mind. They put him back into his cell and left him. I tried to make contact through the wall, but couldn't get a response from him.

"Later, just about dark, *Fidel* came through the yard with an old fan belt wrapped around his fist. He held it tightly. I knew he was going to use it. The turnkey opened the door. *Fidel* entered your father's cell. I heard him yell, 'up'…there was a slight pause, then he said it again… 'up'…there was no response from your father…then I heard the bastard say…sit up…sit up…mullafucker soma bitch'. Then I heard the blow. It was a thump kind of sound. Then he said… 'you not hurt'… 'I hurt you big time mullafucka'. He thought he was faking his injury to avoid further punishment and flogged him again. When your father didn't respond with screams of pain, *Fidel* finally got the picture. They took your father away and we never saw him again." Sutton could see some distress in Jay's eyes. He chose to remain silent.

Jay stared through the porch screen, occasionally closing his eyes and shaking his head. The alarming visions of the evil, wrongdoing Cuban alerted his own dark side and 'Crying Blood' filled his thoughts. Revenge possessed his mind. He could feel the hate well up inside and he clinched his fists to relieve some of the tension. He took in a deep breath in an attempt to settle his thoughts.

Bill was more than reluctant to continue any description of past events. He spoke matter-of-factly. "We never saw *Fidel* again. We all believed he had overused his authority and the Vietnamese Government sent him back to Cuba. Your father's incident came on the heels of another incident in which a prisoner died at the hands of that same Cuban son-of-a-bitch. I was extremely fortunate. I never faced *Fidel*. I will never know whether I could have taken his brutality or not. All prisoners felt the same way. We feel lucky to have survived and we all are racked with guilt that some of us did not make it back. And then there are those who believe some of our POWs were sent to Cuba as bargaining chips. That could account for some of those who are still missing. I personally don't believe that."

Jay allowed for a long pause then asked. "Did you ever hear of the name Guillermo, I don't know his first name?"

Bill responded. "No, should I?"

"I thought maybe you might have heard them call him by his name. Then what about a Benitez Aguillar? Did you ever hear that name? I thought one of those two names might have been the one you called Fidel. I was looking for something that might confirm that."

Bill thought for a minute trying to remember. He shook his head in thoughtful recollection. His face lit up. His recall struck a link to the past and he exploded. "Beanie...Beanie," Sutton couldn't stop mouthing the name. "Beanie... I'll be god damned. Beanie!" Bill Sutton had instantly solved his long awaited mystery. "I heard them call the one guy, Beanie. I didn't understand it until now. So they were trying to say Benny. Well, I'll be damned. So one of them was named Benitez Aguillar?"

Jay nodded. "Maybe!"

"With a name like that he could be tracked down in Cuba and then the trail to *Fidel* and *The Bug* would be possible." Bill stated with a wry grin. "Beanie, huh!"

"I would like to confirm this name, are you sure they were trying to say his name, Benny?"

"It makes sense, but he wasn't *Fidel*. I always believed *Fidel* was trained in speaking slang English instead of real English. Most of his talk was in bar room English. His curse words, his slang, it was all bad English. We do know he was Latino. One of the prisoners who had a Latino background spoke to him and knew he was from Cuba. This was confirmed during our debriefings."

"Do you think he killed my father?" Jay asked showing his intensity.

"Who? Beanie or *Fidel*?

"Beanie."

"I feel certain Beanie didn't kill your father. He was just a gopher, a sidekick. I think *Fidel* did. But not in the traditional sense. He didn't put a gun to his head and kill him. But I do believe the treatment your father received, at the hands of *Fidel*, caused his death. When they took your father away, I was certain he was being taken to a hospital. We never saw him again. And when we were repatriated during Operation Homecoming, the debriefing of other prisoners confirmed he was in the hospital."

"What do you think happened to *Fidel*?"

"That's a good question, one I've thought about for a long time. First of all, I think he was part of an international communist program to test methods of extracting information from POWs. I think he was sent there by Castro to be part of the program. And to be honest, *Fidel* was too arrogant and too intoxicated with power and authority to do a good job. I think your father's death was not intended but that *Fidel* got carried away, got overwhelmingly mad and unleashed his madness on your father. Your father wasn't the only one to die from such treatment. Two young officers in the annex tried to escape and were caught. They were tortured as an example to the prison population and one of them died in the hospital, just like your father. When you received such treatment, the hospital was the next stop before death.

"I think *Fidel* was an aberration. He was driven to the prison every day in a green Russian made vehicle with a chauffeur. While *The Bug* and Beanie rode bicycles to work. *Fidel* was arrogant and power hungry. He was a man they allowed to dictate to everyone far too long. He was overpowering to the Vietnamese. They didn't like being rubbed the wrong way and he constantly did that. None of the North Vietnamese camp commanders liked him. After your father's incident, we never saw *Fidel* again. I believe he was sent back home."

"Where do you think he is today?"

"When I first retired to this golfing community, I had recurring nightmares about *Fidel*. I concentrated on getting it all out of my mind but couldn't. So I stew a little every day thinking about that man. It was the treatment he gave your father that really gets my hackles up."

"Would you still like to track him down?" Jay queried as gently as he could.

"You bet. I'm not sure what I would do with him. But I would sure like to get face to face with him." Bill was fuming at his thoughts.

"That's about the way I feel. Except I'd like to kill him!"

Bill took Jay's comment as a frustrated declaration and didn't think it serious. He assured Jay, "That thought has passed through my mind also. But I have tried to let it go. Be done with it. I would desperately like to stop thinking about him forever."

Jay answered, "Lately, I can't stop thinking about it. My biggest concern and the thing spurring me onward is our own government's intransigence. They don't seem to care. Our politicians only give lip service to the Vietnam War and the veterans. They only have their own agendas to worry about. Not one of them worries about representing the people."

Bill chuckled. "That's nothing new. They've done that for years."

"Do you think I can find *Fidel* or maybe Mr. Guillermo or Benitez Aguillar if I go to Cuba?"

"No, I don't. Not without help. I don't mean to be short with you but I've done a lot of reading about Cuba. You see I also had similar thoughts. You can't travel to Cuba. The U.S. will not issue passports or visas for travel to Cuba. Besides, you aren't allowed to spend money in Cuba. That's against the law. So, you are faced with massive problems in getting to Cuba. Once there, the bureaucracy is such that tracking anyone down would be next to impossible. My advice would be to let it drop. Go back home and honor your Dad's memory." Bill looked deep into the eyes of Jay whom he now felt compelled to treat like a son. "Would you kill this man if you found him or were you joking?"

Jay wanted to please him and was concerned that Bill might call his mother. He responded with caution and a smile. "Naw, I'd just hurt him a little bit and put some scare into him. Besides, I don't have any idea of what to expect. This man would be about fifty-five or sixty years old. He could be dead. He could be out of work and untraceable. No telling where he might be. He could be some where in the political hierarchy, some high level politico. Who knows!" Jay hoped his answers were suitable.

Jay quickly asked another question, changing the subject. "Did you ever make any contacts in Miami or in Little Havana that I might use? Someone who could help in assessing the possibility of success?"

"I did have one man who hated Castro. He had been a wealthy, high level business man in Cuba. His business was taken away by the Castro regime and he was bitter. He still had relatives in Cuba and was sending them money monthly for their survival. His name was Raul Cardenas. I'll have to search for his address. Not certain if I kept it."

Bill brought the subject back to his previous question. "Does your mother agree with what you are proposing? I believe I'd be very discouraging to you if you were my son. I know you loved your father or you wouldn't be here. But planning on doing anything like you propose would be disrespecful of your Dad's memory. I don't think there is anyway he would approve of what you're thinking about doing."

"Yeah! I know. This thing eats away at me each and every day. Then three months ago my Mom and I went to the annual conference for families of POWs and MIAs in Washington D. C. Once again they told us nothing." Jay reached into his rear pocket and pulled out two folded pages.

"I got these two pages from a DOD staffer at the conference. They are pages 28 and 29 of a fifty-six page document from the files of the Defense Prisoner of War Missing Personnel Office of the Assistant Secretary of Defense." Jay handed the pages to Bill. Bill pulled up his reading glasses which were hanging around his neck. His glasses were bifocals and he raised his head to focus through the lower half as he perused them.

Jay interrupted Bill's thoughts. "You can't see on these two pages what I saw when I copied them. I didn't close the lid to the copier fast enough and when the bright light came on its illumination allowed me to see through the blacked out portions. At the top and bottom, behind the blacked out areas, were the red bold letters 'SECRET'. At the top left of the page, also blacked out, was a document stamp identifying the pages with a DIA reference number. It was also in red. I wrote down the number and you can see at the top how I wrote it, DIA#WPP05061980." Jay was on a roll and he had Bill Sutton's complete attention. "But another thing, and this was real curious to me, the FBI was the originator of the document. On the very first line of text, and it was blacked over, were the letters 'FBI' followed by the identifier WPP05061980." Jay allowed Bill the opportunity to visualize the words behind the redacted areas.

Bill slowly offered a comment, "It does seem strange that some words were cut out and others were blacked out."

"Yeah! I thought that was odd. I think the first cut out was a name because it was followed by the identifier WPP05061980 and an asterisk. Then at the bottom of the page with the asterisk was the name Benitez Aguillar but no identifier." Jay attempted to point out that the identifier in the DIA stamp was WPP05061980 just like all the others, also hand written in pencil in the margin were the words 'Cuban/ Miami'."

Jay began again with great enthusiasm. "I have studied these two pages until they are almost frayed from handling. The text mentions the First Conference of Solidarity for the people of Africa, Asia, and Latin America to create a world-wide network of revolutionaries in all third world countries including North Vietnam. I looked this up in the library. This was a conference for all communist leaders to gather and encourage guerilla movements throughout the world. Like you said, Castro aimed this effort at the U.S. He wanted to create a strain on the American image worldwide. He formed a Cuban, North Vietnam, North Korean axis to go directly against the U.S. Somehow, I think this was the genesis for Cubans in North Vietnam. This wasn't a small document; it had fifty-six pages."

Bill listened quietly and attentively. It was obvious Jay had more than just a passing interest in the situation.

Jay started again. "There are four places in these two pages where I think they cut out or obliterated the names of four Cubans. Do you know for sure there were only three Cubans?"

Bill, fully entrapped by Jay, answered immediately. "I only saw three, the one we called *Fidel*, *The Bug* and the enlisted man we called many things, Gopher, Pancho, Chico, and the name we used the most, Hat Rack because everyone used him and he got no respect. I wouldn't mind finding him and shaking his hand."

Bill flipped back and forth from page to page to confirm Jay's reasoning. He spoke nonchalantly, "What do you think the text was all about?"

"I think this was a background document created by the FBI for some reason other than as a report on The Cuban Project in North Vietnam. And when the names appear it was just incidental to the background paper they were creating. But it had to be about or closely related to the Cuban Project you guys debriefed about on your return. And the words Cuban and Miami could be that these two guys are in Miami."

Bill tried to relieve some of Jay's passion. "So what does your mother think about all this?"

"She doesn't want to hear about it anymore!"

"I think I agree with her. I can tell you are very passionate about all this. But if you want my advice, it would be to drop it right now before you further change your course in life. I know you loved your father and probably still miss him but planning on doing something like this, taking it any further, like I said, would be disrespectful of your Dad's memory. There's no way even he would approve." Bill stared deeply into Jay's eyes.

Jay wanting to please him and again concerned Bill might call his mother, offered a final comment. "I can't stand facing each day knowing my Dad and his image in my memory is fading. I don't want his memory to disappear completely from my mind. I fear that one day I will wake up and he will be gone forever. I don't want that! If I could somehow make his death worthwhile, I wouldn't feel guilty about doing nothing. To me, giving of a life should have some meaning! We didn't win that war. His life was taken and it was all for naught. I have to make it right!"

Bill remained silent, he had no profound answers. He changed the subject. "I was in high school during the Korean War. The legacy from that war and the dilemma facing all returning veterans was 'how can you be a good military man in a rotten war'. Many of us Vietnam returnees often think about that question. We proved that you can be. We did our part in the air war. When we were taken prisoner we still had to fight another war. The war of deprivation, silence, lonelyness, hunger, sleep loss, torture, and endless interrogation. We proved you can be a good military man in a rotten war just by being honorable, and we were." Bill got up from his comfortable chair signaling time to stop. "Now you go home and start your life without this misguided effort. Tell your mother we miss her and hope to visit her one day. Tell her we would welcome a visit from her also. We have plenty of room. She can stay right here."

Jay responded with all the cordiality he could muster and left. Driving back to Orlando International Airport, he had tears in his eyes thinking about all he had heard about the pain his father had endured. His most emotional thought was, 'it was all so unnecessary'.

His thoughts for revenge became even more enflamed, creating a sense of rage. He knew beyond all doubt, this wasn't over. Not for him, he was determine to seek out and find *Fidel*, *The Bug*, Benitez Aguillar, and maybe Guillermo, who ever the hell he was.

CHAPTER III

Marcie and Penny were sitting in the downstairs den watching TV when Penny heard the upstairs phone ring. Penny, immediately responding to the first ring, jumped up and almost ran toward the stairs. She instinctively knew it was Jay calling. Penny had insisted on separate phone lines for their upstairs apartment as a means of keeping some privacy. She looked at the hall clock as she rushed pass. It was 10:30 p.m. This stay at home Saturday night with Marcie had been totally blah. She welcomed the phone ring.

Nearly out of breath from running up all thirteen stairs, she answered.

"Hello, Cobb's residence."

"Hi, Penny it's me, Jay."

"Yeah, Dah! I can still recognize your voice!"

"OK," Jay expected some animosity. "I take it from the sound of your voice that my short trip didn't set so well with you. Did you get my note?"

"Yes, I got your note." Penny was haughty. "Hell, what do you expect from me? You just said you were going to see Bill Sutton and to not let your Mom know. Now how in the hell do you expect me to keep it from your Mom. She asks questions and I have to make up the answers." She regrouped her thoughts. "You are a coward! You know that! You forced me to lie for you and to your own mother? What was I supposed to say to her?" Penny's tirade seemed to gather steam as she spoke.

"What did you tell her?" Jay had to know that before coming home.

"I told her you had to make an emergency field trip to Crazy Horse for the 'wildcat' crew which was attempting a diagonal drill and it would be an overnighter." Penny was excellent in hiding the truth when it was necessary. Most of her hiding the truth was about shopping and spending which she was good at. This was the first time she had to lie to Marcie and she didn't like it. It made her very uncomfortable.

Jay liked her answer. "That's good! I've run into a hold up. I planned to be home by now but I'm in Houston. The next flight out to Tulsa won't be for another hour and a half. I'm on Continental Flight 1856 and should arrive in Tulsa about 1:00 p.m. Tell Mom that I'm at the office and need to write up this report and that I should be home in the early morning hours." Jay uttered the words but wasn't certain Penny would use them.

"Listen Jay, you better hope she doesn't ask, because I'm not sure what I'll tell her. I don't like lying to her. I've never lied to her before and I don't want to start now…particularly on this subject. You know how I feel about this. I thought you were going to drop this thing. Suddenly you leave me a note saying you were gone."

Penny wasn't angry, just agitated. "I'm your wife, we should have no secrets. Don't you ever do this to me again!" Penny was three years younger than Jay but had a more logical mind than Jay. She could face any problem and know exactly what to do about it. She felt deep down this problem had some not-so-obvious permanent damage concealed within. That feeling sent shivers of anxiety through her whole body.

Penny calmed herself down. "I didn't mind you going to see Bill Sutton. I thought that might help to clear your mind of this obsession. It was the way you just disappeared."

Jay was very quiet at the other end. In his own mind he knew his search wasn't finished. His determination was stronger than ever. It was just the beginning and he felt pangs of guilt coursing through his own body in not telling her about his intentions.

He spoke. "How is Mom?" Jay thought changing the subject was in order.

"We've been watching TV in the den. She's alright."

Jay offered, "We'll talk about this some more when I get home. Do you have anything planned for Sunday morning? I thought this might be a good time for you and me to take Mom out for a Sunday morning breakfast. How about it?"

"OK, I'll tell your Mom. So what's the time you expect to be here?"

"I'd say about 4:00 a.m. That's allowing an hour's drive from the Tulsa airport to home."

"I'll keep the bed warm for you. We can start on those grandchildren your Mom wants." Penny smiled into the phone as she vainly offered herself. "Be as quiet as you can when you enter and I'll tell Marcie you're on the way home."

Penny hung up the phone and sat on the bed without moving. She stared at the carpet trying to unravel this growing dilemma. Unsatisfied with any of her thoughts, she slowly walked back downstairs into the den.

"Was that Jay?" Marcie asked politely but continued to watch the TV. Not waiting for an answer, she threw out another question which was totally unexpected and was tossed out rather apathetically. "Did his visit with Bill Sutton go as he expected."

Penny stopped in her tracks. She was startled. "So you knew all the time?"

"No! Not until last night when you told me that Jay wasn't coming home for the night."

"Then you knew I was lying to you when I made up that story?"

"Yeah!" Marcie grinned a wry smile. "My intuition kicked in and I called Bill last night and told him he might expect Jay. I figured that was where he was headed." Marcie arched her back to stretch while still sitting in the recliner. Her sixty-six year old bones never liked to be still for too long. She felt a degree of satisfaction and it showed. "I know Jay pretty well. He is the spitting image of his father and just as stubborn. Since we left Washington, this thing has been driving him crazy. He wants to kill somebody. I doubt if you or I can do anything about how he feels. When will he be home?"

"He says around 4:00 a.m. I told him to be quiet when he enters the house or else he would wake you up." Penny smiled back at Marcie as their thoughts connected. "He wants to take us to breakfast tomorrow morning."

"He won't wake me up. I plan to get a good night's sleep now that I know he's OK. I would like to go to breakfast with you two. We can talk then. You just as well should know that I am going to try to rope and hog-tie Jay out of this obsession. It's not a good thing. He has to let go!" Marcie looked over from the television to be eye to eye with Penny. "If he doesn't let go this is going to eat him up. I know! I've been there! And I still can't let go. But I pretend for the two of you. I'm not going to standby and watch him get lost from reality. Can you help me do this?" Marcie's expression telegraphed concern and puzzlement.

"Mom...You bet. I'll help you in every way I can." Penny's mind was going warp speed. "Listen, when we do this, I think you should let me appear as an insider with him. If we both jump on him, neither of us will know what he is up to and never know what he might do. If you allow me to be an insider, sort of half way agreeing with him, then he will tell me things and maybe this way we will at least know what he might have in mind."

"God, Penny! I am continually amazed at your grasp of things. That's good. Let him think you half way agree with him. Jay certainly got a prize when he found you!" Marcie was making a factual statement not offering flattery.

"I'll tell you a secret, Mom. I'm the lucky one!" Penny meant it. "I've just got to keep him."

****

Jay was sitting in the kitchen drinking coffee and reading the paper the next morning when his Mom walked in. He put down the paper and spoke. "Good morning Mom. The coffee is ready."

"How was your trip?" Marcie spoke cordially and politely.

"It was your typical emergency. They didn't need me to get it done!" Jay put his cup to his mouth for a sip.

"I mean your trip to Orlando to see Bill Sutton."

Jay choked on his sip of coffee as he reacted and spilled a small amount to the unexpected question. "Penny told you where I was?"

"Naw, she didn't have to. I spoke with Bill Friday night after Penny told me you wouldn't be home. I knew what you were probably up to." Marcie grinned to herself as she poured her favorite cup full of fresh coffee. She held the cup with both hands and up close to her face to enjoy the smell and feel the warm aroma. She moved slowly to a chair beside Jay. As she lowered herself into the chair, she pulled her robe up tight around her neck and settled down.

"Mom, forgive me. I had to do it."

"Hell son, it's too late now. It's over!" She stared at him, her eyes waiting for an answer. "Isn't it over?"

"I don't know! This thing has taken on a new light. Bill told me things that really got me stirred up."

"Like what?"

"That those four Cubans were the cause of Dad's death!"

Marcie instantly reacted. "He said that? How does he know? And is there any proof?" Marcie was obviously becoming agitated. "Let's drop all this crap. And it is crap. I don't want to hear about it again. I've been there and it did me no good. I don't want you to go through what I've been through. So let's drop this whole affair right now." Marcie grabbed for Jay's forearm and held it firmly. She was strong and the signal being sent could not be misinterpreted.

"Mom, I promise, I'll be a good little boy." Jay was being slightly sarcastic.

"Look at me.... Jay!" Marcie semi yelled to get better attention. "Look at me son, you've got to make me a promise. Nothing short of that will do."

"But Mom, I've got to know." Jay was unshakeable.

"Then let's hire a private detective to find these people if you have to know."

Marcie was only slightly persuasive. She knew her words were falling on deaf ears.

Penny entered the room, still half asleep. She had put her long blond hair into a ponytail before leaving the bedroom.

Even during her sleeping hours, she knew Jay had never been to bed. She was disappointed her offer for a warm bed had been rejected. She approached Jay and slid her arms around his neck, bent over and kissed him on the cheek.

Marcie watched this show of affection and was envious. For more than twenty-eight years she had not been held in a loving, man and woman kind of way. No hugs of romantic importance. Her urgings had completely disappeared and for that she was thankful.

Being an avid horse person she condemned anyone who would geld a young stallion because it took the life out of the horse. Marcie would on occasion say she felt like she had been gelded. Her life had been taken away. Marcie could still remember E. J. and wanting him would never go away. Romance novels filled this void. But she was happy Jay and Penny were still building their moments to remember.

"I'd like to take you two ladies out to breakfast. Where would you like to go?"

Penny answered. "Lord, you've got to wait at least until I've had my chance at the coffee pot." She walked toward the counter and the coffee maker.

"Mom, where would you like to go?" Jay spoke trying to add some cheer.

"Why don't we go down to Jake's Café? You know, down on the lake. All the tourists are gone by now and we could have the place to ourselves. Autumn has arrived and Lake Oolagah should be beautiful."

"What about you Penny?"

Penny nodded in agreement. Then she finally placed the hot cup of coffee to her mouth and sipped. Jay watched her intently. Her blond hair, her doll-like buttermilk skin highlighted by natural rose colored cheeks, allowed him to know he had the most beautiful wife in the entire world. Her robe gathered tightly around her waist displayed her amazing feminine curves. He knew he better not jeopardize this.

Jay had been up all night and enjoyed only seven hours of sleep in the last forty-eight hours. His eyelids were puffy, his eyeballs were like a road map of red veins, and he yawned incessantly. He wasn't in a position to do any kind of arguing. His mind was muddled by sleep deprivation and he needed nutrition. Keeping the conversation away from the subject of POWs, Cubans and death by torture was absolutely necessary. He wouldn't be able to hold his own in an argument with these two.

He let Penny do the driving to Jake's Café and he sat alone in the back seat to doze off if he could. Penny and Marcie carried the conversation during the drive to the café. Jay was exhausted. They knew it and allowed him to doze off. Even after arriving back home, Jay slept in one of the recliners in the den the rest of the afternoon and into the night.

The next day Jay went to work as usual. He was once again refreshed and his mind was in the attack mode. It was a Monday morning and he knew all his contacts would be at work. He called to the Association of Petroleum Geologists.

"American Petroleum Geologists!" The voice answering the phone was instantly recognized.

"Is this Marilyn?" Jay offered cheerfully.

"Yes it is! May I help you?" Marilyn was an excellent receptionist and secretary. Answering the phone was one of her biggest strengths. She always sounded like she had a smile on her face.

"This is Jay Cobb!" Jay responded politely.

"Well Mr. Cobb, we haven't heard from you in over three months. We miss you down here. When are you going to come visit us?" Marilyn's enthusiasm came through in her voice.

"I will visit soon. Is Carl in?"

"Yes sir! I'll tell him you are on the line. Glad to hear from you." She transferred the call to Carl Mitchell, the president of the American Petroleum Geologists Association, in Tulsa.

"Jay!" Carl Mitchell greeted him with excited enthusiasm. "How is our ex-president?" Carl couldn't have been more delighted for the call.

"I'm fine. How are you doing now that you are the new president?"

"I didn't know how much work you had to do until I took office. Now I do and it wouldn't take too much hounding to get me outta here." Both men chuckled in the phone. "I like it all, except for the long hours. I have to drive the forty plus miles from Pawnee everyday and that gets old. My wife is already complaining and I've only been here for three months. I'm afraid the next three years is going to be way too much for her. She likes staying around the house and now she has to go everywhere I go. I'll have to wait and see just how she does." Carl paused from his complaints. "Anything I can do for you, Jay?"

"Yeah, Carl... I noticed in the Geologist Digest that the NRDC (Natural Resources Defense Council) is holding a conference in Miami. What is the date and what will they be doing? Can you tell me about it?"

"Sure, Jay. The conference is the last week in October; about two weeks away the 28th, the 29th, 30th and 31st of October. It's a Wednesday through Saturday deal. It will be held in the Miami Convention Center on Second Street in downtown Miami. The Governor of the State of Florida will be there. By looking at the list of attendees, all the major oil companies will be there, including the four you represent. This will be a lobbyist's field day. Most of the State Senators will be there also.

"The Governor of the State of Florida and the NRDC are hosting the conference. This has proven to be a hot political agenda item. I am getting back channel communications from both the Republican and the Democratic Parties in Florida, each with their own assessment of new oil explorations. I've read more position papers on this in the last month than I care to mention." Carl paused before continuing. "The issue is this; the Governor, along with all the major oil companies desires to open new leases in the eastern Gulf of Mexico for oil exploration. Of course you know all this. You went through this same thing three years ago.

"On the other side of this coin, the opposition believes any new leases for exploration will have a deleterious impact on Florida's natural resources-the beaches, the shorelines, the tourism business, the wetlands and all the other things the do-gooders can think of. The Governor of the State of

Florida asked the Federal Government if he could jointly host a conference with the Natural Resources Defense Council and have a dialogue on the issues. The Governor, beginning to feel the doubts and uncertainties of an election year, wants to ride the fence on this one. He wants to have it both ways and doesn't want to alienate any voters. He's the one that called the conference and will use the outcome to his advantage. If the conference decides it is a good idea to explore for oil, he will use their recommendation to open up new leases and let the NRDC take all the flak. If the conference recommends no new oil exploration, then he will use that recommendation as his position. It is going to be a talking conference and a field day for the news media. It's an effort to take the heat off the Governor. We, of course, are right in the middle and will be there to field questions and answers. Myself and Ben Wakefield, out of Enid, will be there representing the APGA. Do you want to go?"

"Yes. I would like to go. But I can't make all the seminars or the joint sessions, and I don't want you to put me on any discussion groups or committees. I'll pay my own way and get my own hotel reservations. I'll probably get reservations in the downtown area."

Carl responded. "The Clarion is right next door to the convention center and that's where Ben and I will stay."

Jay asked. "If you would, can you send me an information package on the conference and submit my name as an attendee for the American Petroleum Geologists Association."

"Sure can! Do you want to bring Penny also?" Carl didn't wait for an answer. "I'll have Marilyn send out the material today. I am very glad you want to come. I could use your advice and counsel. Want me to send the package to your home or to your office."

"Penny doesn't care much about these things and probably won't go. Send the package to my home." Jay now had a way to get to Miami without either Penny or his mother knowing what he was about to do. Jay's enthusiasm for the trip far out weighed his guilt. When he got off the phone, he pounded his right fist into the palm of his left hand and in a low but audible voice said to himself, Yes!

****

At supper Jay mentioned how his day had gone. "I got a phone call from Carl Mitchell today. You remember? He is the guy that took over my position as President of the American Petroleum Geologists Association. He is from Pawnee, Oklahoma. Anyway, he wants me to go to a conference in Miami. The Natural Resource Defense Council is holding a conference on offshore drilling regarding new oil leases for exploration in the eastern Gulf of Mexico. He asked me if I could come. I said yes. I hope that's OK with you two. The four major oil companies that our firm represents will be there lobbying for the new leases. I believe I need to go." Jay waited for any comments from Penny or from his Mom. None came.

"They will be sending me a package with all the info I need for the conference. The dates are the 28th through the 31st of October." Jay looked at Penny. "Do you want to go? It will be like all the others we went to while I was President of the APGA." Jay used his fork to spear a piece of meat, while pretending nonchalance, waiting for an answer.

Penny spoke up. "Let me think about it. I'm not sure I want to go. Would you like me to go?"

Jay was trapped and hurriedly thought up a response. "If you want to go, I'll make us some good reservations. If you don't want to go, I won't let it bother me any. Ben Wakefield from Enid is going alone. He and I could go together and keep each other company." Jay was pleased with his response and chewed vigorously on his mouthful of food.

Marcie spoke up, "Penny, I think you should go. It'll be fun."

"I'll think about it. When do I need to let you know?"

"Sandy, my secretary will start making the reservations tomorrow. Just think about it and let me know sometime tomorrow. You can call me at the office and let me know. Then I'll have her make the arrangements."

After dessert, the three of them headed for the den, which was their normal ritual. Marcie had her own recliner and Jay had his. Penny was used to being the one who normally used the couch. She didn't mind because she could drop her shoes and recline on the couch with the overstuffed pillows resting her head and providing an excellent view of the TV.

As 9:00 p.m. sounded on the hall clock, Marcie excused herself and went into her bedroom adjacent to the den. Jay and Penny did the same and headed up the stairs to their apartment.

"Jay!" Penny wanted to talk and sat on the edge of the bed watching as Jay undressed. "Didn't you tell me once before that you would like to go to Miami to find out if any of the two Cubans, the two names you have, might be living in the States?"

"Yes, I did." Jay stopped taking his shirt off and sat down in the soft and frilly bedroom rocker. "What are you saying?"

"I'm saying this is the perfect opportunity for you to do that. When you go to Miami you can skip a few of the meetings and go around into the Cuban areas and ask some questions. Maybe look in the phone book, search the county records, try anything to find the names you have. Who knows you might have some luck."

"Strange for you to say that. Bill Sutton told me he had made a slight attempt once before while he was in Miami. He and Janie went there to board a cruise ship for an extended vacation. While in Miami he went to Little Havana and asked around. But he didn't have any names to ask about or to search for." Jay watched Penny for any signs of uneasiness. "He gave me the name of a wealthy ex-business man who fled Cuba when Castro took over from Batista. He met the man and his wife on the cruise ship. His name was Raul Cardenas. I would really like to talk with him. He could at least point me in the right direction." Jay could see he had some understanding from Penny and was more than delighted with her reaction.

"Why don't you come with me?" Jay blurted out his question without thinking. Now that Penny was agreeing with the search, Jay thought the invitation was appropriate.

Besides, Penny could handle any conversation with vigor and was light years in front of his own thinking process. As he thought about it further, he tried to insist that she come with him.

Being pensive, Penny stood up from the bed and began to remove her clothing. She had done this since they were married but it never had the effect it now had on Jay. She could see in Jay's eyes that he was being stirred and she enjoyed the tease.

"If I go with you, would we be together most of the time or do I have to do like before when you were president of the association? You stay gone all day and most of the night while I hole up in the room waiting for a call from you. I don't want to do that. We could have a good time in Miami if you could spend some time with me."

Jay considered her offer and had to think about it. His mind had been diverted as she disrobed. The more he watched, the more he wanted her. He went for the light switch. In the darkness he grabbed her, placed her on the bed and aggressively started removing her clothing just as if they were two teenagers madly in love in the back seat of an automobile on a Saturday night. He could never get enough of Penny nor she of him.

****

The next morning Penny and Jay came down to breakfast together. This was most unusual as Penny was a late riser and never came down for breakfast. The two were holding hands with broad smiles on their faces. Jay was dressed for work in his normal attire; khaki pants, a blue broadcloth button down collar shirt, tie and high top walking shoes. He would be presentable while in the office or he could be called into the field and still be dressed for the occasion. Penny wore a sheer diaphanous house robe tied tightly at the waist and every delicious curve in her body was prominently displayed. It was no wonder Jay was holding her hand.

Marcie was easily put on notice, it appeared the effort for grandchildren had started. She smiled along with the two knowing their secret had been exposed. Marcie wasn't shocked, but happily enjoyed knowing they were both human.

Penny announced, "I'm going with Jay to Miami for the convention!"

"I'm glad. You will have fun." Marcie continued to revel in the thought her son was showing manly tendencies. His dad was a tiger when it came to love making. The thought her son was just like his father brought a smile to her face. Penny's glow could not be mistaken. These two were true partners in every sense.

Penny walked with Jay out to the company owned SUV to say goodbye. Marcie knew something new was up. New ground was being broken and she was there to observe.

When Penny returned Marcie spoke. "It looks like Jay has turned into a renaissance man. Want to tell me about it?"

"I can't keep from smiling." Penny offered with a grin. "Last night was the greatest night I've ever had. It was better than on our honeymoon. I don't know what happened with your son, but I liked it and I hope it stays. He couldn't stop saying how much he loves me and I just ate it up." Penny was outwardly telling all. Marcie listened and vicariously enjoyed the journey.

"Jay wants to go to Miami to try and find the two Cubans and I'm going with him. Does that set well with you?" Penny questioned Marcie.

"We agreed to get him off this subject and get on with living. I think this will get him interested even more in his search. I'm not sure I agree. But at least you will be there to tone things down and keep him from doing something stupid." Marcie's brow wrinkled as she thought this through.

"I'll keep him off track and everything will go OK. I promise!"

"Do you want some breakfast?" Marcie queried.

"No. You know I don't like to eat breakfast. Got to watch my figure."

"You mean to keep everyone else watching your figure." Marcie grinned.

Penny questioned Marcie. "Do you want to go shopping? I think I'll go into Claremore or maybe on down to Tulsa and do a little shopping."

"What in the world do you need?" Marcie asked. She knew Penny's closet was full of fashionable clothing.

"I need some very sexy bedroom things. I am going to capitalize on what went on last night. I want that to happen every night until I am seventy years old. What I have now is sorta nun-like. I want some of those things Victoria's Secret sells. I know they are expensive, but I gotta have some. Penny was close to revealing too much to her mother-in-law.

"Yeah...I'd like to go shopping. I want to see what you buy because that will probably be the last time I ever see them. You've got the body of a Goddess and you would look good in duct tape. No telling how you would look in the right things. I sure don't pity Jay. I would just like to be there for the unveiling." Marcie meant every word of her declaration. She thought to herself, 'getting old is certainly a bummer'.

"When we get to Miami, both Jay and I will have to dress down if we go into the Cuban haunts in Little Havana. I thought I might like to go to a Goodwill or a Salvation Army store to buy some second hand clothing. I know it doesn't sound very lady like or very classy but we need to fit into the crowd. Maybe they are all dressed like we are. I don't know but my guess is that we need to dress down slightly. Jay wearing old jeans and me wearing some old worn hip-huggers. The Hispanics are pretty romantic and sexual. I know I will have to cover up my top to stop all the stares. Jay will be OK. The color of his skin and his jet black hair will match most of those we encounter." Penny paused. "My worry is in leaving the hotel. If we are supposed to be important we shouldn't be dressed that way. If we dress down and get stopped by an acquaintance in the lobby we could be embarrassed. What do you think?" Penny looked at the kitchen clock. Time was 8:30 a.m. She mentally calculated. "If we hurry we can be in Tulsa by 10:00 a.m., do some shopping before noon, have a nice lunch and then shop some more. What do you think?"

"I can't believe your enthusiasm for this. Look, I don't think dressing down is required. All you really need to do is dress casually. You and Jay together, and being in Florida doesn't demand anything but casual. And yes, I want to go shopping also. I'll go get ready." Marcie took one final sip of the coffee that had now grown cold and went into her bedroom.

****

Jay was sitting at his desk completing an evaluation of the seismographics on a proposed site when he had the urge to call Bill Sutton in Orlando. He reached into his handy note book, found his number and dialed.

"Hello." Janie Sutton answered the phone.

"Good morning Janie, this is Jay Cobb. Is Bill in?"

"He sure is. He's out back washing off the golf balls he picked up after the weekend duffers left. I'll go get him." Jay sat back in his chair and waited.

"Hello Jay. Good to hear back from you. Was your mother angry about your trip down here?" Bill queried.

"Only slightly. She called you and I didn't know that. So when I tried to lie about things, I was busted." Jay didn't elaborate but went straight to the subject.

"I'm going to Miami in two weeks. So I would like to talk about my search and to find out what you know that might help." Jay went directly to the point.

"Before I say anything, you've got to tell me your mother knows all about this. I told her I would help get you off this obsession. Does she know and does she agree?" Bill waited for an answer before continuing.

"She knows. She isn't quite sure about the trip. But since Penny is going with me, she's OK with it."

Bill was relieved that he didn't have to turn Jay down on his request. "Well first off, I didn't have any names to search out like you do. I gave you the name of Raul Cardenas. We met him on the cruise ship and he was from Cuba. He departed the cruise ship while we were docked in Bermuda. Maybe he didn't go back to Miami. To get to Cuba you have to go to another location outside the U.S. That might be what he did. But he told me he was in the phone book. You can look that up when you get there." Bill walked to the closed-in patio, took the cordless phone with him and sat down.

"How long do you expect to be in Miami?" Bill asked.

"About five days. Penny is going with me. She's looking forward to another 'honeymoon'. She will be a great help when we have to contact people."

Bill settled into the chaise lounge and started his suggestions. "The best search you want to find is with the *marielitos*. In the early 1980s, about April during the Mariel boat lift, there were one hundred and twenty-five thousand Cubans who entered the U.S." Bill paused. "That would be my start. Some organization in Miami has that list of the aliens who entered the country. It's either the INS (Immigration Naturalization Service), U.S. Customs, the Coast Guard or maybe one of the law enforcement agencies. They were all in on the task of matriculating those people into this country." Bill paused to think of other methods of searching.

Jay interrupted. "I'm trying to take notes, so go slow!"

Bill continued. "I think that every Cuban that entered had to pass through the Krome Detention Center. They stayed there until they were cleared for entry. The papers had to be filled out and filed. Then they had to determine if they had a legitimate sponsor here in this country who could see to their needs, find housing, find them a job, make certain they didn't wander the streets when they were released. So maybe going to the Krome Detention Center would also be a good place to start. It's located south west of Miami in an old Air Force missile site left over from the missile crisis."

Bill hit on a sore subject. "I guess you know that Castro purposely dumped many prisoners out of Cuban prisons and assisted them in going to the U.S. during the Mariel boat lift. Many of those hardened criminals didn't get released. Maybe there is a list of all those detainees you could search through. Of course, you'll search for Benitez Aguillar and Mr. Guillermo. Those are the only names you have. If they are here in the U.S., their names will have to be on a roster somewhere and my guess is it would be with the INS." Bill could tell Jay was busy taking notes so he allowed him to catch up.

"There are also numerous Cuban-American organizations which might be helpful in your search. Most of them are for a 'Free Cuba' and for better 'Human Rights' for the dissidents jailed in Cuba. All these organizations are aimed at liberating Cuba. They probably kept lists of those entering the U.S. which they could use for fund raising. Each day there are more and more groups being organized. My guess is that if you go into Little Havana on S.W. 8th Street, Calle Ocho, you would find more than enough people familiar with those organizations to steer you in the right direction." Bill paused again. "Are you staying close to 8th Street?" Bill asked the question but didn't expect an answer. He didn't think Jay had researched the trip enough to know where to go, what to do, or how to do a search. Bill continued, "In the Cuban part of Miami, Little Havana you will find numerous shops, Cuban souvenir shops, food places, sitting parks and gathering places. The elderly Cubans meet in Domino Park every morning to play Dominoes. You are searching for an elderly person; that might be the place. You might keep that in mind if you want to stroll around and enjoy the Cuban atmosphere. Janie and I did and we thoroughly enjoyed the stroll. It was fascinating."

Jay asked, "Did you feel safe wandering through the streets?"

"Absolutely! I found the Cubans to be very happy people, full of joy, always smiling, enjoying each other, like your father, always joking. Of course, as we walked around we didn't know exactly who was Cuban and who wasn't. We stopped in Domino Park and watched the men play dominoes. The chatter was constant. Everybody talked except the man studying a move. He would be very thoughtful.

Bill asked. "What are you going to do if you find Benitez Aguillar?"

That was a huge and disquieting question for Jay to answer. The phone fell silent as Jay pondered an answer.

Then he spoke. "I don't know. I've thought about it more since I talked with you on Saturday. This man, if I find him, will be in his sixties, maybe infirmed, maybe crippled, hell he could be dead. I don't know what I would do. For certain, I would lean on him to finger the other three. Especially Mr. Guillermo, *Fidel* and *The Bug*.

"The two names, Aguillar and Guillermo always appeared together on both pages of the FBI document, I would expect the two to know each other. If one is in the States, then I would expect the other to also be in the States. One or the other might be *Fidel* or *The Bug*. I need their names. If those two are still in Cuba then I particularly need to know that also."

Jay was very cautious about saying too much knowing Bill and his Mother had talked about this. He didn't want to ring any alarm bells at this point. His own mind wasn't made up about going to Cuba. There were too many obstacles in the way for such a trip. He was not certain he could even go to Cuba. Silence was essential.

"Back to Raul Cardenas. Is he the type of man to talk freely and honestly. Will he answer my questions?" Jay expected Raul to be his first contact in Miami.

"Yeah...he is very social. He is bitter about Castro. Like I told you, by Cuban standards Raul was a rich man. He had his own business, owned a lot of land and lived high. There is an area of old downtown Havana which has a huge thoroughfare leading north to the Bay and into the open waters of the Gulf of Mexico. This boulevard was where all the elite lived. The homes were lavish and ostentatious. That was where he lived during the Batista regime. When Castro came to power, all those people had to quickly evacuate their homes, get all their money and head for the States. Castro and the peasants acted as one monumental effort to redistribute the wealth. Those with wealth had to leave in a hurry and take their bank accounts with them. All their land and homes were taken over by the revolutionaries. Raul is bitter about leaving his homeland after being very successful as a businessman. I think I would be also." Bill paused then continued, "When Raul and his wife got off the cruise ship in

Bermuda, I figured he was going back to Cuba for a visit. He would slip in under the radar and back out again. He told us he had family still in Cuba and visited on a yearly basis. I surmised he was headed back."

Jay asked, "Tell me again about the so called 'Cuban Project'."

"That's a name we attributed to those Cubans in Hanoi. When we returned to the States, many of us were imprisoned in Cu Luc. We referred to that place as 'The Zoo'. We named those Cuban interrogators as *Fidel, The Bug* and their sidekick we now know as Benitez Aguillar or a man named Guillermo. This facility was previously a French Villa. It was in the southern suburbs of Hanoi. As we were debriefed we all referred to our interrogators as the 'Cuban Project'. After that it was placed in public documents and in books on the subject naming it as 'The Cuban Project'. I guess the name stuck. I have since found out that Cu Loc was a high exploitation camp. Public accounts have described four deaths of POWs at the hands of the Cubans. I knew of two, your Dad and another pilot who tried to escape. A North Vietnamese writer by the name of Nguyen Van Thi has described Cu Loc and the Cubans as the Peoples Army of North Vietnam's (PAVN) darkest secrets. I don't know if the Cubans had an official name for it or if it was a special operation or a joint operation with the Russians or if it was supposed to be a diplomatic mission. It has remained 'The Cuban Project' in all books and journals since then."

"What do you think Benitez might recognize it as? Would he know about it if I referred to it as 'The Cuban Project'."

"Naw...He's probably never heard of that name. But he would recognize the name '*The Bug*'. If you should happen to find him, ask about '*The Bug*'. I'm sure he would flinch at the name. '*The Bug*' was vicious and whacked Beanie several times. He'll remember the name."

"I'll certainly keep that name in mind and lay it on him if I should find him. I know this has taken up too much of your time and I appreciate it. I'm not going to do anything stupid, so if Mom calls, tell her I've got my head on straight."

Bill closed, "I'll do that. I hope you are successful. Good luck! Oh, another thing, if you are successful, let me know. I might want to visit with Aguillar and Guillermo.

Jay hung up the phone and gathered his notes. He highlighted the names of organizations he might contact. The INS was at the top of the list.

Jay's secretary Sandy knocked lightly on the open door to get his attention. Jay motioned for her to come in without looking up.

Sandy handed him a list of reservations she made on his behalf. She spoke, "You said you had to be in Miami and available for the first meeting of the NRDC on the 28th of October at 9:00 a.m. The only flight I could get had to be on the 27th. If that is OK, your reservations for two are with American Airlines Flight 3265 departing Tulsa at 4:45 p.m. to Dallas-Ft. Worth, then a connecting flight with Continental Flight 2125 from DFW to Miami, arriving in Miami at 9:45 p.m. EST, the night of the 27th. Your hotel reservations are with The Clarion Hotel next door to the Miami Convention Center. The confirmation numbers are right there." Sandy pointed to the numbers. "If those are OK, I'll get the tickets from the Travel Agency."

"That's good Sandy. Go ahead and get the tickets. And thanks." As Sandy was walking out the door Jay spoke up, "Sandy, one more thing, would you get in touch with some car rental places at Miami International Airport and ask them to reserve a vehicle for us for the night of the 27th for five days. Let me know how we stand on that. We will need a vehicle."

"Sure boss, consider it done. Does it matter what kind of vehicle?"

"Naw...anything with wheels."

At supper time Jay asked numerous questions of his mother. He wanted to know if she was OK with this trip. Jay never mentioned he requested his friend Carl at the APGA to set this up as a personal favor. His mother and Penny accepted the trip as a legitimate requirement for Jay to attend. He knew he would have to be cautious to keep it quiet.

Penny had watched Jay all through the meal for any indication he might remember the previous night's torrid love making and know for sure he enjoyed their encounter as much as she did. Jay was mostly silent and in deep thought. He was challenging himself about the daunting task ahead. He felt that Penny would be a drag if he had to move fast, but also wanted her to be at his side to lessen the drama and ease the conversation. It wasn't a dilemma but it was taking his every moment of thought. His determination had not lessened any. He was more resolute now than ever before. The puzzle would have many pieces but he would not rest until the puzzle was completed.

Often his thoughts turned to the U.S. Government, if they couldn't be successful in searching for the four Cubans then how did he expect to be successful? It was a quandary he lived with for too many years. He had to know!

CHAPTER IV

Checking in at the hotel went quickly. They met Carl Mitchell and Ben Wakefield in the lobby as they were going into the lounge. Neither Carl nor Ben had their wives and wanted Penny and Jay to accompany them for a nightcap. Excusing themselves Jay and Penny headed for their room on the twelfth floor. The twelfth floor was the last floor before the penthouse suites. This convention was no different than the many he and Penny attended while he served as president of the American Petroleum Geologists Association. The penthouse suites would be reserved by lobbyists offering free food and drink twenty-four hours a day. Going up one floor was all that was required to gorge yourself with free booze and hors d'oeuvres. He liked that idea. If he had to be away, Penny could enjoy all the free stuff.

After settling in the room Jay went to the penthouse level to get he and Penny a nightcap. Coming back into the room, Jay took out the huge Miami phone book and started writing down numbers and addresses. His first thought was to look up Guillermo. There were thirty-one entries with the last name Guillermo. Then he looked up Aguillar. Again there were too many entries and not one of the entries was for Benitez Aguillar. Drawing a blank on those two names, he looked up U.S. Government Offices. He found the INS office in the Government Center, on N.W. Miami Court, with all the other administrative offices. He wrote down the address. He looked up the Krome Detention Center. It wasn't under the U.S. Government. He finally found it under the County listing and wrote down the address. At least this was a start.

With only slight satisfaction he turned to Penny whom he had nearly ignored up to this point. "How's your scotch and water?" Jay tried to mend his lack of thoughtfulness toward Penny.

"It's just fine." Penny had been playing with the TV remote while Jay was busying himself in the phone book. She found a 'hot pillow' XXX rated movie on the TV but Jay hadn't noticed.

"Tomorrow I need to go to the first meeting at 9:00 a.m. to hear the guest speaker from The U.S. Department of Energy." He looked at Penny who was on the bed with both pillows stuffed behind her back watching TV. He spoke a bit sarcastically and mused at his own thoughts, "Boring!"

Penny directed his attention toward the TV by pointing with her shoeless foot. "See!"

Jay saw what had been holding her attention and knew she was indeed intent on having a second honeymoon. He gave no disagreement and fell to her ploy.

****

The next morning Jay was up at 7:00 a.m. and hurriedly did his morning shower and shave. He worried whether he should wake Penny or allow for her normal get up time to arrive. Jay quietly closed the door and headed to the restaurant. He knew Penny would rather eat at her own leisure while he was at the Convention Center for the first meeting. The first meeting started at 9:00 a.m. with the keynote speaker enthusiastically outlining the course for the next four days.

Promptly at 10:00 a.m. after the keynote address the meeting adjourned in time for the seminars to begin. Jay left the Center and headed back to the room. As predicted, Penny had eaten breakfast and was putting the final touches to her make-up when Jay entered the room.

"I'm glad you're ready. I'm eager to get started. I want to go to the INS office first. Rather than having to fight for a parking place, I think we should take a taxi. OK with you?"

"Isn't their office in a government complex? If it is there should be plenty of parking. But I don't care, whatever you think is OK by me. Are you going like that. I mean shouldn't you change clothes, be a little more casual like me?" Penny asked.

"Yeah...I guess." Jay yanked at his tie, opened the top button to his shirt, discarded his blazer jacket and declared, "I'm ready."

Taking Penny's advice, Jay decided to drive. The Government Center Offices were located on N.W. 3rdh Street and Miami Court. The valet parking attendant gave them brief directions as four blocks north then four blocks west. The drive sounded easy enough. Time was mid-morning and traffic was only moderate. Jay knew he had made a right choice by driving. After fifteen minutes of driving and intently watching street signs, he made his way to the location and parked in the parking lot. Penny had been right about that. There was plenty of parking.

Entering the building and finding a directory near the entryway, he easily located the INS Office. Penny walked with him as they went down a granite-walled corridor with tiled floors then around the corner to another similar corridor to where the office was located. They entered the waiting room, which was filled with Latinos. It was obvious all those waiting were about four or five complete families with babies, kids and pregnant wives. The loud chatter instantly let you know that English was rarely spoken. There was no receptionist. As you entered you walked across the room to a three by four foot glass window built into the wall. It had a round cutout about chest high for asking questions and another bigger cutout at the bottom suitable for passing papers. You had to wait until someone came to the window.

"*Hola!*" The woman behind the glass wall spoke in Spanish. "*Puedo ayuda usted.*" She asked if she could help them.

Jay looked at Penny in disdain, then turned to speak to the young woman behind the glass, dropping his head to the level of the cutout. "Do you speak English?"

"*Si! Habla usted ingles.*"

Jay turned to Penny again with a disgusted look on his face then turned back to the lady. He declared, "Speak English!"

"OK, I speak English."

"I am looking for a friend. Is there a roster of all the Mariel boat people who entered the U.S.?"

"You must take number. At the door is numbers. You must take number and wait turn."

"I don't want a number. I want to find a list of all the people who entered the U.S. during the Mariel Boat Lift." Jay knew this wasn't going to lead anyplace. "Do you have a supervisor I can speak to?"

"Supervisor not here. Try next floor. Room two-one."

"Room twenty-one?" Jay asked as slowly and as fluently as possible.

"Yes, room two-one."

Jay took Penny by the arm. "Let's go!" The waiting room was an exceptionally busy place. Rubbing elbows with foreigners made them both feel uneasy. Many didn't speak any English, had their entire families with them, babies and all. It was apparent some needed a good bath. Being polite was nearly out of the question. The area was disgusting. Litter was everywhere. Empty drink cans and discarded candy wrappers from the vending machines were strewn over the waiting room. As they left the room, Penny sort of shivered. It wasn't a good thing to witness much less be a part of. After enjoying the obvious visible wealth in the hotel and then mingling with near poverty immigrants was a disturbing experience. The two extreme ends of the money spectrum were readily apparent and in opposition.

Arriving at Room 21, Jay read the label on the door, Permanent Resident Applications. Jay thought that was odd. Why was he directed to Room 21? Below the Permanent Resident label on the door in smaller words were Application Forms with four separate listings; Sponsorship, Green Card, Citizenship, Asylum Application Forms. Jay thought this couldn't be the right place but looked into the room anyway. As he opened the door, he felt he was looking into the same room he just left. It too was filled with entire families of Latinos.

He searched the walls for a cubicle or an office for anyone who might be in charge. There was nothing but Latinos filling out papers on large desks along two walls. He looked at Penny perplexed. Certainly there had to be someone, somewhere, who might be in charge of all this. He searched each wall sign to see if there were any directions. The signs were too numerous to know where to start and they were all in Spanish with small English subtitles. At a nearby door was a sign, which appeared more promising. It had a makeshift doorbell. The sign instructed, when forms are completed, ring bell for assistance. He walked over to the door and rang the bell. He waited and waited. He rang the bell again. Finally a man opened the door. He was about 5'6" with a white shirt showing about its sixth day of wear, slightly portly, no tie and hair that needed attention.

    Jay asked politely. "Do you speak English?"

    The pudgy man answered with no concern. "Certainly."

    "Well finally! Is there an INS roster of all the people who came to America during the Mariel Boat Lift?"

    "I'm sure there is but I'm not certain where you might find it. That was sixteen years ago. Our records are so massive we can hardly maintain what we gather in a month. I would guess you could find a list of the names in Washington. They are probably on a computer printout. Sorry!" The man reached to close the door.

    "Wait a minute!" Jay put his hand out to prevent the door from closing. "I am searching for someone who came to the States during the boat lift. Where would I find that information? Is there a supervisor here in this building?"

    "Try the third floor, Room 328."

    "Who would be there?" Jay was getting frustrated.

    "That is the administrative section, maybe they could help." The short man shut the door in Jay's face.

    "I'll be damned!" Jay turned around to see all those faces staring at him. He looked at Penny. "Should we try room 321?"

    "No, he said room 328. You've got to be calm and think, and yes, I think we should go to room 328 and at least ask."

    Room 328 was a large room with numerous desks, chairs, and cubicles. There was no receptionist, just many workers each busy with their own work. If you needed to talk with someone, you had to walk up to their desk and interrupt them to ask your question. Jay thought about this before approaching anyone.

"Excuse me. Excuse me." He waited for the nice looking lady to answer him.

"Yes...What do you want?" The lady responded like an opponent.

Jay explained. "I am searching for a friend. I think he came to the States during the Mariel boat lift. Do you know how I might query the system to see if he is in the States."

"Does he have a Green Card?"

"I would guess so."

"Then he would be in the system. Go down to Room 21 on the first floor. There is a form for locating family members. Fill it out and turn it in by ringing the bell. Someone will come and accept it." She turned back to her work. "We have signs all over the place to direct people. You should read the signs."

Jay was on the verge of exploding when Penny, seeing his frustration bubble to the surface, grabbed his arm and pulled him toward her. "Let's go honey...down to Room 21 and get a form." Penny was amused at the situation. To a disinterested party, this would have brought a good laugh. Penny mused again, "Bureaucracy, you can't live with it and you can't live without it." She did her best to contain her amusement. Jay could see her body reacting in restrained laughter.

"Damn...this is going to be more difficult than I thought." He walked out of the room in disgust. "These people must be overworked because they are certainly ungracious." Frustration was in his voice. "Let's go back to the car and leave!" They left the building in disgust.

On the way to the car he spoke, "Maybe we should have a bite of lunch or a snack and then drive out to the Krome Detention Center to see if they have a roster."

"I'm not hungry, but I'll have a snack somewhere along the way if you want to stop." Penny had been more than accommodating to Jay. She knew this frustration was working in her favor. When Jay got enough of the run around, he would stop his effort.

As they walked across the parking lot, Penny stopped and grabbed Jay by the arm. "Look at that building." Penny pointed to a single story building across the parking lot. "That is the Social Security Administration building." She continued to point. "See the sign next to the door. Maybe we should go in there before we leave this area and ask about your two names."

Jay agreed and they walked over to the building. Several men were idly smoking cigarettes near the entryway. Both Jay and Penny were startled as they entered the door. The waiting room was large, and completely filled with Latinos. Jay thought to himself, this is a repeat of the INS area. Entire families were waiting. The noise level was deafening with chatter. Jay looked through the crowd and could see a young girl breast feeding her baby, making no effort to offer some dignity to herself and the child's needs.

Both Jay and Penny were being bumped any time they tried to move within the crowd. Jay grabbed Penny by the hand and pulled her through the crowd, out the door into the quietness of the parking lot. When out of earshot of anyone, Jay exploded. "Shit...I feel like we are in a foreign country, no one speaks English. If there ever was any dignity in these offices, it is certainly gone now. All the signs have been changed to Spanish and English takes a back seat. This isn't anything like Oklahoma. Mingling in those offices for any reason makes you feel dirty, without importance and very, very out of place. When did the United States disappear?" Penny nodded her head in agreement.

"Let's go out to the Krome Detention Center and see if there is the possibility of any success there." Penny again nodded in approval.

The Krome Detention Center was about thirty miles south west of Miami in the eastern Everglades. It was swamp land until the USAF started a missile base there for defense against any attack from Cuba. The drive there was easy until you left civilization. Then the road narrowed with nothing on either side but swampland and an occasional alligator sunning itself. Jay stared at the place as he drove up. It was ringed by high chain link fences with concertina wire at the top. It was a prison in every sense of the word and wasn't what he'd expected at all. He had visions of an administrative building with dormitories on all sides. Such was not the case. The dormitories were ex-WW II military barracks. The huge fields in the rear were filled with detainees; some playing soccer, some lifting weights, others playing catch with a softball. It looked like a prison with lots of in-mates.

There were no administrative buildings. There was a single guard on the gate. No cars were allowed into the compound. There was an adequate parking area outside the fence nearly filled to capacity with Government vehicles, U.S. Public Health Service, U.S. Coast Guard, U.S. Immigration Law Enforcement, U.S. Customs Service, and several buses. Jay had to think through what he might say to the guard. He even had thoughts of just driving away. There was no way this would be fruitful to his search. Thinking he should at least try to do something for driving so far in all the traffic, he got out of the car and walked up to the guard. The guard was a uniformed civilian hired by a Security Service. He had only a rain shelter and an interphone system for contacting his supervisor on the inside.

Jay asked, "Do you keep any records here." He tried to be as cordial as possible.

"What kind of records?" Jay quickly decided the guard wasn't trying to be unhelpful, he was just dense.

"Records of the Mariel boat people." Jay watched the eyes of the private company guard and knew he was going to gain nothing from being here.

"Who were they?" The guard asked out of curiosity.

Somehow, Jay contained himself. "Does your intercom go to your supervisor?"

"Yes sir, is there anything wrong?" Again the guard was curious.

"No...but if your supervisor has been around a long time he might be able to answer my questions." Jay still tried to be as cordial as possible. There was no sense in getting haughty with this guard. He was just a required official ornament.

"He's my sergeant. He's been here almost a year now. Want me to call him?"

"Yeah...ask him if he knows about the Mariel boat people?" Jay thought to himself, this could be entertaining.

Pressing the intercom button, the guard spoke. "Sarge... There is a man out here, wants to know about the Mariel people? Do you know anything about those families?"

Now Jay could barely contain himself. He managed to thank the guard and walked back to the car grinning all the way. He knew Penny would get a big laugh out of this. Jay was having frustrated doubts about his proposed effort to search for his father's killers. It wasn't going to be easy. If he was having this much trouble here in the ole U.S. of A., he couldn't imagine his troubles if he had to go to Cuba.

Jay told Penny all about the guard and she did have a good laugh. Jay was shaking his head as he drove away.

"I think I'll head due north until I cross S.W. 8th Street, then we'll go east on 8th. That way we can get a good view of Little Havana. I'd kinda like to get a feel for the way of life the Cubans have found here in the States. All we have ever seen in Oklahoma are illegal Mexicans. The Cubans have to be somewhat different. As a 'people', they are much like us. They have ethnic diversity just like us." Jay didn't realize it, but he was referring to himself as an American instead of as an Indian. Penny liked that.

It would be about an hour's drive to get back to the hotel. Time was approaching 5:00 p.m. and there would be heavy traffic from office workers getting off and heading home. Jay particularly wanted to find Domino Park. Bill Sutton told him Domino Park would be a good starting point for asking questions. He turned east on 8th Street S.W. Much to his surprise it was a wide three lane street with one way traffic toward the hotel area. He thought Domino Park was close to the hotel. It seemed to be a good idea to look for it.

As he drove east on Calle Ocho, his attention turned to the night's activities in the Hospitality Suites at the hotel. Since this was also a business trip, he was anticipating making a few contacts with the conferees.

He spoke to Penny as he funneled through the traffic. "Did you bring that black dress; the one that almost looks like a formal gown with the low cut front."

Penny knew exactly which dress he was talking about and began to tease him in amusement. "You mean the one which allows my boobs to hang out." Penny was more outward in her conversation. I bought that dress for you, not for other men to ogle over. Jay could count on Penny to always be frank and sometimes very awkwardly embarrassing in her tell-it-like-it-is frankness, she added, "You want me to show some cleavage?"

Jay was embarrassed by her comments and his face flushed slightly. Penny's sexual desire was stronger than his. She desired sex more for emotional support than for satisfaction. Having sex two or three times a week kept her urgings down. She could remember when Jay needed sex nearly everyday. His desires in the last year or so had lessened dramatically. The needs of the two didn't match anymore.

Penny knew what caused these changes in Jay. It was his intensity with a project, any project. He gave his all. Doing anything half way wasn't his style. The same held true for his sex life. When he needed it, he was excellent. Penny knew when Jay's mind had captured his spirit. She knew it was this search for his father's killer that had him possessed this time. She wanted it over to allow things to get back to normal. Penny looked over into Jay's face. His expression revealed his thoughts. His mind was elsewhere.

Penny was very extroverted and her thoughts dictated her spoken words, what came up came out. "Are you trying to rope in someone using me as the bait?"

Jay was trapped, "Yeah...Jack Richardson. He owns a trucking company, Mid-West Oil Carriers. He has a fleet of tankers and hauls oil from the fields to the refineries outside Houston in Pasadena and Baytown. He is making mountains of money. The Geologist's Digest had a feature article on him, naming him as a 'comer'."

Jay's attention was suddenly distracted by the activity along the street. He slowed to watch. There was a park area filled with people, mostly young couples. Musicians were playing for tips and some of the couples were dancing. The decorative sign above the entry façade next to the sidewalk read, Maximo Gomez Park. The crowd had spilled over onto the sidewalk. Some had brought their own wine in a brown paper bag, others were drinking beer. Everyone seemed to be having fun. Jay looked for a parking place and found one a block away. He and Penny exited the vehicle and walked back toward the festive activities.

As he approached he took his lead from all the other couples in an effort to blend in. The couples who weren't dancing had their arms around each other and were swaying to the music. Jay put his arm around Penny. Penny, shorter than Jay, put both her arms around Jay's waist and the two also began to swing with the music. There was a saxophonist putting out sounds from memory and a drummer, using wire brushes instead of sticks, offering the mood capturing beat. The people were having a great time. In asking another couple, Jay learned this area was also Domino Park! The table and chairs had been pushed back making room for dancing and merriment. The amorous moves coming from the ladies were sensual and created stirrings in their gentlemen friends. Occasionally, these pent-up urgings caused some pushing and shoving as unaccompanied guys would try to cut in on a couple. But it all appeared to be in fun. Jay and Penny stayed for about an hour, watching and absorbing the fun before heading back to the car and the hotel.

"As I was saying earlier." Jay got back into the subject he had abruptly dumped. "This man Jack Richardson owns Mid-Western Oil Carriers. His operation is out of Oklahoma City. The article said he was going public as Mid-Western Oil Company Inc. It said he planned to retain a fifty-one percent share of company stock and to get into oil exploration big time. Our company has oil leases and mineral rights in three counties in the Cherokee Strip. These leases we believe have massive untapped oil reserves down at the three thousand foot level. Our company is small and we don't have the resources to tap those basins. Besides that is not what we do. We find oil. We research and obtain the mineral rights and then we sell the leases to these rights. As geologists that is our only job and success is our yardstick.

"I would like to cultivate Jack Richardson's new company as a potential buyer for some of our leases. The list of attendees shows his company as hosting in one of the penthouse suites. I want to go up there and chat. I need you to go with me to help break the ice." Jay pulled up to the valet parking area and tossed his keys to the attendant. He and Penny walked into the hotel lobby.

"So you want me to do a number on him. Show him some cleavage to get his attention and you sell him our company leases?" Penny was only slightly agitated. Having her body glorified by others made her feel like a beauty queen again and elevated her ego. She had been sitting at home for the past three months and could use an ego boost. Parading herself in front of strangers for business reasons, however, seemed tawdry, unladylike, and cheap. Jay shouldn't have asked.

"I'll wear that black dress." Penny wanted to be accommodating. "And I'll wear some of the new undies I got from Victoria's Secret. One is a black lacy push-up bra. I know it will make your eyes pop out, but I'm not sure I want all those other men to start staring down my front." Penny was sincere in her comments making Jay feel guilty for making such a request.

"Forget I ever said anything. I shouldn't have asked." It was obvious. Jay knew he had overstepped his bounds and tried to apologize.

Penny asked, "If you want to sell those leases, why don't you sell them to the companies with which you are already have contracts? If you are sure there is oil down there, I'm certain they would gladly purchase those leases. I don't understand."

"It's not just about selling the leases. It's about the 'finder' royalties, which go with the leases. Well established companies like Mobile or Exxon have been around a long time. The company policy on 'finder' leases is set. With a new company getting into the business, success is paramount and they will offer two or three percent more per barrel in royalty fees. Mid-Western Oil I know will be ready to pay bigger 'finder' fees. That could be very lucrative to our future and our security.

"Glad you told me that. Now I can really show some cleavage and enjoy clinging onto the man. I might even allow him to grab me somewhere. Now that I know this is a paid performance; I can really get into doing the job you want." Clearly, Penny was being sarcastic and expressing her displeasure at being used as trolling bait.

Jay began to feel even more guilt for ever asking. As they walked across the lobby, it was nearly impossible to weave through the crowd. The first day of the convention was over and the attendees were mingling slowly through the lobby headed for the penthouse hosting suites for food and drink. All three elevators had suit-and-tie professional men waiting for the next ride up. Jay and Penny were mostly unnoticeable in their casual wear.

****

Penny wore the black dress and Jay was very successful with Jack Richardson. This success almost got him off track from the original reason he came. Ultimately, his resolve remained as before. He was still determined as ever to complete his search for the four men who killed his father.

Jay awoke the next morning with a feeling of exhilaration. His contact with Jack Richardson had been more than promising. Jack assured Jay that he was opening five hundred thousand shares of stock in his new company and the capital expected would allow his Mid Western Oil Company to begin drilling for oil. He asked Jay to come to his office in Oklahoma City to talk about the leases he had available, and...to bring some contracts. Jack was ready and looking forward to it.

The oil business was overshadowed by his eagerness to go back to Domino Park. He left Penny in bed as he dressed and headed down stairs to the restaurant for breakfast. Time was nearing 7:00 a.m. as he entered the restaurant. It was filled with convention attendees. Instead of waiting for a table, he walked out into the fresh morning air and wandered down

Brickell Avenue across the bridge over the Miami River. The morning air was delightful and he kept strolling down the street. As he approached S.W. 8th Street, he walked west thinking he would walk to Domino Park. Not realizing it was sixteen blocks away, he kept walking. This morning stroll turned into a very long walk and gave him time to think. On the way, he stopped in a coffee shop and purchased a cup of coffee. His stroll was most enjoyable and he lost track of time and distance.

His thoughts turned to what his next effort might be. Cuban American Organizations might have a list of Cubans entering the States. He would look in the phone book for names and addresses of some of those organizations.

When he finally arrived at Domino Park, there was one lone man sitting at a table sipping his morning coffee. The concrete and the neatly arranged tile work decorating the area was still wet from the early morning wash-down and cleanup by city crews. Jay walked over to the gentleman who appeared to be in his sixties.

Jay asked, "Do you mind if I join you?"

"Please, have a seat." The elderly gent spoke perfect English. Jay's mind slowed. He asked himself, should I ask if this man is Cuban?

"This is an excellent morning. My name is Jay." He offered his hand. The man responded in like manner.

"My name is Juan." The man was very cordial. "Nobody ever comes out here this early. I come here because this is the one time I can have a peaceful cup of coffee."

Jay asked. "Oops! Do you mind if I sit here?" Jay took the man's comments to believe he wanted his peace and quiet.

"Please sit down. Is this your first time to Miami?"

"Yes it is. I'm from Oklahoma. I came here for the conference going on at the Convention Center."

"How do you like Miami?" The gentleman seemed to offer conversation.

"It is a beautiful city. I haven't been to the water front yet. We just came from the airport straight to the hotel. Haven't seen too much of the city either. My wife has a list of places she wants to see. I wanted to see Little Havana."

"Well, this is it!" The man used both hands in an outward motion to convey his comment.

Jay asked, "Do you come here very often?" He was trying to lead the conversation to some probing questions.

"I come here every day, at this same time. This area reminds me of The Prado in Havana. I can sit here and let my memory wonder back in time. The only difference is a lack of early morning people. In Cuba everybody rises early and the streets fill quickly with activity. You know a new day has started. Everyone is happy and enjoying each other. I come here every day and see no one until almost lunchtime. I used to live in Havana and hope that someday I can go back."

"Do you have family there?"

"No, my family is all here. They all have jobs. I come here after they all leave for work."

Jay approached the subject. "Do you think you might go back to Cuba one day?"

"Yes, I hope!"

"When did you come to the States from Cuba?"

"I came in the summer of 1960, right after the revolution. I had a business and knew it would be taken over by the Castro regime. I left as soon as possible. I got plane tickets for all my family and we flew into Opalocka Airport. We've been here ever since!"

"It is strange that you are from Cuba and I am looking for someone from Cuba. I think he came during the Mariel Boat Lift." Jay was ready to fire his first question. "Is there any organizations that keep records of people coming to the States from Cuba."

"Oh...Yes. There are many." Juan was glad for the conversation. "When my family came, we were the first people to go through the 'Freedom Tower'. It is known as Miami's Ellis Island. It is now a museum provided by The Cuban American National Foundation. They must have good records. They are located on N.E. 6th Street and Biscayne Boulevard." Juan grinned, "They keep asking for donations." Juan paused, offering additional help. "There is also the Cuban-American Assistance Organization on S.W. Twelfth Street in the 1800 block and there is also an Hispanic Library on West Flagler Street." The gentleman smiled as he spoke. There was no sarcasm, just amusement.

"Which one of these organizations would have a list of all Cuban Americans living in Miami?"

"If you are looking for someone, I would go to the Cuban-American Assistance Group. They are the most widely recognized and viable organization. They have files on nearly every Cuban who entered the States. Their files only go back to the revolution by Castro. So 1959 to the present would be the years their files would cover."

"Where could I find this organization?" Jay was eager. He took no notes. He knew he could come back any day and get more information.

"They are down on S.W. Twelfth, 1830 Twelfth Street, I believe."

"Is that very far? Can I walk there?"

"Yes you can. It's only about four blocks away."

Jay had the information he needed. He cordially excused himself. "Maybe I'll see you tomorrow. I like to stroll in the early morning. Let's have coffee again tomorrow."

"OK...I'll be here."

Jay flagged a taxi to head back to the hotel. He had to give the news to Penny. She was still in bed when he opened the door. "You've got to get up! I've got a new lead." Jay's excitement showed. "We need to eat breakfast."

Penny looked up from the bed. Her eyes not quite open fully and her hair drooping around her face. She mumbled some words. "What time is it?"

"It's 9:00 a.m. I've got a lead that I need to check out."

"Hell, go check it out and let me sleep. I did you a favor last night." Her legs began to move ever so slowly under the sheets as she extended them in a sleeper's stretch. She took in a deep breath and blinked her eyes in an effort to wake up. "What do you need me for today?" Her words were hesitant.

"I want you to go shopping today." Jay knew those words would be heard.

Now only slightly alert, she casually threw off the sheets. "What's on for today?"

"I want to go to the Cuban-American Assistance Organization and search for my two names. I would like for you to go find you a new dress, similar to the one you wore last night, and buy it. Tonight we must go back to the Richardson suite and make certain we have him hooked. You've got to look gorgeous. You and the dress you wore last night got me the chance to speak to him. I think we have him hooked. I just need to make certain." Jay was business like in his request.

"You mean, low cut, cleavage showing, sexy display kind of dress."

"Yep...you've got it. Do you want me to wait breakfast for you?" Jay asked.

"I'm not going to eat breakfast. How much can I spend on a new outfit?" She asked to find out how serious he was.

"You have your own credit card, the sky's the limit."

Now Jay really had her attention. She sat on the side of the bed, tussled and scratched at her hair. "You go ahead to where you need to go. I'll be back by 5:00 p.m." Penny yawned and continued to scratch her scalp.

"You use a taxi, I'm gonna take the vehicle." Jay quickly vanished through the door.

Jay was slowly driving west on S.W. Twelfth watching the street numbers waiting for the 1800 block. Once there he slowed even further. The traffic allowed him to observe housing numbers. There it was 1830! The house was old, maybe fifty years old, three stories with an exterior of wooden weather boarding. Parking was easy. He was approximately three miles from downtown.

He rang the doorbell, even though the door was open. The windows were raised and the gentle breeze provided the only cooling. A short, dark-skinned man came to the door. He wore khaki pants and a golf shirt with white tennis shoes. He had a ballpoint pen clipped to the opening of his golf shirt. He was very polite.

"Good morning sir, may I help you."

"Yes, I was told you have records of all the Cubans who entered the States."

"We do, but only from 1959 to the present. Are you looking for someone?"

"Yes, I am!"

"Is he a family member?"

"No, but I would like to find out where he might be."

"We charge a $25 dollar search fee for you to use our archives and 25 cents a copy to make copies of the papers you find." The man opened the door for Jay and turned to walk away. "Follow me!" The man took Jay through two doors to a room full of file cabinets. Jay guessed there were about twenty-five or thirty, four drawer, gray steel file cabinets.

"You need to sign in and state the name you are looking for. Pay first or leave a check on the clip board and you can start." The man explained the system. It was alphabetized with index cards. The index cards identified the subject by number and the file drawer his papers would be in. Jay reached into his pockets and paid his $25 dollars.

"Does your organization take donations?" Jay asked.

"Yes, it is donations which allows us to keep these records and give assistance where needed."

Jay pulled out his folded checkbook and wrote a check for one hundred dollars to the Cuban-American Assistance Organization. The man was very thankful. He left Jay in the file room to begin his search.

Jay went directly to the 'G's and the name Guillermo in the index cards. There were at least thirty entries with the name Guillermo. Jay took the time to write down all thirty names and the year they came to the States. Only three of the names came to the States in the 1980s. That was the year of the Mariel boat lift. He identified those by underlining the names.

He went to the files to find what information might be available on each. The first file was for Alberto Guillermo. His age was twenty-three. The next name was for Manuel Guillermo. His age was thirty-two. The next name was Pablo P. Guillermo. His age was forty-two. None of these names helped. Jay thought for a moment and went back to the index file. He looked under the 'A's for Aguillar. Again there were numerous names. Abedane Aguillar, Abreu Aguillar, Acosta Aguillar, Acevedo Aguillar, Agrego Aguillar, and on for another twenty names. Then he came to Beaton Aguillar, then Benitez Aguillar. Jay stopped transfixed on the name. Bingo, he had a name he was searching for. Jay wrote down the file cabinet in which the papers were located. Grinning to himself and feeling a sense of accomplishment, he found the cabinet, the file drawer and the file. There was only one paper in the file. It was handwritten on yellow legal pad paper. It was beginning to show discoloration due to age. Jay immediately took the file to the copier and made two copies of the paper. He wanted to make sure he had the page and the time to grasp what information was written on the page. He returned the file to its correct place then took a chair and began to absorb the comments.

Benitez Aguillar was a marielito. Jay let his thoughts proclaim, I knew it. This guy came over on the Mariel Boat Lift. He looked at his age; born 1936, entered the country April 28, 1980. No sponsor, height 5'7", weight 165, skin color light, health good, religious preference Catholic, identifying features 4 inch scar left thigh, immunizations all complete. Detained awaiting sponsor. Released May 6, 1980. No sponsor. Country of origin, Cuba, Province of Cienfuegos.

Vocation, farmer. Then there were general comments; able to work, high school education, spent time in the Cuban Army, speaks some English. Jay was very pleased with himself. He searched through the adjoining rooms, searching for assistance. He found the man in charge.

Jay asked, "Did they allow detainees to be released without a sponsor?"

"No, they didn't! Everyone had to have a sponsor or the hopes of a sponsor before they would even consider release. They didn't want to put any of the refugees from Cuba into the population without a means of support. They had to make certain not one of these detainees would become homeless and wander about the streets."

"Look at this one. It states he was released without a sponsor. How did that happen?"

The man stared with a puzzled look on his face. "I don't know, all we do is maintain records as an archive. We don't know anything about the process of matriculating them into society. Maybe you should talk with the INS about this case.

"Are your records typical of the other records?" Jay queried with skepticism. "Is that paper you have all the records that were in this man's file?"

"Yes!" The man answered.

Jay again was getting perplexed at the problems he was running into.

"We usually have more paper work than that. We have follow up information. Where they went. Where they were employed. How they were doing. How much have they become a part of society and their citizenship status. Lots of information like that. We do, however, rely on them to come in or call in the information. Annually, we send out a questionnaire to be filled out and we put it in their file. Looks like we have never heard from your friend." The man was bewildered.

"Is there another organization I might check with to see if they have further information on this man?" Jay needed another lead.

The man took down some notes to find why their files had so little information. He made himself a copy of Jay's page and wrote at the top 05/06/1980. Jay watched as the man wrote down the date. He knew he had seen those numbers before but couldn't remember where. Jay also wrote down the date on his page, 05/06/1980.

"You might try CFC, Center for a Free Cuba, they are the next largest organization here in Miami. You might try The Freedom Tower Museum. Have you tried the INS?" Jay winced at the suggestion.

"Where is the CFC?" Jay was considering going to their location and searching their records.

"They are one block over on S.W. Eleventh Street, 1921 is their street number." Jay wrote down the number. He was more determined than ever to get to the bottom of this.

Finding street number 1921, he parked and rang the door bell. Again these doors were open as were all the windows.

The slight wind helped keep the house cooler. A lady dressed rather colorfully in a long flowing, lightweight skirt and a very flimsy top came to the door. There were signs of sweat under the armpits.

"I understand you keep records of Cuban Americans entering the States."

"Yes we do. Anyone in particular you are searching for?" She was very polite and attempted to dust her hands before offering a handshake.

Jay handed her the copy he had in his hand. "I'd like to find this man."

She read the name out loud, "Benitez Aguillar. He was a marielito, Yes?"

Jay nodded his head in the affirmative. It was obvious this organization was financially better supported. The lady pointed Jay to her computer area on the back wall. "Go have a seat and we'll look up this gentleman."

She followed Jay, sat down at the computer, punched a few keys and the computer came to life. Then she put in Aguillar, Benitez, entered it into search and waited. The screen announced, Search complete, no matches for Aguillar, Benitez.

The lady turned toward Jay. "I'm sorry. We have no Benitez Aguillar in our system."

"Would you do me another search, try the sir name Guillermo."

She asked, "Do you know his first name?" Jay shook his head.

Entering the name Guillermo, the computer came up with thirty-six people with the name Guillermo.

"Sorry, without a first name or some other kind of search information, we can't help you."

Jay tightened his jaw, said thanks and headed back to the hotel. This search wasn't over. He had other trails to pursue.

Jay went back to the hotel believing Penny wouldn't be there. He used a lobby phone to call to the room just to be sure. With no answer he confirmed Penny was still out. He walked over to the Convention Center just to see and be seen. There were numerous meetings going on through out the building. He picked one and sat in the back to listen. His mind remained on his search. Thoughts were plaguing him about his next move. This was his second day, only two more left to complete his search. Tomorrow he would go back to Domino Park and have another chat with his friend. There was a chance he might know something about the *marielitos*. Benitez Aguillar had to be somewhere. He remained in the meeting until it broke up at 5:00 p.m.

Penny was back in the room and humming a tune when Jay walked through the door. "I found the most beautiful dress. You're going to love it. And it will do the trick you want from me." She rummaged through the dress box, pulled out a bright red dress made of a sheer material, and held it up in front of her so Jay could see the purchase.

Jay spoke, "It looks flimsy. That color fit's the sexy part alright. Any cleavage going to show?"

"You bet. Want to see?" Penny was a perfect size 8 and the dress she purchased would fit her like a glove. She stuck her chest forward. "How far out do you want 'em."

Jay felt the tinge of a blush and could feel his eyeballs turning red. "This is strictly to gain attention and for me to show off my trophy wife. That's all."

Penny walked in front of the wall mirror, held the dress in front of herself and turned from side to side admiring it. "This is just right." Penny moved to the closet and hung the dress on the rack. "How did your day go? Did you find your man Guillermo?"

Jay was excited to answer. "No, but I did find the name Benitez Aguillar." Jay's enthusiasm came to the surface. He spoke louder than normal for him. "Aguillar came to the States during the Mariel boat lift in the 1980s. But they haven't had contact with him since he was released on May the 6th, 1980." Jay's face lit up instantly. He ran to his brief case and took out his document. He looked at the reference number. "Well I'll be damn! Look here." Jay pointed to the document where the reference number was listed, WPP05061980.

"What?" Penny readily asked the obvious.

"That reference number we have been watching. That was a date. The 05061980 was the date he was released from the Krome Detention Center!" Jay was beside himself. One small piece to the puzzle had been solved. It made him grin from ear to ear. "Want a drink? I can go upstairs and get us a couple of drinks."

"Yeah...I could use a scotch and water."

Jay left enjoying the idea of his new find.

Penny and Jay left their room about 8:30 p.m. and walked up one flight of stairs to the penthouse suites. Jay was nervous as a cat in a dog kennel. The dress Penny was wearing was making him sweat. His nervousness began to show. His hands were shaking and he had to clear his throat to say anything. The red dress had a top which had multiple folds and the folds were gathered at the waist and held by a black imitation rope which tied and hung to the side. There were opaque panels sewn onto the inside of the top folds along with hidden bra support shielding the possibility of any see-through accidents. Penny told Jay she wasn't wearing a bra as a well intended tease. Knowing this held Jay captive in his own thoughts. The fullness of the gatherings of the top accentuated her hourglass figure. Penny looked sensational.

Jay was proud but equally scared of the reaction the dress might cause. He thought he had gone too far in giving instructions to Penny about how he wanted her to appear. Penny was completely at ease wearing her new dress, displaying her natural endowment and accentuating her curves. She liked seeing Jay squirm. She knew she had him for another night of satisfaction. He wasn't going to be completely in the search mood for long and she knew it.

Penny began a tease just to make Jay squirm more. "How do my breasts look to you." She breathed deeply and allowed her chest to swell. Her best assets stuck out like soldiers at attention.

Jay reached for his collar and ran his finger inside hoping to relieve the tightness slightly. He tried to answer but the words got stuck in his dry throat. He cleared his throat and finally muttered, "Just fine! Almost too fine! Now I feel like I need to hide you and keep you all to myself!"

Those were words of magic. They brought a huge smile to her face. She said, "Good! That's what I'm counting on."

CHAPTER V

It was nearly impossible for Jay to sleep during the night. His mind was totally consumed in locating Benitez Aguillar. Now that he knew Aguillar was in the States, his search had taken on a higher priority. The digital clock sitting by the phone on the night stand was hidden by Penny's body. She was insistent on sleeping on the right side of the bed and her curled up form hid the face of the clock. To watch the time Jay had to raise himself high enough to see over her body. Numerous times during the night he made the same effort just to see the time. Time would not pass fast enough.

 Their room was an interior room and the absence of early morning light did not offer any clues regarding time. In October, Daylight Savings Time acknowledges daybreak at 5:30 a.m. and it seemed like an eternity waiting in bed for time to pass. As he raised himself to view the clock, the red digitized numerals announced a time he could finally get up. It was 6:15 a.m. He softly raised the sheets with his right hand and slid out of bed slowly trying not to wake Penny. He always did this for Penny and it wasn't necessary. She was a sound sleeper and it usually took a stronger effort to wake her up. But Jay still recognized her need to sleep and did his best not to disturb her.

 Once dressed he slipped out the door and pushed the recall button for the elevator. Arriving at ground level, he swiftly crossed the empty lobby, went out the automatic doors and started walking the entire sixteen blocks to Domino Park. He felt an urgency to talk to his new found friend, Juan. He stopped for coffee just like the previous day. Arriving at Domino Park, he saw Juan sitting in the same spot and moved in that direction to join him. Juan already had his coffee.

"Good morning Juan." Jay very casually greeted his friend.

"You remembered my name." Juan smiled his greetings.

"Can I join you." Not waiting for an answer, Jay continued. "I know you come here for a quiet, undisturbed cup of coffee, and I don't want to infringe on your ritual." Jay was exceptionally polite.

"I welcome your company." Juan spoke perfect English and only occasionally could you detect any accent, which would identify him as a foreigner.

"Did you go to any of those organizations yesterday? Did you have any luck?"

Jay eagerly welcomed the question. "Oh yes I did! I found the name Benitez Aguillar but I didn't find the other name. They were very helpful. Thanks for the tip." Jay allowed for another question or two from Juan, trying not to show his impatience. But he was bursting with anticipation to talk about his situation. He was in his third day, tomorrow would be the last day of the conference and he knew there had to be a stroke of luck or genius if he was to successfully find Aguillar.

Juan queried again, "Did they have a biography on Aguillar?"

Jay was more than thankful for Juan's asking. "They had very little information. He came to the States in the Mariel boat lift and that was about all the information available."

"How old was he?"

"He was born in 1936 in Cienfuegos Province. I went to two organizations. The second organization didn't have his name at all. It was like he just disappeared after he arrived." Jay watched Juan for any expression that might give him other clues for his search.

"So he is sixty years old. Was their anything about a sponsor?"

"No, he apparently had no sponsor. No forwarding address. No kin folks listed. That was the end of the trail."

"Did you try the INS?"

Jay almost laughed at the suggestion. "The INS seems to be too swamped to help anyone with any problem." Jay wanted to expound on his disgust with the INS and too many foreigners working the system, but he didn't. He needed Juan and maintained his cool in an effort not to antagonize Juan. Jay looked off into the distance searching his mind for any avenue he might use while Juan was available. "Do you need another cup of coffee? You're about empty and so am I." Jay reached across the table to grab Juan's cup.

Juan nodded his head. Jay left with both cups to find a refill. He had seen a coffee shop on the corner and headed in that direction. Looking into Juan's nearly empty cup, he could tell Juan liked it black. Returning after a couple of minutes, he handed Juan his coffee. Now Juan would have to be helpful.

"Are there any other organizations that might follow or list those Cubans who escaped from Cuba during the early 1980s?" Jay was trying to keep the conversation going and the search from ending.

"Did you try law enforcement, Customs, the Coast Guard, the Sheriff's Office, the local Police, the county records? They might be helpful. All those agencies had a hand in moving the *marielitos* through the system. You wouldn't have believed it unless you could have seen it. Every bus available was used to transport my countrymen from Key West to Miami. There was no system set up to handle that many people coming to the States. They used school buses, commercial carriers, city buses, rented vans, every shuttle bus available from the hotels and motels. They shuttled people from Key West to Miami. It was a mess and it took about three days for the system to get set up for the influx of people. If your man Benitez came during the first three days, he could easily have been lost in the system. If he came after that, then there has to be a record of him somewhere." Juan shook his head and grinned.

"Should I try Customs?" Jay knew he didn't have enough time to go through all the agencies in search of a name. They would all still be swamped even after sixteen years. And more people were still coming from Haiti, and all the Caribbean Island countries, not necessarily looking for asylum, but for a better life. Jay waited for Juan to answer.

Juan thought about his answer. "No, it would just be a wild goose chase. They aren't interested in extra work."

Jay thought about the comment 'wild goose chase'. This man has been truly blended into American culture. Only an American would use those terms. He waited for a useful thought. None came. He sat there quietly enjoying his coffee and knew this was the end of the road. Juan was equally quiet. The two sat and watched while the city crews cleaned the area from the night before. They were later than usual. As the wash-down crew came closer to their location, they raised their legs to allow them to clean under their table.

Jay asked, "What time do you usually leave here?" Jay needed this information in case he had more questions.

"I'll stay until all the old men come to play dominoes, usually around 10:30 or 11:00."

Jay thought this to be a humorous comment. He was talking to an old man who referred to the others his age as old men just like Bill Sutton did.

"By the way, what is your full name?"

"You'll be surprised. It's Jaun Tomaso."

Jay showed some bewilderment. "Isn't that an Italian name?"

"Yes, it is." Juan answered genuinely in agreement.

"So…You are Cuban…Right?" Jay's consternation was obvious.

"Yes, I am Cuban. My father was an Italian American. I was born in 1930. At that time the Mafioso was using Cuba as a base for illegal operations. My mother, rest her soul, became pregnant with me and used his last name for me in the hopes I might become an American. My father took me back and forth to America while I was young. So I am half and half."

"That answers how you are so fluent in English. I am glad to make your acquaintance." Waiting a few more minutes, Jay finally shook his hand, excused himself and started back to the hotel. He was slightly disappointed in this morning's lack of enlightenment.

He was walking through the lobby when he remembered he should have asked about the other name, Guillermo. Jay left the hotel in a rush. He needed to catch Juan while he was still in an approachable mood. In a rush, he flagged a taxi for the ride to Domino Park. Since Calle Ocho was a one way street east bound, the taxi driver went west on S.W. 7th Street until beyond Gomez Park then came eastward to Domino Park.

He arrived and went directly to Juan's table. "I forgot something. Did you ever hear the name Guillermo?"

"Antonio?" Juan questioned.

"I don't know what the first name is. How old would you say Antonio is?"

"He's in his sixties."

"Do you know where he lives?" Jay was beginning to feel eager to see Antonio.

"If you wait here for about another hour, he will be here. He comes here everyday. He brings his own fold-up tabletop and his own box of dominoes. Usually there is an American made Cuban cigar stuck in his jaws. There is the El Credito Cigar Factory three blocks east and all the tourists and Antonio buy their cigars direct from the factory. Antonio is an avid domino player. Everybody knows him and many come to watch him play.

"He usually shows up about 11:00 a.m. and stays for three or four hours. He never gets up out of his seat to stretch. When playing dominoes, he's oblivious to his surroundings. He has become a legend in this park. Many opponents watch his dominoes closely, thinking he has marked them somehow and cheats."

"You think he will be here in about an hour?" Jay's eagerness was obvious. His impatience was even more obvious.

It seemed like the hour wait was taking too long. Juan got up from his chair to leave and said, "Watch for an elderly man with a foldable board under one arm and a box of dominoes in his other hand. That is Antonio." Juan left.

Jay completely blended into the area quite well. His skin color was similar to all the Cubans, and he was very casual. He knew he didn't want nor need another cup of coffee, but he left for the coffee shop anyway. The cup of coffee would give him a prop he could hide behind.

As time approached 10:45 a.m. he saw a man walking up 8th Street. He was carrying a cardboard panel under his arm and a small box in the other hand. Jay thought, that's my man. He waited for him to find his normal seat, unfold his tabletop, and dump his box of dominoes onto the table. He was about 5'6" and appeared to weigh approximately 165. That should be my man, Antonio Guillermo. Using his coffee to sip and being as nonchalant as possible, he approached Antonio Guillermo.

Two other men approached as well. It was obvious they knew Antonio and could be his playing mates. Both men were younger than Antonio. They greeted each other very cordially and spoke only in Spanish. Jay grinned as he approached. He didn't want to move too quickly. The men began their first game. Jay watched closely. He had never seen or played dominoes before. He made an effort to understand the game. One of the younger men asked Jay. "Want to play?"

Jay was surprised. "No, don't know how, I'll just watch."

"Take a seat anyway."

Jay was thankful for the offer, pulled out a chair and sat down. The men continued to speak in Spanish and Jay felt out of place. He watched as Antonio, deep in thought, made a block with a double six. Antonio smiled and looked toward the other two players. Several comments in Spanish passed between them. Jay knew the younger men were being slightly hostile toward the move.

Jay made an offhanded remark loud enough to be heard. "That's the kind of move *The Bug* would make." Antonio slowly looked away from the table into Jay's eyes. There was an unspoken connection between the two. Antonio quickly looked back to the table.

While they each studied their next moves, Jay asked, "Do any of you know Benitez Aguillar?"

Antonio instantly looked up. His puzzled expression showed on his face. Jay knew he had struck a nerve. He tried to engage again. "I need to find him!"

"What for?" Antonio tried to hide his inquisitiveness.

Jay had to think quickly. "He seems to have disappeared. He knows a man called *The Bug* whom I would like to locate."

Antonio's face flashed immediate concern. Antonio was startled by the comment. He attempted to hide his agitation and casually asked, "Why do you need to find him?" It was difficult for Antonio to return his mind to the game. Wondering who this stranger might be plagued his brain. He hesitated when his turn came.

One of the younger players spoke, "It's your turn Antonio. Make your move!"

Antonio sat motionless, trying to hide his inner turmoil. "Are you from the INS or some other agency?" He threw the question toward Jay.

Jay responded, "No, I just need to find him or *The Bug*." Jay was not thinking fast enough to derail the questions. He sat quietly for the next thirty minutes watching Antonio's every action.

Antonio continued to cast glances at Jay. All his stares were peering and probing. It was obvious to Jay he had found something. He didn't yet know what. Jay continued to sit opposite Antonio and return each and every intense look. Finally Antonio got up from the table, stopped the game, made some comments in Spanish and began to fold up his cardboard table top. The two younger men gathered his dominoes and placed them into the box. Antonio spoke a few more words to the young men and left. Jay followed.

As they walked west on 8th Street Jay, about ten feet behind, kept his distance consistent. He expected to follow Antonio to his home. Antonio attempted to speed up his gait. Jay did also. It was now very clear to Jay that Antonio was disturbed about his inquiry and was trying desperately to disengage from this stranger following him.

Finally Antonio couldn't take it any more and certainly did not want to let Jay follow him all the way home. Antonio blurted out. "What do you want."

"I want to know how I can find Benitez Aguillar."

"That's impossible!" Antonio was adamant. "So leave me alone."

"I can't. If you know something you need to tell me." Jay responded.

"What if I don't?" Antonio threw back.

"I'll keep following you until you do." Jay had his man captured and he knew it.

"I can't tell you anything about Benitez Aguillar. And you better leave me alone before I call the police. You can't just follow me."

Jay knew that was true. He also knew Antonio was rattled and he might be on the verge of getting something out of him.

Antonio turned away and continued to walk down 8th Street. He turned left at the next intersection and walked south for two blocks. Jay walked with him and slightly behind. Antonio was very irritated. For a sixty year old, he was fairly healthy and his walk was brisk. He stopped abruptly and again turned to Jay. He asked Jay. "Do you have pencil and paper?" Jay nodded in the affirmative. "Then take down this number....555-9657....ask for Sam Bascom... and don't contact me again, or come near me again." Jay wrote down the information.

Jay had to consider his next move. What if the number was bogus and merely an attempt to get rid of him. He decided he needed to stay with Antonio at least until he knew where he lived. They walked south at the next intersection for two more blocks to Twelfth Street. Jay recognized the street. It was the same street where he found the Cuban American Assistance Organization the day before. Antonio turned left, crossed the street and walked through a short gate into a yard. Antonio spoke. "This is my home. You can't come in here. I respectfully ask that you leave me alone."

"OK...I'll leave. My name is Emanuel J. Cobb and you will hear from me again." Jay accepted his wishes, turned and walked away. Jay wrote down the street number of the home. He was truly onto something and could hardly wait to get back to the hotel to call the number Antonio gave him.

Antonio watched from inside his home. As the stranger left the premises, he got the phone and called FBI Agent Sam Bascom. He reread his instructions to make certain he was correct. The instructions ordered him to call Sam Bascom anytime he felt he was being watched or being hassled. Antonio told Sam Bascom about the incident with a man named Emanuel J. Cobb.

After the conversation with Antonio, Sam Bascom called Washington to the Defense Intelligence Agency and asked for Special Agent Stewart Carter. For three months Agent Carter had waited for this call. Sam Bascom told Stewart Carter that Jay Cobb had finally appeared.

"Damn! I knew it. I damn well knew it. This is going to work after all. I had nearly given up hope that Emanuel Cobb was going to show at all."

"Well Stew, unless I miss my guess, he is going to be in my office in about two hours. You need to contact your boss and make sure this thing is still on. I know how to handle Cobb, I just need to know if it is a 'go'."

"I can guarantee it, but hold the line and I'll walk into his office to find out."

After a few minutes Stewart Carter came back on the phone. "It is a 'GO'!
Somehow when I handed Mr. Cobb those papers at the next of kin annual meeting in Washington three months ago, I knew he was our man. It's going to happen!"

Sam Bascom affirmed. "OK, then I'll take care of the next step."

Time was approaching 12:30 p.m. and Jay was hungry. He decided to wait until he got back to his room and get Penny so they could eat together. When he entered the lobby he impatiently sought out a house phone and called the number for Sam Bascom. His excitement was reaching a crescendo. The number rang once before being answered.

"Federal Bureau of Investigation." The receptionist answered delightfully. "May I help you?"

Jay was dumbfounded. He couldn't speak. Why the FBI? His thoughts were muddled.

He answered. "Is Sam Bascom in?" Thoughts were still rattling around in his head.

"Who shall I say is calling?" The receptionist continued just as she was taught.

"My name is Jay Cobb." He worried he had stumbled into something more than he was prepared to handle.

"One moment please."

Jay thought about hanging up the phone and going to lunch with Penny to allow himself more time to think. Suspecting he was in over his head, he moved to hang up the phone. When he heard a response in the receiver, he listened further.

"This is Agent Bascom. Can I help you?" The voice was polite enough.

"I'm Emanuel J. Cobb. I just met Antonio Guillermo. He wouldn't answer any of my questions and gave me this number to call." Jay in his haste spoke up. "What's going on? Why am I talking to the FBI? Who is Antonio Guillermo?" Jay sputtered out all the thoughts he had.

"Tell me again who you are and what you want with me." Sam Bascom responded as professionally as he could.

At first Jay was silent, then he explained who he was and why he was in Miami and that he was searching for Benitez Aguillar.

"I'm Agent Bascom, can you come to my office, say about 3:00 p.m.. If you can, I'll wait for you. Our office won't be open tomorrow. It's closed on Saturdays.

Jay spoke out again, "What's this all about?"

"Can you be in my office at 3:00 p.m.?"

"Yes, where is it?" Jay was unsettled and dazed with this confusing turn of events.

"It's in The Federal Building on S.W. 1st Street across from the Dade County Courthouse. We are on the second floor, Room 214.

"I'll be there!" Jay was puzzled and bewildered. He hung up the phone slowly as his mind churned. He reluctantly moved away from the phone in deep thought. This was baffling to him. He went up to his room in a mental fog.

Penny was in the room preparing herself for lunch. Jay thought it was time he spent some quality time with his wife. "I want to take you out to a nice place for lunch. Where would you like to eat?"

Penny answered. "Some place nice. You mean 'very' nice?"

"Yes, very nice. We haven't had much time together. I need to make it up to you. Let's start with something good to eat."

Jay used the room phone. He requested the valet parking service to have his car ready in ten minutes. Waiting for Penny didn't help his thought process any. He was hyper, needing to know more information. He couldn't decide whether to tell Penny or not. This might ruin her day and her trip. He remained silent.

Jay spoke while Penny was completing the final touches to her hair. "I thought we might drive north toward the MacArthur Causeway and find a unique restaurant along the waterfront." Jay had already looked up the location on a local map in the lobby and knew exactly where he wanted to go.

Penny mumbled her response. "Uh huh."

Driving north from the hotel, Jay watched for 1st Street. He was more focused on where the FBI Office was located than searching for a restaurant. Reaching 1st Street he found the street to be one way eastbound. At least he knew where it was. He would wait for the return trip to find it. Penny pointed out a nice restaurant as they got further north of downtown.

Jay never mentioned the FBI or his encounter with Antonio Guillermo during their meal. He allowed Penny to enjoy her food and tried to be as cordial as possible. But his mind was elsewhere. He kept looking at his watch. Penny asked several questions and Jay's answers were tale-tell that his mind wasn't with her. Penny knew something was up.

After lunch Jay dropped Penny off at the hotel and drove straight to the FBI Office. It was only 2:15 p.m. but he didn't care, he had to know what was going on. The directory indicated the FBI Office was on the second floor. Jay walked up the stairs. The stairs were wide and designed to architecturally be a part of the ornate appearance offering institutional grandeur to the structure.

Jay found the Office. An opaque half glass mahogany door with gold leaf, three inch high letters 'FBI' identifying the office. Opening the heavy door, Jay moved toward the receptionist's station. She was sitting at a huge ostentatious mahogany desk. The woodwork shined like it was maintained on a daily basis by a very meticulous and caring cleaning crew. The room smelled of air freshener. Jay thought to himself, it has the aroma of pine.

"Is Agent Bascom in? My name is Jay Cobb and I have an appointment for 3:00 p.m."

She used the phone to announce Jay's arrival. Dropping the phone back into its cradle, she pointed toward a single door immediately to her right. Jay knocked slightly before entering. Agent Bascom was on the phone when he entered and Jay had to wait nearly five minutes for Sam Bascom to finish his call. This was a standard but typical ruse to fake a phone conversation to make the customer wait and feel intimidated. Jay never felt intimidated. He was urgent in his presence. The agent never indicated for Jay to take a chair and sit down. He made him continue to stand until the conversation was over.

Jay looked around to assess the importance of the office and the agent. The wall to the right side of the agent was nearly covered with a bank of five foot tall, four drawer file cabinets. Each of the file cabinets was double locked. There was a steel rod passing through welded hasps at the top and bottom and through each drawer handle disallowing entry without removing the steel rod. Each hasp had a lock holding the steel rod in place. There were numerous Certificates of Award hanging on every wall. The agent's desk top was very neat. Papers were all in proper placement. Jay had the thought, this man isn't busy at all, too much time to be neat. Agent Bascom hung up the phone and without getting up from his heavily padded, leather swivel chair, reached out his hand toward Jay to shake his hand as an introduction.

"Good afternoon, I'm Agent Bascom. What can I do for you?" The agent spoke as if he wasn't expecting Jay; another intimidating tactic.

"I met Antonio Guillermo this morning and questioned him about Benitez Aguillar. I could tell by his actions he knew the man, but he wouldn't answer any of my questions. He told me to contact Sam Bascom. I called the number only to find you are an FBI Agent. I need to know what's going on." Jay blurted it out showing some concern in his voice. Still he wasn't intimidated by the planned reception.

"Tell me who you are and why you want to know." The agent rocked back in his comfortable high back swivel chair.

Jay began. "Three months ago my Mom and I went to the POW/MIA conference held by the Defense Department annually for the next of kin. I was there and I got two pages from one of the briefers which had been redacted but there were still two names listed. The margins had a penciled entry, two words 'Cuban' and 'Miami'. The two names listed were Mr. Guillermo and Benitez Aguillar." Jay paused to allow the agent time to follow. Both pages had the same entries in the margins.

The agent spoke, "So what is your interest?"

"My father, Emanuel Jayhawk Cobb was a POW in Hanoi for five years and ten months. We were told he was a prisoner. When all the POWs were repatriated, he wasn't one of them. In talking with other families of POWs and POWs themselves, it came to light that some prisoners died in captivity. We were told later that my Dad had died in captivity. Contacting my Dad's backseater, also a prisoner, we learned my Dad was tortured to death by Cuban interrogators. Piecing together the puzzle, I surmised that the U.S. Government knew this but was withholding information which would confirm it." Jay paused for words and thoughts. "The two names on the two pages convinced me that Guillermo and Benitez Aguillar were Cuban and could be somewhere in Miami. I wanted to talk to them to put an end to our family's misery and get some closure." Jay stopped and watched Bascom's face for any sign of commiseration. None showed.

Agent Bascom stood up, reached into his pocket and pulled out a key ring. He searched the ring for the correct one and went over to the bank of wall cabinets. One of the drawers was labeled with the letters WPP. The agent took off the lock, pulled the securing steel rod right out the top, placing the rod behind the cabinet and opened the WPP drawer. He rifled through all the files finally pulling out a very thin file. He took it back to his desk and sat down.

The cover folder had its circumference printed with a one inch red band and the words SECRET in bold half-inch letters printed at the top and bottom. This entire action took no less than five minutes and the agent uttered no words of friendly politeness in the process. Jay didn't let this intended show of importance get to him. He sat stoically waiting as long as the man wanted him to wait.

The Agent spoke, "Let me take a moment to review this file. I haven't opened it since 1980." The agent started flipping through the pages. After about a good ten minutes, the agent closed the file and looked up at Jay. He stood up trying to convey his concern. Stuffing his hands into his pockets he finally offered. "I can't tell you anything you want to hear."

"Why not?" Jay showed his irritation. "If you have something, you need to tell me. All this crap about secrecy is a bunch of bullshit." Jay angrily stood up and pushed his chair back. He reached for the file. Agent Bascom beat him to the file and picked it up. Bascom showed some displeasure at his intrusive nature. Jay was getting pissed.

Jay allowed his anger to show. "What about this man Guillermo? He knows something. I could see it in his face when I asked about Benitez Aguillar. Is he a Cuban living in the States? Was he an interrogator in the Cuban Project? You better tell me the truth. Why would Guillermo give me your name? What is his interest to the FBI?" Jay paced back and forth in front of the large pretentious desk. "I better get some answers," Jay stared into Bascom's eyes. "NOW!"

As he blurted out his demand, Jay leaned over the edge of the desk, put both hands in the middle of the desk to support his weight and came almost nose to nose with Agent Bascom.

Bascom withdrew backwards. He was now the one who was intimidated.

"Just settle down. I'll tell you what I can do. I'll call my superior in Washington and ask if I can release anything to you. It is the DIA I have to deal with and this is Friday afternoon. If I can get some answers before 4:00 p.m., I'll call you and set up a time to meet with you again tomorrow. Where are you staying?"

"I'm at The Clarion Hotel, 100 S.E. 4th Street." Jay wasn't satisfied with the answers. It would be easy for Bascom to come up with many excuses why he couldn't reach his superior and this would all be gone. Jay thought quickly. "You call him now! I'll wait."

Agent Bascom was uncertain what he should do. He knew he had Jay riled up and that is what he wanted. Bascom picked up the phone and asked the receptionist to get his Washington contact on the phone. A few minutes later, the phone's red light lit up as it rang. He picked up the receiver, "Agent Bascom, your contact is on the line."

"Hello Stewart." The two passed some words of friendly chatter. "Stewart, I have a man here who needs some information concerning Antonio Guillermo and Benitez Aguillar. Do you know those names?"

Jay was only hearing one side of the conversation but he knew Agent Bascom was doing what he wanted him to do. Jay heard him give out the case number WPP05061980. Jay immediately recognized those identifiers. It was the same identifiers on his two pages. He listened intensely to the rest of the conversation. Finally Agent Bascom said to his contact, "When can you get back to me. This man is very urgent and slightly irate. I need to know as quickly as I can. OK!" Agent Bascom hung up the phone then looked at Jay.

"Here's what he is going to do. This case is very touchy. He has to contact his superior and get permission to release any information to you. He said he would get back to me as soon as possible. I told him you needed to know today or early tomorrow morning because you were leaving tomorrow. He said he would give it his best shot. I'm afraid that's all I can do."

Jay wasn't satisfied. "Why does this man Guillermo live in the States under your supervision?"

"I can't answer that."

"When and why did he come to the States?"

"I can't answer that."

"What in hell is going on. I want to find Benitez Aguillar. I know he was an interrogator in Hanoi and I know he had something to do with my father's death. And I'm going to get to the bottom of this if I have to get very physical with this man Antonio Guillermo. And that is a threat. You arrogant assholes are sitting on critical information, withholding it from the public. What in the hell gives you the right to juggle the lives of U.S. citizens while protecting foreigners?" Jay was becoming livid. He hadn't been this mad since he was falsely jailed as a teenager simply because he fit a bigoted profile and was obviously an Indian.

"When in the hell am I going to get some answers? Or do I have to go rough up this guy Guillermo to get you moving on this?" Jay slammed his fist against the desk top to show his resolve that he expected action. Agent Bascom got the message.

"Why don't you go back to your hotel. I'll have an answer for you before this day is over." Bascom wasn't too reassuring.

Jay, very irritated, shoved his chair aside and left without any remarks. He could be intimidating as well as they could. He showed he was mad and Agent Bascom knew it. The man followed Jay to the door making certain he was gone. Then he called his contact at the DIA.

"Stewart, he's gone and he took the bait hook line and sinker. He is all riled up and ready to get physical."

"Good, I knew he was the man when I handed him those two pages. I believe now we will get the names of the Cuban interrogators out to the press and it won't have to be us who does it. Unless I miss the mark, this man will get physical with Aguillar, get the names of the other two interrogators and take them to the press and to all the POW/MIA organizations. We will finally get those identities into the public domain against our standing orders and we won't be blamed or fired because of it. This man will get it done for us. Good work."

Bascom's contact in the DIA seemed relieved. "I've been wanting to hand these identities over to the press ever since we got those names from Benitez Aguillar in May of 1980. None of the succeeding administrations wanted to allow the names to be publicized. That was so wrong. Each SecDef has gone along with the policy and withheld these names for sixteen years. At least now we can wait and see what our boy does to get them out there. He was a right choice. You did good."

"What do I do now?" Bascom asked for the next step.

"You contact him again and get him back in your office after hours, when no one is around. Make a big deal about swearing him to secrecy and then hand him the file." Stewart Carter thought better of his idea. "No, don't hand him the file. Tell him what's in the file. And tomorrow you allow him the pleasure of being surprised when you introduce him to Aguillar. That sort of surprise should really get him fired up. Then leave and let him do the rest. We'll just wait and see." Again the contact in Washington offered congratulations to the FBI agent.

When Jay got back to the hotel, he told Penny what had transpired. His anger was obvious and Penny had difficulty following the entire intrigue of his visit to the FBI Office.

She burst into a tirade. "You shouldn't have gone. You should have told me before you went there. Now we have all this business to relive, and for what? You told your mother you wouldn't get all caught up in the affair again. Now you have really jumped in way over your head. It is going to kill our family life and ruin our marriage. I came here thinking this would be our chance to have a second honeymoon, to really enjoy each other. I've done everything you wanted and now you throw this out like it was just another bend in the road." Penny was getting madder with each word. "This is absolutely the worst possible thing you could have done to both your mother and to me. What were you thinking?"

Jay began to feel guilty about what he was doing. "I just believe my Dad would agree with the 'crying blood' philosophy, an eye for an eye. He would like for me to find out what happened and why. It isn't so much about revenge as it is about knowing. I need to know!"

Angry, Penny spoke, "OK, let's go eat and we'll talk some more about this."

Penny knew this Friday evening was going to be a long one, Jay visiting with his cronies from the oil business and she being as social as possible. Not too many women were at the convention and she would be stuck throughout the night with every Tom, Dick, and Harry who thought she was good looking. For that reason Penny dressed more conservatively purposely intending not to stand out while in the hosting suites on the upper level. The new red dress stayed in the closet.

After supper they went back to their room to freshen a bit before starting their business social on the upper floor. They were about to leave their room for the penthouse suites when the phone rang. Jay answered. After a few words he hung up.

"That was FBI Agent Sam Bascom. He asked if I could come to his office right now. I said yes." Jay watched Penny expecting another tirade.

"Well, I'm damn well going with you. Like I said, I'm not letting you out of my sight. Let's go."

Jay wasn't completely happy about this but did nothing to turn her down. Both promptly went downstairs. The parking valet was too backed up for them to wait. Jay had the doorman to flag a taxi.

It was well after hours for the FBI office to be open. Time was nearing 8:30 p.m. and the halls were empty. Reaching the second floor and the FBI Office, Jay tried the doorknob. The office was locked. He tapped on the door. Agent Bascom came to the door. He showed surprise when he saw Penny with Jay. Jay made some excuses about stopping off before going to a party and that was why Penny was along.

"OK, she can wait in the outer office." Bascom led Jay in to his office and shut the door.

"I got permission from both the DIA and the Assistant SecDef." Bascom lied about the Assistant SecDef. "Here's what we have to do. I have to swear you in and have you sign a form declaring you will not under any circumstances reveal what I am about to say. Are you OK with that?" He paused waiting for an answer. Jay didn't like the idea. Bascom continued, "If so hold up you right hand and repeat after me." Jay took the oath. Bascom reached into his desk drawer and pulled out Form 413, which was a nondisclosure form. Jay signed immediately without even trying to read all the legalese involved. The bogus ceremony completed, Bascom offered a seat to Jay. "You call me Sam from now on. OK?"

"Here is the story on BenitezAguillar. He came to the States on April 28, 1980, during the Mariel Boat Lift." Sam Bascom referred to his file. "He came on the ship Caliente Mujer. He was with 79 other refugees. When he arrived, they were escorted by the Coast Guard into Key West Naval Station. They were then transported by bus to an x-missile base south west of Miami, out in the eastern Everglades, an absolute swamp land. This was the same station which a few days later became known as The Krome Detention Center. Everything there was makeshift. This influx of people caught all agencies by surprise. The INS, The U.S. Customs, The Border Patrol, The Health Department, and Law Enforcement Agencies, all were caught off guard. They hired as many commercial carriers as could be leased. It was a virtual nightmare for all of us involved.

"Most of the detainees came because they had family here in the States and they were already waiting for the opportunity to leave Cuba. When Castro semi-gave permission for the boatlift, he also opened his prison gates and allowed many hardened criminals to leave. He even provided them with transportation to Mariel. They were placed on boats." Bascom paused then began again. "Back to Benitez Aguillar. He had no family and therefore no sponsor. If he had a sponsor he would have been released. He was detained. After a few days of detention, he asked to see someone in the federal intelligence community. He said he had information which he would trade for his release. The INS didn't exactly know who to contact. So they called our office, the FBI in downtown Miami. I was only a new comer at that time. My boss told me to go down to Krome and interview Benitez Aguillar. I did.

"It came out during the interview that he had been, he called it, a prison guard in Hanoi and had information about four American POWs who were murdered while in prison in Hanoi. I took down everything he told me and came back to the office. I briefed my boss. He told me to call the DIA and the Defense Department Assistant for Intelligence and tell them we had a man with possible information they might want.

"The next day an Air Force Major from the Joint Chiefs and a representative from the DIA, a man named Stewart Carter, arrived with recorders and note pads. I took them out to Krome for another interview with Aguillar. Aguillar told them everything he told me. During further and very intense questioning they were able to get even more information. He ultimately said he was sent to Hanoi with a delegation. He and two others were to instruct the Vietnamese on interrogation methods. These were the same methods Castro used on imprisoned dissidents to obtain information on subversive activities. He wouldn't give us the names of the two other men unless we would grant him asylum. None of the three of us had the authority to grant him asylum. We disengaged and left with the information."

Bascom knew the names of the other two individuals but purposely withheld that from Jay. Bascom knew he couldn't go too far. His plan to expose the names of all three would certainly rest on his shoulders. Since he and Stewart personally set out to effectuate this task of exposure, neither wanted to lose their positions and certainly didn't want anything to be traced back to them.

Bascom continued. "We asked that he be granted asylum. No agency would agree. Finally the DIA leaned on the FBI to place the man in the Witness Protection Program. My boss got approval from headquarters and we did just that. Benitez Aguillar was released from Krome on May 6th, 1980." Bascom showed the file number to Jay, WPP05061980. You might have pages from a document with that number on it. My contact in Washington alerted me to the fact that there had been a slip up during the Next of Kin Conference and he gave two pages to someone. That identifier means Witness Protection Program (WPP) and the release date of May 6th, 1980 (05061980). In that manner, the U.S. Government became his sponsor. We had no choice but to hide his identity."

Jay thought to himself, he was finally getting somewhere. He believed Sam Bascom was being straight forward with him. He appreciated it and said so.

Jay asked, "Where is Aguillar now?"

"What are you doing tomorrow?" Bascom tossed out the question. "Say around 11:00 a.m.?"

Jay answered quickly, "Nothing."

"Then I'll come by your hotel, pick you up at 11:00 a.m. and take you to see Aguillar. You've got to promise me not to make a scene and not to become physical with him. You can't hurt him and you can't divulge his identity to anyone. Remember you swore to hold this information confidentially and the nondisclosure form you signed will hold you to that. This is all hush-hush. Not even your wife can know. Do you understand what I am saying?"

Jay had trouble agreeing to that, but did. He wasn't sure he could hold all the information to secrecy. He knew he must tell Penny something and must also tell his Mom. He had no allegiance to this man or his agency. And he certainly had no allegiance to anyone in the Defense Department. After he meets Benitez Aguillar and understood what kind of a man he is. Only then would he decide. He was certainly not going to be swayed by any signature or promise until he knew the names of the other two men, namely *Fidel* and *The Bug*.

As he left the office, Jay turned to Penny and loud enough to be heard by Bascom said, "It's all over. I've finally got what I was looking for." Jay shook Bascom's hand and took Penny by the arm and left.

After leaving the building they walked a short distance to a main thoroughfare and waited for a taxi to drift by. The long wait and the walk had Penny fuming in anger over the entire episode. Her silence signaled total disagreement.

Jay told Penny, "I have absolutely no respect for the way our high paid politicians and government workers behave. I don't know what to think about all this. I believe I was just handed a pile of horseshit! All this secrecy makes me want to puke. This is our country too and they treat all us citizens like we don't have enough brains to act responsibly. This ain't over!" Jay was adamant.

"What do you mean? You just said it was all over!"

"I know I did. I did that for his satisfaction. I'll wait until tomorrow. He said he'd introduce me to Benitez Aguillar at 11:00 a.m. tomorrow morning. If he doesn't, then I'm going to really be pissed off!" Jay's jaw muscles tightened as he clamped his mouth shut. His determination was visible. Morning couldn't come soon enough.

CHAPTER VI

Jay's eagerness to meet Aguillar left him with a sleepless night. Penny now knew all the facts. When Jay came out of the office door after his two hour meeting with Agent Sam Bascom, he was elated and excited with enthusiasm and anticipation. In the taxi on the way back to the hotel he started telling her the entire tale. Penny reacted unexpectedly. She had been waiting in the outer office for two hours for Jay and Bascom to finish. She was all dressed and eager to socialize. The overly long meeting was too much for her to accept. The room had no comfortable chairs and there was nothing for her to do except sit silently. Her dress was getting wrinkled, her panty hose were becoming uncomfortable and her back was killing her from being forced to sit up straight in one of their lousy chairs. Knowing her beauty preparations were all for naught, she was rightfully angry. When Jay walked through the office door, she was more than eager to leave. Her unmitigated disappointment in being ignored was obvious.

 The taxi ride back to the hotel allowed her the opportunity to vent her frustrations. She wasn't interested in what went on in the agent's office. She felt put out from being neglected for such a long period. Penny's character was not complex at all. She was raised in a Christian family, had good moral values, was more passive than proactive, accepted everyone without preconceived thoughts and always carried a smile because she was always happy. She was very accommodating to Jay. She allowed him to use her as a conversation shill during his need to be social. Penny, Penelope was her given name and one she hated, was Miss Stillwater of 1985 and that was who she was, a beauty queen with an affinity for meeting people and the ability to hold a conversation with scholars as well as the homeless. She was outgoing to the point her beauty was often overlooked. But sitting alone in a quiet office for hours was irritating.

Relieved after her tirade, she allowed Jay to speak, she listened with eager anticipation knowing he had new information. When he told her about going to meet Benitez Aguillar in the morning, she was as excited as Jay. Maybe this would end it all. She wanted to invite herself to go with Jay; but knew it was an impossibility. Jay was most forthcoming in telling all. He dismissed all thoughts of his sworn statement and the nondisclosure form he signed not to reveal information. He wasn't in the military nor did he hold a government position which would demand he remain silent for security reasons. He told all. Penny knew everything Jay knew and that soothed her disposition. Time was approaching 11:00 p.m. She knew many of the conferees would soon be going back to their rooms. She asked Jay. "Do you still want to go to the hospitality suite to visit with Mid-Western Oil?"

"Naw...Let's go to our room and enjoy a good night's rest."

Penny was more than agreeable. Even though dressed, she was glad to have Jay to herself. Penny knew that after the coming morning meeting with Aguillar, Jay might be more distracted and her importance to him might be cast aside. She eagerly anticipated the night alone with Jay to reclaim her own status.

Except for the enjoyable diversion of loving his wife, the night went poorly for Jay. His anticipation held his mind and thoughts in check. He couldn't reach the nothingness state, which would allow peaceful sleep. He tossed and turned most of the night. He took a peek at the red numerals of the digital clock on the nightstand too often. He watched as each minute flipped to the next. When it read 6:00 a.m. he arose from the bed slowly, quietly dressed and left the room. Penny never budged. The night with Jay, without any doubt, should have put a smile on her face. After such an interlude, she passed instantly right through the REM state into deep sleep and hadn't stirred since.

Getting coffee from the continental breakfast bar in the lobby, Jay sipped the coffee making his usual sounds, which Penny had always kidded him about. He made a sucking sound drawing in very small amounts of the steaming hot, awakening fluid. He had done it all his life and it was more than a habit. It was his very own identifying ritual. Jay sought a comfortable chair to enjoy his first morning cup.

Looking at his watch, he realized it would be more than four hours before he was to meet Agent Bascom. He decided to take the long walk to Domino Park. At least he could talk with Juan Gonzales again. He was the one who pointed him toward Antonio Guillermo. He walked south across the Miami Canal from the hotel the four blocks to Calle Ocho, then the sixteen blocks to the park. The streets were fresh from the street sweepers and still slightly wet. When he got to the park, as expected Juan was sitting in his usual chair at his usual table with his usual cup of hot, chicory darkened coffee.

"Good morning Juan." Jay offered.

"Yes it is." Juan tried to be polite but it wasn't genuine.

Jay knew something was wrong. "What's wrong, you seem almost unfriendly?"

"I was told last night that you were following and harassing my friend Antonio Guillermo. What was that all about?" Juan stared at Jay.

"It was strictly personal." Jay attempted to placate Juan.

"Has he done something to you? Why is it personal?" It was apparent the subject wasn't going to be dropped easily. Jay was in a quandary. He didn't know how to answer. It was apparent he was in territory where everyone knew everyone else. They were close enough that word spread too easily. Jay tried again.

"It was nothing. He had information which led me to another man. That's all. He told me what I wanted to know. It's over with him. If I need to apologize, I will." Jay wanted it to be dropped.

"He was upset about you following him to his home. Yes, I think you should apologize!" Jay acknowledged the comment with a head nod.

"OK...I'll come back here today after a meeting I have and I'll apologize to him."

This pleased Juan. The two continued to sit in peace and enjoy the morning breeze. The mid October breeze was a welcomed change to the Miamians. The summers were too hot and the winters were perfect. This change in the weather brought the tourists to Miami. This was the tourist season and Miami was on the verge of its annual change, room rates would double, its population would triple, and the need for employees would quadruple. Juan was oblivious to the change. It meant very little to him. His life was stable and routine. Changes didn't affect him.

After an hour of visiting, Jay became too uneasy with waiting for the time to pass. He excused himself and left. The walk back to the hotel seemed terribly long. Walking through the lobby of the hotel he met Carl Mitchell. Jay went to a late breakfast with his friend.

"I understand you and Jack Richardson have come to an understanding about some oil leases." Carl inquired.

Jay answered, "Yes, we have. How did you know?"

"Last night in Jack's hospitality suite, he was telling everyone about going public with his new company and sort of asking for investors for his stock offering. That's when it came up."

"It was kind of strange to me." Jay commented. "I couldn't understand why he would be here about off-shore drilling. That's an expensive operation and he won't have that kind of capital even after he goes public. So I couldn't understand why he was here and why he spent the money for the hospitality suite. Now I know, he came here looking for investors. That makes sense." Jay had another mystery solved. He thought to himself, 'I hope Jack finds enough investors to buy my leases'.

After breakfast Jay went to the room to freshen a bit before meeting with Agent Bascom. He found Penny still asleep. He quietly completed his personals and went back to the lobby to wait for Sam Bascom.

Promptly at 11:00 a.m., Agent Sam Bascom pulled into the portico area. Jay saw him pull in and instantly walked over to the government leased vehicle, a new Lincoln town car. They greeted each other and drove south across the bridge to 7th Street, there Bascom turned right into the west bound one way traffic. Reaching S.W. 16th Avenue he turned left and then left again onto Calle Ocho. Bascom pulled over and parked. Saturday was a slack day and finding a parking space was not a problem.

Jay spoke, "I've been here before. This is Domino Park."

Bascom answered, "Yes, it is."

Jay was confused. "Are we meeting Benitez Aguillar?"

"Yes. I'll introduce you to him."

They each got out of the car. Jay followed Sam into Domino Park over to a table where four people were playing dominoes. Jay easily recognized Antonio Guillermo as one of the players. Bascom motioned with his index finger toward the table for one of the players to come over. Antonio got up from the table and came over.

Jay knew he had to apologize to Antonio and thought this was what it was all about. As Antonio neared, Jay spoke up. "I want to apologize Antonio for following you yesterday. If I upset you, I'm sorry." Jay did what he had to do and thought it was over and now they could go see Benitez Aguillar.

Agent Bascom spoke. "Jay Cobb, this is Benitez Aguillar! He is also Antonio Guillermo."

The startled look on Jay's face was instant. He was astonished. His brow wrinkled and his head dropped. His mind spun around in circles. This was unbelievable. Jay couldn't respond with any comments. He was completely taken by surprise. He just stood motionless and speechless. He began to shake his head slowly from side to side trying to figure out this unexpected turn of events. Jay looked at Agent Bascom with a questioning stare.

Finally his mind cleared and he spoke. "What the hell is going on?"

Bascom motioned with the back of his hand for Guillermo to go back to his table. Then he turned to Jay. "We need to talk more."

"You're God damned right, we need to talk!" Jay was in between curious and furious. He turned away from Bascom for a moment in absolute disgust. His jaws tightened; he wanted to hit something. Bascom was a thin man and four inches shorter than Jay. Jay knew he could take him out if he had to. "You've got to tell me what's going on! This is dogshit. You've been taking me on some kind of a controlled odyssey. Does all this have some kind of government approval. What in the hell is going on?" Jay was becoming red-faced in anger. This wasn't Jay's personality at all. He was normally a passive, accepting individual. Never finding fault with anyone or anything. This surprise stirred his character into aggressive hatred.

Bascom added, "Let's go over to that table." He pointed to a table out next to the sidewalk. "I have to bring you up to speed."

"You're damn right! You have one helluva lot of explaining to do."

Agent Bascom pulled a folded paper from his chest pocket and sat down. The paper was a copy of the nondisclosure statement Jay had signed the night before.

"I want to remind you of this piece of paper. Revealing what I am about to tell you is punishable by fine or imprisonment. Is that understood?"

Jay was reluctant to answer. "Yes, I understand!" He was less than pleased with the way the conversation started and blurted out to Bascom. "Don't you dare give me the runaround. I'll smash you like a bug!"

Bascom offered again. "This is absolutely confidential information." He spoke slightly above a whisper, looking around to make certain no one was listening. Jay rolled his eyes around, visibly stating his objection to all this clandestine stuff. He leaned toward Agent Bascom to make certain he missed nothing.

"Antonio Guillermo is under the Witness Protection Program and has been since May 6th, 1980. The U.S. Government is his sponsor. We provide him with certain benefits. If he dies while in the program, we will bury him. He can't leave this area and go anywhere else without our knowing about it. He is a Cuban refugee and everyone in his living orbit recognizes him as a marielito. He has to remain that way. Understood?"

"Yes, I understand all that. Is he an Ex-Cuban Army soldier and was he in Hanoi as an interrogator?" Jay stared at Bascom waiting for an answer.

"Yes…he was Benitez Aguillar, an Army Sergeant and he was in Hanoi under the auspices of the Cuban Government as a trainer for the North Vietnamese. Prior to going to Hanoi, he was a prison guard at Ariza Prison in Placetas, in the Province of Cienfuegos. Army soldiers were often used as prison guards, especially where mostly political prisoners were incarcerated. He was familiar with the ways they extracted information from the dissidents. He himself was an interrogator in the Cuban prison system and was picked to go to Hanoi because of his knowledge.

"The Joint Chiefs of Staff and The Secretary of Defense signed off on the approval for the FBI to place him in the Witness Protection Program in exchange for certain information. So we, the FBI, didn't just decide to place him in the program. We were asked if he could be eligible for the witness protection program. I checked it out. Allow me to quote… 'the witness protection program is eligible to any person who has knowledge of or has information about the commission of a crime and has testified or is testifying or is willing to testify to such' is eligible.

"My bosses and all the Defense Department higher ups put their heads together and decided Benitez Aguillar met the requirements. While under the program he was to receive security protection, immunity from prosecution, secure housing, assistance in obtaining a means of livelihood or a subsistence allowance, SSI benefits, reasonable traveling expenses, free medical treatment, and if needed free burial benefits. The military wanted the information he had and the WPP was the trade-off for the info. To make the choice more politically acceptable there was a lot of communications between agencies to classify what transpired in Hanoi as War Crimes." Bascom waited for questions from Jay.

"Who were the other two or other three interrogators who went to Hanoi with him?"

"We don't know. He has never revealed their names." Bascom was lying. He did know. But for their plan to go as expected, he couldn't reveal that information. He had to rely on Jay Cobb's persistence and ingenuity and allow him to expose the other two names.

"Was there two others or three others?" Jay, in piecing the puzzle, now knowing Guillermo and Aguilar were the same person, he believed there might be only two others.

Bascom answered. "I think there were only two."

"Has this man confirmed that U.S. POWs were tortured to the point of death by these two Cubans?" Jay was striking directly at his problem.

"Yes...He has confirmed deaths in the POW population in Hanoi prisons."

"Did he name those POWs?" Jay especially wanted to know this. "Did he say where they were buried?" Jay got slightly off track in his haste to gain any information he could about his father.

"He named one POW, it wasn't your Dad, on the very first interview while he was in Krome Detention negotiating for asylum. He told of all the methods used, the treatment by the North Vietnamese, and the conditions the POWs endured. He appeared straightforward in passing us the information. I prepared a fifty-six-page document on the interview. It was the first document I prepared for the FBI and I was proud of it." Bascom was making his play for Jay's inquisitiveness.

Jay commented. "I can't believe you didn't get the other two names from Aguillar. He seems like an average guy. Being in the U.S. should give him the protection he wants. So why didn't you guys lean on him to name his cohorts. Hell...why don't you do it now. He's here. You're here. Go get it!" Jay hit the nail right on the head.

"After such a long period, we can't touch him. He is established in the system. He is a 'non-threat channel' and the word we get is, 'don't rock the boat'. The issue with the POWs being tortured by the North Vietnamese has died down considerably and no politician desires to have it resurrected. It is a political hot potato. Our instructions are specific, 'don't stir the waters'." Bascom could see his information was being accepted. He waited for additional questions.

"Can I talk with Aguillar?" Jay asked calmly.

"You can but only in my presence. That is part of the WPP."

Jay was not accepting anymore appeasing comments. "So, we have an ex-Cuban Army Sergeant, a man who interrogated our POWs, a man who tortured our POWs, a representative of The State of Cuba, a Revolutionary Communist Country which espouses anti-U.S. sentiment and we provide him with asylum and living subsistence, paid for by the U.S. Government and we can't touch him! We don't get all the information we need and you can't touch him!" Jay truly displayed his anger. "You people are unbelievable. You don't do shit but gradually give our country and our assets away to foreigners." Jay was explosive in his rhetoric. "I tell you what I'm going to do. I am going to damn well put a stop to his living conditions. I am going to tell all the Congressmen, the Senators, all the POW/MIA organizations...we'll bring some level-headedness back to this situation. And you can damn well believe I will!" Jay was boiling mad. "I don't need your ride back to the hotel. I'll walk. You are all assholes. You know that!" Jay stomped away from the table and briskly walked toward his hotel. He didn't wait for a response from Agent Sam Bascom. He was mad as hell.

Sam Bascom tossed a final comment toward Jay who was already about ten feet away. "You're not going to do anything stupid are you?"

Jay Cobb continued walking, his back toward Agent Bascom, he lifted his right hand into the air and made a waving gesture with his middle finger acknowledging his comment. Jay spoke in gesture, 'Screw you'.

Bascom went back to his office and Jay went straight to the hotel. Both had serious things on their minds. Jay needed to tell Penny what had happened and Sam Bascom needed to tell Special Agent Stewart Carter of the Defense Intelligence Agency how the meeting went.

Sam Bascom dialed a special unlisted phone number for Special Agent Carter.

Carter answered the phone expecting Sam to call. "Hello, Stewart Carter here." The line was a monitored line and Sam had to talk in code. "Sam Bascom calling, meet me on the second story." Stewart answered. "I'll meet you there in two minutes." This was their private code for Stewart to return Sam's call on a secure line. It was used often when an active case was being investigated. Stewart returned the call almost immediately.

"Hi Sam, it's me Stewart." Carter spoke up enthusiastically eager to know results. "Well, tell me how the meeting went."

Bascom responded. "It went just as we expected. Mr. Cobb was extremely surprised. With the introduction complete, he became very silent. I knew he was in a state of shock. I motioned for Guillermo to go back to his game of dominoes. After he walked away I watched Mr. Cobb simmer then he got hot under the collar and exploded with a myriad of questions. I watched his every reaction. He is not going to stop with this simply because I introduced him to Benitez Aguillar. He left in anger. He vented his anger on me. He thinks I'm nothing but a bureaucratic government employee. I tell you, he is going to be our man. There isn't anything that is going to get in his way to get the information he wants. You know what? I truly expect him to go back to Domino Park, get Antonio and haul him off somewhere until he gets the names he's looking for." Sam Bascom grinned into the phone, pleased with the outcome.

"That's really good. He is playing right into our hands. So are you going to get lost for the next few days, at least until Mr. Cobb leaves town?" Stewart queried.

Bascom replied, "I'm not going to respond to any phone calls. I believe Antonio will call when Mr. Cobb confronts him and I won't be available at either of my three numbers. If Mr. Cobb calls again I won't be available. I never let on that we knew the names of the other two Cubans. I expect him to get the names from Antonio. I expect Antonio to also tell him that he gave the names to me. That is a confrontation I don't want to be around for." Agent Bascom passed along all the details he could think of.

"Do you think we went too far?" asked Special Agent Carter. "Do you think someone might get hurt? We don't want Antonio to be roughed up enough for local law enforcement to get involved. We just want him to pass along the names of the two remaining Cubans."

"Yeah...I know. I don't think so. I could get one of our surveillance vans and watch out for Antonio. You think that would be advisable?" Sam asked his contact.

"Naw...let's drop our involvement, just liked we planned. We'll let nature take its course. I truly don't think Mr. Cobb will get too violent. He could get mad and shake Antonio a bit, but he won't rough him up too much. I'll hang my hat on that. We need that son-of-a-bitch Antonio to go back to Cuba. We can't deport him because we think Castro won't allow him back into the country. So we can only hope Mr. Cobb scares him enough that he will leave the country. Hell, he could go to Mexico if he wanted to and live out the rest of his days. I want all payments, subsistence and other benefits to stop. I hate having to talk to all those families of POWs and MIAs and withhold information. I feel like I'm being treasonous. Let's keep our fingers crossed that Mr. Cobb will rise to the occasion and advertise Benitez Aguillar's name throughout the POW/MIA Organizations and let them know who he is and where he is. That should get him some more visitors. Too many irate visitors and he will leave the country. Let's hope this does the trick. Do you think we've pulled this thing off? Does all this make as much sense to you as it does to me?" Stewart waited for a response.

"Yeah...I think so and I agree with all that. I'll lay low and wait for a newspaper story or something to indicate Mr. Cobb has intervened like we've planned. I know we did the right thing."

Sam Bascom hung up the phone; then closed his desk and left the building.

******

Jay was steaming mad when he entered the hotel. He saw several friends in the lobby but kept right on going to the elevator. He needed Penny. She had to hear the latest twist. Jay was ready to explode. To his total disappointment Penny wasn't in the room. He went back to the lobby, searched the restaurant, searched the lounge, looked into the gift shops; she was no where to be found.

Jay tightened both fists. He tried to calm himself down but that wasn't possible. Hyper with adrenalin flowing, his blood pressure climbed even higher as he waited. Jay knew he had to go back and face Antonio. He needed two more names and needed them now. He had to do something and do it quickly or else he was going to be a victim of his own impatience.

He rushed out of the lobby and took a waiting taxi to Domino Park. He found Antonio comfortably sitting at his usual table with four friends and players. Jay walked over to the table and just glared at him. The piercing stares made Antonio uncomfortable. He cast quick glances at Jay. It was very obvious that Jay Cobb wasn't going to leave him alone as the FBI Agent had instructed. He felt the hatred in the stares and knew his FBI safety umbrella wasn't going to be very helpful. Between glances and game moves, Antonio was loosing the game, which wasn't his style. He never lost.

Jay continued his intimidating eye-to-eye contact with Antonio. This was making Antonio very nervous. He was terrified and could feel the hatred. For sixteen years his life had been quiet and peaceful. Now he had the perception it was coming to an end. His entire body started to shake. He couldn't hold a game piece still while he made his move. His friends sitting at the table noticed his anxiety, hands shaking, seemingly unable to think. Antonio was asked if anything was wrong. He finally announced he had to leave. He picked up his games pieces, placed them into the box, folded his cardboard top and walked away.

Antonio was a slight man. Even in his sixties, his hair and eyebrows remained jet-black. His eyes were beginning to depress into their sockets as his weight deteriorated. Crows feet lines were prominent at his temples. His skin was becoming loose as his body weight lowered to approximately 145 pounds. Old age was creeping in.

Jay tossed over in his mind how he might get the names of the other two Cubans out of this man. He also needed to know which one was *Fidel* and which one was *The Bug*. Jay once again followed Antonio staying ten feet behind. This made him extremely nervous. The stalking continued until he walked through his white, wooden yard gate. Again once inside the gate, he turned facing Jay.

He blurted out, "What do you want from me!"

Jay responded, "You were in North Vietnam. You tortured my father. He died in prison at Cu Loc. I want to know who killed my father."

Antonio fired back, "It wasn't me. I never hurt any prisoner."

"The hell you didn't. You were right there and had a hand in it. I'm gonna beat your ass to a pulp unless you tell me who killed my father." Jay was completely out of character. To threaten to beat someone was totally unlike him. Jay grabbed the gate and started through.

"You can't come in here. This is my house. You stay out!" Antonio was beginning to feel this man had every intention of intruding on his ground and could possibly hurt him. "What do you want from me?"

"Did you ever hear the names *Fidel* and *The Bug* while you were in Hanoi?"

Antonio looked shocked. He stepped back to avoid Jay's forward movement. "Yes…I've heard the names of those two. What do you want me to say?"

"I want you to give me those names, their real names!" Jay continued to walk into Antonio pushing him back. He could see that his threat was getting a reaction. "I want you to give me those names, right now!" Jay shoved him back toward the house using his left hand and pushing against his chest. You know I can beat your ass and I'll do it right now if you don't give me those names!" Jay grabbed him by the shirt collar with both hands and nearly lifted him off the ground. Antonio dropped his box of dominoes and the folded tabletop fell from his underarms. Antonio felt helpless and cornered. His home should be his refuge, but now it was being invaded and he could do nothing. He prayed for a friend to come by and see his predicament. No one passed by. It was just the two of them.

Antonio was terrified he was really going to be beaten up. The eyes he was staring into meant business and he couldn't get loose from the grip. He burst into tears and wet his pants. Jay felt slightly sorry for the man and released some of his grip allowing him to put his feet solidly on the ground. The tears streamed down the side of his face and he shook in fear. He searched the ground for his dominoes, his most prized possession. They were scattered everywhere. Antonio began a muffled cry. His chest heaved in a whimper as more tears came. His manhood dwindled to nothing and he was vulnerable to more attacks.

"I can't tell you! The FBI won't let me talk to you." Between sniffles Antonio tried to explain his instructions. "Mr. Bascom says they will send me back to Cuba if I talk. I don't understand anything. Why do you want to hurt me? Why are you here? Why are you doing this to me? Why did Agent Bascom bring you to me?" Antonio was so shaken words hung in his throat.

"I want to know who killed my father. His name was Emanuel J. Cobb and he died in prison at Cu Loc in North Vietnam. You and two other men identified as *Fidel* and *The Bug* were his interrogators. All three of you killed my father. Now give me the names of your two buddies!"

Antonio responded haltingly. "I have already given those names to Agent Bascom and Special Agent Stewart Carter." Antonio grabbed a quick breath. "They have those names already. Why do you threaten me? If they have the names why didn't they give them to you instead of bringing you to me?"

Jay thought to himself, that's a good question. If Agent Bascom has the names why didn't he say so. He became enraged and his victim could see the fire in his eyes. Jay declared back to Antonio. "I don't know and I don't care, you tell me the names, right now!"

Antonio began to cry again. "You...let me...call...Agent Bascom, if he says it's OK...I will tell you."

"No! You tell me now! You were a guard in North Vietnam. You tortured American prisoners...right? You were known as Beanie...right? Your two partners were called *Fidel* and *The Bug*...right? You three were in the Cuban Army...right?" Antonio nodded his head yes after every query. "Then give me their real names and where I might find them. I'm going to kill you if you don't!" Jay made his threat appear real.

Antonio became fearful of losing his own life. He shook his head from side to side, knowing he could be deported if he spoke out. He also knew if he was deported back to Cuba his days of luxury were gone forever. Tears flooded his face. He began to whimper in waves of tearful weeping.

Jay was truly beginning to feel sorry for the old man. He withdrew his grip completely and watched as the old man sagged under his own weight. Jay was now facing his own nature. His feelings of sympathy for the man took hold and he just shook his head back and forth. The old man lowered himself to pickup his dominoes. Jay watched. He tried to regain some control of himself.

Jay was having second thoughts about himself and what he was trying to do. He had already made up his mind to find those people and let the world know who they were and where they could be located. He questioned if he had the character to pull it off. If he had to get physical again, without being totally mad, he knew he could not hurt anyone. It wasn't in his make-up. He must find a different way to gain the information he was so determined to obtain. Now as he helped the old man gather his dominoes; he was ambivalent about what he should do next. How could he extract the information from this scared old man?

The old man had all his dominoes but one, he still whimpered like a baby as he stared at the ground searching through his tear filled eyes trying to search out the missing domino. As Jay watched he knew he better be strong and not give in to his impulses to comfort the man.

He pushed the man backward. "You have a phone... right?" Jay asked. He saw the old man bend over to pick up his last domino. He closed his box.

"Si...I have a phone."

Jay knew that if he didn't get the names now, he probably never would unless he was to make a second trip to Miami. He and Penny were scheduled to depart tomorrow, Sunday morning, on Continental Flight 385 for DFW at 9:30 EST. There wasn't going to be enough time to do this all over again before then and he wasn't certain he would be able to sell a delay to Penny. Now Jay found himself between a rock and a hard place. He had to move now!

He pushed the man backwards again. "I tell you what we are going to do Antonio." He spoke as sternly as possible. "We are going into your house and call Agent Bascom and you are going to get permission to tell me the names and location of your other two cohorts. Got that?" Jay was as stern as he could be. He knew he had to show resolve or his threats wouldn't work. He had already shown physical violence was possible, now he had to rely on unyielding resolve if he was to be successful.

Antonio gave a slight nod that he understood. He picked up his folded tabletop, soft covered cardboard mat, tried to dust it off, placed it under his arm, and the two entered the house. Jay tried to pinpoint readily identifying features of the house in a concerted effort to place it indelibly in his mind's eye.

The house exterior was painted in a light blue pastel color with dark blue trim. The yard was well maintained, the grass was nicely manicured and smooth as a golf course putting green. There was a single stone monument to the left facing the street. It appeared he had purchased an oval, concrete birdbath, placed it length wise on a pedestal of stone and made a perch within the shape where he had placed an image of the Virgin Mary. Jay had the thought, this old man was very religious.

The floor of the small porch was painted a battleship gray. Some of the tongue and groove flooring was buckled upward from moisture. As he entered through the doorway, he saw a small 17-inch television in the corner. There was a mantle over a false fireplace. On the homemade mantle sat a foot tall, porcelain image of the Virgin Mary. Next to the doorway into the bedroom was a wooden cross, the image of The Crucifixion. A string of prayer beads was coiled on the mantle. There was a well-worn cloth recliner, which obviously had been used too often. The armrests were worn through in spots and batting could be seen under the thin covering. Jay saw the phone sitting next to the armchair. He went over, picked it up and handed it to Antonio. "Here…Call Agent Bascom…now!" Jay had harshness in his voice.

Antonio dialed the number. He waited for an answer. There was no answer. After a long period, Jay grabbed the phone away from Antonio purposely showing anger. "What's the number?" Jay had determination in his voice.

"It's 555-9657." Antonio's voice broke as he offered the number.

Jay dialed the number and also got no answer. "Do you have an alternate number?" Jay was forcing his zeal on Antonio. When the old man gave him a second number, he dialed it quickly. There was no answer. Jay looked at the old man, his brow wrinkled and his stare piercing. His intentions were obvious. The old man started to shake once again. Fear showed on his face. He was afraid of what Jay was going to do.

"OK old man, you either give me the names or I start roughing you up again and I don't want to do that." Jay reached out toward the old man attempting to grab a handful of shirt and convey the beginning of a bad time. The old man reacted by moving backwards.

"Wait…I'll give you the names, just don't hurt me!"

Jay backed off. "OK…what's the name of the man everyone called *Fidel*?"

"His name is Lieutenant Colonel Miguel Fuentes."

"Where does he work?" Jay kept showing his zealousness.

"When I left, he was with the Ministry of the Interior." Antonio could barely speak. "He worked in the Headquarters building of The State Security Department (DSE) at the Villa Marista prison in Havana."

Jay had to make an effort to clear his mind of all extraneous thoughts and concentrate on remembering these details. The information he was getting was what he came for. His cognitive span had to be pointedly focused. He bundled his information, Miguel Fuentes, Lt/Col, Minister of Interior, Havana Province, *Fidel*. He used this method during his college days. Bundle the information, remember it, and let it be the foundation for discussions, presentations or an essay. He continued to listen intently.

Antonio continued. "He was responsible for all Comites para la Defense de la Revolucion (CDRs) in Cuba. Every block in every town in Cuba has a CDR. The CDRs are like a neighborhood watch here in the States, except the CDR warden watches for and reports on any political activism or any anti-government sentiment within the neighborhood. There is harsh judgment and harsh punishment for anyone crossing this boundary. That's why the prisons are full of dissidents. If you don't like someone, you can report them and they go to jail."

Antonio continued trying to satisfy Jay. "Miguel Fuentes was a school teacher in the small town of La Boca. When the invasion of Bahia de Cochinos, The Bay of Pigs, happened in 1961, Miguel was teaching high school in La Boca. The defense forces traveled past the high school and the word got out that there was an invasion underway. Miguel left his teaching post and joined the defense forces to assist in repelling the invasion. During the invasion he shot down an airplane and Castro saw him do it and immediately gave him a position in the Fuerzas Armadas Revolutionaries (FAR) with the rank of Lieutenant. He became a Re-Education Officer in the prison system. Part of re-education was to interrogate prisoners. He started a process, which ballooned all over Cuba. The process began to include torture. At first moderate but under Miguel it got worse and worse. He invented extreme torture for prisoners. When Castro wanted to send a delegation to North Vietnam, Major Miguel Fuentes was his obvious choice. I don't know where he is today." Antonio shyly peered into Jay's eyes to see if he was satisfying his need for information.

"What about the other guy, *The Bug*?" Jay kept his demeanor strong and his glaring eyes intense.

Antonio responded quickly. "I hated that man, he was very violent. He was just as bad, if not worse than Miguel Fuentes. His name is Captain Raphael Almarales Pardo. When I left in 1980, he was in charge of Kilo 8 also known as, LA 26...La Especial. It was a prison in Camaguey Province for political and special prisoners."

Jay again bundled the information into memory parcels... Raphael Almarales Pardo, Captain, Kilo 8, Camaguey Province, *The Bug*.

Antonio continued. "Many well known dissidents were under his watch. That man is bad. He's vicious. He has a violent nature and an affinity for inflicting pain. He will strike anyone just for the pleasure of causing pain; the harder the strike and the louder the cry, the better he likes it. He is power thirsty. Maybe he is still there. I don't know. He is a man you should stay away from." Antonio seemed to relax slightly.

Jay finally had the names he was after. His effort in Miami was over. Jay was relieved he didn't have to go any further with Antonio. Oddly, he felt like making a huge apology to Antonio Guillermo. But thought better of it and just left without so much as acknowledging his departure. He kept his face stern and his jaws tight as if sealing his departure with anger. On the inside he had slight hatred for what he did.

As he walked back to the hotel he was racked with strong but ambivalent emotions toward himself. One side of him sought congratulations for being successful. The other offered condemnation for taking advantage of an old man. Thoughts of continuing his search were on the skids. He was drowning in self-conflict in a big way. It made him pensive and self-assessing. He had thrust himself into a dark abyss and he knew it. He was looking forward to seeing Penny. She always had a soothing affect on his nature. Bewilderment had flooded his being. God knows, he didn't know what to do next. Returning to his room, he immediately sat down and put all this information on paper and placed it into his briefcase. His thoughts then turned to the convention and the other reason he was in Miami.

****

Mentally returning to the convention, Jay felt obligated to attend the final event. The reservations were made. It was the final banquet and the speaker was the Governor of the State of Florida. He knew he had to be there. He had to see and be seen. It was his personal philosophy to make himself important. Penny was going to wear the same black dress she wore to the Mid-Western Oil hospitality party. Jay was glad she was going to wear it. She would garner more visibility for him. Attending the banquet would help seal the proposal chats he had with Jack Richardson of Mid-Western Oil.

Everything went well at the banquet. They were seated at the same table with Ben Wakefield and Carl Mitchell of the American Petroleum Geologists Association and enjoyed the night. The next morning they scheduled their time to be at the airport for the trip homeward. Jay had not completely told Penny everything which went on with Benitez Aguillar. He was slightly ashamed of himself and casually deferred all of Penny's questions until he thought the time was right.

****

Antonio sat at home the rest of the day after Jay left. Thoughts were churning through his mind as he tried to think about his future. He believed his life under the Witness Protection Program was coming to an end. His future life in Miami could be in jeopardy. He liked being in the States as a ward of the government and to have the freedom to think and do as he pleased. In his confrontation with Mr. Cobb, he knew his future was in danger. Thoughts of what to do next were plaguing his mind. He had complete freedom since going into the Witness Protection Program. No outside interferences from anyone. He blended into the community instantly. Attended church regularly and supported it with his presence and donations. He was recognized within his community as a friendly, personable individual, always willing to help anyone in need and was revered by many. Juan Gonzales was one of his closest friends. They were the same age, attended the same church, did volunteer work for any group when it was needed. The events of the last two days were disturbing. Seeking a solution he went to his church.

Antonio sat in the sanctuary of St. Vincent's Catholic Church for hours on Saturday night waiting for others to leave. He knew some immediate action was necessary. St. Vincent's maintained a private room with a leased long distance phone line direct to Cuba for all the families in the church to use. Anyone could use it to talk with their families remaining in Cuba. Antonio used the phone frequently to call to Cuba. The phone room was excellent for his purposes. The phone wasn't monitored, the room small and very private. Conversations had a twenty-minute time limit. Antonio dialed the number he used many times in the past.

"*Miguel..es Benitez.*" Benitez spoke.

"*Beni, que pasa? Hace mes que no oimos de ti.*" Miguel responded.

"*Oye,e llamo de San Vincente, estoy en peligro, me han descubierto. Este muchacho de Oklahoma se aparecio aqua. El estaba determinado en obtener la informacion de nuestra delegacion a Vietnam del norte el 1967.*" Benitez advised.

"*Parece que su padre se murio despues de una de nuestra interrogaciones.*"

"*Que tu quieres que hagamos con el. El nos puedo causar problemas.*" Benitez again advised.

"*Beni, le distes nuestros nombres? Si. Se los tuve que dar, era eso o dejar que me goliard?*" Miguel asked.

"*Tu crees que el hara mas dano? No se, mi contacto Sam Bascom me hecho oara alante y me lo dejo a mi. No se por que pero asi fue. Ya mi identical esta conocida, y mi trabajo clandestine esta en peligro.*" Benitez offered.

"*Que tu queres que you haga? Nada. Sigue como si nada hubiera pasado. Si el regresa, corre! Tu tienes tu passaporte, vete a Cancun y ahi te recogemos.*" Miguel asked Benitez.

"*Tienes sufficient dinoro? Si. Tengo dinero Escondido!*" Benitez Answered.

"*Esta bien, mantente listo para correr. Tu y Rafael teinen que estar viigilando a este tipo. Mi position aqua me permite detonable. No te preoccupies, yo le aviso Rafael.*" Miguel advised.

"*Sigue mandando tus informes.*" Benitez responded.

The conversation in English.

"Miguel...This is Benitez."

"Beanie...It's about time you checked in. Where are you calling from? Is it secure enough to talk? We haven't heard from you in a month. Anything wrong? You never sent us your report on the shoot downs back in February. I need to congratulate you again on passing that information to us. You did good."

"I'm calling from St. Vincent's Catholic Church family center like I have always done in the past. Miguel! I think I have been compromised...my cover has been blown. This kid out of Oklahoma showed up. He was determined to make me give up the names of our delegation to North Vietnam in 1967. It seems his father was one of the POWs who died in Cu Loc prison after several sessions with us. I need to know what you want me to do about him? He could be trouble."

"Did you give him our names?" Miguel Fuentes asked.

"Yes...I had to. He started getting rough with me, pushing me around. I faked weakness to get him to stop. He stopped, apparently accepting my act."

Miguel asked another question. "Do you think he will do anything more?"

"I can't tell. My handler, Sam Bascom led him to me. I don't understand why. I'm supposed to be in the witness protection program and he revealed my identity to this kid. I don't know why. But my identity is blown and our undercover work might be in jeopardy. What should I do?"

"Nothing right now. Continue as if nothing has happened. If he comes back and it gets bad, you need to run. You already have a passport to Mexico. According to our plan, you need to run to Cancun and await a flight on Cubana Airlines. We'll pick you up there and bring you in. Do you have enough money to escape?"

"Yes...I have about three thousand dollars U.S. stashed away in a religious monument in my front yard. I'll check out flights to Cancun. If I leave through Miami International, passing through customs could be a problem. That's the first place they would place a checkpoint. If I have to run, I think I would do better making a charter flight out of Opalocka airfield to Orlando or some other location and then catch a flight to Cancun."

Miguel, slightly concerned asked, "Sounds good. You be ready to disappear. Did this guy from Oklahoma indicate he was coming to Cuba...to continue his search for me?"

"He didn't say. But you and Raphael should be on the alert for him. His name is Emanuel J. Cobb, Jr. He's about six foot tall, square shoulders, slightly dark skin, and heavy course black hair. Put him on your national watch list and leave it with Customs. You need to turn him around as soon as he arrives."

Miguel answered, "I am glad you touched base on this. Also...make sure you send us a communication on the latest political campaigns. I believe we were able to side track all the political talk about a democratic change for Cuba by creating that international incident when we shot down those two Cessna aircraft in February. Keep up the good work. Anything else?"

"No...I wanted you to know about this kid. I smell danger from him."

"Thanks, we can handle it from here. We've been able to avoid all efforts to find us since we left North Vietnam in 1968. That doesn't bother me. I am in a position to stop anyone and anything. If he shows I can give him special treatment. I'll pass this information along to Raphael. Keep us informed. We need more information about the elections and how they are going, especially the issues."

Benitez hung up the phone. Feeling much better he started home.

Miguel, now in charge of the Department of Security within the Ministry of the Interior was in a position to handle any interference, which might come his way. Miguel surmised it was about the deaths of American POWS which occurred while they were imprisoned. It was the reason his group was declared *persona non grata* in North Vietnam and was sent back to Cuba.

Benitez was greatly relieved after talking with his old friend Miguel, at least he now had a place to go if circumstances got out of hand. The thought of returning to Cuba was greeted with eager anticipation. For sixteen years he had been away from his homeland. He would always have a sense of pride regarding his land of birth with a desire to return some day.

Cuba is a desirable country to live in. It has beautiful bays, rivers, beaches, mountains, valleys and excellent weather for year round farming. The beauty of the countryside, the atmosphere, the people, the weather, every natural factor contributes to the physical enhancements of the country. All Cubans living in exile have a strong desire to return someday, and Benitez was no different.

CHAPTER VII

The early Sunday morning hotel shuttle to Miami International Airport was an uneventful trip for which Jay was thankful. During the night he had the chance to unwind slightly but not until he was completely satisfied all the information he bundled in his memory was written down as correctly as possible. Neither Penny nor Jay had eaten breakfast and were looking forward to having a leisurely morning meal after check-in. Jay was emotionally renewed and his mind was clear. He was successful obtaining the names of the three Cubans and successful with Jack Richardson and Mid-Western Oil. The moment had to be just right to let Penny know everything.

The speaker system announced Continental Flight 385 for DFW loading at Gate 22. Jay looked at his watch. He wanted more time before loading. He paid the breakfast bill and the two rushed to Gate 22. Time on the ground went quickly and soon they were at 29,000 feet cruising toward Dallas-Fort Worth International Airport.

Penny allowed Jay the opportunity to maintain his silence. Her intuition suggested something was bothering him. She was confident her husband of four years would tell everything when he was ready. His silent demeanor since leaving the hotel suggested he was preparing to discuss the details of his search for Benitez Aguillar. She calmly waited for his revelations.

As predicted, Jay put down the magazine he purchased at the gift shop and started talking. "Penny...first, I want to apologize to you for being so disinterested and ignoring you through most of this trip. You have to know, I couldn't have done any of this without your support. You made my contact with Jack Richardson of Mid-Western Oil easy and he agreed to purchase some of our leases. I'll have to go to Oklahoma City to close on the contracts but I know it's a done deal. You helped do all that. This is going to bring in a lot of money for us. I mean a lot of money!"

"Just how much money?" Penny causally asked.

"Maybe millions." Jay watched as Penny's expression showed disbelief.

"Oh, my God! You mean like millions of dollars?" She exclaimed.

"Yep! Millions of dollars!" Jay enjoyed her excited response.

"Oooh, ooh, oh, my God!" Penny had trouble letting it sink into her brain. "When did you know this?" Penny wanted to know why he was telling her now. She felt Jay should have told her sooner.

"I wasn't really certain until last night. After the banquet while you were in the restroom, Jack told me to come to Oklahoma City as soon as possible. He wanted to obtain some oil leases. Then he winked and gave a thumbs up. I took that to mean he was ready to sign."

"Well, I'll be damned; evidently he liked my black dress. You'll have to keep him away from me for a while. Twice last night he put his arm around my waist and pulled me close. I laughed it off. But now, since there is money at stake, a lot of money, I sure as hell don't want him to assume anything." Penny was delighted over the money but that was as far as it was going. She didn't want Jack Richardson any closer than he was last night, leases or no leases.

Jay took her comments well. "OK...OK! He's seen all of you he is going to see. You're all mine!" Jay was sitting on an aisle seat in the first class section. There was plenty of room for him to spread out, but he moved closer toward Penny as he spoke. "Regarding my effort to search for the names I was looking for, I was successful in that also. We made a clean sweep in getting what we came here for." Jay reached across the armrest for Penny's hand. He squeezed her hand affectionately. She looked at him, searching his eyes for a reason to this show of affection. When their eyes met, she understood fully. Jay was being as sincere as he knew how. He wasn't one who outwardly displayed his affections. She smiled quietly accepting his unspoken message. He appreciated her and was grateful for her support.

"I got the names I went there to get." He paused, "You are going to find this strange." Penny looked at Jay waiting for his comment. "Benitez Aguillar and Antonio Guillermo are the same person. Aguillar is under the Witness Protection Program and they changed his name to Guillermo. Our own government is protecting him and paying all his bills. This doesn't make any sense at all."

"Is he the man you came here to find?"

"Yes! He sure is and our government has known who he was since 1980." Jay let that morsel of information sink in before continuing. "*Fidel*'s real name is Miguel Fuentes and *The Bug*'s name is Raphael Almarales Pardo." Jay paused for a moment. He squeezed Penny's hand again. She turned to look into his eyes. Instinct told her something was not right. She laid her other hand on top of Jay's soothing his anxiety, calmly waiting for his next words.

"I had to get rough with Aguillar to get those names!"

"I thought you expected to do that?" Penny sort of shrugged her shoulders gently against Jay's.

"I found out something about myself. I can't be mean!" Jay searched for words. "This old man cried right there in front of me. I had to make him fear me and show my determination." Jay looked up and stared into the distance. "That really bothered me. I still hold the image of that old man kneeling on the ground and sobbing like a baby. He was kneeling to pick up his box of dominoes which I knocked out of his hand." Jay paused and pursed his lips. "He thought I was going to hurt him and it caused him to wet his pants." Jay shook his head back and forth as he stared at the seat in front of him. "I'm not up for this. To be honest, I thought I could be strong and determined; able to do whatever was required. I can't!"

Penny reveled in his declaration. "That's no surprise to me. There isn't a mean streak in you. You're not telling me anything I didn't already know."

"I feel miserable about treating that old man the way I did. I don't think he deserved it. When we get home I've got to call Bill Sutton and get his feelings about this man. He was there in Hanoi and observed what was going on. If he tells me this man deserved harsh treatment, then I will feel better." Jay closed his eyes to envision the scene all over again as if purposely punishing himself.

"This man is very religious. He has monuments and statues around his house for daily meditation. He appeared gentle and soft spoken. He was liked by his friends at the park. I hate I had to get rough with him to get the names I needed." Jay's jaw muscles tightened. He was thinking harshly of himself.

Jay continued. "I think I have released a basket of snakes and someone else will have to round 'em up and put 'em back in the basket. Originally I planned to pass these names along to anyone and everyone who would listen. Now I'm not so certain. If I do, it will destroy this man's life." Jay stopped talking and warmly rubbed Penny's hand, searching for comfort.

Penny responded by turning closer to Jay and grabbing his hand in hers. "That's not your problem. If he was involved, he needs to suffer. It's like a murderer getting released on parole. If he did the crime he needs to finish his time. I'm sure there are other families out there, just like us, who want and deserve their pound of flesh. You haven't done anything wrong. It's your character that's in your way. The man I fell in love with is kind, loving, gentle, and compassionate. If you were any other way, I wouldn't love you as much as I do. What you just said confirms what I already knew." She displayed a warm smile of understanding. "Don't beat yourself up for being who you are. I love you for it." She leaned her head across the seat to touch Jay's in a display of affection.

"Something else bothers me. That man Benitez or Antonio, whatever he uses, he's here in the States because the U.S. Government under the witness protection program is sponsoring him. Since he's under the witness protection program, he gets a monthly subsistence allowance. He has his home rent-free. He gets SSI benefits, medical care and protection. I don't understand all that. But this is the kicker and bothers the hell out of me. The FBI Agent and a Special Agent for the DIA have had these names since May of 1980! They have been telling us they had no information. This makes my head spin. This whole affair could have gone differently. Most of my anger is out of frustration with our own government." Jay closed his eyes. Penny waited for more.

Jay's anger was showing so he purposely dropped the subject. "You know what? I will have to go to Oklahoma City when we get back to close with Mid-Western Oil. Why don't you and Mom come with me? We can have a nice short and very expensive vacation. I have to go and I would like both of you to go with me. This should be a very lucrative deal for all of us! Maybe we should start spending some of the money."

Penny offered a wide grin and nodded in the affirmative. She believed things would be better and spending money always made her happy. Now that Jay had the names of those Cuban interrogators to publish to the world, he should be happy too.

Arriving back home, Penny immediately brought Marcie up to speed on all the events which took place. She told her that Jay's search for the truth had ended. He found the first man and obtained the names of the other two. He was satisfied.

Jay's plan was to release the other two names into the public domain but planned to withhold the name of Benitez Aguillar. She explained how Jay felt after his encounter with Benitez. Marcie understood and was grateful to know his search was over. Penny told Marcie about the planned trip to Oklahoma City for the three of them to celebrate the oil lease contracts. Marcie agreed and glad to be asked.

After Jay greeted his Mom, he bolted straight up the stairs into their apartment. He was eager to get on the phone to Bill Sutton and pass along all the information he had, especially about Aguillar and Guillermo.

It was Sunday and Bill stayed off the course away from the weekend duffers.

Bill answered. "This is Sutton's residence."

"Hey Bill? This is Jay Cobb."

"Well, well. How did your trip go?"

"It went well. I found Benitez Aguillar and after some persuasion he gave me the names of *Fidel* and *The Bug*. Now that I have their names I am going to send them out through the press and to all the POW/MIA organizations." Jay felt a sense of exhilaration. "I don't think I will tell anyone about Benitez Aguillar. He is in his sixties and to be honest I kinda feel sorry for him. I had to rough him up a bit to get the names and I am really sorry I had to do that."

Bill blurted out, "Why? What did you have to do?" Bill was concerned.

"I hardly did anything, I grabbed his shirt collar and he began to cry and he wet his pants. He was afraid of what I would do to him."

"Don't feel bad! He damn well deserves anything you might have done. All you did was to make him remember and sweat a little."

"But I thought you said you would like to find him and shake his hand?"

"I said that for your mother's benefit to get you to back off. Benitez was the guard that dragged your father out of the interrogation room and took his lifeless body back to his cell. Then the next day after *Fidel* beat him some more, it was Benitez and a North Vietnamese soldier who carried your father to the hospital. You should have asked him about your father's condition when he left him at the hospital. No sir!" Bill emphasized. "Don't you feel bad about Benitez. He was as bad as the other two. He hit me several times during my interrogations. I don't like him at all! He deserved whatever you had to dish out." Bill Sutton paused and Jay thought over his comments.

"Where did you find his ass?" Bill asked.

"He plays dominoes everyday in Domino Park on S.W. 8th Street in Little Havana. Everyone knows him. He has a nice house on Twelfth Street. I followed him there to put on the pressure for the other two names." Jay rocked back in his chair at the phone table. He was beginning to feel a little better about himself.

"What are the real names of those other two bastards?" Bill Sutton was eager to know.

"The man you call *Fidel*. His real name is Miguel Fuentes. He is a Lt/Col and works in the Ministry of the Interior in Cuba. The other guy, *The Bug*, his name is Raphael Almarales Pardo. He is a Captain and is the prison warden at Kilo 8 in Camaguey Province. Apparently it is a special prison for hardened prisoners."

Bill quickly thought about this and spoke. "I think I'll go to Miami and look up that SOB Aguillar myself. I've always wanted to be face to face with any of those three bastards."

Jay heard Bill's words and became a little confused. It sounded like Bill Sutton was changing his position. When Jay got physical with Benitez, he remembered Bill's previous words, 'I'd like to shake his hand'. Those words had hampered his physical determination, made his effort a little harder and made him feel guilty. Jay didn't understand where the boundaries were then or now. Finding that boundary separating intimidating efforts from out and out violence should have been easy. It wasn't.

Bill's original words had interfered. Now Bill was ready to jump on the bandwagon and go see Benitez himself. Jay was bewildered. His most inward thoughts came to the surface. His initial effort to seek revenge was becoming relevant again. Avenging his family's crying blood became foremost on his mind.

Bill declared through the phone, "I'm going to see that man as soon as I can."

"What will you do with him?" Jay was more than curious; he needed to hear Sutton's degree of hatred.

"I'd like to smash his face in. When I remember all the bad things he helped accomplish, I fume. I'd like to vent some of my anger straight on him." Bill sounded determined. "Don't you ever believe he was a good guy. He wasn't. Yeah… he is getting older but so are we. Some of those he tortured didn't have the opportunity to grow old."

Jay was reassessing his view of the situation. If Bill Sutton felt that strongly, then there were many others who would feel the same way. The basket of snakes Jay released, were already beginning to be gathered by someone else. Jay had to think this thing through all over again. On the plane ride back his mind was set. He decided what he was going to do. Now after this conversation with Bill, he wasn't as certain. One side of him said let it drop you have done enough. The other still demanded revenge. Avenging his father's death would please his dark side and that was frightening! His dark side was beginning to scare him a little.

After his revealing conversation with Bill Sutton he was even more troubled. Jay went back downstairs and joined his Mom and Penny in the den where they were quietly watching TV. Thoughts of reconsidering his actions swirled in his brain.

His Mom jumped directly to the question. "Well son, what's the verdict? Are you really finished with this obsession?" His Mom needed to know so she could go back to a normal life and normal expectations. She hated seeing her son so distracted and isolated from day to day events.

"Yeah...I think my effort to get some closure is over. I have the names of those three killers and I plan to let the world know who they are and where they can be located. Why should they be allowed to live normal lives? Our lives were badly upset by their outrageous acts. Let us offer them some misery for a change." Jay appeared satisfied. At the same time he let his mind roam over the subject again and again. Crying blood revenge still remained in his thoughts.

Jay changed the subject. "Mom, are you coming with us to Oklahoma City? We'll make a vacation celebration out of it if you come. There are lots of things to do in Oklahoma City, The Museum of Art, The Botanical Gardens, The National Museum, Oklahoma City Central Park and you don't have to drive to any of these places. You can do all this on the Metro Transit. I would personally like to visit and pay my respects at the Alfred P. Murrah Federal Building Memorial." Jay paused to let it all sink in. "We'll stay at the best hotels, eat at the best restaurants, you and Penny can shop 'til you drop' and I'll go take care of business." Jay was up beat in his invitation. Besides he had a lot of thinking to do about The Cuban Project. A little diversion would suit him too.

Marcie, delighted with the prospects of a fun trip and glad to be included, readily accepted the invitation. "I want to have my own room. That's a must...OK? I want you two to have some alone time together. I need grandchildren and I'm still waiting."

"Whatever you say Mom! You and Penny both deserve to be spoiled a little bit. I haven't been around the house too much lately. If I'm right, we should come back with millions of dollars." He smiled at the two ladies in his life and felt good about himself.

****

Jay pushed his eagerness aside and waited two days before contacting Jack Richardson in Oklahoma City. He didn't want to appear too eager. He expected Jack would need the time to settle back into his daily routine before discussing the new venture. From his office in Claremore Jay phoned Jack and asked if the lease possibility was still under consideration. To Jay's surprise Jack said, "Hell Yes. I thought you would call as soon as you got back." He told Jay he wanted to set a date for Jay to come to Oklahoma City to close on the deal.

Delighted, Jay set the date for Friday morning. They would drive the hundred miles on Thursday allowing plenty of time to get settled into the hotel. It would also give Jay the luxury of additional time to prepare for meeting with Jack Friday morning at 9:00 a.m. Jay busied himself putting his lease packages together. His company had six leases to sell. Two leases were in Creek County, two in Okfuskee County, and two were in Nowata County. Jay's company had researched and purchased the mineral rights and completed the seismographic and geological assessments. The positive evidence indicated oil was there. It just had to be extracted.

Each lease had its own package of papers. When Jay prepared to put them in his briefcase, he realized there was way too much to fit into one. He would need a second to carry it all. He found his partner's briefcase, emptied it and put the remaining papers into it. His partner was on location for a major oil company assessing a new location. Jay took both briefcases full of papers and headed to their lawyer's office for one final check. He knew when they drove to Oklahoma City on Thursday, he must have everything needed to close the deal without any glitches.

Early Friday morning, Jay began preparing himself for his meeting. He wore his navy blue blazer and khaki colored pants. They seemed appropriate for a brisk fall breeze with temperatures in the high sixties. When he was leaving the hotel room, he took a final look in the wall mirror before walking out. He thought he looked like a case lawyer carrying all his material to trial, a fully loaded briefcase in each hand. It was an amusing thought. He was ready for the meeting.

After his meeting with Jack Richardson on Friday morning Jay couldn't contain himself. He had signed a deal for six million dollars plus a lucrative per barrel royalty! When those wells come into production, Jay, his partner, his company, and both families could live in wealth the rest of their lives. Jay's excitement and exhilaration soared. Winning a lottery could not have been more exciting.

He left the Mid Western Oil Company offices carrying the two now nearly empty briefcases. The offices were located on the eighth floor of the Executive Building on Broadway Boulevard. When the doors to the elevators closed, Jay at last was able to express his overflowing enthusiasm. He waited until the floor enunciator indicated he was between floors and he yelled out loud...YES!

Jay left the building and briskly walked down the endless row of professional office buildings towering above the downtown area. He had a definite bounce in his walk and a grin which would not go away. As he approached the Broadway Hotel, he walked into the lobby area searching for a courtesy phone to call Penny.

When Penny answered he exploded. "We did it...We sold our leases...Six million dollars! Go tell Mom...Can you believe it...Six million dollars!"

Needless to say Penny was delighted with the news. Jay exuberantly told Penny to take Mom shopping and buy anything they wanted.

When he hung up, he finally came down from the clouds and looked around. The street level foyer to the hotel was a shopping plaza with several tourist-oriented businesses. He strolled through the plaza to unwind, still carrying the near empty briefcases. Jay noticed a large poster in the window of a travel agency listing the beauty and pleasures of Caribbean vacation destinations. Now feeling he was soon to become wealthy, he stopped in to consider a real vacation trip.

Once inside he was greeted by a nice, well-dressed lady. As he looked at all the travel brochures for Jamaica, Puerto Rico, and the Virgin Islands, his thoughts turned to Cuba. He realized going to Cuba and finding the remaining two interrogators remained foremost on his mind. Out of curiosity he asked the lady if it was possible to visit Cuba. She offered him a seat and began to bring up information on the computer regarding Cuba as a destination.

Cordially, she talked as her rapidly moving fingers called up data on the computer. "I did this for a young Latin couple about six months ago. They wanted to go to a Caribbean destination for ten days. There was not one vacation spot which matched their budget. As I worked the problem, I came up with a ten day excursion to Cuba at half the costs of all the other locations. I set them up with that tour. When they returned, they came back to tell me their tour was most delightful. They said the Cuban people were happy to welcome them. The people were so nice to them, they hated to leave. And the countryside...there weren't enough words of praise for them to express the beauty they saw. They actually wanted to book another trip." The lady paused to read some information off the computer screen.

"Are there any restrictions on going to Cuba?" Jay asked before she could begin her presentation.

"Yes...there are a lot of restrictions but none of them are enforced. Our laws say no citizen can leave the States and go to Cuba. However, if you are Cuban-American and have family there, you are excluded from this."

"Then how did they get permission to go?" Jay scratched his head.

"You have to join a tour group and let them do all the work for you," The lady grinned.

"What tour group did you find for them?" Jay quizzed.

"I found them a tour group called *Ensenanza de Cuba*. It was an 'educational' tour group. A New England University through the Center for Cuban Studies in New York was authorized to offer this tour every three months as an adjunct to its academic studies. Strangely enough, anyone can join the group. Back then it cost about $780 dollars for a ten-day tour. There were a few other extraneous expenses. If my memory serves me well, they had to meet with the group in Cancun, Mexico. From there everything was paid in advance. The tour group procured a tourist card for everyone. This replaced the passport for entry into Cuba. I think that was an extra $25." The lady remembered more than she thought she could.

"The tour group, *Ensenanza de Cuba*, was a creation of the Center for Cuban Studies and was licensed through the Office of Foreign Assets Control under the U.S. Treasury Department. They are the umbrella through which certain Universities are allowed to arrange for such tour groups to Cuba. The University's Department of Latin Studies booked and handled all registrations for the tour." She gave more than enough background for the offering.

"Are there any restrictions specific to the tour group?" Jay's interest was strong.

"Under this particular educational tour, as a minimum you must go to the University of Havana for four hours in the morning on two different days where you are lectured on the culture, the history, and the heritage of Cuba." The lady offered as an aside, "They also offer a brief Conversational Spanish course, if you want to learn to speak the language."

Jay was impressed. Out of nowhere and with little hesitation he asked about the next tour, when it would depart and if the travel agent could get him booked.

The lady readily agreed to handle all the arrangements saying she would send him a contract with a package detailing all the particulars. Jay gave his office address for receipt of the package. He also said he wanted his flight to depart from Oklahoma City.

Astonished with his own impulsiveness and the ease of travel, somewhere in this lengthy discussion with the travel agent, Jay went back to his original plan to find *Fidel* and *The Bug*. Feeling wealthy and still harboring this passion, he whimsically decided to make the journey. This abrupt and unexpected choice placed him at odds with himself. Should he or shouldn't he make the trip. As best he tried, rationalizing his choice was difficult. He ultimately decided it was like dreading a visit to the dentist for a root canal procedure. You could dread it only so long. After a while you just wanted it over. That's where he found himself, he just wanted it over. The only answer was to go to Cuba.

If he was going, he knew he did not want Penny or his mother to find out about it. If they were to find out, his plans would be side lined. Since his earlier chat with Bill Sutton, his plan to find these people and dish out some sort of revenge had resurfaced more focused then ever.

After leaving the travel agency, Jay asked himself more probing questions. Being absolutely honest, it wasn't curiosity about Cuba. Searching out the two Cuban interrogators was his driving force. Visiting Little Havana in Miami had stirred his interest and talking with Bill Sutton had cinched the deal. Going to Cuba would be a way to settle this score and get it over. His mind was made up once and for all. His attitude was one of firm determination. Cuba would be his next stop.

That night Jay took his Mom and Penny out to a fine restaurant to celebrate their newfound wealth. Already beginning to create his cover for the trip to Cuba, Jay directed the conversation to the leases. Jay told them he would need to spend some time in Oklahoma City and at the drilling sites consulting on the process of bringing in new oil. He assured them he felt obligated, especially for the first location, to guarantee success of the effort. Both women agreed it was necessary and spurred him onward with the task. Jay felt a little guilty lying to them but he had his alibi.

Upon returning home, Jay made himself a list of all the things he needed to do to complete his journey to Cuba. Getting a passport, even though not required for Cuban entry, was needed for any contingency which might occur. It was at the top of the list and he needed to start that process as soon as possible. He spoke on the phone daily to the travel agent keeping track of the plans as they developed. After three days he received his travel package at the company office in Claremore. Reading all the material created more enthusiasm for the trip. Eager to make the trip, he found himself getting into the spirit of traveling to a foreign country.

Before leaving Jay knew he must talk further with Bill Sutton and try to get detailed descriptions of the two men he hoped to find. His conversation with Bill Sutton had to be well scripted or he would surely tell Jay's mom and that would be the end of it.

Jay, sitting in his office in Claremore dialed Bill's number.

"Hello." Bill's wife answered the phone.

"Good morning Mrs. Sutton. This is Jay Cobb. Is Bill in?"

Jay heard her drop the phone and a yell in the background. "It's for you!"

The wireless phone was picked up on the patio. "Bill Sutton."

"Hi Bill. This is Jay Cobb again." After all the amenities of greeting him, Jay spoke. "I am writing a paper on those two men, *Fidel* and *The Bug*. I plan to send this out to all the POW/MIA families I can. What I need from you is their physical description. You gave it to me once before but I didn't pay that much attention to the details. I am ready to write down your words, so if you would, please tell me their identifying features."

"OK...Let me see...*Fidel* had a tattoo on the underside of his left arm just above the wrist. It was some kind of pentagram, artwork instead of an image." Jay wrote down the information.

"Another feature was his eyes. He had different colored eyes. One was green and the other was dark brown." Jay highlighted this data.

"His skin color was light tan, sort of honey colored, just like your father's. He was tall, about 6' 2" and very official looking. He always carried a leather bound baton like he was a general or someone important. The way he looked at you was intimidating. You could feel his eyes boring holes right through you. His laugh was sinister sounding. It was like he was laughing at you, jeering and taunting, making you feel small. That son-of-a-bitch was sadistic as hell and he always had to win. If he felt you were competing with him by not complying and answering his stupid questions, he would beat the hell out of you just for recreation. Anyone going before him knew they would be beaten and tried to steel their nerves to handle his abuse." Bill paused. "Is that what you wanted to know?"

"Yes sir. What about the other guy, *The Bug*?"

"*The Bug* was vicious. He was also about 6' 2" and stood erect. He was always neat. We all thought it was way out of place, for someone to be so neatly dressed yet viciously mean. He was light skinned, didn't speak much English. Hell, he hardly spoke at all. He carried a riding crop." Bill stuttered into the phone. "No wait a minute, I'm getting myself confused." Bill thought for a minute then continued. "No. I was right. It was *Fidel* who had the leather wrapped baton. *The Bug* carried the riding crop. He had a slim line mustache and a pointed goatee. That's how I remember him. Somehow because of his neatness, I always had the impression he was a ladies man, a real peacock. That's all I can remember about him right now."

Jay spoke with excitement. "This is great information. I will include it with their names and locations. Hopefully the U.S. Government will get enough pressure from all these families until they'll be forced to react in some manner." Jay further asked, "Are you still thinking about going to see Benitez Aguillar?"

"I sure am! And I've passed his name and his location along to others who might plan a little visit as well. He should have a real party on his hands." Bill laughed into the phone.

"Thanks for the info! And tell Mrs. Sutton I said Hi!" To keep Bill from calling his mom, he added, "Oh yes...my Mom says Hi also." Jay hung up the phone and tried to visualize the two men who changed so many lives. He needed these two descriptions imprinted into his brain. The more he thought about the two evil men, the more he knew he would have no peace without some type of revenge for his father's death.

CHAPTER VIII

Jay drove away from his home in the early morning hours the first week in November. His good-byes were said the night before. They believed he was going to Oklahoma City to be a consultant for the new leases and knew he would be out of touch for about ten days. Both Penny and his Mom accepted his departure as part of his job.

In fact Jay was headed to the Oklahoma City International Airport to catch his flight to DFW with connections to Cancun, Mexico. His passport was in hand and in his pocket was $1,000.00 in U.S. bills. Jay purchased a money belt where he had $5,000.00 in large bills stashed away for anything which might occur. He was on his way for a ten day excursion to Cuba with a touring group.

Packing his luggage was a problem. Temperatures in Oklahoma in November were anything but summer-like. But for the next ten days he would be in the tropics and needed lightweight summer clothing. Penny helped him pack stuffing warmer working clothes in his luggage. Without voicing objections Jay let her do the packing. Arguing would only bring questions. If he was to have summer clothing he would need to buy it.

Jay's tour group instructions were simple. Meet the group at the Cancun Airport terminal on the date and time as set. There were a total of 21 people registered for the tour. Jay was the only unaccompanied individual. His instructions were to meet by a sign in the open concourse of the Cancun terminal and ask for a lady named Triana Travis. She would be the group leader and guide. Triana would hand out schedules for the next nine days, hand out the tourist cards to be used instead of the passports and name badges for identification. Jay easily found the tour group. The large floor sign in the lobby announcing *Ensenanza de Cuba* Tour couldn't be missed. Triana Travis was already there greeting everyone. She was short, a little chubby but not obese and very comfortable to look at. Through her loose fitting clothes, it was easy to see she had definite feminine curves. Being slightly portly didn't interfere with her good looks. She was Latino and very fluent in English as well as Spanish. Her smiling face was very pleasing to the eyes. Jay thought she was in her forties. Like most Americans with an overworked affinity for nicknames, he started to call her T.T. When he voiced it to himself for the first time it sounded like an off color insult and he discarded the idea.

Jay had an aisle seat on his previous flight from Miami to DFW and didn't have the opportunity to view any of the waters of the Gulf of Mexico. On this flight from Cancun to Havana he sat in a window seat and could watch the Gulf throughout the flight. Departing Cancun he looked in awe at the greenish blue waters. Being from a land locked state, seeing the ocean or the gulf was a new experience. The flight on Aerocaribbean Airlines aircraft, an IL-18 Russian made jet liner, took less than an hour to arrive at Jose Marti International Airport. During the short flight, Jay had his eyes glued to the window watching the water. The gulf was much different than that of a large lake. The colors were fascinating.

Approaching the shoreline, he witnessed a most magnificent view of tropical waters. The water gradually changed from a deep blue, into a greenish blue, then into the most brilliant emerald green color closer to shore. As the waves began to tumble approaching the shoreline, an ivory white line of breakers cascading over each other gave him a marvelous view.

He sat back in his upright seat as the plane began its approach continuing to envision the water's edge. All the time his thoughts were about Penny and how he wished she could be sharing this beauty with him.

The group disembarked from the jet liner, retrieved their baggage and was directed by the tour guide straight into Customs. Triana had already informed the group about the

Customs process, saying it would be relatively pain free. The Customs Officers normally made only a cursory look at the baggage and the entire group should pass through in less than five minutes per person. All were delighted to hear this.

As Jay walked up to the counter with his bags in hand, he was greeted warmly with a smile. The Officer looked at his tourist card, also referred to as a visitor card. He then looked at his nametag. Each person in the group was wearing prominent nametags handed out by the tour guide during the initial welcoming in Cancun. These were to be ice-breakers to facilitate introductions. His name Emanuel J. Cobb, Jr. was readily apparent.

The officer asked, "Mr. Cobb?" He had a slight amount of difficulty of pronouncing Jay's first name. "E...man..u..ell J. Cobb?"

Jay responded, "*Si*. Emanuel J. Cobb." He articulated his name slowly.

"*Uno momento senior.*"

The Customs Officer went over to a wall-phone and made a brief phone call. Jay sensed something wasn't right. Triana, the ever vigil guide, came toward Jay. She had already been checked through and left her baggage to come to his aid. A happy, smiling person, ready to laugh at anything, she easily took charge.

"*Que tiene de malo equipaje?*" Her smile was as warm as possible. Is there anything wrong with the baggage.

"*Dar largas...no tener alternative.*" He has to wait. These are my instructions. Triana and the officer continued their conversation for about three minutes, occasionally being confrontational. It was easy to see she was disgusted.

Triana turned to Jay and tried to explain the delay. After her brief explanation, she had Jay step aside to allow the others to make their way through Customs. He stepped back and became even more suspicious regarding his delay. He watched every move the officers took. They continued their inspections, with the remaining part of the group, as if nothing happened.

The rest of the group cleared Customs in about twenty-five minutes. Soon two men in casual dress, both wearing sunglasses, approached the group and spoke with Triana. Jay knew he was under suspicion for some reason as the three of them continued to speak and intermittently glanced toward him. Both men were wearing white '*guayabara*' shirts, a styled dress shirt sometimes with ornate stitching for wearing outside the trousers in tropical climates. The taller and older of the two was obviously Caucasian while the other was darker skinned. He could hear their conversation but didn't understand a word of the rapid tongue Spanish being spoken.

Triana came over to Jay. "I'm not sure what's going on, but they have instructions to detain you for further questioning. They told me to take the rest of the group and leave. They would see that you were returned to the group after their questioning. Do you know of any reason they would want to detain you? Do you have any contraband, of any sort?"

Jay shook his head no. "Did they say how long my delay would be?"

"No, they didn't say. We have a bus waiting outside to take us to the hotel. I will go ahead and take these people to the hotel. I am so sorry about this, but I can't keep everyone here waiting for you to clear. I'll get you registered into the hotel.

"After these two gentlemen finish with you, you can take a taxi. Our reservations are in The *Hotel Nacional*. Any taxi driver should know where it is. If you can afford it, give the driver a five-dollar bill and he will take excellent care of you. None of the taxi drivers speak good English. They aren't taught English in the middle schools or high school in Cuba. So speak slowly. Our hotel is in the *Vedado* area off *Calle 'O'*. The streets are named alphabetically. *Hotel Nacional* is on 'O' Street." She looked at her watch. "It's almost lunchtime. Why don't you meet us in the lounge on the top floor? We will be there having sandwiches for lunch. You will like the hotel. It overlooks the Straits of Florida, excellent view. I am terribly sorry. I can't stay with you. I must get these people settled into their rooms. We'll see you at the hotel."

Jay asked, "Did they give you any clue about why I'm being delayed?"

"They only said, they have instructions to question you."

"Did they say who they are? Are they police, customs. What?" Jay was starting to get a little concerned about his safety.

"Just be polite and answer their questions and I'm certain they will let you go without too much further delay." Triana smiled, turned and walked away.

The two men grabbed Jay's luggage and indicated for him to follow. They walked through a door into a nearby room. There were no windows and only painted concrete walls. There was a large low table in the middle of the room. It looked like a place for thoroughly inspecting baggage. Jay believed this was a continuation of his customs declaration and search. When in the room, his luggage was tossed onto the large table and opened by the dark skinned individual while the taller man appeared to be guarding the door.

Jay assumed these two men were customs officers. The one officer, going through the bags, pulled each individual item out of his bag and thoroughly searched it. Jay couldn't believe what was going on. The officer would take out a sock, run his fist down to the bottom, stretch out his fingers and then hold it up to the light to peer through the fabric. There were ten pairs of socks. The socks alone were a slow process. After a while Jay began to think these two would fit the category of the mentally challenged. They continued their nonstop chatter while searching his bags and having some good laughs as they did. Jay remained standing. He was never told to sit down even though there was a chair close by. He stood and watched. They seemed to ignore his presence.

After an hour of this nonsense, the two switched places. The man guarding the door came over to search his things while the other took his post at the door. This person spoke some English.

"Meester Cobb, you born in United States?" Jay was glad to hear English. It made him feel a little better.

"Yes, I was born in the United States."

"Have family in Cuba. Yes?"

"No, I don't."

"Why you here?"

"I want to study the culture. This is an educational tour for me."

"You know Havana?"

"No." Jay was beginning to get the feeling that all this show of imagined concern was truly bogus. He went along with the charade.

"You know Little Havana?"

"You mean in Miami, that Little Havana?"

"Yes...you visit Little Havana...yes?"

"Yes, I have." With this question Jay instantly got the picture. Benitez Aguillar must have fingered him to the authorities in Cuba. It had to be Benitez. Why else would they ask about or even know he was in Little Havana?

Jay asked, "Are you men with customs?"

The man standing in front of him shook his head no.

"Who are you with?" Jay was still trying to piece the puzzle together.

"We ask questions, not you!" The answer was sharp and intended to put Jay back into a passive mode.

"Why you interested in Cuba?"

Jay tried to think up a legitimate reason which would pass. "I am a geologist. I find oil, petroleum deposits, for companies. I think there is oil right here in Cuba. If I can study the history and make a few field trips, I might find something to go on, something which could indicate there is oil here. If I do I plan to get permission from your country to investigate further." Jay thought this should boggle their minds.

"What is schedule while you here?" The man held up a shirt to inspect.

Jay thought maybe this one isn't as dumb as he thought. "I am scheduled for a four hour lecture tomorrow morning at the University of Havana. Then I also have a four-hour lecture the next day. After that we have field trips into the surrounding areas.

"You look for oil?" He turned the shirt over to continue the inspection.

"Yes...I will be looking for signs of oil." Jay inwardly grinned; these two seemed to be buying his tale. Soon they would release him and he could go to the hotel.

"You have gun? Pistola?" The man raised his right hand and pointed his finger as if holding a gun.

"Absolutely not. I don't like guns."

"Guns restricted! You have knife?"

Jay reached into his pocket and pulled out a small penknife. "Yes, just this small one."

"Toss on table." Jay placed it gently on the table. "Take off shirt!"

Jay was concerned now, apparently they weren't buying his story after all. He removed his shirt and laid it on the table.

"Take off pants." Jay unbuckled his belt. He was concerned they might inspect his belt and find his five thousand dollars U.S. hidden inside the secret pocket. He unzipped his pants quickly to divert any attention to the belt. Shaking his right leg he stepped out of his pants one leg and then the other. He tossed his pants on the table, trying to make sure the waistband and the belt were covered by the pant legs.

"Take off shoes." Jay dutifully kneeled to untie his shoes and push them away. "Take off socks." Jay did as he was told.

"Raise your hands and place them behind head." The officer made eye contact with his partner. They grinned at each other. "Don't move. Stand up straight." All these instructions were beginning to get on Jay's nerves and piss him off. The entire process was totally uncalled for. After a short time, Jay dropped his hands to the dismay of the officer.

"Put hands back up." The officer barked his instruction with obvious force.

Jay put his hands behind his head again.

"Now...Don't move!" The officer looked around Jay to the man standing at the door. He made a slight nod. In a louder voice he said, "Don't move!"

The two men walked out the door. Jay was left standing with his hands behind his head and naked except for his boxer shorts. His belongings were strewn all over the large table. Jay continued to look straight ahead at the blank wall, expecting the two men to reenter the room at any time. Jay made a quick turn of his head to his left and took a peek at his watch. Time was approaching 1:00 p.m. He had been detained now for two solid hours. His concern grew. He thought again that Benitez Aguillar was the only person who could have possibly fingered him. His anger grew as he thought about Beanie, the interrogator. "That son-of-a-bitch! I won't ever feel sorry for that bastard again!" Jay declared to himself.

After what seemed like an eternity, Jay again turned his head and peeked at his watch. Only thirty minutes had passed. He was still holding his hands behind his head. Even though he had his knees locked to relieve some of the pressure on his legs, it was putting extra strain on his back muscles. He moved his body from side to side to keep blood circulation flowing. Occasionally he would drop one hand at a time and shake it rapidly to keep the stiffness down. He continued this routine for at least another hour. Sneaking a peek at his watch, time was approaching 3:00 p.m. He went back into his stance. Mentally, he kept questioning what this was all about. He had no answers. He fully expected the two men to burst back into the room at any time. Then he asked himself, what can they do to me if I relax? His profound answer was, nothing. He began to take one hand down at a time.

When both hands were at his side and no one came to correct him; he relaxed his stance and bent his knees to start circulation. He waited for at least another twenty minutes and when no one came; he decided to put his clothes back on. Once dressed, shoes, socks, and all, he walked over to the door, cracked it open enough to look around. Everything looked normal. The customs officers were very busy with new arrivals. The place was flooded with people all moving quickly through the exits. He opened the door further. Not one person noticed him. Jay's thoughts darted through his mind. He was being harassed by those two goons, but he didn't know why and he couldn't see them anywhere.

Jay went back to the table and repacked all his belongings. He pulled himself together and walked out of the room into the large waiting area filled with travelers. He blended into the crowd and walked through the exits. He was free. Free from what, was his question?

Many transients were waiting for taxis. Jay walked away from the front concourse exit down the line of waiting taxis and was accepted by a driver who readily jumped out of the driver's seat, met him on the sidewalk and grabbed his bags. After Jay got into the taxi and the driver started the vehicle, he flashed a five dollar bill. "*La direccion es Calle 'O', Hotel Nacional.*"

The driver answered with a big smile, "*Si, amigo. Hotel Nacional.*" While enroute the driver, rapidly speaking in Spanish, became a tour guide announcing the landmarks they passed on the way to the hotel.

Jay understood some of it. He recognized *Nuevo Vedado* as the name of a town. Since there were many Mexicans in Oklahoma, he knew what *nuevo* meant. The driver became animated as he passed the *Plaza de la Revolucion*. Jay didn't understand a single word he said. Jay did understand the words *Universidad de la Habana* as it was pointed out. That was to be the location of tomorrow morning's session of learning the culture.

Arriving at the hotel Jay proceeded to the desk and asked for his key. Time was nearing 5:00 p.m. He went to his room, dropped his luggage and immediately headed to the top floor lounge. He hoped that Triana Travis would be there. Maybe she could answer some of his questions.

Triana was in the lounge. Part of her duties was to be the first person to arrive at every location. The group's dinner was to be served soon. The first day's dinner was planned for getting better acquainted with all traveling partners. Jay walked directly to her table.

She asked, "I see you were finally allowed to leave."

Jay wasn't sure how to answer that question. Instead he opted to tell her what went on. "They didn't do anything. I was there for four and a half hours. They completely upset all my belongings, dumped them onto a large table, made me stand naked for an interminable amount of time, left me and never came back." Jay was more than disgusted and Triana couldn't blame him. She was perplexed also.

"What was their purpose?" She asked, "Did they say anything to indicate why they treated you as they did?"

"It was merely for harassment! You have made this tour before, right?"

"Yes...many times."

"Have they ever treated anyone else like this before?"

"Never!"

"Then I think it was for pure harassment. They picked me out of the group for some reason. I don't understand the treatment. Can you do anything about it?"

"I plan to certainly try. I have to know if this is going to become a regular thing. If it is, I'll stop making these tours. I can't have my groups being harassed in this manner."

Jay felt confident she was good to her word. As they remained at the table, more of their group began to show. There were couples from California, Arizona, Alaska, Michigan, North Dakota, and five couples from the University of New Hampshire. The evening meal and drinks went well. Everyone was enjoying the company of the others. Jay was the loner. He was still fuming over his treatment.

Many of those on the tour had thoughts of him carrying contraband and were somewhat aloof in their behavior toward him. Since he was alone, their feelings were compounded by suspicion. Jay attempted to be as cordial as possible but his explanations didn't make any sense.

Again he had thoughts Benitez Aguillar had made contact with someone and announced his coming. He was targeted! He certainly couldn't discuss this with his traveling partners. Silently Jay was determined, more than ever, to complete his purpose to find Miguel Fuentes and Raphael Almarales Pardo. He believed the two were behind his reception. This indicated to him that he was on the right track.

Before going to his room after the dinner, he wanted to walk to the waterfront and enjoy the beautiful sights. The hotel had two entrances. There was an entrance facing the Straits of Florida with chairs for sitting and enjoying the view. There was another entrance, a main entrance, for vehicle arrivals in the rear and numerous exit doors throughout the first floor. For such an old building, it was well planned. The literature handed out before the trip said that in the 1930s, the *Hotel Nacional* was Cuba's symbol of prosperity and celebrities visiting Cuba often stayed there.

The hotel had small local area maps as handouts. He picked up one to help direct his walk. As he walked through the doors facing the water's edge, he came face to face with the two men who searched him at the airport. They were standing along the steps. Obviously, they were waiting for him. He purposely walked over to goad them into some explanation...this was getting old.

They spoke first. "Meester Cobb, you go back home! Not stay Cuba!"

Jay stared them down and walked past deciding not to engage in anything.

One item on the map caught his eye, the monument to the USS Maine. He knew from the Spanish wording, *Monumento al Maine* and from the location of the hotel, that he was close. He looked to his left across the park area along the shoreline highway, called the *malecon*, and saw the tall monument. It was the USS Maine Memorial. He walked along the shoreline and enjoyed this piece of history. Looking out across the Straits of Florida, he thought this was one of the most breathtaking sites thus far. The map also indicated three blocks west on Calle 'L' was a location marked U.S. Interests Section. He thought to himself, maybe he should go there and mention how he had been harassed. Jay started in that direction. Thinking better of it, he would ask Triana's opinion first about what he should do.

He pulled himself up to a thick, waist high wall marking the boundary of the *malecon* and perched himself on top to look around and relax. He began to smile as he realized how peaceful it was. He was enjoying this quiet pleasure. Looking back over his shoulder, he was shocked to see the same two men standing in the shadows of the streetlights watching him. He knew he was truly targeted and being shadowed. Now his concern was really growing.

Jay left and walked rapidly down a street blocks away from the hotel. The two men followed him. He walked faster and the two men speeded up their gait. Jay turned right at the first street he came to. He had wandered too far from the hotel and feared the two men might try to pick him up on some bogus charge. Finding himself in such a tenuous position was unsettling. He walked around a blind corner. There were a goodly number of people wandering the streets and Jay knew he could easily elude the two.

When out of their sight, he ran for two blocks and again turned right. He stopped running and walked to the next corner where he turned right again. There was a bar on the corner. He walked into the bar and positioned himself on a stool beside a window so he could watch to see if the two men had followed. The bar was lively, music playing, couples dancing, everyone laughing and having a good time. He saw a red and white lighted neon sign on the rear wall advertising La Tropical Beer. When the waitress came he ordered one. He peered through the bar window expecting to see the two men at any moment. They never showed.

This left Jay with his jumbled thoughts. Who were these men? Why were they following him? Did they truly follow him or was it just his imagination. This was a set of circumstances he had never anticipated, especially so early in his trip. Stories about Latin prisons were common knowledge and none of them were good.

Jay was having second thoughts about why he was here. He was certain Miguel Fuentes and Raphael Pardo were the reason he was being targeted. He knew Benitez Aguillar had fingered him and it must have been to Fuentes and Pardo.

When he left the bar, he continued to be warily on the look out for the two men. He searched up and down the streets before he stepped onto the sidewalk. He calculated the hotel was about two blocks straight ahead. At every corner he looked four ways searching for the two. They were nowhere in sight and he was more than relieved.

His relief was short lived. Walking into the lobby of the hotel he came face to face with the same two men. He stopped and stared deeply into each face with a glare. He stepped toward the man on the left. As he did both men backed up. Jay had made his point. He took another step toward the two. They moved backwards.

"What do you want from me?" Jay was angered.

"Meester Cobb, you go home! Not stay Cuba!"

"I don't know who you are." He looked at both men, staring directly into their eyes. He knew they were intimidated by him. "Who sent you?" Jay was on a roll and could feel he was over powering the two. "Go tell your boss, I am coming after him." As soon as the words were out of his mouth, he knew he shouldn't have spoken. It was like asking for trouble. Not smart!

Jay took in an elaborate amount of air and this time stepped forward forcing the two to step aside and let him through. It worked. He continued to the elevators and up to his room for the night. He locked his door and placed a chair against the doorknob. If anyone tried to enter he would know about it first.

Jay had to know what lengths these two men were instructed to go. These thoughts left him with a nearly sleepless night. The next morning he had plans to discuss it all with Triana and ask more questions about the U.S. Interests Section. What was their purpose and what would they do for a U.S. Citizen? At this point Jay was primarily irritated. He felt certain he could intimidate them. Was this harassment coming from a higher authority or were the two men merely working as a favor to one of the people he wanted to find? Whatever the answers, he now knew his task wasn't going to happen without a hitch. He worried about his next step. Were they going to block his efforts?

The next morning Jay showered early and went to the lobby before going to the restaurant for breakfast. Much to his surprise, sitting in the lobby were the same two men from last night's incident. Jay knew what he had to do. He would have to secretly change hotels.

Jay ate breakfast and met the group in the lobby for their shuttle bus trip to the University of Havana. Strangely enough the two men didn't follow. He put this bit of information in the back of his mind. If this were true, then getting a new hotel should solve his problem. He could come back to the *Hotel Nacional*, enter through an alternate doorway, meet with the group and proceed with the tour. This would maintain the impression he was staying with the tour group. His course of action was taking shape. From now on he would become the hunter instead of the hunted. At least he would be free while they thought he was occupied with the group.

Like a good student Jay sat through the entire four-hour lecture with breaks every fifty minutes. After it was over Jay walked up front to speak with the lecturer. He asked if she knew anyone who might do some research for him and one who could speak English. She mentioned there were students who could do it but they would have to be paid. Jay was more than agreeable. The lecturer, a professor in the History Department, told Jay there were several people willing to do research as part of their thesis exercise and gave him some names.

Jay asked, "Could you have one of them meet me here in two hours, say around 2:00 p.m. I'll meet them in the hallway outside this lecture hall. My name is Emanuel J. Cobb and I'll pay whatever they ask."

Jay left the group. He told Triana he was meeting a researcher and would miss the afternoon bus trip to the art museums. He walked down Calle 'L' to the *Habana Libre* Cafeteria and had lunch. He walked back to the University for his meeting with a researcher at 2:00 p.m.

The researcher was a cordial lady also in her mid thirties just like Jay. She looked the part of a true academician. Casual dress, her hair rolled in a bun on the top of her head with a pencil protruding from the right side and she had an armload of books. With her load of books, she still had a spirited bounce in her walk and her demeanor was delightful. She smiled continuously and was glad to meet a foreigner.

Jay started the conversation. "I am a history major and I need some research on a project I refer to as 'The Cuban Project'. There may be another name for it in Spanish. It would be a military project started in 1967 and ending in

1968. It had to deal with a Cuban Delegation going to Hanoi during the war in South East Asia. I am trying to tie the delegation to the First Conference of Solidarity held right here in Havana in 1966 with world leaders from three different continents, Asia, Africa, and Latin America. Then in 1967, Castro dubbed the year as 'The Year of Solidarity with Vietnam'. I have researched all the records I could find in the U.S. It is my hope you might be able to search Cuban National Records and come up with some helpful information. You needn't write a report on it. Just give me what notes you might find. If I were to do it, I wouldn't know where to start and most of your records would be in Spanish. So I am most willing to pay for your services and hope you might can find additional facts for me."

Jay watched the lady's eyes for understanding. As she thought she started talking. "I could go back through some newspaper accounts for those two years, I could search the library here at the University, and I could also use the Museum of the Revolution. There are some papers and documentary evidence of world happenings in those archives. I'll search them all. I charge five dollars U.S. per hour. For an eight hour day the cost would be forty dollars." She looked at Jay for confirmation that her price was acceptable. He shook his head to acknowledge agreement.

Jay asked, "How long do you think it might take?"

"I'm free tomorrow and I'll work on research the entire day. Give me your phone number, or how I can reach you, and I'll let you know tomorrow night how it went."

Jay responded, "Better still, can you give me your number, I'll call you. My schedule is fairly tight with this tour group." She gave Jay her number and the two departed.

Jay used the map from the hotel and walked the six or seven blocks back. He passed the Capri Hotel enroute. On a whim he stopped in and registered. It was not a deluxe hotel but it was upscale enough for all rooms to be air-conditioned. Other comforts didn't matter to Jay. He planned to leave his luggage in the *Hotel Nacional* as a cover and only use the Capri Hotel for sleeping. He decided it would be necessary to continue to use the *Hotel Nacional* only as the meeting place with his group. If he needed fresh clothing he could return and collect anything he needed. It appeared like a good plan.

To make it work, he would need a means of getting in and out of the *Hotel Nacional* without being noticed. He decided to search the hotel for the entries used by their utility services; laundry, food service, maintenance and any of the other exits.

When Jay entered the lobby, both men were still waiting for him. His assumptions were correct, these two goons were staying close and using his hotel as the point of maintaining contact to guard his coming and going. He took the elevator and stopped on the second floor, there he searched for a stairwell. He walked down one flight of stairs and opened the door slightly to see where the stairs were located. They were well off the lobby and not readily visible. He walked out to search for an outside door. In the far western end of the building he found an exterior access door. His point of exit was identified. Jay walked up one flight of stairs then took the elevator to his floor. He was comfortable with his plan as long as the two guys remained uninterested in following the tour group, everything should go well.

The schedule indicated the tour group was to eat dinner in the hotel restaurant at 6:30 p.m. Jay showered, put on fresh clothes, and went to the top floor lounge to await dinner. He looked at his watch; it was only 5:30 p.m. There would be an hour wait before the group gathered. He expected no one from the group to be there. As he entered the lounge, the faithful Triana Travis was already there waiting for the group. He walked over to her table.

"Good afternoon Ms. Travis." Jay was cheerful.

She nodded. "Yes it is. We missed you on the art tour this afternoon."

Jay felt compelled to tell about his dilemma. "Listen Ms. Travis, I am having trouble with those same two men who detained and searched me at the airport. They are following me everywhere I go. If I go on your scheduled tours, it appears they don't follow. When I take a walk or stroll along the waterfront, they are right behind me watching every step I take."

Triana was surprised. "I thought all that was over!"

"It's not over by any means. If you will observe while you are in the lobby, you will see both of them waiting for me. When I walk through the lobby, they will be right behind me. I don't know why and I don't know who they are. But for some reason, unless I want them to trace my steps, I have to evade them." Jay paused before asking his next question. "Were you able to find out anything?"

"I talked with the hotel manager. He told me they were there for a purpose and had been ordered to watch our tour group. Needless to say, I was shocked to hear that. The manager advised me to contact the DSE. That is the Security Directorate under the Minister of Interior. When he told me that, I admit I was alarmed. You see, I know what that directorate does. I am Cuban-American. I fled Cuba in 1985. My family had several run-ins with the DSE before we left. My father was the editor of a newspaper and was constantly under threat about his writings. So we decided to leave for the States for our safety. The DSE is tasked with policing crimes, espionage, sabotage, and all offenses against the State." Triana looked directly into Jay's eyes. "I've been through our group list searching for a reason they would be watching us. I can't find anything about anyone which might alert the DSE to our presence. Is there something you need to tell me? Who you are and why are you really here? I need to know!" Triana was polite but business like.

Jay was beginning to feel trapped. He had been singled out and the tour guide knew it was him causing the trouble. He knew it was time to confess something if he was to gain any help from Triana.

Jay spoke. "Before coming here, I was in Little Havana in Miami. I did have a run-in with a local Cuban-America. I believe he called ahead and told somebody to make certain I was harassed and watched. And that is what has been happening. I never dreamed this would happen or that I would cause any problems for the tour group." Jay paused and watched Triana for compassion for his predicament. He continued, "I promise you, I shall stay away from the group as much as possible. I don't want this to interfere with your tour." Jay thought long before confessing further. "Let me tell you what I have already done. I have taken a room in the Capri Hotel a couple of blocks away. I will leave my baggage here in my room but I will spend each night at the Capri. I am doing this to make certain nothing will interfere with your group. Nor do I want them following me everywhere I go. I am in Room 316 in the Capri if you should have to get in touch. I hired a researcher at The University to collect some information for me. With that in mind, I still need to go with the group to the University for tomorrow morning's lecture. After that I will do my best to stay clear of your group. I sincerely hope I haven't given you or your group a bad name." Jay was genuine in his explanation. "After tomorrow's lecture, unless you happen to run into me in the lobby, I won't see you again until departure time. I will contact you the day before our scheduled departure to see if anything has changed. If not I will plan to meet with you at the airport for departure."

"I am glad you told me. I will try and keep your whereabouts a secret. But let me give you some advice. If what you are doing can be construed in any way as anti-government, you run a big risk of being jailed. They really don't even need a reason to jail anyone here. My father was jailed for an editorial he wrote. He got out after three months in confinement and we left the country immediately. If you are put in jail, you will have one helluva time waiting for justice. That is a fact! You need to be very careful. I would be unable to help you in any way except for notifying your family once we return to the States." Triana was candid with Jay and he appreciated it.

Soon all twenty of the other members of the group arrived and they all went to dinner together in a reserved room. It was a pleasant dinner. However, Jay could feel some of the disparaging glances cast his way. The others were wary of him. Jay excused himself. As he left he looked at Triana, exchanging a look of understanding. He knew he could count on her for all the help she could safely provide.

Heading back to his room to brush his teeth, he kept thinking about his circumstances. His hatred for Benitez

Aguillar was heavy on his mind. That little son-of-a-bitch has made his trip miserable. If he could get to him again, he would do more than push him around and he certainly would not feel sorry for the old man. The connection Benitez had with Cuban authorities began to worry Jay and placed a dark cloud over his effort to find Fuentes and Pardo. Following through with his search forced him to be more clandestine than he had anticipated. He would have to disappear.

Wisely or not, Jay deliberately walked through the lobby to pick up his two shadows. He was determined to find out how serious they were. He walked out the front toward the shoreline highway and again sat on top of the protective wall separating the *malecon* from the walking traffic. There was a reasonable amount of foot traffic doing the same thing he was doing. All the tourists wanted to view the water's edge. He gazed over his right shoulder to see if he had been followed. Sure enough the two men were standing under a streetlight. It was as if they wanted him to know they were watching.

Jay walked eastward then down Calle 'N' toward the Capri Hotel. He turned right, away from the waterfront at the first corner and again tried to lose the men using the same tactic as the night before. It worked once again. He lost the two at the second corner. He found another bar, *Casa de los Infusiones.* He entered and walked through the elbow-to-elbow crowd toward the bar.

At first he felt out of place. Most of the people were young, in their early twenties. The music was blaring, young couples were dancing anywhere they could find the space and all tables were full. The sheer size of the crowd dimmed the amount of available light. Candles on the tables offered little light. Pushing forward to the bar, Jay was finally able to get an elbow onto the bar and ordered a beer. When he paid in U.S. dollars, he received the bartender's full attention. Looking around was impossible. All he could see was the person standing next to him. The crowd made him feel safe.

When he could, he was able to catch a glimpse of the women dancing. Cuban women were exceptionally sensual. They swayed when they walked and when they danced everything jiggled. They purposely dressed to accentuate their feminine features. Short dresses to reveal their legs appeared paramount. It was obvious they spent lots of time preparing for a night out. Once into the nightlife they enjoyed every minute of it. Enticing men's glances was their forte and what better place to tease than on the dance floor.

As he enjoyed the view, a well-tanned arm pushed through the crowd across his back to get a beer from the bartender. Jay leaned forward slightly allowing the arm to get a foothold at the bar. As he turned around, he was surprised to find a lady going for the beer. It was readily apparent she was a nighttime girl. He had been warned by Triana Travis about the *jiniteras*, the good time girls, seeking favors from foreigners. Jay smiled as he allowed her to the bar. She smiled back. Jay purchased the lady's beer. To introduce herself, she put her head close to Jay's ear and spoke, "Rosa...Rose..ah. My name!"

Jay responded, "Jay! My name is Jay." He spoke hardly any Spanish and the only English she knew was bar room English. Still they were able to converse above the noise. She was in her late twenties, bra-less which was most obvious when she moved. She was wearing an extremely short dress, not only showing her well-formed legs but the lower part of her butt. She lured Jay into dancing. All the swaying, the bouncing, the rubbing and the way she melted into Jay's body was a turn on. He had to hold himself in check. Rosa was in the nightly process of tagging herself a man. Jay was thoroughly enjoying the dance floor seduction by Rosa.

In his interlude with Rosa, he didn't notice the two men as they entered the bar. After their steamy dance, Jay and Rosa were accommodated with a table from a waitress who knew Rosa. Rosa moved her chair closer to Jay and kept an arm on his shoulders at all times claiming her catch.

Jay was too enthralled with Rosa and didn't see the men approach. Both men came over to their table. "You come with us!" Jay was startled.

Rosa wasn't about to lose her catch. She became angry. Speaking harshly and fearlessly in rapid fire Spanish to both men, she nearly caused a scene.

Whatever she said made a difference. The two men backed off. When it was time to leave, Jay was fearful they might try to arrest him for something. As best he could, he conveyed his concern to Rosa. She understood exactly. Night time escapes were her forte. She physically pulled Jay to the dance floor. They swayed to the music and moved slowly through the crowd toward the back of the bar. The crowd worked in their favor. Rosa led Jay through the maze of people and they disappeared through a rear entrance.

Jay was faced with a quandary, he couldn't allow Rosa to go with him to his hotel. Yet he needed someone of Rosa's talents to stay with him and act as his protector against any unforeseen circumstances. He was offering Rosa money to be his 'guide' not for her nightly pleasures. That wasn't exactly what she had in mind but after some pleading, she accepted his offer and made arrangements to meet again. Rosa could do things Jay couldn't and would be a great asset. He offered her lots of money. She reluctantly accepted the alternative to a night of physical pleasure.

"Where can we meet tomorrow? Late in the afternoon." Jay asked.

"You know *Paladares Carabelas*?"

"No! Where is that?"

She explained that a *paladares* was a privately run restaurant, very small. It would be an excellent place to meet and have dinner at the same time.

Jay pulled out his map of *Nuevo Vedado* and Rosa marked the location of the *paladares*.

"I'll meet you there tomorrow at 6:30 p.m."

Rosa reluctantly walked away. This was not the way she wanted the night to end. This guy was a good-looking man with plenty of U.S. dollars to spend. Maybe the next time would be different. Jay never told Rosa at what hotel he was staying. He expected to keep that secret.

Time was approaching midnight and Jay walked past the *Hotel Nacional* toward the Capri. He spent a restful night, knowing he would have Rosa to lead him anywhere he needed to go which added a myriad of great possibilities to his plan.

The next morning Jay left The Capri early. He went to the far side of *The Nacional*, entered through the side door, walked up the stairwell to the second floor and used the elevator to his floor. In his room he showered, brushed his teeth, put on fresh clothes and left. He took the elevator to the top floor restaurant for breakfast where he met the tour group. Jay sat by himself apart from the group.

When they left, he left. Passing through the lobby, Jay and Triana both saw the two men waiting in the lobby as usual. They were talking to another two men, similarly dressed, wearing sunglasses and short-sleeved shirts. Jay studied the faces of the two new arrivals so he could recognize them again. He believed a new crew had been alerted. Triana watched the men and Jay's reaction, trying to form her own opinion about what was taking place. All twenty-one of the group boarded the bus and headed for the University for their morning's lecture.

Jay was only slightly concerned. If they hadn't arrested him by now, they weren't going to arrest him. On the bus Jay spoke briefly to Triana, advising her he wouldn't be taking the bus back after the lecture and not to wait for him.

Jay wanted to wait around and make contact with his researcher to see if she was making any headway on his project. A sense of relief came over Jay, knowing he wasn't going to be arrested. However, being constantly watched was a problem.

His plan was taking shape. He expected Rosa to be his biggest asset. She could direct him away from trouble and talk their way out of any jam. The information from the researcher would be his starting point. There should be historical facts documented somewhere in Cuban History related to their worldwide involvement with foreign countries. He fully expected the two names for which he was searching to appear in the Cuban Archives somewhere.

He planned not to tell anyone the names of the men for whom he was searching, not even the researcher. That could spell disaster for his success. Jay planned to disappear from his group after today's lecture and seriously pursue whatever leads his researcher might find for him.

CHAPTER IX

After the second day's lecture and during the lunch break, Jay walked to the front of the room and asked, "Can I get in touch with," he pulled a note from his breast pocket and used it as reference, "Gabriella Saurez, she is doing some research for me."

"Wait just a moment." The professor moved toward the rear wall, picked up a wall phone and pressed the intercom button, "Gabriella Saurez, *auditorio...uno!*" She spoke to Jay. "If Gabriella is in the building she should be here in a few minutes."

"Thanks, I'll wait."

Jay sat down in one of the seats toward the rear of the room and waited for Gabriella. He believed he could recognize her from the previous day's introduction. When she walked into the room Jay stood to greet her.

"Hi Gabriella, have you made any progress yet?" Jay was eager for a response.

"Yes I have. The library archives have excellent newspaper coverage for that period of time. I went through lots of newspaper clippings and I think I found some of the information you were looking for." She pulled out a notebook and flipped through some pages. "In January 1966 Fidel Castro hosted The First Conference of Solidarity. It was known as The Tri-Continental Conference. It was at this conference that Fidel Castro made an agreement with North Vietnam to send assistance. The year 1967 was the year that the assistance began. That year became known as "Year of Solidarity with Vietnam." She flipped a page. "I also had a reference to the *Primer Groupo De Asistencia Militar* (First Military Assistance Group). I looked up that reference and found an Order Number authorizing the assistance and a table of organization. Attached to this document was a roster of the Unit." She read straight from the roster. "Major Miguel Luis Fuentes was the Officer in Charge of one thousand, nine hundred, and eighty-three men. His overall next in command was Lieutenant Raphael Almarales Pardo. The enlisted man in charge was Sergeant Benitez Aguillar."

Jay had difficulty holding his excitement in check. Trying not to show his eagerness he spoke. "That's very good information." He had additional thoughts about his own government in their efforts to find these three men. He found one in Miami, and this student found the other two in the library. Rationalizing, he decided there were only three possibilities. The U.S. Government found them, or the U.S. Government didn't try to find them, or the U.S. Government did find them and wouldn't tell. Jay decided, if he and this student found them, then the U.S. Government also found them and wasn't telling.

She began again, "I only made a copy of the first page of the roster which has the three names and ranks of the persons in charge. The duties described were numerous, nearly covering the full spectrum of any military organization. I did find another reference where it was called a Diplomatic Mission. This afternoon I thought I would go to the *Museo de la Revolucion* (Museum of the Revolution) and try to search these three names for you. Since these three were career military men, sometimes their names will appear at other places." She watched for a sign from Jay, hoping to see a show of enthusiasm for her work.

"That fits with the research I did in the States. Do you think it might be possible for me to get an interview with the three men you named?"

"It will be up to them. I will try to find out where they are now and give you their addresses so you might call and set up an interview." Gabriella was pleased Jay was happy with her results. "If you have nothing else, I will go to the Museum of the Revolution."

"Thank you very much, Gabriella, you have done well. Will you still be at the Museum at 5:00 p.m.? If you are I could meet you there and we could discuss what you find and I will pay you for your services."

"OK...I'll meet you at the museum at 5:00 p.m."

Jay was more than delighted. He knew he was on the right track to complete his task and come face to face with *Fidel* and *The Bug*. Confirming the names was a great success. Now he knew beyond all doubt there was an authorized Cuban Project in Vietnam, a delegation formally sent by Fidel Castro. Jay was on a high. He smiled and savored his moment of success.

******

A major success arriving out of The Cuban Revolution of 1959 was cleanliness. The streets were cleaned on a daily basis and garbage wasn't allowed to collect anywhere. Each night an army of cleaning crews sweep through the city of Havana. A fleet of garbage trucks filter the city of its previous day's refuse.

Earlier at daybreak, one such truck moved slowly eastward along *Calle Calzada* to Calle 'L'. The driver stopped the truck at the rear gate to the U.S. Interests Section compound. The silence of the early morning hours was broken as the driver started the hydraulic crusher to compact the collection of garbage.

One of the two men hanging onto the rear of the truck stepped off and walked slowly toward the rear guard gate. The rear entrance was used only for utility services and a guard stood watch. The garbage man was wearing a lightweight cotton jump suit for personal hygiene and protection from the filth and stains. The guard permitted his entry.

The area within the compound was overly lighted by security floods allowing the man easy footing. He entered the shadows of the building, walked along a concrete walkway and disappeared behind a protective hedge row at least six feet tall. As he approached a side door he looked around making certain no one was watching. The door was secured by an electronic coding device. He punched in the six letter code. The sound of the entry lock solenoid withdrawing the door lock allowed the disguised man entry. He walked through the door quickly.

Behind the door was a maze of electrical and electronic equipment. The entire room was bathed in red night lighting much the same as a photo processing darkroom. Every piece of equipment was alive with its own symphony of digital sounds and glowing red and green lights. The tall man walked to a corner cubicle and sat down in an office chair in front of a General Electric Model S200 International Phone Scrambler. The box about two foot square and three feet tall was an antiquated piece of phone equipment. In a normal world, its usefulness would have been replaced years earlier by a plethora of updated versions of secure communicating devices. Since the revolution of 1959, this unit remained the only communication unit to U.S. Agencies.

He selected an automatic dial-up and could hear the dial tones as they rang the end destination. The call was instantly answered.

"Hello!" The short response was normal and expected. The night duty officer in the Ops Room of CIA Headquarters, Langley Virginia reacted to the call.

"This is 'Copperhead', patch me through to Agent Stewart Carter at DIA."

******

One hour later another call was made through the interagency States side system.

The secretary/receptionist in the FBI Office in Miami buzzed the intercom for Agent Sam Bascom.

"Yes...what is it?"

"I have Special Agent Stewart Carter on the line for you. Line three."

"OK...I'll take it." Bascom pushed line three button. "Hello Stewart, this is Sam. What's up?"

"Meet me on the second floor in two minutes." It was their special code for contacting on a secure line. After two minutes Sam picked up on the secure line as soon as it rang.

"What's up Stew?"

CIA Special Agent Carter spoke. "Do you remember Emanuel J. Cobb?"

"Absolutely. Our man Antonio gave him the names he wanted. I confirmed that with Antonio after his visit here."

"Guess what?" Stewart paused. "Jay Cobb is in Havana!" Stewart waited for Sam to explode at the shocking news.

"You've got to be kidding me. Neither of us expected that. What's he doing in Cuba?" Sam Bascom was surprised and hoped Stewart had an answer.

"He's searching for Fuentes and Pardo."

Sam asked, "How do you know that?"

"I just got a call from my CIA contact in Havana, Carlos Rodriquez. You don't know him. He is an undercover CIA mole within the Department of Security in Cuba. We talked on the scrambler. He asked me about Emanuel J. Cobb. He said Emanuel Cobb was there in Havana. He and his local partner within the Department of Security were ordered by Fuentes to follow Cobb and make him return to the States. They have been following him for thirty-six hours and Cobb isn't thinking about leaving. He asked if I knew anything about Cobb being there. I told him I didn't."

Sam Bascom was subconsciously shaking his head no. "I don't know anything about that!"

Stewart acknowledged. "OK, but if you are ever asked anything about Cobb being in Cuba, you have to deny any knowledge about this! Our butts could be hanging out...far out! I also told him to be very careful, this could develop into an international incident if it went too far. He said that was his concern also. He didn't want this to escalate." Stewart paused as he let the news sink in with Sam.

"I asked Carlos how he was going to handle the situation. He told me he had it taken care of. He had another agent, Rosalita Guttierez, to 'tag' Jay and stay with him. He tried to tell me how well the set-up came off. Rosa 'tagged' Cobb in a bar. Then Carlos Rodriquez and Rosa got into a shouting match over Jay Cobb. Carlos and his partner backed down rather than creating a scene. Jay now wants her to be his guide." Stewart stopped as he grinned into the phone.

"Carlos said 'you should've seen Rosa last night. She had on the shortest dress he had ever seen. Her beautiful legs were standouts and any time she bent over you could see her ass'. Carlos said he about flipped when he saw her. She is a good looking woman anyway and when she dressed the way she did, no man could have resisted. Rosa moved right in on Cobb and he didn't have a chance. Her play as a *jinitera* was too believable. She left the bar with Mr. Cobb. If that man didn't spend the night with Rosa, then I have no respect for his manhood." They both smiled at the thought. "She knows not to let him out of her sight and keep him under control." Special Agent Carter was concerned this turn of events had the potential to be explosive and he was the one who caused it. It had to be handled correctly. Carter spoke, "About three or four years ago I went through a refresher course at Quantico dealing with new technology. There were only six people in the class and Carlos Rodriquez and Rosalito Guttierez were two of my classmates. They were there under some sort of a special agreement. That's where I met them both. They are both Cuban born and are Special CIA Agents. Carlos doesn't have a law degree but Rosa does. She was born in Cuba but raised in Miami and received her law degree from Florida State University. No one knows just how far she has her neck stuck out. Being Cuban born, if she should ever wind up in jail, the U.S. Government can't do one thing about it. Rosa does a good job and likes what she is doing. For a twenty-nine year old, she knows the ropes and just how far she can go without being caught. She is a real beauty too! When Carlos told me she was undercover as a prostitute, I wanted to go down there and solicit her services. Man, she will make you want to pump iron all day. I hope Mr. Cobb appreciates what we are doing for him! I know I would like to be in his shoes right now. I've got to go. How are things in Miami?"

"OK for now. The political campaigns are heating up and I am constantly on alert for something. I think I should go visit with Antonio and have a long chat. I haven't kept contact with him like I should. There are too many irons in the fire. Since the Brothers to the Rescue had two Cessna aircraft shot down, and with all the political campaigns, I have been very busy. You and I have to stay in touch to follow this situation." Agent Bascom felt a tinge of concern and immediately decided he must visit with Antonio Guillermo as soon as possible.

"I agree. I'll call you tomorrow." Special Agent Carter hung up the phone and remained in his chair in deep thought.

****

Jay was pleased with the information he received from Gabriella and left the University. He spent the remainder of the afternoon killing time, playing the tourist role. With the information he received he knew this might be his last chance to see the sights of Cuba. He hired a cyclo-taxi. These were pedestrian movers unique to Cuba. It was a three-wheeled bicycle with a sun protective roof and a seat for two people mounted over the two rear wheels. It was cheap transportation and it was ideal for getting a slow street level view of the surroundings. The drivers were adept at moving through traffic in congested areas. Jay used his city map to point out where he desired to go.

He first pointed to Parque Central. The pedal cab driver nodded his head indicating he understood the destination. The cyclo-taxi driver turned his vehicle around and headed east along Calle San Rafael. It took only twenty minutes to travel the 2 mile distance to the park. Parque Central was a spacious area filled with tourists and local people enjoying the peaceful pleasures of the stately Royal palms, the orange flowered Poinciana trees and the shady almond trees. Jay exited the taxi and briefly surveyed the park before returning to select his next destination. Everyone was very cordial in their greetings.

Jay searched his map and selected the Castillo De La Punta on the west side of the mouth to Havana harbor. The driver instantly knew his directions and wheeled straight northward along Paseo De Marti, locally referred to as The Prado, toward the open sights along the waterfront.

During the drive from the park, Jay could see some of the remaining vestiges of the Revolution of 1959. Many of the old stately office buildings were converted to tenements. The past grandeur and impressive professional facades were gone. They were replaced by overcrowded apartment dwellers. The ornate wrought iron balcony rails on each floor now displayed bed clothing and daily wash as they were hung out to air and dry. Jay thought redistribution of wealth could not be more evident than in living conditions.

Visiting the Castillo De La Punta and viewing the Straits of Florida, Jay was beginning to develop an ambiguous outlook toward Cuba. It had tastes of modern day capitalism and apparent poverty intertwined as one. It was confusing to understand. He viewed across the harbor at the Morro Castle on the eastern side of the harbor. Having the opportunity to visit and see this part of Cuba was a plus.

Jay reentered the pedal cab and pointed to the Castillo De La Real Fuerza, the Plaza De Armas, and the Palacio De Los Capitanes General as his next destination. The driver studied the map before turning around. He drove around the Maximo Gomez monument to get to Calle Tacon. Jay wanted more time to study these locations. Time was passing fast. He enjoyed being the tourist and absorbing the sights of past history. He wished Penny could be with him to also enjoy the views. Time was approaching 4:00 p.m. As he studied the map he believed there was enough time to stop at one more location. He chose the Plaza De La Catedral as his final destination for the day. The driver headed north on Calle San Ignacio toward the plaza. On arriving at the plaza, Jay knew he had not allowed enough time to thoroughly appreciate the Plaza De La Catedral. The cobbled square and its 18th Century baroque architecture demanded to be studied. After spending too few minutes passing through the square, he mentally noted he would come back if time allowed.

The driver pedaled north on Calle San Ignacio to Calle Chacon then westward to the Museo De La Revolucion for his meeting with Gabriella.

Time was approaching 5:00 p.m. and Jay was eager to meet with Gabriella to see what she might have found in documents stored in the Museum of the Revolution. The museum was located in the old Presidential Palace vacated by Batista after the revolution. Since his departure, it had been used as a museum. In front of the museum was a display of a Russian made SAU 100 Stalin military tank mounted on a concrete stand. Jay stood beside the display waiting for Gabriella.

Promptly at 5:00 p.m. Gabriella walked slowly through the high columns supporting the portico to the entrance. Jay immediately recognized and walked toward her. She smiled warmly as he approached.

Jay was the first to speak. "Did you find anything?" He was more interested in the information than he was in politely greeting her.

"Yes, I did. You need to go in there and look around yourself. You'll like it." She was still being the academician, papers shoved not too neatly into a notebook and a handful of pencils. "Let's walk around to the side of the building and sit down to discuss what I found." As they walked she continued. "I found references to those three names in the *Primer Groupo De Asistencia Militar* to North Vietnam. Major Fuentes, Lieutenant Pardo, and Sergeant Aguillar." Arriving at a park bench, both sat down. Jay watched Gabriella intently waiting for more.

"The first man, Major Fuentes, has a history with the Revolution. There is a photo of him and Castro taken right after The Bay of Pigs invasion. Castro was pinning a medal on him and giving him a commission as an officer in the FAR (*Fuerzas Armadas Revolucionarias*). The caption relates that Fuentes was awarded the medal for shooting down an aircraft and Castro witnessed him doing it. Fuentes wasn't in the FAR but only a schoolteacher in the village of La Boca. It was national news that he was able to take over a gun and use it successfully to make the shoot down. At the time he was a national hero. Of course, we know he was El Comandante of the 1st Military Assistance Group sent to North Vietnam. After he came back, he was placed in the Department of Security. From that start in the Ministry of the Interior he has been elevated to the top executive authority for the DSE, one step below the Minister. The Headquarters for the Department of Security is located in the old Villa Marista Prison building in Vivora. It has been converted into an office building and Fuentes' office is located there. You asked me if you might interview him. I would guess you could. I don't know. Maybe you should call his office first." She finished speaking from her notes and handed them to Jay.

"The second man, Raphael Almarales Pardo, came up through the FAR. He was with Castro in the very beginning while they operated out of the Sierra Maestra Mountains even before they defeated Batista's forces. After the overthrow, Castro made him a Lieutenant. He held a position in the prison system for re-educating dissidents. The newspapers, mostly Miami papers, sighted numerous complaints against him. But I could not find any official reference to it. The news accounts stated complaints were filed against him for over stepping his boundaries as a Re-Education Officer in the prison system. He invented methods of torturing dissident prisoners as part of the re-education process. It didn't say why he was chosen to be a part of the mission to North Vietnam. He was second in charge of the Diplomatic Mission to North Vietnam under Fuentes.

"Since 1969, Pardo has constantly been in trouble. Again, newspaper accounts cited his tastes for illicit behavior as reason enough to discharge him. Apparently, he drinks too much, is always soliciting prostitutes and has beaten up several women. And as far as I could tell, officially his record is clean.

"He was transferred from his assignment at Kilo '8' prison to a small local prison in Majagua, in the Province of Ciego de Avila. I found a reference note regarding a recent article in a Miami newspaper in which he was accused of torturing a political prisoner to near death. The Miami paper stated, 'it took the victim six months in a hospital to recover'. I believe that was why he was transferred. Again, I don't know about an interview." She handed Jay all those notes as well.

"I didn't find anything about Benitez Aguillar. He just dropped out of sight."

Jay congratulated her. "I must say, you did the job well. With these notes, I should be able to complete my research on The Cuban Project." Jay pulled a wad of small bills out of his pocket. Counted out five ten dollar bills U.S. and handed them to Gabriella. She was overly appreciative for the money. Jay was most cordial in his departing comments and immediately left.

Jay looked at his watch, time was 5:30 p.m. and he had to meet Rosa at the *Paladares Carabelas* at 6:30 p.m. He again referred to his map. Rosa had marked the location. Jay searched for a cyclo-taxi. It was the best and cheapest mode of transportation for around town. There was only one other cheaper mode, The Camel, which only cost one peso but it had a normal route to follow. Jay guessed the distance to be approximately two miles. He could easily have walked the distance but he would need some time after he got there to locate the restaurant. One of the tricycle taxis came by and Jay used it to head toward Nuevo Vedado where the restaurant was located.

When the driver got to the destination, he stopped. Jay looked around for the restaurant. There wasn't any. He tried as best he could to ask the driver if this was the restaurant. He pointed to the map. The driver nodded. "*Si...Si...Aqui, aqui!*" The driver pointed to the front door of a private home. Jay paid the driver. Hoping this was the place he had no choice but to wait for Rosa. As he looked down at his watch, he still had twenty minutes before Rosa was to arrive. He walked up to the screen door and peered in. He saw a woman in the front room and talking through the screen asked, "*Paladares Carabelas?*"

"*Si senior, Paladares Carabelas!*"

Jay was surprised. He expected a restaurant. This didn't look like what he would call a restaurant. Inside he saw only two tables, each with four chairs. The tables were set as if expecting customers and only a very few customers. He turned back to the street and waited for Rosa. He would occasionally shuffle the papers he was holding from hand to hand.

He looked both ways, up and down the street. In the distance about two blocks away, his eye caught a glimpse of a lady. Somehow, even at great distances, a man can catch only a slight view of a woman and know she is beautiful. An unexplainable phenomenon, beauty to a man is a magnet for his eyes. This lady was walking with a sway and the hour glass figure magnetized the eyes of every male she encountered. As she came closer, Jay wasn't certain but he thought it was Rosa. The night before in the bar he never got a chance to study her face. The dim lighting hadn't helped either. Jay knew she was a good time girl of the evening, a *jiniteras*, and really hadn't bothered to look closer. He paid very little attention to her during the night and sort of cast her looks aside. While they were dancing with her pressed close he didn't have the chance to really consider her. His mind was absorbed by the way her femininity passed freely into his spirit. The way she melted into his body told him she was good at her trade.

Now seeing this woman in the light of day, wearing street clothes, he instinctively felt it was Rosa but wasn't absolutely certain. This person was Caucasian, her hair was brunette with an auburn glow. Her dark eyebrows accented her face and were fitting for those large dark eyes. She was wearing a colorful skirt which fell below the knees and a top held up by spaghetti straps exposing her shoulders. This lady was stunning. He hoped it was Rosa.

A huge grin automatically formed on his face. He adjusted his shirt, pulled at his pants to bring them back up to his waist, and tried to breathe deeply. He wanted to appear as gentlemanly as possible. Rosa certainly did not appear as a *jinitera* today. With a well-proportioned hard body, strong and physical, she looked like a gym instructor or a personal trainer. The sway in her walk had to be a practiced kind of a stroll. Apparently she liked to draw attention. His thoughts carried him back to his collegiate days, 'she's built like a brick shit-house'.

She came toward Jay. As she approached, Jay spoke out, "Are you Rosa?"

"Si, Rosalito Guttierez." She smiled warmly.

Faced with this gorgeously attractive lady, Jay had trouble getting his words to roll off his tongue. "Are you..." Jay cleared his throat to hide his growing nervousness. "Are you ready to eat?"

"Si!" Even as she spoke, Jay could feel her strong feminine presence.

Jay felt proud to walk into the *Paladares Carabelas* with Rosa on his arm. Again he had thoughts this wasn't a real restaurant. Obviously, it was more like a private home which served meals, much like a bed and breakfast. Both tables in the front room of the house were neatly set, a linen tablecloth, place mats, fresh flowers in a small vase and silverware. It was kind of nice for it to be different, a new experience. It was a very private and intimate setting.

Rosa addressed the waitress in Spanish. The waitress immediately jumped into action and brought glasses and a bottle of wine.

"Want chicken?" She asked Jay.

"Yes. Chicken sounds good to me."

"This place, *Paladares Carabelas*, only have chicken. Beef...can't get!"

"OK, we'll both have chicken."

Rosa did the ordering in Spanish and their service was excellent. During the meal Rosa asked many questions. Always in broken English.

"What we do tonight?" She asked.

"I don't know yet we'll decide later, after we have eaten." Jay noticed Rosa as she ate. He could tell she had class. She ate small bits of food, sat erect in her chair with her shoulders back, placed her napkin neatly across her legs and chewed slowly with dainty like motions. She was beguiling with an unquestionable allure. He believed Rosa was born and raised in class. Lately she must have run into some bad luck to be a lady of the night.

Jay opened the conversation with why he was in Cuba. Since the tale he passed to the researcher worked well, he continued to use it. "I have been doing some research in the States about a Cuban Diplomatic Mission to North Vietnam during 1967 and '68. Do you recognize the name Lieutenant Colonel Miguel Luis Fuentes?"

"Si. He big man in Security Department. Next to Minister."

"Do you know how to find him and could talk with him?"

"Yes...I take you. Tomorrow?"

"How about Raphael Almarales Pardo? Do you know him also?" Jay waited attentively for a response.

There was a strained look on Rosa's face. "Not sure. Where he work?"

"I think he works for the Department of Security in the prison system."

"OK...OK...OK. We find Pardo also."

Jay couldn't believe his luck in finding Rosa. She was perfect for his search, and being a woman of the night had street sense to offer. Besides she was very pleasing to the eyes. It was difficult for Jay to keep his temperature down sitting across the table from this beautiful Cuban lady. He didn't understand why she was working the bars. She apparently had class and without question could have any man she wanted. It didn't add up, but Jay didn't care. He was glad to have her along for the ride.

As best he could, he tried in vain to figure out how much information he should pass to Rosa. Jay knew without a doubt, when he got close to either of the men, he would have to tell her something more. If he didn't she wouldn't know there might be danger. He had to tell her. But when?

"Do you recognize the name Benitez Aguillar?" Jay tossed out that name as bait for conversation.

"Where he work?" Rosa couldn't speak English well, but tried.

"I don't know. He was in the FAR in the 1960s." Jay watched Rosa for any signs of recognition. She shook her head and pursed her lips sloughing off the question. She daintily put the napkin to her mouth and dabbed her lips gently. This small insignificant gesture revealed her past. There was no sign of any make-up and her shoulder length hair was freshly washed and dried. Her dress was of normal length and also fresh. Jay continued to admire her looks and readily thought about the class structure in Cuba. He wondered why a woman with obvious class would become a woman of the night.

"Those three names are the people I would like to meet. If you can help me find them, I would be most grateful." He waited for a response.

"Miguel Fuentes, I know! I find Raphael Pardo. Benitez Aguillar, I not know. Maybe have to search." Rosa raised her brow and smiled, assuring Jay she would find them.

"Where would we find Miguel Fuentes?"

"He in Vivora! Office in old *Villa Marista prison, Apartamento Calle Obispo*. I see many times. Tomorrow morning I show." Rosa placed her napkin to the side of her plate and sat upright in her chair, announcing she was finished. "Where we go now?"

Jay offered a half smile. He had to think. In his eagerness to get on with finding his targets, he hadn't thought about how to fill the rest of the evening. He responded, "I would like to see if those two men are still waiting for me; the same two men who were in the bar last night. Remember you argued with them. To do that I need to go to the *Hotel Nacional*."

Rosa jumped to the question, "You stay *Hotel Nacional*?"

Jay didn't know how to respond. He was just beginning to understand it would be necessary to tell Rosa more about his circumstance sooner then he had expected. Jay stood and gentlemanly helped Rosa out of her chair.

Rosa turned to waitress, "*La cuenta, por favor. La comida estuva deliciosa.*"

Jay pulled out a handful of U.S. dollars and let Rosa pick out the right amount for paying the bill. He thought to himself, this is going to work well. Finding Rosa was a huge stroke of luck.

As the two walked away Rosa asked again, "You stay *Hotel Nacional*?"

Jay knew he better tell her something. "Yes, I have a room in the Hotel." He thought again, "I also have a room in the Capri Hotel. When those two men kept following me, I left *Hotel Nacional* through a side exit and registered at the Capri. So now I stay at the Capri and meet my tour group at the Nacional the next day."

"OK...tonight I stay Capri with you!"

"You can't stay with me, the desk won't allow it."

"It's OK...you say...my wife."

"No...you can't stay with me. I only have one bed."

"I have no place for night. Must stay with you."

Jay started thinking about this, trying to rationalize in his mind how delightful it would be if she stayed with him. "Let me think about it!" Jay attempted to divert the conversation.

Rosa also tried to divert the discussion. If she were to be successful and truly stay with Jay at all times, she would have to be more enticing. "We go to bar...OK?"

Jay agreed, "OK!"

"We take taxi...OK? We go *Dos Hermanos*!"

Jay nodded his head in agreement. He didn't realize it at the time, but was to find out later, where they were headed was a famous hangout for Ernest Hemingway.

When they flagged a taxi, Rosa gave directions. "*La direccion a San Pedro eh Calle Sol...Dos Hermanos*!"

The driver made many turns and stopped at numerous intersections. At first Jay tried to remember locations and directions but it got so complicated he decided to just sit back and enjoy the ride. The final destination was on the wharf facing Havana Harbor. The streets were filled with night people-seaman and *jiniteras*. The bar was unique but mainly catered to the locals. Jay didn't see anyone he might consider a tourist. Rosa put her right arm around Jay's arm and leaned into his shoulder just as they entered the noise infested dark grotto of a bar. She purposely wanted to convey the message that he had been tagged and other *jiniteras* should stay away.

The atmosphere inside was rustic, quaint, and antiquated. There was no band, just a lot of noisy chatter and women of the night holding on tightly to their mark. Rosa did likewise. Jay somehow, felt honored that she remained tight against his side. Strange as it was, he even felt a sense of pride that Rosa was with him.

Rosa spoke to one of the waitresses at length and was able to commandeer a table ahead of others still waiting. Jay was enthralled with all the sailing artifacts and memorabilia hanging from the walls and ceiling. He wasn't concerned about assessing the crowd. It was strange to him, but he felt absolutely safe with Rosa. He believed nothing would happen to him with her at his side. The night was way too enjoyable for Jay and he began to forget about his motivation for the trip.

****

Jay never made it back to the *Hotel Nacional* and ultimately agreed to Rosa's request to stay with him at the Capri. The night desk manager did nothing to interfere with Rosa entering the hotel.

As Jay unlocked the door and politely indicated with a gesture of the hand for Rosa to enter, he spoke in an accommodating tone. "You can sleep in the bed, I will sleep in the chair." He nonchalantly pointed to the chair.

"*Ni hablar*!" She realized her mistake and came back in English. "No...no! You stay in bed, I stay in bed." She smiled as she spoke. "Night time be good!"

Jay had to think this comment over. He had more to lose by being unfaithful than he had to gain from a night of pleasure, no matter how great the pleasure. He rationalized to himself; both could sleep in the bed without becoming intimate. He restated his position. "OK...we both sleep in the bed."

As they undressed for the night Jay quickly realized that Rosa had no bed clothes. It seemed not to matter to her. She slipped into bed without anything on. He had a lump in his throat as he viewed her perfect hard body. He began to sweat and his hands showed his nervousness. His strength of character was being sorely tested. He was determined to remain faithful.

Jay normally slept in his boxer shorts. While Rosa was under the sheets nestling down into the soft mattress and pillows, Jay turned out the lights and lay down on top of the sheets. He tried to get the temptation completely out of his mind. He was doing just fine until Rosa rolled his way and put her arms around his middle and snuggled her warm body up close to his. As her hands began to wander, he grabbed them firmly and made certain they would wander no more. The night turned into the longest night he had ever endured. It was totally sleepless. Rosa however dropped off and slept soundly throughout the night.

The next morning Jay didn't have to wake up; he never slept. At 6:00 a.m. he arose from the bed and took a cold shower, trying to get his senses back in order. Rosa heard him in the shower and sat on the edge of the bed waiting for him to get out of the bathroom. When he emerged, she went straight to the bathroom. She seemed to have no modesty. Walking naked in front of him didn't seem to bother her in the least. It bothered him tremendously. He was having second thoughts about her staying with him. He couldn't let it happen again. He needed sleep.

They left the Capri to have breakfast some place else. Jay sought privacy.

"Today...go see Miguel Fuentes...Yes?" Rosa asked politely. The only difficulty she encountered during the night was Jay's reluctance to give in to her advances. Cuban women are different than American women. Sex was a normal requirement for living, a lovely experience and not one to be shunned. Rosa felt the same way.

In the new post revolution Cuba, living conditions were crowded and large families lived in one or two bedroom quarters. Many husbands and wives as well as couples had to seek out privacy to become intimate. Often simply scheduling private time or sending the children outside. When scheduling didn't work out, motels and rooming houses accommodated the need by renting rooms by the hour. Sex was a fact of life and not a sordid affair between a man and a woman, even when completed outside marriage. Jay's background was different. His cultural background clashed with hers.

"Yes...can we go see Miguel Fuentes?" Jay asked.

"Want to speak?" Rosa asked.

"No...I just want to see him. I want to know what he looks like. How old he is. And can he be easily approached. That's all." Jay allowed his thoughts to explore circumstances. "Can you approach him, say a few words, and indicate to me that it is Miguel Fuentes? That is all I want you to do."

"Yes? I do that."

The new day was wonderful. Temperatures were in the low 70s and the northeast trade winds offered a gentle breeze. November was the season of change. In Cuba there are only two seasons, the dry season and the wet season. November was the start of the dry season and the lower humidity provided an enjoyable breeze.

Rosa flagged down a taxi and gave directions to the Security Department building which was about ten miles away in the Havana suburbs on the eastern side of Havana Bay. Jay offered his idea of what they were to do. He wanted to pay off the taxi and then hire a cyclo-taxi. In this manner, he could remain in the vehicle some distance away unnoticed; and Rosa could position herself near the parking area where Fuentes would arrive. With this plan she could walk up to him, say hello, and that would be the identifying gesture.

The taxi ride took about twenty minutes to complete. Jay paid the driver. Both flagged down and hired a cyclo-taxi. Jay and Rosa sat in the pedal cab to finalize their instructions.

Jay spoke. "This man Fuentes should be in his sixties. He is about six feet tall. He has a tattoo on the underside of his left arm just above the wrist."

Rosa looked at Jay bewildered by his comments. She didn't know what to think and mentally questioned what she was hearing. She said nothing, just listened.

"The tattoo is not an image of anything, just artwork, a pentagram with five points." He continued and Rosa listened in disbelief. "His other identifying feature is eyes of a different color. One is green and the other is dark brown." Jay was glad to pass this information along to Rosa.

Rosa stared at Jay and couldn't contain herself. She blurted out loud. "You son-of-a-bitch! You know this man too well already!" She lost her composure and her broken English accent. "Why am I here to identify him for you? What are you up to? Are you getting me into trouble?" Without thinking, Rosa had burst into excellent spoken English. Jay's comments had completely taken her by surprise. She was dumbfounded. Here was a man she was trying to help and he didn't need it. She refused to get out of the vehicle. Her anger intensified. She further added. "Who the hell are you? And what are you doing here? What are you trying to do?"

Jay was astonished. The broken English and the bar talk was all a ruse. He started to feel threatened. The woman pretending to be a woman of the night was not that at all. Her spoken English was truly American. He too had a lot of questions for this woman.

Rosa immediately ordered the driver. "*Taxista... Go... Rapido! Capri Hotel.*"

Jay attempted to get Rosa settled down. "Why are you mad? I'm not sure what I did wrong! Did I say something wrong?"

Rosa responded. "Yes! You sure did. I thought I could help you. But I'm afraid you aren't here for a good reason, and until I find out what that reason is, I am going to dump you like a hot potato." Rosa was steaming mad. "This isn't a game we are playing. You could get us both thrown in jail. Until you know how it is here, you are treading in quick sand. I suggest you turn around and head back home to wherever you came from and don't look back. You better grow up and learn this is very serious business you are dabbling in." Rosa made her point and looked straight ahead, fuming.

Jay had to think long and hard before answering. After a few minutes he softly responded. "You're right. I have done an underhanded and terrible thing. I'm sorry I brought you into this." Jay was quickly trying to get his thoughts together.

He wrinkled his brow in a puzzled look. "But you don't add up either. All of a sudden you speak perfect English! Who do you work for? Why are you here with me? Who sent you? Don't you think I have a right to know more about you also? Since I arrived, I have been hassled by somebody. The Customs officer called someone about me and from there everything went to hell. I've had to leave my tour group. I've had to change hotels. Right now I truly don't know what I am doing here. Can you enlighten me? If you can't, then I may have to leave. I'll buy another ticket and take the first plane out of here."

Rosa softened slightly. She looked into Jay's eyes and could feel his sincerity. His good old American naiveté was obvious. She offered a gentle grin. Rosa allowed it to break into a smile, finally a laugh.

Jay looked on in bewilderment. "What?"

"You guys are all alike. You need a woman to steer you in the right direction." She laughed again, apparently enjoying the humor.

"Well, you tell me who you are and what you are doing. Then I will tell you what I am doing here. Deal?" Jay spoke of his willingness to follow her lead if she would come clean.

Rosa was guarded in formulating her response. "OK...I guess!" After a few moments of thoughtful contemplation, she began. "I work for the U.S. Interests Section. I also work for the *Asistencia al Viajero*. I am Cuban. What I do is to help travelers stay out of trouble. Your travel guide Triana Travis called the U.S. Interests Section and made us aware of your situation. That's why I am here." She paused and in all seriousness spoke. "If you get into jail, I can't help you at all. It is too late to help. All we can do is call your family and tell them how they can get in touch with you." She allowed that comment to sink in with Jay.

She started again. "Our dedicated purpose is to keep tourists out of jail and away from trouble." Rosa paused to allow Jay to think about what he was hearing. "I also have other contacts. I was told by one of them to stay close with you until you leave. Now, my suggestion is for you to do exactly that...leave. Somehow, someone higher up has targeted you and placed a tail on you, to make certain you leave the country. The only alternative to this, is that you never leave the country. I don't know why and I don't know who. Can you tell me why? Is it Fuentes?" Rosa again waited for a response. "Now it's your turn to come clean. How about it?"

Rosa watched Jay to see if he might accept her advice. She was well aware the immediate solution to the problem was for Jay to leave the country. She needed a positive reaction from Jay. Helping him stay out of trouble could be very dangerous for her. She desperately needed to know his situation. When Jay gave her such specific identifying features for Miguel Fuentes, she knew something wasn't right. Jay had too much prior knowledge of this man Fuentes, and could be stalking him. She had to protect herself and her job.

Jay started to open up, then thought better of it. "I'm not sure I can tell you why I am here." He stared straight ahead, his thoughts running rampant through his mind. "How confidential and private can we be with each other? Do you go away and tell someone else, and then I go to jail?" Jay was thinking. He needed some assurance. What happens when I tell you? What do you do with the information?" Jay then watched Rosa for any sign of assurance. He didn't know this woman. He was concerned she might be someone other than who she claimed to be. It was all a matter of trust.

"Can I trust you?" Jay watched her face.

"You can trust me to help you and to keep you out of trouble. Without knowing your real intentions, I can't say." Rosa appeared to be disinterested and watched the passing scenery as the pedal cab moved slowly through the streets toward The Capri.

Jay had a lot of thinking to do also. He quietly considered his options. If he tells her what he planned, then his trip is in vain and he would, out of necessity, have to return to the States. If he makes up a cover story, she might be smart enough to see through his fabrication and he will still have to return to the States. He began to realize he had no options. He had to speak the truth.

He started. "OK! I am from Oklahoma. My father was a major in the Air Force. He flew aircraft in South East Asia. He was shot down over North Vietnam. He bailed out and was a POW. He was tortured to death while in prison. The men who tortured him and caused his death were Lieutenant Colonel Miguel Luis Fuentes and Captain Raphael Almarales Pardo. I have a score to settle with both." Jay watched for acceptance. He continued, "I went to Miami and found one of the three people involved in my father's death. His name is Benitez Aguillar! He escaped Cuba during the Mariel boatlift and lives in Miami, getting his house rent free, getting subsistence to live on, and has medical benefits paid for by my own government. I think that's a bunch of crap and someone like me has to settle the score. Somehow make things right. The score is three to one, and my family is the loser."

Rosa spoke up. "What do you plan to do when you find Fuentes and Pardo?"

Jay shook his head with the honest realization he wouldn't be able to complete his task and also with a slight touch of shame "I don't know. I have worried about that for twenty-eight years. I can't just let it go. I have to do something to set it right." Jay stammered. "My people were Indians, we were removed from our homes in the Carolinas and marched for two-thousand miles to Oklahoma. We lost many lives. The President of the United States did that. Now, the same U.S. Government won't do anything to find these people who caused the death of my father. My heritage says I can. When family blood is spilled, I can seek revenge. It was crying blood that was spilled and I have the right to avenge it." He stopped grinding his teeth, took a deep breath, and sat motionless.

Rosa waited to speak. "Do you want to hurt these two people or do you just want to let them know you know who they are and you might challenge them at any time?" She waited while Jay thought through his answer.

"I don't know!" He hated himself for not being stronger. His mind went into a thoughtful mode. With his left hand he subconsciously reached to the base of his neck and with two fingers pulled out the small pewter image of the Thunderbird he wore on a silver chain around his neck. He rubbed it gently over his lips, and spoke.

"I want to face them. I want them to know that I know what they did." He bowed his head way down in disgust. "I'm not certain I could hurt anybody." Never before in his entire life had he felt such futility in such a hopeless situation. After following his perceived instincts to seek revenge, Jay knew in his heart he wasn't up to the challenge. Rosa's questions had placed him into a position of honest reality. Jay shrugged his shoulders and stared at his feet in deep thought. He was mostly disgusted with himself.

Rosa watched as Jay slumped forward placing a hand to his lips in puzzled disgust. She wanted to be helpful and was sympathetic to his cause. Parts of her own life had been interrupted by hatred and she knew the feeling well.

"Let me tell you what we should do. We should take tomorrow off. Take a break for a few days and think this thing through. How many more days before your group departs?"

Jay counted quietly. "I think six!"

"OK." She was hopeful he would allow her to help. Coming back to reality she spoke honestly. "You have to know right now, I can't leave you alone. I will have to stay with you every step of the way until you get on that airplane back to Cancun. That is a fact!" She smiled as she said it. "So you are stuck with me no matter what. That means we will stay in the same room again, like last night. I can not let you out of my sight. Understood!"

Jay nodded his head affirming he agreed. "Can I still see this man Fuentes?" He looked at his watch; the time was 8:30 a.m. He offered, "Maybe he hasn't come to work yet. Let's go back and you point him out to me. That's not asking too much."

"You'll have to promise me you will stay in check and do nothing. OK?"

"OK...I promise. Turn this driver around and let's head back."

Rosa gave instructions to the driver of the pedal cab. He turned around and headed back to their original location.

When they arrived, Rosa told the driver to wait and they would stay seated in the cyclo-taxi.

They waited. No cars arrived for at least thirty minutes. Both Rosa and Jay were beginning to think their effort might have been in vain. Then a 1955 four door Chevrolet drove up to the building. Rosa spoke to Jay. "Put your arms around me, quickly. Hug me. Act like we are lovers." He gladly accommodated her instructions. She watched the man get out of the vehicle. Jay took the opportunity to kiss her on the cheek. His lips against her warm cheek sent an unexpected need through his body. He continued to hold his face against hers in a long moment of pleasure. Rosa watched the man get out of the chauffeured vehicle. She was very observant of his activities. As he exited the car, she whispered to Jay. "That's him. That man is Miguel Fuentes. Look!"

Jay turned slowly to watch as the man left the vehicle and walk toward the building. "So that is Miguel Fuentes. He doesn't look too intimidating. Are you certain that is him?"

"Absolutely! That man is Fuentes. I know. I have been to parties with him. I know that is him!" Rosa continued to allow Jay to hold her tight until the man disappeared into the building. Then she gradually pushed him back and instructed the driver to turn around and head back toward the hotel. The distance to the hotel was about ten miles and it would take too long for the pedal cab to get there. She suggested they pay the cyclo-taxi driver and get a real taxi back to the hotel. Jay agreed.

On the ride back to the hotel, Jay was rather quiet. Rosa could feel his disappointment. The morning so far had not gone well. She spoke. "It is only 9:15 a.m., what would you like to do the rest of the day?"

She watched Jay for a reaction. He shrugged his shoulders apathetically.

"We don't have to sit in a motel for the rest of the day. How much money do you have?"

This got his attention, "Why?"

"I know some good places to go which might get your mind off things. I am a brunette and you apparently don't like me. I can take you to where there are nothing but blondes and they all sun themselves topless on the beach. Does that sound like a good way to spend the day?"

She had Jay's attention. He came to life. "I have enough money. We can have a nice time." He needed to ask the next question. "Why do you say I don't like you?"

"Last night you had the chance and I was disappointed you didn't want me. You need to think like a Cuban. Love and sex are practiced for pleasure. I had the feeling you didn't want me or that I wasn't attractive." She waited for his response.

"You are the most attractive woman I have ever seen. I am married and I love my wife. You and I in the same bed is torture for me knowing I shouldn't touch you. I'm not sure I can survive you being in the same bed for six more nights." Jay smiled as he spoke the words directly to Rosa hoping she would understand.

Rosa accepted his words with a warm smile. She knew the pain he placed on himself. "What about me, don't my needs count?" She offered gratuitously but in jest. Jay couldn't answer without lessening his determination.

"We can hire a taxi, or take this taxi and go to *Playa Santa Maria*. That's a beach area about forty miles from here. Cost you about fifty dollars. You can lay on the beach and get a tan, or you can eat along the beach, or you can drink on the beach, or you can just watch all the blondes on the beach. The sand is a light golden color and very fine. The water is a beautiful aquamarine and turquoise blended into an emerald color close to the shoreline. I think it is just beautiful. What do you say? It will take us about an hour or so to get there?"

Jay didn't have to think twice. "Let's go!"

Rosa spoke to the driver. This driver couldn't make the trip but he knew of another driver willing to take the trip. The deal was made.

Jay asked. "Can we buy bathing suits when we get there?"

"Yes, if you want. I don't need one. I'll just pull up my dress to expose my legs and pull down my top to expose the rest of me."

Jay shook his head. He knew he would have to have something to hide his modesty.

The beach was just as Rosa had explained. The area was populated with blonde European women, most without a top, sunning happily and sipping drinks. Somehow, he surmised he had arrived in male paradise. Oklahoma certainly wasn't like this.

CHAPTER X

"Jay! Jay!" Rosa called his name in an effort to wake him up. She shook him gently by his left shoulder. "Wake up."

Startled, Jay gradually began to come to life.

Rosa raised herself onto her right elbow facing Jay, "Wake up."

He opened his eyes and looked at Rosa. She was facing him without any bedclothes over herself and he stared right at eye level into two of the most beautiful mounds of flesh he had ever seen, soft and invitingly close. Less than six inches from his face, temptation was waiting.

"Damn...damn, Rosa!" He tried to be pleasant. "You are bound and determined to make me blow a gasket! How much of this do you think I can take?" Jay voluntarily pulled the sheet up over her exposed breasts.

"That's not what I want. I was thinking during the night how we can find Raphael Almarales Pardo."

Jay pulled himself up on his left elbow and faced Rosa, being careful not to disturb the location of the sheet. "How?"

"What is on the schedule today for your tour group? Do you know?"

Jay had to think for a moment. His groggy mind slow to awaken. "I'm not sure." His thoughts slowly began to function. "This is the fourth day...I believe this is the day we were scheduled for the *Pinar Del Rio* excursion. It is to be an overnight trip. Why?"

"I need you to slip into the *Hotel Nacional* through a side door unnoticed, change your clothes like you are going on the trip and then go through the lobby. You have to be seen again by those two guys. If they don't see you again, they will report your disappearance to Fuentes and there will be an all points lookout for you until they find you. That's why."

"What time is it?" Jay reached for the night stand and his watch. "Hell, it's only 5:00 a.m. The tour group will never leave earlier than 8:30 a.m. They told us that at our first meeting. We have three and a half hours before they leave. What's the rush?"

"It's me. I need the time to bump into those two guys in the lobby and get some information. Both of them will know Raphael Pardo and where he might be. That's what I'm counting on and I have to have the time to work them. You will have enough time to shower, shave and change clothes. Your reappearance has to be established. OK?"

"I guess." Jay reluctantly pushed himself out of bed and threw off the sheets. He looked at Rosa. "Holy cow! At least cover up. I can't take much more of this. My testosterone levels are over flowing now!"

Rosa smiled and was reassured. She knew Jay was nervous about her sensuality and she enjoyed the tease. "OK...I don't have any night clothes."

It was only a short ten-minute walk to the *Nacional* from the Capri. The two separated before getting close to the entrance. Both stayed in the early morning shadows totally out of sight. According to plan, Rosa was to wait twenty minutes before approaching the doorway. This would give Jay ample time to get to his room.

After the twenty-minute wait, Rosa adjusted her clothing. She rinsed out her top the night before and smoothed it over as she placed the spaghetti straps at just the right place. She shook her hair lightly and pushed it behind her ears. Taking a last deep breath, she walked toward the entrance.

Approaching the entry she didn't see either of the two men. She guessed the time to be approaching 6:30 a.m. and activity in the lobby was just beginning to increase. She once again shook her hair, took another deep breath and made a grand entrance. Her stride was physically enthusiastic and a broad grin was all over her face. She appeared as fresh as the morning breeze and as lively as a bouncing ball. There was a flurry of looks from all the males in the lobby. Her entrance couldn't have been more glorious even if it had been announced over a loud speaker. She enjoyed being observed.

It swelled her ego and caused a warm tingle to course through her body.

She saw the two men sitting in a chair. Both appeared sleep deprived and were absorbed into the overstuffed chairs. They too witnessed her entrance and they were as suddenly awakened by her fascinating intrusion into the somber lobby. One of the men stood up. She walked straight to him. It was her contact Carlos Rodriguez. She greeted him with a passionate kiss as if she hadn't seen her lover in quite some time. Carlos was embarrassed. She was working her role of a *jinitera* and he knew it was a ploy of some sort. He went along. She allowed her body to fuse into his and whispered into his ear. "I need to talk to you."

Carlos acknowledged her request with a very slight head nod. He put his arm around her, winked at his partner and together he and Rosa ambled into a quiet area in the elevator corridor.

As they ambled out of sight, appearing amorous to everyone, Rosa spoke. "Where can I find Captain Raphael Almarales Pardo? He is a prison warden at some location. Don't ask questions, just tell me how to find him."

Carlos was taken aback by the request. "Why do you want to know? Are you going to feed that information to Mr. Cobb?"

"Don't ask, just tell me where he is. You have to trust me on this."

"OK! Pardo is in a lot of trouble and Fuentes has been hiding him away from the press. He is still the captain of the *Prison de Majagua Municipio* about two hundred miles east of here along the main highway. He has his own quarters, I'm not certain where, but he frequents the bar in that village. Fuentes tries to take care of him." Carlos paused to look around to see if anyone was watching. "He is an alcoholic and won't take to any advice. If you find him, be very careful. I'll find out if Fuentes has someone looking after him. If not, he should be accessible in any bar."

"Thanks, that's what I needed. When will you know if Fuentes has someone looking after him?"

"Come back here this afternoon. I should have it by then." As he spoke, his partner came around the corner to see what was happening. Rosa saw him first and grabbed Carlos again in a passionate love hold and planted the longest kiss directly on his lips. She played the role of a *jinitera* to the hilt. Her body was the ideal distraction. Men felt guilty when they observed her and whatever she did or was doing went unnoticed. Carlos' partner witnessed the love hold and immediately turned away. A typical reaction, he felt guilty viewing a private affair.

As Carlos' partner turned the corner, Rosa spoke up. "I need that information as soon as I can get it. I'll come back here this afternoon. Do you think you will have it by 3:00 p.m.?"

"Yeah…If I can get it, I will have it right after our lunch break. We both go back to headquarters for any additional instructions and that's when I'll find out. The assignment should be on the scheduling board. If one of our people is assigned to *Prison de Majagua Municipio*, then it should be on the board. OK?"

"That's good. I'll show up here right after lunch. But I won't come in until I see you return. Now you grab me and hold onto me until I pass through the lobby."

Carlos was glad to accommodate her.

As Rosa left through the entrance, she began to think through the day. Realizing she hadn't told Jay what to do after his reappearance; she was disgusted. It was not in her character to miss details like that. Maybe Jay was getting to be too much for her to carry. He was a good looking man. She stood 5' 8" in her bare feet and Jay was around 6'2". They matched well together even when she wore stiletto heels. She was drawn to him and liked him more than her position would allow. This rattled her brain. She knew she would have to wait until the tour group left to know what Jay would do. She positioned herself on a bench further away from the hotel and waited. The bus didn't leave for the next two and a half hours. Since this tour was an overnight excursion, the group had luggage to load and everyone was slow gathering themselves for the trip.

She watched Jay get onto the bus without any luggage and hoped this infraction wouldn't be noticed by the two men shadowing him. Rosa knew she must get a taxi and follow the bus until there was an opportunity for Jay to exit the bus easily. He had to know she was following before he would exit. Rosa hailed a taxi and instructed the driver to follow the bus on its westward travel until the opportunity presented itself.

The bus driver went westward along the *malecon* to a major intersection where he could turn left to join the six lane *autopista nacional*. Rosa took her shot at the intesection. The taxi driver pulled along side the bus, Rosa jumped out and got Jay's attention. He was startled to see her but grinned a huge smile back to her. He walked forward and asked the driver to let him off the bus. Jay turned to Triana Travis who was sitting immediately behind the driver. He told her he would not be making the trip and debarked from the bus elated over the circumstances.

When the bus pulled away from the *Hotel Nacional*, Jay had a sinking feeling he had been abandoned. While the driver drove further and further away from the hotel, Jay's concerns increased to the point of desperation. He felt stuck in the tour group for the next two days. Seeing Rosa shot his spirits to a new high. When he met her, he pulled her close to him and hugged her tightly. It was a most sincere show of affection and relief. Rosa responded in kind. They held onto each other.

"God! Am I glad to see you!" Jay's face was aglow with excitement and relief.

"Me too! I'm sorry I didn't give you instructions about what to do. But you pulled it off well. I believe those two goons will leave you alone for the period of the tour, the next two days anyway." They embraced again. This was the first time Jay showed true affection toward her. Her warm smile trickled through her entire body as they held each other tightly. Rosa dragged her moist lips across his cheek until her lips found his. She planted another passionate kiss directly on his lips. Jay felt the genuine emotion. He allowed their connection to persist for minutes.

Rosa spoke, "The taxi driver is waiting." She pulled away to catch her breath and straighten her shoulder straps.

Reluctantly Jay disengaged. "OK! What do we do now?" Calmly he grabbed her hand still keeping her close.

Rosa began to explain why she went to the hotel. "I will have the information after lunch where we might find Raphael Pardo. In the meantime, I want you to take me to breakfast. I haven't eaten yet." The two entered the waiting taxi as Rosa gave directions to the driver. "You will have to pay the driver for his fare. I took the taxi and haven't paid anything yet. You don't know how glad I was to see you enter the bus with the rest of the tour group. That made my day. I had the taxi driver to follow the bus. We both did good. Now we are free for at least the next two days."

Jay nodded his head in agreement. His high was still running his mind and he put his arm around Rosa and squeezed. "Rosa, I have a confession to make. When I didn't see you as we left the hotel, I thought I had been completely abandoned and I felt sick to my stomach." He relaxed his arms. "Do you know what 'homesickness' feels like?" She nodded her head. "When my father left us and went away to South East Asia, it made me sick. For three or four weeks I had this horrible feeling. My stomach felt empty. That emptiness went from my stomach to my heart and back again over and over and over. I couldn't get over it. I was homesick for my Dad." Jay paused. "When you weren't outside waiting for me, that same feeling came over me. God, I'm so glad you followed us.

"When I first saw you outside the bus, my heart jumped through the ceiling." Rosa could feel the sincerity in his voice. "You will never know how happy it made me. Leaving the hotel and not seeing you anywhere, I had the feeling you were gone forever. I didn't feel safe. Please, don't ever scare me like that again."

During breakfast the two eyed each other like high school sweethearts. Neither ate diligently, but stirred their food with their forks. It was obvious both were in deep thought. Occasionally Rosa would reach out for Jay's hand just to touch it. Their feelings were preoccupying their minds. Each felt the spirited magnetism drawing them ever closer together. But giving in would spell disaster.

Rosa broke the silence. "Where would you like to go for the rest of the morning?"

Jay answered. "Aren't we on the west side of town?"

"Yes, we are."

"How far do you think it is to Mariel, the bay where the boat lift began. I would like to see that area."

"It's about forty miles from here. The *malecon* only goes part of the way but the remaining highway has four lanes and an excellent drive. Do you want to do that?"

"Yes, I do."

"I hope you know what you are in for. Mariel is different from what you might expect. It is very dusty there. The biggest cement factory in Cuba is there and the dust gets on everything. There are docks with fishing boats but it isn't as active nor as attractive as it once was. If you just want to see the place, we'll go." She displayed a devious grin. "I will have a surprise for you."

"What's the surprise?"

"Can't tell you. Wait and see!"

"OK...surprise me." Jay wanted more conversation. "Did I tell you what I think about the Cuban in Miami, Benitez Aguillar. He was one of the three I searched for, remember? He left from Mariel and went to Key West. Seeing Mariel could help me understand all the details. Here is another concern, Aguillar still has connections here in Cuba. I know he was the one who called Miguel Fuentes and told him I was coming. Why would there still be that connection? It would only be there if he were some sort of an informer. He doesn't have any family in Cuba. He has no ties with Cuba except as an informant for the Security Department. Since he and Fuentes were together in the past, it seems natural he would continue to pass information. I think he was also the one who told the Cuban authorities about the Brothers to the Rescue mission when two Cessna aircraft were shot down."

Rosa listened with intensity. Her face displayed concern regarding this information. "That is very interesting. Someone should look into that." She appeared to dismiss the information but seriously planted it into her memory. This could be a break. She and her contacts had known for years that information was filtering back into Cuba about all the happenings in Miami. They mostly attributed it to family information with low-grade credibility. But there always seemed to be action taken to thwart any unannounced upcoming actions. There was suspicion but little beyond that. This truly was excellent information for a lead.

Jay told Rosa that Benitez Aguillar was under the Witness Protection Program with the FBI under the name of Antonio Guillermo. He also told her where Benitez lived in Miami.

Again Rosa appeared to disregard the information gathering it into her memory for future action.

They left the restaurant. Found a taxi for hire and immeiately left for Mariel. Rosa told Jay they had to be back in the early afternoon. He agreed.

The driver took highway 2-1-3. Jay and Rosa watched the scenery mostly in silence. The two rode quietly and appeared to be out of thoughts. Such was not the case. Each had very serious thoughts about the other. Circumstances had thrust them together making one a part of the other. Being silent admitted nothing and reduced the tension.

As they approached Mariel from the north following the harbor toward the town, Rosa spoke to the driver. "*Taxista... gire a la derecho.*" She ordered the driver to turn right. When the small road approached the dock area she spoke again. "*Taxista...gire a la izquierda.*" After a short distance she spoke, "*Parada...aqui.*"

The driver stopped the vehicle and Jay and Rosa got out of the vehicle. She led him down to the dockside wharf. As they approached Jay heard a man shout out loud, "*Rosalito... Rosalito...sensational sobrina!*" The man jumped over the gunwales of his boat and came running toward the couple. He appeared to be in his late fifties and was gray at the temples. He had a sea tan, skin like leather and deep crows feet at the corners of his eyes from smiling through the years. He was muscular and physically fit. As he approached Rosa, he held out his arms for a big hug. They hugged each other and spoke in rapid flowing Spanish. He swirled her around lifting her off her feet. Both were overwhelming in their greeting to each other. When the chatter finally died down, Rosa spoke. "Jay Cobb this is my Uncle Julio. He is my father's oldest brother." Uncle Julio grabbed Jay's arm in a strong boisterous welcome. He hugged him also.

"Come to my boat." The boat was large, maybe seventy feet long and all steel. He led the couple down the docks to a gangplank leading onto the deck. Jay noticed the boat's name, *Caliente Mujer*. He had seen that name somewhere before. Suddenly it came to him. He remembered this was the same boat which carried 79 passengers to Key West during the boatlift and one of those passengers was Benitez Aguillar. This appeared to be an unbelievable coincidence. He never mentioned this. He didn't want anything to intrude on this warm family welcome.

Uncle Julio and Rosa continued their non-stop talk. Sometimes in English, most times in Spanish. It was clear this was a very close-knit family and a very warm, loving one. Jay was seeing a side of Rosa he had never seen before. He knew beyond a shadow of doubt, her role pretending to be a *jinitera* was way out of line for her. The change was a complete metamorphosis.

She was now a kind, happy, personable family member glad to visit with relatives. She was just as proud of Uncle Julio as he was of her. Neither could stop smiling. Rosa was totally enjoying this visit. She appeared to drop back into her childhood and out of respect let her uncle do most of the talking. The smile on her face would not go away. Jay had the thought, 'this is a most memorable meeting'. He had never enjoyed this kind of greeting from anyone in his family. He wondered why and was slightly jealous.

They visited for three hours before Rosa reminded Jay they had to be back at the hotel before 3:00 p.m. It was time to leave. The goodbyes took forever to complete. Uncle Julio did not want her to leave. She gave him a farewell hug that lasted for minutes. They were glad to have visited but sad it had to end.

When Jay and Rosa finally got back into the taxi, she burst into tears and Jay comforted her as best he could. He put his arm around her, occasionally wiping away her tears until they both erupted in laughter at such a show of sentimentality. The ride back gave both a chance to decompress. The occasion came back to reality.

Rosa spoke first. "I'm sorry you had to see that."

"My God...Why? I was moved by it and by you. What I saw was the part of this world I wish was everywhere and forever. Nothing bad, just loving family." Jay was most sincere. "That's what I have missed with my father being gone. He didn't have to be dead. It was at the hands of those three Cubans!" Jay realized he shouldn't have spoken those words. He was being too critical of all Cubans and his comments ruined the joyous feelings. "I'm sorry I shouldn't have said that."

Rosa smiled at his offer. "I'm sorry you had to see that side of me. What I do is a job. It is also a needed service. It isn't good for you to know that side of me. Sometimes I have to pretend to be someone else, an entirely different person. I didn't want you to see me cry." She wiped at her eyes with the back of her hand.

Jay couldn't believe that someone could do what she was doing. It would take experience and cold heartedness. Out of curiosity, he asked. "How old are you?" He had no idea how old she was.

"I'll be thirty in a couple of months."

"You mean you are only twenty-nine years old?" He was dumbfounded.

"I guess that is an admission of age. I don't want to be thirty. That's like having lived half your life away. It scares me."

Jay tried to think of some good, soothing words. There were none.

Rosa instructed the driver to take them to the Hotel Capri. They would have to end their journey there. Rosa could walk to the *Hotel Nacional* from there to make the meeting with her contact.

Rosa spoke out. "Is your room paid for at the *Nacional*? Was it pre-paid?"

"Yes, it was. Why?"

"I don't see any reason for you to stay there anymore. You can slip out the exits with your luggage and move all your stuff into The Capri. On occasion you can appear in the lobby to satisfy those two goons. I think we can easily get away with it and we won't disturb your tour group anymore. Depending on the information I receive regarding Captain Raphael Pardo, we might be leaving Havana for a couple of days."

Jay looked directly into Rosa's eyes and witnessed determination. She was going to help him! He couldn't speak fast enough. "OK...I'll move my stuff out."

"When you do, you keep the key. You might need to go there again."

The driver stopped at The Capri. Jay paid him and both got out. Standing next to the entrance, Rosa asked. "Do you want to follow me, get your stuff and walk back here? Or what?"

"I'll go with you."

Jay and Rosa walked the two blocks to the Hotel *Nacional*. She told Jay exactly what she was going to do. She would enter the lobby, get the information and leave. It shouldn't take more than five minutes.

"Who has this information?"

"Don't ask!"

Jay tried to keep his curiosity from interfering with his task. He certainly wanted to know where she was getting the information. But he was at ease more than ever with Rosa. His trust in her was without question.

They separated well out of sight of the hotel. Jay went to the west end of the hotel and Rosa walked straight toward the arrival entrance. Approaching the portico, Rosa saw both men standing next to the steps. She put a broad smile on her face, increased the bounce in her walk and with her right hand, ran a finger through the spaghetti strap on her right shoulder, pulling one strap down over her shoulder. This made her top loose and allowed some cleavage to appear.

She walked straight toward Carlos allowing their eyes to make direct contact. Carlos turned to face her and was ready to react to her lead. Rosa spoke an appropriate greeting to the two men. Getting real close to Carlos, she grabbed him by the waist with both hands and pulled him tight against her. Carlos put both arms around her capturing her arms within his grasp.

Rosa put her face against his and whispered. "You pull me around the corner."

Carlos accommodated her command. Once out of sight, Carlos gave her the information. "Captain Raphael Pardo is in *Majagua, Ciegi de Avila Province*. It is located inside the province border, just beyond Sancti Spiritus Province along the *Carretera Central*. Pardo has been physically replaced but still holds the title of warden in the local prison. He doesn't report to work anymore because he has a drinking problem and he beats up women. The international press writes articles about him all the time regarding prison conditions and treatment of prisoners. The man engages in outlandish and inhumane treatment. Fuentes replaced him. He lives in a tenement in town overlooking the river. Anytime day or night he can be found in the only bar in town, *El Heuvino*. It is on main street and also faces the river. No one has been assigned to watch after him. Captain Pardo is out of favor with Colonel Fuentes. It should be clear sailing to get to him. Can you remember all that."

"I sure can, and thanks. Now grab me again and move us around front toward your partner." Rosa gave a wink to Carlos' partner as she left. Walking away from the entrance, she readjusted the right spaghetti strap, stood up straight and moved casually down the walk toward The Capri.

Rosa was the first to arrive at The Capri and waited for Jay. Soon he appeared carrying three black carrying cases, two in one hand and the biggest in his other. Needless to say, it was a chore and he was out of breath and sweating under the strain. Rosa laughed when she saw him.

The two went to Jay's room and she exchanged the information with him.

"Tomorrow we will go about two hundred miles east of here to the town of Majagua, along the Majagua River. We should find Captain Pardo in the El Huevino bar in downtown." She paused. "Tonight we should hire transportation for tomorrow. We don't have to leave too early, say around 9:00 a.m. The drive should take about four hours. How is your money holding out? Do you have enough for this trip? Cost will be about one hundred fifty U.S. dollars. Do you have enough?"

"Sure, no problem. What is the plan?"

"You are going to have to do what I say, and nothing more. I will see to it that you get to face this man. You will have to tell me if he is the right man. Do you have identifying features for him just as you did for Fuentes?"

"This man Pardo can't be readily identified accept by name. He is tall, about six foot and light skinned, nearly white. Years ago he was neat and wore a thin line type mustache with a spiked goatee. He should also be about sixty years old. He is a vicious individual, mean and enjoys hitting anyone within reach just to enjoy the pleasure of inflicting pain. Of course he may have changed since then. If he is a true alcoholic, there is no telling what he might look like now." Jay stopped and fingered the Thunderbird pendant around his neck. "All I know is that his name is Raphael Almarales Pardo. Since I was in Little Miami, I have that name indelibly imprinted on my brain."

Jay started a confession about himself. "When I finally tracked down Benitez Aguillar in Miami, I had the opportunity to hurt him, I couldn't. It just wasn't in me to hurt a sixty year old man. I actually felt sorry for the man. I really have to think back to my father and how senseless his death was. That's when I regain my hatred for what these three men did. Many times when I think about my father I get very angry. This can all end if I have my chance to face both these men, Pardo and Fuentes. Right now killing and hurting are not on my mind. I just want all my sad feelings to go away, to end it all, now!"

"OK...here is what we will do. We will drive to Majagua, arrive in early afternoon, locate the bar, have something to eat and go to the bar around six. We will find him and you can face him. Remember you've got to listen to me. My butt can easily be thrown in jail for this. I am Cuban. I am not a U.S. citizen like you. If I get put in jail, and Fuentes can do that, there is no government which can come to my rescue. You remember that. OK!"

Jay agreed and then spoke up. "Let's think this thing through and make a definite plan. This man Pardo has three personality traits which stand out. He is mean, he likes women and he is an alcoholic. We should develop a plan which counters these traits. Take them away from him. Make it so he can't enjoy those pleasures anymore."

Rosa queried. "That's OK to talk about, but just how do you propose we do that?"

"I was thinking about AIDS. Cuba has the best AIDS preventive program in the world. It is highly advertised and it is a disease which is under control. The people educated to it understand the gravity of it. How can we give him AIDS? That would ruin his future exploits with women." Jay watched Rosa's face and could see her mind working over this statement.

"Another thing." Jay tossed out a new idea. "There is a drug called Antabuse. It is a therapeutic drug for the treatment of alcoholism. If the drug is in the system of an alcoholic and he drinks, it makes him deathly ill. They have attacks of vomiting, nausea, dizziness and heart palpitations. Let's give him a dose. At least for a while until the drug wears off, he would have to stay away from drinking."

Rosa understood as the ideas sunk in. "You don't have to hurt him, just take away women and alcohol and you ruin his life." Jay was nodding his head in agreement.

Rosa added, "I know a pharmacist but getting the drugs could be a problem. Most Cuban pharmacies compound drugs. Maybe we could get him to compound a few pills. Without a prescription compounding the drug would keep the pharmacist out of trouble. There is less accountability for compound drugs."

Both considered defeating his pleasure with women. Rosa spoke. "What if we tattooed the letters AIDS on his forehead. No woman would touch him if they suspected he had AIDS." Rosa grinned at her suggestion.

Jay laughed. "That's good thinking. On the forehead is a bit too much. Why not have those letters tattooed on his forearm?"

Rosa added, "Every small town or community has a tattoo parlor. It would be easy to get an artist to do it if we pay enough."

"Then let's do it." Jay responded. "I'll give the artist a big tip if he keeps his mouth shut. That's decided! How about the drug? Do you think it is possible?"

Rosa thought it over. "Yes, we should go take care of that right now."

Jay added. "Let's think about where? When we find him, how do we get him someplace where we can pull all this off?"

"Don't worry about that. I'll get him to take me to his residence. We will do it there."

"Sounds like a start anyway." Jay was getting excited about seeing Pardo. "I will need an old automobile fan belt."

"For God's sake, why?" Rosa wrinkled her brow, puzzled.

"I just want to scare him with it. I want him to think I'm going to beat him with it. I would also like for him to think we were going to torture him, just like he did all his prisoners. It would be like poetic justice."

"What about his meanness? Got any ideas about that?" Rosa queried.

"Naw...I'll have to think about that some more. Let's go get something to eat. It is almost 7:00 p.m." He had a renewed appreciation for Rosa. She was his partner, his friend and now was someone he couldn't do without. Jay took great pleasure in her company.

"Let's take a taxi and go to the pharmacist first and find the drug you talked about. I know right where to go. It shouldn't take long."

Jay agreed. They went straight to the pharmacist near the U.S. Interests Section building. Rosa knew the man in charge and easily convinced him of her needs.

Finding a *paladare* for dinner was easy. Rosa seemed to know where they were. If Jay had to find one, he wouldn't know where to start and if he looked at one he wouldn't know what it was. Walking the streets and holding hands with Rosa was enjoyable. Jay knew something was happening. He hadn't thought of Penny or his mother since arriving. And now Rosa was continually on his mind. He tried in vain to block her out of his brain. She was constantly there.

As they ate, Jay questioned Rosa incessantly. It was as if he couldn't know enough about her. The setting was intimate and fit the occasion.

He spoke. "Where do you live?"

"I live on the top floor of the U.S. Interests Section building. It has multiple floors, only the street level belongs to the Office. It is a special place to live. I have a view of the Straits of Florida and the *malecon* roadway. It is in a compound and safe."

"Do you need to go there and get some things for our trip tomorrow?"

"It might be a good idea. We could swing by there before leaving and I could pick up a few things."

Jay looked at Rosa with questioning eyes, "You are not a *jinitera*! So how do you dress most of the time?"

"I dress mostly just like this. When I dress this way, I can get into any place I want to. If I let myself hang out, the men never notice anything but my topside. Anything I do goes unnoticed. Now when I am put on a case like yours, I usually dress more lady like. But I was told you were in a bar, so I put on bar clothes. It works for me!"

"Do you do this often? I mean wear your bar clothes and pretend to be a prostitute?"

"Seldom! But I am called often to help individuals that have gotten themselves in a hard spot. So I wear clothes that could go either way. Here in Havana the temperature is tropical, so everyone dresses lightly. That works well for changing a disguise. You can be demure or you can be loose. Whatever it takes."

Rosa thought about the next day's events. "I am slightly familiar with the town of Majagua. It is very small. I am certain the bar will be small and filled with local people. To do what I have to do, I will have to look and act like a *jinitera*. I know you won't like it. Just don't think about it or what is happening to me. Accept it as going with the territory."

Jay asked. "What about me? What did you decide about me? You know, when you first saw me?" Jay eagerly waited for a response.

"You were easy, a mister nice guy. I tagged you without any problem. And I had to move in before a real *jinitera* came along. You are a good-looking man. I had no trouble getting close to you. Getting away from those two goons that were following you could have been a problem. But you had already taken care of that."

Rosa thought long before speaking again. "Sleeping with you was my idea. I was immediately drawn to you." She paused and fondled her fork searching for the right explanation. "What I do doesn't allow me to have a normal relationship. Since I took this job and left the States, I haven't had a loving relationship. Sometimes I want to love and to be loved like everyone else. The job doesn't allow it, and a 'one nighter' doesn't have any appeal. You were different. You are what I remember as the perfect guy. I wanted to sleep with you." She reached for his hand and placed hers on top of his.

Jay was surprised by her comment. He tried to think of an appropriate response. Letting her know how he felt seemed to be in order but he couldn't bring himself to meet the challenge. What he did say was all wrong and it changed the subject. He knew it the minute he spoke the words. "How long have you been doing this job?"

"This is my fourth year."

"How much longer will you continue to do it?"

"I don't know. I really love Cuba. I think it is the most beautiful country in the world. Many people think Miami is just like Cuba. It isn't. It takes a lot of money to enjoy Miami. Here you can enjoy anything for next to nothing. The people are happier, there is no class structure, it's like this place caters to the people, not the other way around where the people cater to the location and spend money. Cuba is quaint, steeped in heritage, it is multi-ethnic and everyone is happy.

"In Miami, all the people are unhappy with someone or something. There is too much traffic and too many people in small places. Happiness, I mean true happiness, doesn't exist there. You saw my Uncle Julio today. He is a happy man. That kind of happiness doesn't exist in Miami."

Jay appreciated her comments. She was honest and he knew it. Finished, Jay reached into his pocket to pay the bill. Rosa spoke to the waitress and reached across the table. She began pulling bills out of Jay's hand to pay the tab.

They walked back to the hotel, arm in arm. Jay was pleased she was clinging to him. It felt good. They just fit together and he knew it. Rosa never asked any questions about Jay. He already mentioned he was married. She didn't want to hear more knowing it would interfere.

Rosa again brought up the subject of the next day's events. "Tomorrow we can enjoy the ride and I will act like your tour guide, telling you where we are and what to look for. But when we get to Majagua, you will have to let me lead. Your skin color is perfect for you to blend in. But you will have to loosen up. Look as if your clothes don't fit, and allow your hair to look uncombed. Don't do any talking. When we locate this guy, Pardo, I will make some moves on him, get him drunk and under control. Then I will arrange for him to take me to his quarters. You will have to follow closely behind to see where we go. Once I enter his residence, I will see to it that the door remains unlocked. You come in and we will complete our plan. Somewhere in that schedule, either you or I will have to go get the tattoo artist. I think it should be me." She was comfortable with the plan.

Rosa wanted to emphasize another thing. "Dammit now, remember! You cannot hurt him. That is the most important thing. If we hurt him, they will find you and me and put us both in jail. Understood! And we don't want to be identified as being together. Being separate and alone in a small town is really important. We won't be as noticeable if we separate. Being unnoticed is absolutely necessary."

Rosa continued to make certain he understood. "Do you know what a CDR location is?" She didn't expect an answer. "Every block in Cuba has a CDR (*Comites para la Defensa de* la Revolucion). Your man Fuentes, in his position is in charge of the CDRs. These are neighborhood watches who maintain peace and strike down malcontents. Anyone we might run into could easily be a representative or work with a CDR. So we have to be extremely careful. We haven't done anything as yet which might cause Fuentes to send out an alarm. What we are planning might just do it. That's why I thought it best to hire a vehicle and slip out of town. So when we arrive in Majagua we have to be extremely careful not to disturb anyone or bring ourselves under suspicion, at any time. Have you got all this?"

Jay nodded his understanding. Holding to his earlier commitment he said, "I promise, I will not hurt him and I will be invisible." He thought further. "But what if he gets rough with you? Can I stop it? What? I know I won't be able to contain myself if he hurts you in any manner."

She answered in all honesty. She enjoyed and appreciated hearing he would have to intervene if Pardo hurt her. "I don't know. I can usually keep things under control, especially in a bar. Pardo is a man with a fondness for women. I know I'll have him under my spell in no time.

"After we leave the bar, his roughness could be a problem for me. So you stay close when we leave. I'll do my best to get him drunk enough before we leave the bar. You'll have to give me enough pesos to buy a full bottle of Bacardi rum. I'll medicate him with that. We'll just have to wait and see."

Back in his room at The Capri, Jay began to unpack some of his things before bed. He took a shower. When he returned Rosa had undressed and was wearing one of his tee shirts. She lay on the bed. The long tee shirt was excellent for her bedclothes. She was ready for a good night's sleep. Jay thought, since being together and knowing her better, she has suddenly become modest, a change of character.

Jay was wearing a fresh pair of boxer shorts. He lay on the bed beside Rosa. It took a long time for him to go to sleep. He wanted desperately to roll toward Rosa and hold her tightly. Thinking about that kept him from falling to sleep. His quandary over Rosa only deepened. She was a good person and he liked her more than he wanted to admit.

Jay slept intermittently during the night. His thoughts were about Rosa and her safety. Going into a small town to find an alcoholic malcontent didn't seem like the ingredients for a safe encounter. Every time the thought came to his mind, he would turn and look at Rosa. She was sleeping soundly. He liked watching her breathe.

Being in a strange country and not understanding the different customs, offered uneasy concerns about tomorrow. He seriously considered calling it off. His determination to face this man was too strong. As he thought about *Fidel* and *The Bug*, his anger and hatred returned. He wanted, more than ever, to face this man. Jay continued to think of *The Bug* in an effort to psyche himself up for the job ahead.

CHAPTER XI

Jay was restless throughout the night. He never entered into a soundless sleep; Rosa weighed on his mind. Visions of her were persistent. Trying to understand his feelings was impossible. When the early morning light came through the window he welcomed the opportunity to get out of bed. After twenty-eight years this was another one of those long awaited days. Seeing Rosa sleeping soundly, he made the effort to quietly raise himself out of bed and into the shower.

Rosa stirred from under the sheets. With her right hand she reached over to feel Jay beside her. He wasn't there. She quickly opened her eyes, sat up in bed and surveyed the room. Hearing the shower, she flopped backwards and began a much slower awakening. She too was looking forward to this day. It was one day closer to getting Jay onto an airplane safely and ending her present assignment.

There were very mixed emotions running through her mind and body. Ending this journey was not going to be easy. In the past she had always been able to maintain an arm's distance away from the people with whom she worked. Jay was different. She found in him the qualities she admired. He was the epitome, as she envisioned him, of her perfect man. Keeping her distance was impossible right from the start. The first night caught her off balance. She let her guard down and wanted to be involved. Now as the time approached for ending this encounter, she struggled within herself, knowing heartache and sadness were waiting. For the moment, waiting for Jay to appear and greet her was an expected pleasure.

When Jay appeared, hair wet, towel wrapped around his waist, he looked at Rosa and smiled broadly. "Good morning!" He walked to the mirror and combed his wet hair.

"How do you feel about meeting Captain Pardo?" he asked Rosa.

"OK…I guess. I'm not looking forward to it. If we don't do it right, we will be in trouble." She backhandedly cautioned Jay.

"It's going to be OK! I can feel it."

"I wish I felt the same way." She rose from the bed, still wearing the long tee-shirt belonging to Jay and disappeared into the bathroom. She yelled through the door. "I'm going to take a shower. OK?" The sound of water running could be heard. Jay smiled to himself. It felt way too comfortable to know there was a strange woman taking a shower in his room and he was enjoying the feeling. After yesterday's events, he knew his feelings were too real.

They dressed and went down to the hotel restaurant for breakfast. Talk during the meal was trivial and polite. Both were struggling with their thoughts.
Rosa turned the conversation toward this day's planned events.

"There are several things we should do before our departure. I'm guessing you still have enough money. We are going to a small town. We should convert some of your dollars into pesos. Then we need to go to my quarters so I can change my clothes. I have to play the bad role again today. Don't be surprised by what I wear. You may need an overnight kit. But make it as small as possible. No need to pack clothes, we should be on our way back here tomorrow morning." She stopped to think things over. "The taxi driver…we want to keep him. Maybe he can sleep in his taxi. He better be available anytime we might need him and on a moment's notice. It is also possible; we may not be able to get a room and may have to sleep in the taxi. It will be a four-hour road trip. If anything more comes up, we can discuss it during the trip." Rosa finished her meal and stirred left over morsels with her fork, deep in thought. "What about your money? How much do you have left?"

"Enough." His reply was short. "How much do you think we should convert to pesos?"

She answered with a grin. "Enough!" Jay got the jibe.

Time soon approached 8:30 a.m. After a last stop in Jay's room, they left and went outside to the line of taxis waiting for a fare. They hired one for the day and left for the U.S. Interests Section building.

"Calle 'M' and *malecon!*" Rosa instructed the driver.

Arriving in front of the building, Rosa got out and looked at Jay. "You can't come up. I'll be right back after I change." Jay nodded.

When Rosa reappeared, Jay was shocked. She was wearing the same short dress she had on the first night he met her. Her blouse was an off-shoulder, almost see-through sheer, flower design material. Large, gaudy, brightly colored earrings hung from each ear. Her shoe heels were nearly stiletto height. As she bounced through the entrance gate, Jay knew she was unquestioningly into her character as a *jinitera*. He didn't like seeing her like this. Knowing her better, caused his concern to become immense. He shook his head slightly with some disgust.

He opened the car door. "Why do you have to dress like that?"

She could see concern all over his face. "For anonymity! We are going into a very small town. If I dressed any differently, we would stand out like sore thumbs and would be remembered. We don't want anyone to be able to describe us as we are normally. When they describe me as a prostitute, my real identity isn't recognizable. The same for you; I don't want you to be identified either. We'll work on that during the trip. Don't take this the wrong way. We have to be very careful. This man Pardo, likes and uses women. This is what I have to do if I am to get close to him. Dressed like I am, he will come after me. And that's when we have him. OK?"

"I guess." He smiled at her, then a big grin formed. "You look absolutely horrible!" Rosa laughed with him. She instructed the driver.

"*Autopista Nacional...este, por favor.*"

The driver understood and turned around and headed toward the south side of Havana to join the *autopista nacional* eastward.

Rosa still laughed at Jay. "Just sit back and enjoy the ride."

After an hours drive they passed through the foothills into the open plains. The land was low and on occasion swamp forests could be seen on the south side of the road. The roads were excellent and traveling by car was comfortable and enjoyable. Rosa didn't do much explaining in the first hour.

In the second hour they entered the flat lands of the Matanzas Province. The flat areas were dotted with sugar cane fields and banana plantations. Heavy rows of palms flowed gently in the northeasterly breeze. Rosa began to explain the farming and agriculture in the area.

Approaching a cross roads near the village of Australia, she spoke of the often referred to Bay of Pigs invasion which took place about twenty-five miles south of the *autopista* at the beach, *Playa Larga* and *Playa Giron*. Jay wasn't interested. His main thoughts were still about the way Rosa was dressed. He was certain it would cause problems. Admittedly, jealously was also driving his concerns. He didn't want others looking at her.

Jay commented regarding the location. "This area looks pretty swampy in places. Doesn't seem like a place for an invasion. Maybe that's why it didn't work."

Rosa knew his mind was preoccupied with distant thoughts. "Then how about the scenery? Isn't it the most beautiful view you have ever seen?" Jay nodded in agreement. He was sitting on the passenger side of the seat and had a terrific view of the countryside to the south.

"Looks swampy." He continued with his own thoughts of what might take place. Preparing for the next several hours and how best to make it safe was his concern. He was finally going to face Raphael Pardo. He tried to psyche himself up by creating visions of his father's torture. He subconsciously fingered his Thunderbird image around his neck. This worked. He was filling his mind with hatred for the man, *The Bug*.

Another hour passed, they passed over the Hanabana River into Cienfuegos Province. The flat lands began to turn into rolling hills. Further travel put them back into mountainous terrain. Jay could see hills to the north and mountains to the south. Rosa remarked again how beautiful the country of Cuba was. Anything and everything a person could ask for. The *autopista nacional* was still under construction just ahead, so they turned off onto the Carratera Central highway before nearing Majagua.

Rosa turned to Jay. "Don't take this all wrong." She was right behind the driver. As she spoke she leaned forward in the seat, reached under her blouse and pulled off her bra. Jay watched in horror. He could see right through her top.

"What are you doing?" He couldn't understand why.

"This man Pardo, he has two weaknesses. alcohol and women and I am going to see that he gets both."

"But is that really necessary?"

"I was told and you confirmed it for me, this man is rough. I'll have to make it easy for him. I don't want anything ripped apart. This way I'll keep my clothes intact. Don't worry. I'll be OK." Her comments weren't too reassuring to Jay.

She continued, "Give me some of the pesos; maybe fifty dollars worth, enough for a bottle of dark Bacardi rum."

Jay took out his roll of bills and let her pick out the right amount which she placed in her small hand purse. She began to go through their plan. "Here is what we have to do. You have to go in first." Rosa reached over to Jay and pulled some of his shirttail out above the belt and tussled his hair, totally enjoying the process. She then unbuckled his belt and let it out one notch. "After you are in, I'll wait about fifteen minutes before I walk in. I don't want anyone to place us together. We need to be single and alone. Don't you do anything to pick this man out of the customers! Just go to the bar and order a beer and then sip on it.

"Allow me a full fifteen minutes and then I'll come in and go to the bar. I will chat with the bartender. I'll make a move on you. We will get cozy, and then I will look around. When I find this man, or the one I think is him, I'll go over to him, make some gesture which he will acknowledge, and then I'll sit down next to him. Please don't be embarrassed about what I do. I am doing this so you can face this man. OK?

"From there on, I will feed him as much alcohol as possible. If this man is a true alcoholic, it will take a lot of booze to get him drunk. When he is about blind drunk, but still walking, I will talk him into taking me to his residence. You follow us closely and we will do what we planned. You can face him in the privacy of his own home...Right?" She waited for an answer

"OK, I have all that. Yes. I just want to face him. After that we can both leave and it will all be over." Jay was concerned for Rosa's welfare.

The taxi driver waited for instructions. They drove slowly through town searching for a tattoo parlor. Rosa noticed a small business sign, Tattoo, on a side street and ordered the driver to turn. She walked into the tattoo parlor and made the arrangements promising a big tip when it was over. She told the artist she would be back in approximately an hour or so. Returning to the taxi they continued to look for the only bar in town.

Rosa discovered the bar, El Huevino. The sign was small and hardly noticeable. It didn't need to be prominent, only the locals used it and they knew where it was. Rosa had the driver park the taxi a short distance away from the bar.

She spoke. "What's the time?"

"It's 5:30 p.m. I'll expect you in fifteen minutes. Do we need a signal to let each other know things aren't going well and we should leave?" Jay asked.

"Yes, raise your left hand if you want to leave."

Jay exited the taxi, walked toward the bar, and entered. He walked straight to the counter and ordered a beer. He was doing his best to be casual and blend in. Thanks to Rosa, his pants were lower than he normally had them around the waist and the bottom of his pants touched the floor. His shirt was partly out and he looked the part of a local. As he drank his beer he looked around. There were only four people in the bar, a couple at a table, another man standing at the bar, and in a dark corner in the rear was a man leaning heavily on his table as if it were holding him up. He was wearing military styled, army green utility clothing. He was sitting alone in the dimly lighted corner. The way his head bobbled he appeared to be drunk. It was late afternoon and too early for anyone to be drunk. That had to be Pardo.

After the allotted fifteen minutes, Rosa strolled in. She swayed displaying her wares and came straight to the bar. Like any *jinitera*, she spoke to the bartender first. It was part of the routine for any *jinitera* to allow the bartender the opportunity to say no to their presence. With the bartender's approval, she moved close to Jay. Her standard move was to touch shoulders with her mark. As she did, she moved ever so close to Jay and asked him to buy her a drink. Jay ordered the drink. The plan was moving as rehearsed. The next move was unexpected and the plan changed slightly.

The green suited man staggered toward the bar, bumping into chairs along the way and went straight for Rosa. He spun her around with one strong hand and spoke. Jay didn't understand any of the slurred Spanish. He assumed the man asked her to join him at his table. He watched as Rosa nodded agreement and finished a sip of her beer before going to his table.

The bartender spoke softly to Rosa. "*Hombre...no muy bien! Cuidado prudente!*" He was advising her to be careful. This man is bad. Rosa acknowledged his remarks, but walked over to the darkened table anyway. She sat down with her back toward Jay. It was purposeful. She did not want Jay to observe too much of what she expected to happen. He had seen her at her best. This exercise was going to show her at her worst. They were getting too close to each other and she felt some shame for what she was about to do. Once seated, Rosa signaled to the bartender for his attention. She ordered a full bottle of Bacardi dark rum. When it arrived, she paid for it and immediately poured a drink for her new mark.

He gave his name as Raphael Pardo. Sure enough, Rosa had the right man and the plan could proceed. The man immediately moved his chair closer until they were side by side. Rosa, without flinching, accommodatingly moved closer to her mark. She filled two shot glasses of Bacardi. Jay watched as they touched glasses before downing the first drink. There was obviously a lot of chatter accompanied by boisterous laughter. Pardo did most of the talking.

Rosa poured him another drink. This time she didn't pour herself one. Jay was fully observant and liked her effort to refrain from more drinking. Pardo appeared sluggish, drunk and slurring his words during the first introduction at the bar. As Rosa and he sat together in the dark corner he was beginning to come back to life out of his stupor. He hadn't moved most of the day. Sitting in the dark corner by himself had dulled his senses. With the excitement of a woman perched next to him, his spirit was revived. Soon his hands started to move all over Rosa.

At first she was accommodating. Much sooner than expected she had difficulty keeping him at bay and wished she had moved more cautiously. He was like an octopus. Hands were everywhere. They disappeared under her blouse in front and in back.

Jay strained to see what was happening. His character and patience were sorely tried. Holding himself in check to keep from interfering was more than difficult. He couldn't tell whether Rosa was handling the situation well or not. He knew there was too much action going on.

One time as he looked at them in the dark corner, he could see the raw flesh of her exposed back. He knew the S.O.B. had pulled down her top and was fondling her breasts right there in the bar. This was more than difficult to watch. Shivers went up and down his spine. He needed to go over and stop this. Jay closed his eyes and turned away not wanting to see more.

Finally he could take no more of it and started to walk over. Rosa knowing Jay would have trouble accepting this turned to see if he was watching. She saw him coming and immediately jumped up from the table. She pulled her top up, excused herself politely and walked toward the bar where Jay was standing. As a ruse, she asked the bartender for another glass. She spoke to Jay in a whisper, "I'm OK...don't you do anything."

Jay looked at her in disbelief. He wanted to call it off. Rosa shook her head ever so slightly at Jay, indicating for him to be calm.

Jay blurted out, "You've got to make him stop!" Jay was emphatic. She only acknowledged with a nod.

Rosa swayed back to the table and poured Pardo another glass of rum. She was counting the number of glasses he drank. This was his third glass. She calculated it would take one more drink before she could gain control. Enduring just a little longer to get that last drink into him seemed worth it. Pardo began his fondling all over again. He was like a man gone wild. Jay watched in horror. This was becoming impossible for him to observe. He tried desperately to hold himself in check, by taking in a large drink of beer. It was not just difficult, it was chilling down to his bones, harming to his nature. This spectacle of incivility and complete lack of respect for womanhood was more than Jay wanted to watch. This treatment of women was way beyond the scale of any standard. This guy had to be the world's worst sadomasochistic son-of-a-bitch he had ever seen.

Jay's jaw muscles stuck out as he gritted his teeth. His eyes began to water, fearing Rosa would be harmed. He hoped Rosa would hold up her left arm and they would leave. She didn't. She allowed the disgusting pawing and clawing to continue. The man was an animal.

Pardo again pulled down her top and began fondling her breasts. She tugged at her top using it to at least slow him down. He was too energetic to be slowed and too rough for her to allow it to continue much longer. He pinched one of her breasts so hard it hurt and he just laughed as she yelled for him to stop. After a few minutes Rosa jumped up. She pulled herself together and this time went to the restroom.

There was only one restroom for both men and women to use. Jay also headed there to talk with Rosa and convince her to call it off. The restroom door was latched. He waited for her to exit. Before she came out, Pardo showed up. Jay jeered at him when their eyes met in the hallway and walked off.

Jay watched the hallway from the bar, waiting for Rosa to reappear. She didn't appear as soon as Jay thought she should have. He again walked toward the restroom. There in the hallway, Pardo had her cornered and was fondling everything. He had her short skirt pulled up to her waist and was squeezing her butt with both hands and kissing her on the cheek. Jay bumped the man hard on the back and said excuse me.

In a startled state of his drunken stupor, Pardo, distracted, stopped and walked back to the table holding a death grip on Rosa and keeping her tight against his side. He was laughing loudly and falling over chairs along the way. Rosa indicated to Jay that she had things under control. He knew that couldn't be the truth.

Once Rosa had Pardo seated at the table, she poured him his fourth drink and thought this would do him in. She endured his fondling waiting for the drink to take affect. Pardo's elbows were beginning to slip off the table occasionally and Rosa knew he was close to being totally blind drunk. Pardo's hands continued to grope. He went for her legs and moved his hands up and down her smooth skin. His hands moved inside her thighs as far as he could reach. Quickly and without warning with his right hand, he grabbed for the soft warm folds of skin between her legs. Jerking a handful of sheer panties, he ripped them out of the way and went for more pleasure with his fingers. A forceful thrust caused a sharp pain, Rosa had to yell responding to the pain. Pardo was more than rough, he was forcefully going beyond fondling. She cautiously put her hand between her legs to feel for any injury. When she withdrew her hand there were spots of blood on her fingers. Rosa challenged herself whether to stay or not. She decided to continue realizing their goal was close.

Jay started to come to her rescue. Rosa knew Jay would react and stood up, motioning for him to stop. It was up to her, this man had to be taken out of the bar. She whispered into the ear of Pardo. Offering to go to his home for sex, the man smiled and kissed her on the hand. Rosa grabbed the bottle of Bacardi and they left. She had to support her mark to make it out of the bar. Relying on Pardo to give directions to his residence was difficult. All he could do was point in the direction they should walk.

Jay followed the two, not too close behind but just enough to watch all their moves in case Pardo fell. Rosa eventually made it to the Cabanas del Rio Majagua and she was relieved when they entered his apartment.

Jay entered the apartment nearly at the same time they arrived. He was very close behind. His first comments were to Rosa.

He asked, "Are you OK?"

"He hurt me in the wrong place. I think I am bleeding." She spoke barely above a whisper. Her face showed pain and distress. She was out of breath from carrying this guy. She looked down at the inside of her thighs and could see small spots of blood. She held pressure against her lower abdomen with both hands.

"What do you mean." Jay was startled. He looked down at her thighs and also saw spots of blood. It frightened him. Let's get the hell out of here. This ain't worth it!" He pulled a handkerchief out of his pocket and handed it to Rosa. She folded it and placed it between her thighs and held them tightly together. She didn't know exactly when or how she lost her panties. But they weren't there.

She spoke. "Hell, we've come this far, now let's get even!" She was fuming. "I'm going to beat the hell out of this bastard myself. He shouldn't be let loose. Somebody needs to whack him!"

Again feeling between her legs, she confirmed there were no remnants of her panties anywhere and she needed them to hold the handkerchief in place. This sadistic bastard was going to pay. "I have never had anyone to treat me the way this man did. He likes to hurt people and he enjoys it. If he stands up I am going to kick him in the groin so hard it would send his balls to his throat. This guy needs to be dead."

Pardo, resting on the side of the bed, looked at Jay puzzled. As if to say, who are you? Pardo continued to stare at Jay in bewilderment.

Jay spoke to Rosa. "Are you OK? I mean are you injured?"

"I'm OK. I don't think anything is hurt too badly!"

"Do you feel well enough to get the tattoo artist or do you want me to go?"

"No, I'll go! I'll need to do the talking." She left, walking with her legs held as tightly together as possible. Rosa took their hired taxi to get the tattoo artist. Rosa was glad to leave the room. It would give her a break from this ordeal.

The old man was staggering drunk and unable to walk. He tried to get up and fell to the floor. Jay was hoping he was still sober enough to know what was happening. He pulled Pardo up onto a stool and thought it would be appropriate to start referring to Pardo as *The Bug*.

"Captain Pardo," Jay addressed him. "I am the son of a POW you killed in North Vietnam. I am here to kill you! You are *The Bug*...Right?"

The old man looked up still puzzled and slightly surprised, "Are you Meester Cobb?"

Nodding his head yes, Jay asked. "Do you know Benitez Aguillar?"

The old man gathered himself in an effort to appear sober. "*Si!*"

"Benitez is the man who gave me your name and where I could find you. I promised Benitez I wouldn't kill him if he told me where I could find you. Now do you want to bargain for your own life?" Jay made the offer seem real.

The old man nodded his agreement.

Jay acknowledged with a nod, "Then tell me where Fuentes lives and where I can find him." He thought to himself, this might be easier than originally planned.

The old man spoke out. "Fuentez live *Habana Vieja* on *Calle Colon* along the *Paseo de Marti* in tenement. Has girl friend. Weekend both go to *Playa Varadero*. Stay Hotel Pullman, *Calle 49*. Hotel not big. Have 15 rooms. OK...I live now!"

"Maybe! What is his girl friend's name?"

"Name Maria Castro. Rich woman...*mucho dinero*."

"Is she a relative of Fidel Castro?"

"No...no. She from Venezuela."

"How does Fuentes travel. What kind of transportation?"

"Fuentes have 1955 Chevrolet. Take always." The old man was getting more nervous. "I live now? You let live. No kill!"

Jay tried to think of more questions. None came. Jay walked toward the closet.

He rifled through the contents for a wooden clothes hanger. He found one and an old necktie. He grabbed the old man by the arms and pulled both arms behind his back, inserted the clothes hanger between his back and his arms and tied his arms together with the necktie just above the elbows. Once his arms were bound together behind *The Bug*'s back, Jay took another hanger, forced it between the elbows and the tie, then started twisting the hanger like a tourniquet, drawing Pardo's arms together. Once it was very tight, Jay walked in front of the man and asked. "Does that feel OK?" Sarcasm was in his voice.

The Bug spoke, "Are you Meester Cobb?" The old man repeated himself.

"So you know who I am. I am glad you do. For twenty-eight years I have waited for this day. I am going to kill you right here but not until I have tortured you unmercifully. You were in Cu Loc, North Vietnam in a torture camp where you exploited prisoners for information. I am going to do the same to you right now. I am sorry you are drunk. I would enjoy it better if you were sober."

The Bug understood every word and suddenly became very sober. He had fear in his eyes. He watched every move Jay made expecting at any moment to be struck by something. Jay walked around behind and took several more turns of the tourniquet. "How does that feel? How do you think those POWs in North Vietnam felt when you tortured them?"

"I am old, I not take too much." *The* Bug begged. "I need drink."

"Can't do that, you have to know when and how I am going to kill you, you son-a-of-bitch." Jay was putting on a good act. He could actually see fear in the old man's face. He walked behind him again and took several more turns of the tourniquet. "Let's see how you like it?" The old man groaned.

"You say, no kill!" Yes?"

"Not true!" Jay continued to let the old man suffer.

"How about a hotfoot?" Jay pulled out a book of matches. Bent over and pulled off a shoe and a sock, exposing the old man's disfigured toes. He struck a match and held it right against the man's foot. The old man jerked his foot away and yelled. "I nearly burned your toe off and all you did was yell. Guess I need to try the other one...OK?" Jay kept his ruse going.

"That woman you were fondling, that's my girl friend. You lecherous bastard." Jay drew his hand upward conveying an oncoming blow across the face. The old man closed his eyes and winced, waiting for the blow.

"Let me see...how many POWs did you kill?"

"No! I not kill. Fuentes, he kill four!" The old man was truly fearful or he wouldn't have uttered his boss' name.

"So, Miguel Fuentes killed four POWs."

The old man was eagerly nodding his head in agreement. "Need bathroom!"

"Too bad, it doesn't matter now. You'll be dead in ten minutes anyway." Jay was beginning to get into this torture thing. He could get satisfaction as long as he showed resolve. Jay walked into the bathroom and looked for a prescription bottle. The medicine cabinet had only one bottle of medicine. Small little gray pills were inside. Jay didn't understand the label. He reached into his shirt pocket for a small wrapping of paper which contained the pills he and Rosa had acquired the night before. He unwrapped the pills and put them into the same bottle on top of the others. The four pills were the Antabuse. In drug terminology, disulfiram. The drug used for alcoholics in recovery therapy. If this old man took any of the pills inadvertently, it would make him deathly ill. It could also kill him. Jay didn't care.

Having to watch as this man totally disrespected Rosa's body, made Jay almost as angry as thinking about his father's death. Pounding this man into the floor would be a huge pleasure. He grasped a straight edged razor he picked up in the bathroom and walked back out in front of the old man.

"Where do you want to die? In bed? On the floor? Where?" I am going to cut your throat and let you bleed to death." Jay flashed the razor. The look the old man gave him displayed nothing but stark terror. He never answered. Jay thought it was time to get physical. He drew back a foot and kicked the base of the stool showing his anger. The old man again winced, closed his eyes tightly and with a deep frown waited for another blow.

"You were with the First Military Assistance Group to North Vietnam... Right?" Jay looked at the old man and waited for an answer. *The Bug* just nodded.

"Miguel Fuentes was the man in charge...Right?" Again *The Bug* nodded.

"Tell me again, who killed my father?"

The old man spoke up. "Fuentes kill!"

Jay walked around behind Pardo, grabbed his head and pulled it back like he was preparing to slit his throat. The old man quivered in his grip and wet his pants out of fear. Damn Jay thought. This was the second time it happened. Benitez did the same thing. It was fortunate for the old man when Rosa returned at just the right moment.

Rosa walked in the door with the tattoo artist close behind. She spoke in Spanish to the old man. Jay didn't know what was said, but whatever it was it relieved the old man's tension. He offered a slight smile and begged incoherently.

The tattoo artist plugged in his inking needle while Jay untied the old man's arms. In less than an hour, the tattoo artist placed the letters AIDS on the old man's forearm in a bold red font where it could always be viewed by anyone. Beneath it the Spanish word, *CONTAGIAR*, was imprinted. This prominent display would notify any woman to stay away from this man. The ultimate revenge...this man would never touch another woman! Jay paid the artist well for his skill and for his silence. Rosa walked with the artist out to the waiting taxi and instructed the driver to return the artist to his place of business and come back immediately.

Jay looked at Rosa, they grinned. Jay asked, "How are you doing?"

Rosa answered with hatred in her voice. "I'm OK, but I am going to get even with this son-of-a-bitch, somehow." Jay knew she meant business.

She saw the straight edged razor in Jay's hand. "What are you doing with that?" She asked.

"I'm going to slit his throat and let him bleed to death." Jay winked at Rosa.

"Maybe we need to pour some rum down his throat before you slit it open!" She reached for the bottle of rum on the dresser, unscrewed the cap and held his chin up. "Have a drink?" With extreme anger she made him take several gulps. Rosa entered into a tirade of Spanish verbiage. Jay didn't know what she said but he knew the implications. Rosa was giving him hell. Rosa reached down to his crotch and grabbed a hand full of *cojones* and squeezed. The old man yelled out in pain.

"How does that feel, you bastard? Fun?" His head was down as he writhed in pain. Rosa pulled his chin up so he could look her in the eyes. Jay could feel the hatred in the air and waited for Rosa's next move. She deserved to do anything she wanted with this man.

Suddenly and without warning the old man's head dropped against his chest. He was out cold. He passed out from too much alcohol.

"What do we do now?" Jay asked.

"I don't know about you but I am not through with this bastard yet." She knew it was cowardly to hit a drunk. She didn't care and hauled back and slapped the shit out of the son-of-a-bitch right across his left eye. "That should make a black eye before tomorrow. Feeling some relief in being able to explode, she turned to Jay. "Don't the Indians have what the teenagers called a 'mohawk' haircut?"

Jay was astonished at her question. "Why?" He asked.

"I feel like giving this bastard a haircut, and it's going to be a 'Mohawk'. You know what I'm talking about, a two inch strip of hair down the middle of the scalp."

"Yeah...I know. You mean we are really going to cut his hair off and leave a strip in the middle?" Jay had to laugh as he took in the suggestion.

Rosa spoke. "This is just another way to get back at him and keep him away from other women. He will look horrible. He will either have to wear it or shave the rest of his head." Rosa was serious and went into his bathroom searching for soap or shaving cream. She came back with Pardo's scissors and shaving cream. She used the scissors to cut off most of his hair and then she created a line along the top of his scalp and began to shave his head leaving a two-inch strip across the top. She also shaved off the remnants of his unkempt mustache and beard. When she finished, she stood back and marveled at her artwork.

They attempted to clean up their mess. The hair was placed into a paper sack and put in a garbage container outside in the hallway. All the chairs were put back into there original locations. Shaving items were returned to the bathroom. Jay looked around. It all looked in order. Jay could see that a red and dark blue color was forming around Pardo's left eye.

"He looks unsymmetrical." With that comment Jay struck the man across his right eye. He could have hit him much harder but felt that would be just enough to blacken it.

Rosa still angry was forced to laugh at Jay and said. "We need to get out of here right now! No telling who or what might happen next." She walked through the door toward the taxi. Jay lingered behind to make certain things were tidy. He dumped the old man onto his bed and pulled his legs up into the bed. He double-checked the bathroom guaranteeing they left nothing behind which could place them at the scene.

Rosa got into the waiting taxi. Stepping into the rear seat she felt some sharp pains where Pardo had grabbed her and forced a finger into soft flesh when he jerked her panties to shreds. She needed to see if there was any more bleeding. There was no light and this wasn't the place. Her left breast was hurting also where he pinched her. She was glad she got the chance to hit that S.O.B.

It seemed to her Jay was taking entirely too long to come back. When he returned and stepped into the taxi, Rosa quickly ordered the driver to return to Havana.

"What did you do in there?" Rosa queried Jay as he settled in his seat.

"Nothing!" He responded.

"I know better than that. Is he dead?"

Jay was shocked she asked such a question. "Certainly not! I didn't hurt that man any more than he was already hurt."

"What did you do? What?"

Jay smiled and chortled to himself. "I'll tell you before I leave Cuba."

"If it was anything bad, you need to tell me now. We have our necks stuck way out and don't need the Security Department coming after us."

"I only cleaned up the place and put him in bed. He's OK."

As they left the town of Majagua, Jay felt compelled to apologize to Rosa.

"I want to tell you how much I appreciate what you did, but if I had it to do over, I would call it off. I couldn't stand seeing you go through that again." Jay apologized as best he could. "You could have been killed by that man. You didn't know he wouldn't kill you. So why did you do it? I couldn't have done this without you. You did it for me and I am ever so grateful." Jay paused for other thoughts. "I can't understand how you can dress the way you do. I just don't understand how you can be two people so easily." Jay looked away shaking his head. He looked out into the dark night. The world was black now and the visibility was only as far as the vehicle lights would extend. Jay stared at his watch looking for the time. It was about 8:30 p.m., adding the four hours travel time he told Rosa, "We should be back by 1:00 a.m."

Rosa didn't answer. She was still hurting. Pardo's actions were much worse than expected. There was no way she could have known just how rough he was going to be. This was her worst encounter while doing her job and one she would never forget.

Rosa wanted Jay to understand. "My role is to smooth out as many bumps as possible for our American tourists and keep them out of trouble. I must say, you have been a challenge." She offered a smirk as she spoke. "I don't have any political leanings. One day things might be better and this beautiful country will prosper. I truly love Cuba and want to have a future here. So I help to make it better."

She casually leaned her head against Jay's shoulder. "You Mr. Cobb, have been one of my best customers. Helping you was reward enough. I believe men like you are a gift to the world. Please don't change." She gently put an arm around Jay's chest. He responded by placing his arms around her. He held her tightly against his side. Jay's manly protectiveness was what she needed to get over her bad ordeal with Pardo. Both remained silent for the first part of the trip. Rosa would doze off intermittently in the comfort of Jay's strong arms. The quiet time was essential to decompress and get back to some normalcy. Nearing Havana both became alert to the next step and their minds toyed with the problem.

There was only one other hurdle in the way, Lieutenant Colonel Miguel Luis Fuentes. She dreaded that one. He was too high up the ladder of power. She knew it could prove costly. He could be the downfall for both of them. It would be a grave challenge. She must try and talk Jay out of it.

For conversation Jay offered. "While you were out getting the tattoo artist, I was able to get some information out of Raphael before he passed out. He told me that Fuentes was the one who killed my father and he lives on Calle Colon along *Paseo de Marti*."

"Along the prado!" She confirmed. "He could have an extremely nice apartment there."

Jay continued. "He said he had a girl friend and each weekend they stayed at the Hotel Pullman in the town of Varadero. Do you know where it is?"

She looked at Jay thinking, here we go again. "Yes I know where Varadero is. It's about eighty miles from The Capri Hotel. You go east along the main highway 2.1.3 out of Havana through Matanzas then to the beaches area. We used the same highway 2.1.3 when we went to Mariel, except we went west."

"Now that I am finished with Raphael, we could spend the weekend at The Pullman Hotel." Jay offered.

"Wait a minute. That is like playing the jail card. You go directly to jail. That man Fuentes is nothing to take lightly. He does his job of keeping the national peace by putting people in jail. Haven't you heard any of the news accounts about dissidents being placed in prison and given inhumane treatment? Go buy yourself a Miami newspaper. I don't want one of those people to be either you or me.

"Let's not move too fast all over again. I think we have been extremely lucky. Pardo was a drunk and an easy mark. This man Fuentes has guards around him anywhere and anytime. You won't be able to get close to him. You have to know that if we go after him, we will be courting with danger." Rosa paused to think up other discouragements. She knew Jay was determined. The disgust and disappointment showed on her face. "If we do go after him, it will have to be on my terms, and I'm certainly not ready yet. We have to think this thing with Fuentes over very carefully. First, I have to get to the hotel and check myself. Treat my injury if necessary. I don't believe it's serious just uncomfortable. Just think we can't have sex anymore." Rosa grinned at her sarcastic rebuff.

Jay smiled at Rosa's little joke and spoke out. "I know Fuentes will be tough to get to. When I go for him, I want it to be all me. I don't want you in the picture at all. My plan is to do it without you. Never again will I place you in jeopardy like I did tonight. If you will help me plan it and maybe set him up, I will do the rest. You don't know how difficult it was for me to watch as Pardo groped at you." Jay paused to think. "Pardo told me it was Fuentes who killed my father and three other POWs. Fuentes has to go down and it has to be me who does it. He is my pound of flesh." Jay fell silent in his thoughts. He subconsciously fingered the Thunderbird image around his neck. Crying blood had to be avenged!

CHAPTER XII

The mid-day sun in November was in its southern course disallowing heat to build as it did in the summer months. A gentle northeasterly breeze fluttered the flags hanging on the outside balconies of The Capri Hotel. Street noises filled the air with sounds of people, vehicles and an occasional horn from a tourist bus recalling its passengers. Room temperature and the breeze made for a comfortable wake up. There was no need for air conditioning.

Jay was the first to awake. He found Rosa with her arms across his chest. Her steady, rhythmic breathing was warm against his neck. Jay was remaining faithful to his wife but his strength of character was sorely tempted. The woman next to him was perfect in every way. She was beautiful, strong, extroverted, kind and trusting. Further, she cared and wanted to help him. Being tempted by desire was a tormenting spear aimed straight at his heart. Thoughts of giving in to his urgings for Rosa plagued his very existence. He lay as still as possible, allowing this cherished moment to continue as long as it could.

Finally Rosa began to stir, slowly at first, with only gentle movements of her legs. Her eyes remained closed not wanting the peaceful sleep to end. Her mind still muddled in the throes of awakening. Her eyes opened slowly. Jay's throat and neck filled her field of vision. Moving her head ever so slightly to see his face, she witnessed his eyes meeting hers and a warm greeting smile glowed on his face.

"Good morning." Jay spoke softly in an effort not to break the silence too harshly.

Rosa grinned back. "What time is it?" Those were the only words she could think of.

"It's almost noon, we both got a good night's sleep." He waited for her to gradually come to life.

Rosa never moved her arm from across Jay's chest and even forced a slight pressure as if claiming him for life. In a move which seemed so natural, she pulled herself closer to Jay and moaned those happy sounds usually attributed to newly married couples. Those pleasured sighs conveyed her thoughts to allow this to never end. Yearnful urgings could also be discerned.

Jay allowed her to stay in this comfortable hold. He too, enjoyed it. After several minutes, he knew she wasn't going to fall back to sleep. The silence, however, was as welcomed as her closeness. He remained silent and waited for Rosa to begin the day.

Eventually, with an undeniable urge to use the bathroom, she arose from those cherished moments and made the reluctant move. Jay had been awake for almost an hour and sat up in bed waiting for her to return. The tee shirt she was wearing allowed her legs to be displayed to their fullest. Jay had those temptation demons permeating through his entire body. They could make his hair ache. He tried to look away but couldn't. She sat down on the bed as close to him as possible. After squirming a bit in her process of nestling next to him, she turned directly to Jay and smiled her most warming smile ever.

Nervously he asked. "Are you OK? Is everything in good shape?"

She knew exactly what he meant. "Yes it is. It must have been his fingernails which gouged me slightly. It's all OK!"

Jay was glad. He felt a sense of responsibility for her injury. If his desire for an encounter with Pardo was less, it would not have happened. "I'm so sorry. I should never have come here. But I am so grateful, and so glad that I got to meet you. I have never in my whole life met anyone like you. You are incredible!"

Rosa allowed a warm smile to form. Her face glowed. A blush rushed from her toes to the top of her head. Strong emotions filled her soul. She was overwhelmed by his remarks and didn't know how to respond. Time stood still.

Breaking the mood, she leaned over and kissed Jay on the cheek.

"I'm hungry, we need to go eat." She jumped off the bed. Realizing she had only the clothes she wore the night before and no underwear or panties, she asked. "Can we go by my apartment before we eat? I can't wear these clothes in public anymore. As a matter of fact, I am going to burn them as soon as I can."

Jay understood. "Yes. We need to go by your apartment first." Jay started going through his luggage to find fresh clothes. He took out a pair of khaki pants and short sleeved, broadcloth shirt with a button down collar. It was his favorite clothes. The shirt was new and hadn't been opened. He took out a myriad of straight pins before putting it on.

"My apartment isn't far, we could walk, except I don't want to be seen in this dress ever again. I want to dress in ordinary clothes. Be like every one else." She spoke as she tried to put on the soiled skirt.

"Let me buy you a new dress?" Jay spoke without thinking. "Hell, let me buy you an entire new wardrobe!" He wanted to do this for her.

Rosa looked at him, puzzled. "Are you rich?"

Jay offered a grin. "Yes I am. I'm rich. So let me buy you some new clothes." The sincerity in his voice was direct.

She stared at him in disbelief. "You are rich? Wealthy? You have lots of money?"

"Yes. Yes. And yes to all three of your questions.

"So that's what you meant when you said you had enough? You meant you had plenty?" Rosa laughed a mumbling kind of laugh.

Jay finished dressing before Rosa and he had more clothes to put on. She tried in vain to make herself presentable. The short skirt just wasn't acceptable anymore and she knew it.

They left in a taxi heading toward the U.S. Interests Section building and Rosa's apartment. Jay waited in the taxi while Rosa changed. When she reappeared she looked stunning once again. She was wearing a calf length wrap around skirt and an open collared blouse. The skirt had pockets and

Rosa liked keeping her hands casually in her pockets. This was the real Rosa.

Jay complimented. "You look gorgeous!" Then added. "Where do you want to eat?"

"Let's go to the Hotel Savilla. There is a nice restaurant on the top floor. You can stand at the windows and see Havana Harbor and the Florida Straits to the north. It is a very pleasing place to eat. Besides it's already lunchtime. We missed breakfast."

Rosa instructed the taxi driver. The ride was short, maybe only six blocks.

As they ate, Jay brought up the subject of Fuentes. "Why don't we hire a taxi and go to Varadero." He tried to be as diplomatic as possible. "Just to look around, nothing else."

"OK...It's your money. It will take about two hours to get there and two hours back. It will take the rest of the day."

"That's OK. We don't have anything else to do." He waited for Rosa to agree before saying anything further. He knew they would talk during the drive and he was more than eager to get to Fuentes. He relied on Rosa's expertise and knowledge to get there. Talking to a taxi driver she was able to negotiate the trip for eighty dollars U.S.

The driver took the tunnel across the harbor to the east side for connections to highway 2.1.3 for Varadero. Due to heavy traffic the trip took longer than expected. It was about 3:30 p.m. in the afternoon when they passed through the city of Matanzas. Varadero was still twenty miles away.

Jay's eyes caught a glimpse of familiar faces. He looked closer. His tour group was parked near the *Plaza de la Vigia* in the center of Matanzas. The group was outside the bus and the two goons who had followed him were having an animated conversation with Triana Travis and two of the group members. Jay slid down in his seat and pulled Rosa down with him until after they were past.

Rosa was startled. "What's up now?"

Jay lifted himself slightly and peered out the taxi window. They were beyond the group sufficiently. "Something's going on. My tour group was back there and those two goons had them stopped and were obviously asking questions. I know something's up."

Rosa thought for a moment, going through every detail of the previous day's encounter with Pardo. Suddenly as if a light were switched on. "When you went back into Pardo's room after I left, did you do something I should know about? At the time I asked, 'what did you do'? You said you would tell me before you left Cuba. I need to know now! What did you do?"

Jay was trapped, "I gave Pardo two of those pills, the Antabuse."

Rosa became edgy. "For God's sake, why did you do that?"

"I wanted to do more to that man. He was getting off too easy."

Her mind was rapidly churning over possibilities. "Could they have made him so sick that he died?"

"I wouldn't think so. Maybe he had to go to the hospital or something." Jay offered a counter possibility.

"I hope Pardo didn't die. If he did, we could be in a lot of trouble. You said that Aguillar told Fuentes that you were coming to Cuba to find Fuentes and Pardo. Right?" Jay was nodding his head. "Then Fuentes knows you were out to get him and Pardo. Right?" Jay nodded again. "If something has happened to Pardo, then Fuentes will believe you had something to do with it. Right?" Jay again nodded.

Rosa continued. "Then we have to believe they are looking for us."

Jay had to agree. She was right on everything. "What do you think we should do?" He asked, quietly considering the situation.

"I think we should get a disguise of some sort and lay low. We should also find a newspaper and go through it to find anything we can which might explain what happened to Pardo. This won't stop us from going on to Varadero. That city is a vacation spot. They are trying to make it the Cancun of Cuba. Many tourists from Europe, South America, and Canada go there year round. We can get lost in the crowds in

Varadero. But when we return to Havana we need to be very careful." Rosa was thorough.

"Why don't we hire this taxi to be our own personal tour bus and keep him as long as we can. That should keep us off the streets and safe."

Rosa nodded in agreement. "We are close to Varadero, tell me again the name of the hotel."

"It's the Pullman Hotel on Calle 49."

Rosa passed the information to the taxi driver. She asked Jay. "What do we do when we get there?"

"I thought we might go into the hotel, see how big it is, see how friendly it is, find out whatever we can about the place. Fuentes and his girlfriend stay there every weekend. I'm sure when he's with his lady, he'll want privacy. He won't have any guards around. That's my chance to have a face off with him, somewhere private and without his guards."

Rosa laughed at him. "You are beginning to figure all this out for yourself. I can see what you expect me to do." She was staying ahead of Jay. "I am supposed to go in and ask questions about this woman. Find out whatever information I can get. Make friends. Right?" Rosa's mind worked at warp speed.

"The lady's name is Maria Castro." Jay tossed out the name before she asked.

"Maria Castro!" Rosa exclaimed in surprise. "Maria Castro owns the hotel. She belongs to the socially elite here in Cuba. Her name is always in the news. So that's who I have to ask questions about?" Rosa didn't wait for an answer. She knew Jay wasn't going to respond. "We better go to a gift shop and buy us both a tourist looking hat and sun glasses. We have to blend in better or we are going to look suspicious." Both Rosa and Jay were dressed enough like typical tourist to get by. With hats and sunglasses they would blend in well.

Rosa knew the Pullman Hotel was on a back street and showed the taxi driver where to turn. Finding a place to park was difficult. The dry season, which was just starting, always had heavy tourist traffic during this period. The Varadero area was bustling with people and vehicles, mostly taxis and rented or hired vehicles. Varadero was a long peninsula and all traffic had only one way in and one way out. When people came and stayed the roads became a bottleneck impeding the flow. Eventually the driver found a place a few blocks away from the hotel. Rosa again instructed the driver not to leave. Indicating he would be well paid.

Jay and Rosa departed the taxi and walked toward the hotel. Passing a gift shop, Rosa grabbed Jay by the arm, pointed out the shop and pulled him through the entryway. She tried on several wide brimmed sun hats and sunglasses until she was satisfied. Jay only looked for the right size hat and took the first selection available. It was a white, Caribbean Plantation hat. He grabbed a pair of sunglasses and thought he looked quite fashionable, just like a tourist.

Continuing their walk to the Pullman Hotel, Rosa began to ask many questions. What specific information did Jay need? Was he anticipating staying the night sometime? How quickly did he plan to have his confrontation? With each question, Jay shrugged his shoulders. He didn't have a clue as to what he wanted to do. He did know he had to see the place first. See how it was laid out so he could devise a plan.

Arriving at the hotel, both saw exactly how 'private' it was. The restaurant was open-air and breezy with only a few tables. The pool was very small and sitting areas by the pool were sparse. There was a small gift shop and it looked to be the best place for asking questions. The lady managing the gift shop seemed pleasurable enough.

Jay looked over all the merchandise while Rosa talked with the shopkeeper. Jay selected several useless gifts in an effort to mask their real purpose. Within fifteen minutes Rosa had the full story about the place, its use by the owner and the owner's male friends. Rosa hung onto that morsel of information. If Maria Castro had male friends, then Fuentes wasn't an exclusive escort. This might be good to know. Without this knowledge both could have been embarrassed or caught by taking actions based on bad information.

Rosa asked where the owner stayed when she came for the weekend. There was a 'honeymoon suite' where she stayed. It was never rented for the weekend but always held for the owner. Rosa was even able to get the room number from the gift shop lady. The owner had her own airplane and flew into the Juan Gualberto Gomez Airport every Friday around 11:00 a.m. Her schedule was pretty much a ritual. Luckily, it appeared this fifty-five year old heiress was habitual if nothing else. This made Jay's choice of actions easier than he expected. Jay paid for his selected gift items and they left.

Before they started back to the taxi, Jay wanted to look around. He also wanted to spot where the 'honeymoon suite' was located. The suite was the only room with an entry into the pool area. He let Rosa follow him outside to admire the pool area. He could see that the sliding glass doors were less than secure. That surprised him. The layout was simple for a fifteen-unit hotel. All the rooms were at street level and they all looked less than secure. A real thief could have a field day. He noted the room number immediately across from the 'honeymoon suite'.

Walking back to the taxi, Rosa began to tell Jay all the facts he wanted to know. As he absorbed the information, his plan was formulating in his mind. They left Varadero to head back to Havana.

As they approached the *Plaza de la Vigia* in the town of Matanzas on their return, Jay watched intently to see if the two goons were still harassing his tour group. He didn't see anything unusual and knew they were gone.

Rosa queried Jay, "Well, what do you think?"

"I think arranging a face to face encounter with Fuentes will be easy, that is if you will help set it up."

"What do you have in mind for me to do?"

"Right now, and this may not hold as I think about it some more, right now I would want you to call Fuentes and tell him you are Maria Castro and you arrived early. Temptation should get him out there sooner than the weekend. When he shows I will have him all to myself. Does that sound feasible to you?" He needed her opinion.

"OK…I can do that, except I will leave a message for him. He probably knows her voice. I couldn't possibly imitate her voice. Now tell me what you plan to do?"

Jay knew that question was coming and he didn't have an answer. "I don't know yet. I'm hoping something comes to me by tonight. Tomorrow is Thursday and I must have this over before Friday. So tomorrow is the day. It has to be done tomorrow."

Rosa had to say something. Jay was stewing over his incomplete plan. "Is it possible that you could just call it off? I mean not do anything. We believe those two goons are looking for us already, so why chance it?" She made her point.

Jay pursed his lips, shaking his head. "I've got to do it now...or never! You don't know how badly I want this to be over. Facing Fuentes is my last step to make it all go away. I have to do it. Not only for me but for my entire family. We have enough money to live a good life without worries." Jay stopped to stare into space through his passenger side window. "All the money in the world won't make this go away. Facing Fuentes will. God...I don't know what I will do when I face him. But I just know I have to." He sat quietly for the next half hour. Rosa allowed him the quiet time to think through his plan.

As Rosa looked outside, she ordered the taxi driver to take a different route back to Havana. It would be a faster trip. She also wanted a Miami evening newspaper, and this route would allow her the opportunity. She watched diligently for the next newsstand. Rosa suddenly asked the driver to stop. There was a newsstand in the flea market area on the opposite side of the street. Asking Jay for some change, she purchased a paper. Thumbing through it she found what she was looking for.

Inside was a feature story by a prominent Cuban exile living and writing in Miami. The title read...VIOLENT WARDEN RECEIVES VIOLENCE. Rosa had a full grin on her face as she read more. The photo, taken in the hospital, showed a badly bruised face with two black eyes and a 'Mohawk' haircut. The article speculated the attack was from a released inmate who endured similar treatment at the hands of Captain Raphael Almarales Pardo. Pardo had been removed from intensive care and placed in a step down unit where he was undergoing treatment for vomiting, extreme nausea and dizziness. His physician stated he might have taken some type of drug that made him require hospitalization.

Rosa handed the paper to Jay. "Here read this. It will make you feel better."

Reading the article brought laughter to his face. Every few seconds, Jay would laugh out loud. Finished, he turned to Rosa and gave a thumbs up sign. They laughed together.

Jay asked Rosa, "How does the Miami press get the news so fast about happenings here in Cuba." News was being put to press in Miami before the Cuban newspapers even knew about it.

"It's money. Miami pays better. There are people here who work for the Miami newspapers. With so many Cubans in Miami, it is a necessity. What happens here is news in Miami. There are air couriers which deliver pouches direct to Miami several times a day. Your man Pardo, has been getting a lot of Miami press about his inhumane treatment of dissidents. When he showed up at the hospital, looking like he did, it was news. It should be in tomorrow's Cuban papers."

Jay was pleased with her answer and continued to look out the window in deep thought.

"Jay!" Rosa drew his attention away from the window. "We'll have to stay at my apartment tonight. You do know that. Right?"

"No! I don't. Why?"

"Because those two goons are seriously looking for you now and they will search every hotel around. I'll bet you registered at The Capri using your own name. Right?"

Jay blushed. "Yes."

"That's why. You can't let them get to you now. We have to stay at my place."

Jay responded. "I don't mind doing that. I just don't want to inconvenience you in any manner. You have already been more than I could wish for. You have your own life to live and watching out after me wasn't part of the bargain." Jay hoped Rosa would insist. He did need a place to stay the night and her apartment was an obvious choice.

"Come on now. You know you can't go back to the hotel. You don't have a choice, just do it!" Rosa insisted.

"OK...I don't have a shaving kit or anything?"

"You can use my toiletries. Don't start giving me a bunch of excuses. It will be fine for you to stay the night with me. Besides, there has never been a man in my apartment. You'll be the first."

He tried in vain to think of some appropriate and profound words, but couldn't. "How big is your bed?" His words were trivial.

"It's a standard double bed. Like the one in your hotel. What does that matter?"

"Like I said, I don't want to inconvenience you more than I already have."

She looked at him questioning his thinking. "You better be thinking about how you plan to work Fuentes tomorrow. And don't worry about the sleeping arrangements. I'll stay on my side of the bed. Got any new ideas about tomorrow?"

"Not yet!"

Rosa directed the driver to the U.S. Interests Section building. She turned to Jay. "What about the taxi? Want to keep him or let him go?"

"Let's let him go. Tomorrow morning we'll hire another taxi for the full day." Jay had another thought. "Unless of course, you want to keep him and go out to eat."

"I have food. I'll fix dinner for the both of us."

Rosa asked the driver for the fare charge. As usual she took enough of Jay's money to pay the bill.

Jay felt honored as they walked through the opened, heavy steel gate to the entrance. "So I'm the first?"

Rosa nodded her answer and spoke. "It's not much, but I call it home." She grinned and Jay laughed at the remark. "This building, in pre-revolution days, was the U.S. Embassy. It serves much the same purpose now with consular duties provided to U.S. citizens. But there is no ambassador."

The building was completely surrounded by an eight-foot high decorative wrought iron fence. The grounds were well manicured and the building was truly like an embassy. The entry was official looking and they gained entry using an electronic code. The marble and tiled foyer was immaculate. Not one spot of dust anywhere.

Jay was stunned by the grandeur of its institutional appearance and the untarnished cleanliness. "How do you get to live in a place like this?"

"My good looks."

They took an equally clean, polished, stainless steel elevator to the third floor. At the doorway, Rosa pulled up one edge of the rug and picked up her key. She unlocked her door and replaced the key before opening the door. Entering, Jay was again astonished and thunderstruck by the interior. He expected feminine warmness, instead he was greeted by utilitarian furnishings. This apartment was similar to the foyer and gave the appearance of a bank. The floors were tiled with twelve-inch marble squares. The wainscoting was made of white marble slabs and both rooms to the apartment were bathed in chandelier lighting. It was also fastidiously clean and bold. As he looked around, he marveled at the size. He knew this was previously two offices that were converted to living space. Rosa made a few attempts to warm the area. A 9 X 12 throw rug on the floor did offer some warmth and muffled some of the hollow sounds. Furnishings were sparse. Jay walked into the bedroom. It too had the same flooring and wall coverings, but Rosa had taken great pains to make it more pleasurable. The bed was neatly made, all clothing placed neatly in the closet, not much to suggest that someone lived here. It was almost too clean.

Rosa started taking off her clothes and went to the closet for a robe. Then walked to one corner of the larger room to an area she referred to as the kitchen. Jay followed her every step. There was a refrigerator, a microwave oven, stove and coffee pot, but not much else. Its appearance indicated it was seldom used. At her direction, Jay opened a closet and observed ceiling high shelves completely stocked with a wide variety of American labeled canned foods.

She asked, "What would you like to eat? Pull out anything you want."

Jay responded, "Anything." He was still in a state of shock over the cavernous apartment and now the fully stocked shelves. How can she afford all this and how does she rate such an apartment? Does she ever cook here? Question after question put his mind in overload. This was way over the top of what he expected.

Rosa opened several cans that Jay selected and quickly prepared a 'get by' meal. The table was very small, mostly for only one person. She pulled in another chair for Jay.

"So...what's your plan for tomorrow?" Rosa queried.

"I think what I have to do is lure Fuentes to the hotel. Wait for him to arrive and then try to find a place where we could talk. I will have to wing it from there."

"Don't you think that is slightly naive? He will know what happened to Pardo, at least by then. You know he will be on the lookout for you. He won't allow you near him. You'll have to take him by surprise."

"OK...How do I do that?" Jay asked.

"We should rent the room directly across the hall from the 'honeymoon suite'. We leave our door opened slightly and while he is opening his door with his back turned, push him into the room. Then close the door, and do whatever you plan to do with him. Then you've got to get the hell out of there as fast as possible."

Rosa was thinking more soundly than Jay. "Another thing, you should turn in your return flight ticket and exchange it for the next flight out to Cancun. Have you thought of that?

"Fuentes will be after you and he has many more people he can put on your trail. I am not even certain we will be able to drive back to the airport without being spotted and picked up." She thought some more. "You will have to make sure he has no means of communicating. If he has a hand-held radio, you will have to smash it. To keep him from using the room phones, you will have to jerk the line out of the wall before you leave. You will have to tie him up and place a gag in his mouth. Lets only hope the maid service doesn't find him until after we make our get-a-way. It will take next to three hours to get back to the Havana airport from Varadero. That's a pretty long time." A new idea struck her. "There is an airport in Varadero, maybe we should hire a flight in a small aircraft and fly directly to the Havana airport."

Jay spoke, "To do all that is a big order!"

"I know. I also know you shouldn't do this. Just think about this, it could be a life-changing venture. It isn't going to be easy and everything you plan has to come off like clock work." She watched Jay's eyes for any indication he might drop it.

"Think about it and if you still want to do it, you'll have to go to The Capri Hotel tonight and get your luggage. Tonight we should also check into the flight schedules off the island. I think we might be able to make arrangements for a standby chartered aircraft to be available at the Varadero airport. This way you can make a fast departure for Jose Marti Airport and get there before they start searching for you in a big way. After you leave Fuentes you need to stay out of sight."

Jay got excited. He slurped down the remainder of his food. "I'm going to get my luggage right now." He stood up to leave.

"Wait a minute. I have to go with you. Let me dress." Hurriedly she rifled through her closet and pulled out one of her short skirts again. She knew there could be a need for distractions, and a short skirt always did the trick.

The Capri Hotel was only four blocks away. Unable to flag down a taxi, they walked. Nearing the hotel, Rosa told Jay to stay behind and let her see if the way was clear. The way was clear. She thought. As she got closer, the two goons were standing next to the doorway. Immediately turning back, she warned Jay. Again he would have to enter through a utility entrance to get to his room unnoticed.

"That's what I expected!" Rosa had to exclaim. "You registered using your real name. They found it and are waiting for you to appear. Now! Tell me I was right!"

Jay grinned and nodded his head granting her the reality check mark.

Rosa wasn't certain she should approach the two men. If there was a lookout bulletin for the two of them, approaching the two men could be devastating. She told Jay to go ahead and find an alternate way into the hotel and she would keep watch on the two men. If necessary, she would chance an encounter to get him back out safely. Jay left and Rosa became the lookout. The two men stayed at their positions without changing. Jay came back in about fifteen minutes with all his luggage and they walked back to Rosa's apartment.

Back in her apartment safely she advised Jay. "I think you should allow me to call the Varadero airport. Hire a plane and have it standby for our get-a-way."

"OK...Will they hold it without a deposit?"

"They will if I tell them how much we will pay for the service!"

Jay took off his money belt; unzipped it and pulled out large bills of U.S. dollars. He placed them in front of Rosa. "There is five thousand dollars. I'm willing to spend it all to pull this off."

Rosa stared at the bills in amazement. "OK...I'll do it. You must really hate this man Fuentes!" She immediately called to the Varadero airport to the Aerocaribbean Airlines desk. Rosa talked for nearly fifteen minutes. Jay waited for her to finish before getting the information he needed.

Rosa told Jay everything was set-up. The private charter from Varadero airport to the Jose Marti Airport would cost three hundred U.S. dollars. Jay agreed. She further told him there was an Aerocaribben Flight each Monday straight from Varadero to Cancun. If he was willing to wait until Monday, they had an opening for Monday's flight. The airlines desk also informed Rosa, they could exchange his flight ticket in Varadero for his departure from the Jose Marti Airport on the first available flight. He needed to check in with the desk when he arrived at the airport to do this. They would additionally check his baggage through to Cancun from there. He would need his tourist card to get his luggage passed through Customs. Jay understood the information and was glad.

He told Rosa, "I am banking on my tourist card to get me through Customs at both airports." He asked Rosa, "Can we leave early in the morning and allow ourselves enough time to go to the airport, check my luggage through to Cancun, and then find the charter company and pay in advance for the flight?" He wanted to make certain the charter was set-up. The get-a-way charter was most important as an option to stay ahead of any searches which might be ordered.

"What do you plan to do with Fuentes?"

"I need to buy some rope, just enough to tie him up. When I talk to him, he will understand who I am and why I came to Cuba."

"You are not going to hurt him are you?" Rosa wanted his promise to stick to that plan. She knew if Fuentes was hurt in any manner, Jay's chances of escaping Cuba would be slim to none. "You have to remember this man is very high in the military and in the Security Department. He puts people in jail and throws away the key. Don't hurt him and you may have a chance to escape unharmed."

Jay talked through his plan. "I'll make sure we separate him from all communications like you said. I will take care of his hand-held radio. I'll smash it to pieces and I'll jerk the phone out of the wall. He will have a radio in his vehicle. His car radio is instant communications with all police and law enforcement agencies throughout Cuba. It is important we disable that radio too." Jay thought for a moment. "His vehicle has an alternator which supplies AC current to the radio. The alternator only works when the engine is running. If he does get loose, he will have to use a house phone and that will be slow. He will probably go straight to his vehicle to use his car radio. We have to disable his vehicle. Do you know what a distributor cap is?"

Rosa shook her head. She had never heard of a distributor cap before. Jay started to explain.

"Under the hood on top of the engine is a piece of hardware with six wires coming out in all directions. The wires lead to the spark plugs. That is the distributor cap. Take it off, there will be spring snaps holding it on and then pull out the little mushroom shaped rotor on the inside. All you have to do is pull it off." He could see Rosa didn't know what he was talking about. "Forget it, I'll take care of that when I get there. That should buy us a little more time if we need it. Maybe enough time to get to the Varadero Airport, get on the plane, and head to the Havana airport. Remind me before we pull away. I'll pull out the rotor. That should give us about a three hour lead."

Jay was thinking fast. "One other ingredient like you suggested, we need the room opposite the 'honeymoon suite'. If we get there early enough we have a chance to get that room. Maybe we should call and reserve that room for tomorrow."

He watched Rosa. Jay sensed she was beginning to get an uneasy feeling about this. He asked. "Are you going to be OK with all this?" She only nodded. It wasn't easy to talk, now that it appeared like it would happen. She wasn't in control and it scared her. If things got out of hand they could both go to jail for life. Every detail had to go off without a hitch. That appeared impossible. "I'm not sure we want to do this. I feel trouble coming."

Jay felt her turmoil and put his arms around her. He offered words of comfort but they did little to dim her concern. Little did he know her thoughts were also about his leaving. When they went to bed, Jay held her close until both fell asleep. As he dozed off, he had a good feeling about everything, especially Rosa. She felt good in his arms as she melted into his side and slept peacefully.

The next morning Jay rose early, took a shower and shaved. This was the day. For twenty-eight years he held hatred for the perpetrators of his father's death, now it was coming to an end. He woke Rosa. She was a sound sleeper and didn't hear or feel Jay get out of bed. Jay packed his things and prepared for his departure, making certain he had his ticket, his passport and his tourist card handy. He waited while Rosa prepared herself for the day.

Once outside in the clear morning air, Rosa hailed a taxi and bargained for the full day of service. Jay didn't understand any of the words but held out a hand full of bills for Rosa to complete the transaction.

Rosa picked out several bills. "I'm only going to pay him half now and the other half later. That should be a guarantee we have the service as long as we need it."

They arrived in Varadero early. The first thing accomplished was to secure the needed room at the Pullman Hotel.

Then they drove to the Varadero airport and went straight to the Aerocaribbean Airlines desk. Jay exchanged his flight ticket for an earlier flight out of Jose Marti Airport and then checked his bags through Customs. They were tagged for a through flight to Cancun, Mexico. Next they searched for the charter flight. It was in a small office on the outside of a hangar. Jay and Rosa went in to make certain the arrangements were complete and prepaid for the charter to the Havana airport.

The next stop was to find a gift store or a fishing and bait shop to purchase some rope. They found a bait shop and purchased fifty feet of quarter inch nylon anchor rope. Every detail was complete. After the purchase Jay looked at Rosa, took a deep breath and smiled. "I think we are ready to go back to the hotel and make the phone call to Fuentes." Rosa reluctantly nodded her head.

Jay again sensed her uneasiness. "Relax, it will all be over soon!"

They returned to the hotel before noon time and were given early access to the room. Rosa made the phone call to Fuentes' office. Posing as Maria Castro, she told Fuentes' secretary to give him the message that she arrived earlier than usual and would like for him to come to the hotel as soon as possible. She hung up and looked at Jay, "I hope this works and he takes the bait. How do we want to work it?"

Jay looked at his watch. "The drive here will take him two hours. We will just have to wait it out. If he doesn't come, I promise you I will call it off." Rosa smiled her agreement.

Jay couldn't get the details off his mind. "We leave our door open, stand there holding each other, when we hear his footsteps in the hallway, clutch each other until he has his door opened. Then I will push him through the door, gain control of him and tie him up. You pull the door closed and go to the parking lot. Watch out for anything suspicious and make certain the taxi is available."

Rosa ridiculed Jay, "Shut up. Every time you talk about this, I get a lump in my stomach. I'm afraid this might not work. We should call it off!"

"We can't now. Hopefully Fuentes is already on his way."

As time neared the two-hour estimate, Jay opened the curtains slightly to watch the parking lot. He was nervous as a caged tiger. He would pace away from the curtains, walk back and forth, then return to the curtains and look out. Fuentes never appeared within the two-hour estimate and Jay got concerned.

Rosa said, "He may not come. How long do we wait for him?"

"Shit...I don't know. He has to come!" Jay's agitation was growing.

"I still think we should call it off." Rosa goaded.

"Don't keep giving me more things to worry about." He went back to the curtain to peek out. His frustration was obvious.

Finally the four-door 1955 Chevrolet pulled in. Jay got excited and pulled the curtains closed. "He's here! We're on!"

Jay nervously looked at his wristwatch, retrieved the rope and stood in the open doorway of their room. Rosa came closer as planned and Jay put his arms around her. When they heard muffled footsteps nearing in the hallway, Jay moved Rosa to his right to get a better view. He put his lips to her cheek and stared into the hallway. Fuentes appeared, looked briefly at the couple, and put the key into the lock. As he started through the doorway, Jay lunged at him forcing the sixty-year-old man through the doorway and face down onto the bed. Rosa closed the door to the 'honeymoon suite' and went straight to the parking lot as a lookout.

Jay was forceful with the man. He lay on top of Fuentes until he got his arms above his head. He gripped the man's arms together with one hand. He raised the man off the bed, pulled a chair over, and placed him on the chair. He released his arms and stood in front of him.

"I am Emanuel J. Cobb. My father's name was Emanuel J. Cobb. You tortured him to his death in North Vietnam."

The man responded. "You Meester Cobb? We look for you. We find you and put you in jail, forever."

Jay saw the hand-held radio on the floor. He picked it up and smashed it against the corner of a dresser. Looking around the room he spotted the phone next to the bed and jerked it out of the wall. "Now you can't call anyone."

The man grinned at Jay. His grin was evil, displaying disdain and hatred. He looked venomous. His stare was intimidating. He threateningly flaunted his power.

"You mullafucker. I take you apart." Fuentes tried to take control. "I not scared of you. You bastard American!"

Fuentes immediately stood up and lunged at Jay with hands outstretched going for Jay's throat. Jay reacted and quickly put his right knee directly into Fuentes' groin area. The old man bent over in pain, both hands over his *cojones*. The blow took his breath away. Dropping to his knees, then to the floor, he writhed in pain. The blow had been incapacitating. Jay waited for him to recover. He waited for minutes before the man could catch his breath and stop groaning.

"American bastard, eh!" Jay tried to be civil. Seeing the man in pain didn't bother Jay. "You killed my father, and I am going to kill you. Don't you have any remorse at all?"

Fuentes looked up at Jay. He grinned at him, still clutching his groin area. He coughed before speaking. "American's weak, not strong. We beat your ass. Mullafucker shit head!" Fuentes fearlessly continued to taunt Jay. He grinned again with even more wickedness in his evil eyes of two different colors.

Jay grabbed the man's left arm to search for the tattoo above the wrist. It was there. Without question this was the right man. Jay pulled him off the floor and positioned him back onto the chair.

Jay spoke, "Do you know Benitez Aguillar?" Jay didn't wait for an answer. "He told me who you were and where I could find you. You are the man who killed my father. I am going to kill you!"

"With what?" Fuentes continued to show no fear.

"With this rope! I am going to hang you in the bathroom so your girlfriend will find you hanging from the showerhead. Before I do, you're going to be tortured just like you did to so many POWs in North Vietnam. I am an Indian. We scalp our enemies. You are my enemy."

"You somabitch. You no have guts!" It was as if Fuentes was taunting Jay to do it. The man laughed out loud deriding his attacker. "You weak mullafucker!"

Jay wasn't intimidated. "How many other POWs did you kill in North Vietnam."

That same wretched grin reappeared. "None!" He laughed again at Jay, a boisterous laugh with sinister wickedness. Again flaunting his power not to be intimidated. "You somabitch you can't hurt me!" With his last words Fuentes reached into his shirt and from around his neck pulled out a necklace with a pewter image. All the while laughing boisterously at Jay; a villainous, victorious kind of gibe, taunting and daring action.

Jay looked at the image, astonished. That looked just like his own Thunderbird medal. Rage came to the surface and his head began to swirl. His face turned a blood red in anger. He could feel his pulse pounding at his temples. Jay put his head back and as quietly as possible made the blood curdling sound of an Indian warrior. The same sound his father taught him. Every muscle in his body became hard as steel. The adrenalin heightened his strength. He gritted his teeth together until his jaw muscles extended. The veins along the side of his neck expanded. He clinched both fists into a tight steel grip. All these reactive actions occurred in a microsecond. Seeing the image caused Jay to explode.

He reached forward and jerked the necklace clean off Fuentes' neck. He immediately turned it over. Just like his own medal, the letters EJC were deeply engraved. This was without question, his father's medal! Rage overcame his spirit and he lost all self-control.

With his clenched fist holding the medal, he drew back and hit Fuentes with all the strength he could muster knocking him clean off his chair. With his adrenalin spurred strength, he easily jerked him straight up off the floor and dropped him back into the chair. With the image still clutched tightly in his hand, he backhanded Fuentes across the face with all the strength he could bring forth. The second blow knocked him off the chair again. Jay grabbed two handfuls of his shirt and jerked him back onto the chair.

His teeth covered in blood, Fuentes laughed at him. "You American fool. I put you in jail forever!" This power crazy, barbaric monster wasn't going to relent.

Jay didn't take the comments lightly. It felt good to put his fist into the man's face. His rage was insistent he continue. He used his left fist against Fuentes' right jaw. His head swiveled but Fuentes never fell off the chair. Jay sorely wished he had a fan belt to use it on him just as he had on many others. He would like to make him suffer through a few good whacks across the face. Instead Jay grabbed the man by his ears, pulled his head down and brought his right knee square into his face. Blood splattered from his nose and bloody streams oozed into his mouth.

His rage somewhat subsiding, Jay took out his pocketknife and cut a couple lengths of rope. He tied the man's hands behind his back with one piece and bound his feet together with the other. He wasn't finished. Remembering the haircut Rosa gave to Pardo, Jay decided to do the same thing to Fuentes, but let him think he was being scalped.

Once he had him secure, Jay walked into the bathroom searching for a shaver or a razor blade. When he came back his hands were shaking but he had a shaver and a straight edged razor.

"Say your last words! You are going to lose your scalp!" Jay used the straight edged razor and began dry shaving Fuentes' scalp. The shave wasn't going well. Fuentes jerked his head to the side. The straight edged razor dug into his scalp. It started to bleed. There was a good amount of blood. It filtered through his hairline over his forehead into his eyebrows and eyes. Obviously Fuentes believed he was being scalped because he started yelling. Jay quickly stuffed his handkerchief into his mouth to muffle the noise. He took a pillowcase from the bed and using his knife ripped a strip for the gag. He tied the strip of cloth around Fuentes' head over the handkerchief in his mouth. "Now scream you bastard. I know this is going to hurt. Try yelling now you son-of-a-bitch, your scalp is coming off. It will be over in one slash of the blade." By now blood engulfed Fuentes entire head.

Feeling the blood streaming down his face and the back of his neck, Fuentes began to shake anticipating the excruciating pain. His fear became uncontrollable. He tried to yell against the gag. His eyes displayed stark terror. He started shaking his head back and forth to hamper Jay's efforts. Jay's confidence soared, he had him fooled. This was putting real fear into the man and he relished in it.

Jay grabbed a handful of his remaining hair and tugged hard at the man's scalp, jerking his head around. Fuentes began straining at his bindings. The muffled yells turned into moans of crying. His breathing became labored. Abruptly and without warning he passed out from pure exhaustion.

With a smile on his face, Jay took this opportunity to shave Fuentes' head into a Mohawk haircut. He felt that would be poetic justice. This partial head shave took about five minutes to complete. Jay looked at it and was pleased with his artwork.

Fuentes regained consciousness. His eyes were glazed over and a distant stare froze his eyes. With blood still flowing down his face and seeing all the hair on the floor, Fuentes truly believed he had been scalped and knew he was dying. He started whimpering.

Jay took another length of rope and tied the man's arms together behind his back at the elbows. He dragged him into the shower and trussed him to the showerhead by his elbows. He pulled him up high enough that he could only touch the shower floor by standing on his toes. The same way Fuentes did to POWs. Jay knew it would cause real pain. Pain that would never be forgotten. Jay took the opportunity to clean himself up. He washed the blood and hair off his hands. Using a towel he wiped a few small blood splatters off his pant's leg.

Jay turned to walk away leaving the old man hanging by his elbows from the showerhead. Before walking through the bathroom door, he turned around to offer a final comment. "I'm weak...huh?"

Jay looked at his watch. This entire episode had taken only seventeen minutes. He walked out the door looking for Rosa. She was waiting in the parking lot next to their taxi.

Jay was still shaking from his ordeal with Fuentes. He opened the hood to the Chevrolet and quickly pulled out the distributor rotor. He pushed Rosa into the waiting taxi. "We've got to leave right now. Tell the driver to hurry!"

Rosa stared at him with a puzzled look. His face was red, his eyes were red and his hands were quivering uncontrollably. She knew things didn't go well but was afraid to ask. Rosa gave the driver instructions to hurry to the airport. During the drive she tried to ask Jay about what happened. For the thirty-minute drive, he would only shake his head to ward off talking about it. He was only slightly calmer when they arrived at the airport. They went straight to the charter operations office.

By the time they reached the office, he was a little more settled and able to speak a few words. He allowed Rosa to take enough bills from his hand to pay for the taxi plus a generous tip.

The flight to Jose Marti Airport outside Havana took only twenty minutes. On arrival Jay and Rosa went to the Aerocaribbean Airline desk which was in terminal #3 on the north west side of the Airport. He checked his ticket and the flight schedules to notice how long he would have to wait for the next flight out. There was a three-hour wait. He took Rosa to the restaurant. Neither had eaten since breakfast. Jay barely ate anything.

Rosa continued to goad Jay until he began to talk.

Jay spoke, "I wasn't going to hurt him. I put up with his mouth. I told him who I was. He scoffed at me and taunted me. Even after he tried to physically attack me, I decided to tie him up and leave him sitting there in the chair. But then Fuentes pulled out this medal," Jay took it out of his pocket and showed it to Rosa. She held the necklace with the pewter image dangling. She immediately recognized it was identical to the one Jay always wore. He told her to turn it over and look at the back. She observed the letters EJC engraved on the back. Jay reached inside his shirt collar and pulled out his medal. He leaned toward her, "Look at the back of mine!"

She exclaimed. "Oh my God! They are identical. This was your father's medal!"

Jay nodded his head. "That's when I lost it. I saw that medal and I went berserk." Jay paused and held his own medal to his lips. Then he held the two together. "This one belonged to my father." Jay held it in his fingers and stared at it. "They were identical. When I realized Fuentes was wearing my father's medal, I went crazy! I mean I lost it big time! I couldn't hold myself back. I didn't care that he was an old man. It didn't matter to me." Jay stopped talking while he tried to quell his seething anger. "That guy deserves to be taken off this earth but I didn't do it. I hurt him pretty bad and he deserved it." Jay wasn't remorseful but somewhat disturbed with himself and what he did. Jay found a dark side of himself he didn't know existed and he didn't like the view.

Holding his father's medal in his hand, Jay knew it was proof beyond any doubt, his father was gone forever. Letting his Mom see and hold it in her hands should offer some comfort to her. It would bring back old memories, but it would also bring closure. For that reason alone his trip was not in vain.

Finishing their coffee, Rosa spotted some gray uniformed policeman, many more than normal. They were scurrying through the terminal. She had a disturbing feeling they were searching for Jay. She alerted Jay and they departed. Jay went ahead and completed the Customs check-thru and walked through the departure gate. With so many policemen evident he had to rush. Jay and Rosa barely had time to say their goodbyes appropriately.

Rosa continued to watch after Jay's welfare. She saw another carload of policemen unload at the arrival check-in area. She told Jay to go through the gate to the flight line and hide among the ground support vehicles. Jay took her advice and walked to the flight line. He looked at his watch. There was still two hours remaining before his flight. He knew he had to hide well. He found a baggage cart and sat on the side away from the terminal out of sight. Rosa sitting in the lounge continued to watch Jay and make sure she knew where he was at all times.

Rosa was startled when she was tapped on the back of the shoulder. She jerked around quickly. It was her contact, Carlos Rodriquez. She was relieved to see it was him. He spoke quietly but emphatically.

"They are searching for you and Cobb. You better leave now."

"Why, I had nothing to do with Fuentes. He never saw me at all."

Carlos answered. "This isn't about Fuentes. It's about Raphael Pardo. He died last night. Fuentes already had Cobb's name and we were looking for him. The travel guide, Triana Travis linked you with him, and the bartender in Majagua identified you. You have to lay low and plan on leaving the country immediately. They have already alerted the entire police force, and it wasn't Fuentes who ordered it. Nobody knows where Fuentes is." Carlos caught the import of Rosa's comments. "And what about Fuentes, did you two do something to him too?"

Rosa acknowledged with a nod of the head.

"What did you do?"

"I don't really know. I wasn't there. But I'm sure Cobb didn't go easy on him."

Carlos spoke emphatically. "You better leave and don't waste any time doing it. Don't go back to your apartment. They will be waiting for you at your apartment gate for you to show up. I'll take care of your belongings when it's safe. The trail to Cobb has been established. It will only be a short time before he's arrested." His final remark. "Don't waste any more time. Leave now!" He gave her a departing nod of the head and winked. He walked away.

Rosa couldn't think straight. She was totally surprised. How did they connect us together? We were very discreet not to allow ourselves to be identified. Following Carlos' instructions she casually looked around to observe the crowd, then got out of her seat. Trying not to draw attention she walked slowly through the departure gate toward the flight line. She knew where Jay was and went directly to the baggage cart.

Jay was surprised to see her. The startled look on her face told the full story. There was trouble! Jay had never before witnessed any fear coming from Rosa. She grabbed for his hand to pull him up from his seated position.

"Come on...We've got to leave fast!" She quickly gazed around the area for an escape route. There was a vehicle drive-thru gate off to the right of their position about sixty yards away. "Let's head for that gate. Walk slowly and don't draw any attention. Put your arms around me and let's just stroll nonchalantly through that gate."

Jay didn't answer. He knew there was big trouble working against them. He did as he was told without questioning her motives. He knew Rosa well enough to know she had a good reason. Whatever it was putting fear into her, had to be big. Her fear was contagious. Jay became fearful. The two strolled slowly across the sixty yards to the open gate. It seemed like an eternity.

CHAPTER XIII

Passing through the open gate, Rosa looked around. They needed a taxi fast. The taxis were all lined up in front of the terminal waiting their turn for a fare. She knew they should walk in the opposite direction. She turned to Jay. "Let's just keep walking. When we pass outside the terminal area then we can speed up and hustle as fast as we can."

Jay followed Rosa's lead. He was puzzled over what was happening. He kept his right arm around Rosa's waist as they walked faster and faster. "What's going on. Are they looking for me?"

"No! They are looking for us. They are looking for me too."

"Why? Fuentes never saw you. I made sure you were always out of the picture so they wouldn't come for you."

"It isn't about Fuentes. It's about Pardo. He died in the hospital last night."

"Holy shit! I am sorry as hell Rosa. I didn't want this to affect you."

"It's too late now Jay. They apparently put the pieces together and tied me to that incident. That tour guide of yours, Triana Travis, was the one who fingered me. And the bartender in Majagua, he identified me also. Now they are searching for both of us. Let's keep walking and looking for a taxi."

They went in the opposite direction away from town traffic. A Police vehicle with four officers inside drove by at a high rate of speed. Jay and Rosa hurriedly rushed down a small path away from the highway. They cautiously watched to see if the vehicle turned around. It didn't, but it heightened their fear.

Rosa knew the punishment which was certain to come if they were caught. Her shortness of breath came as much from fear as from their fast pace. The urgency of their escape forced their blood pressure to soar, their breath to become labored and feeling a slight amount of dizziness all at the same time. Seeing Rosa's fear caused Jay's to escalate. He was physically in excellent shape but this taxed his body beyond normal limits. He could see himself becoming a prisoner in a system touted as inhumane and one from which he would never return. His thoughts flashed to Penny and his Mom. Would he ever have the chance to have his own children and grandchildren. Seeing his life coming to an end was a definite reality. His fear grew moment by moment.

They walked for nearly a mile before seeing another taxi. Rosa flagged it down. They entered the taxi. *"Vedado, por favor.* It will take us about thirty minutes to get into town. What do you think we should do now?" Rosa asked.

Jay answered. "Find out first if the driver speaks any English."

Rosa queried. *"Habla usted ingles?"*

The driver shook his head no to the inquiry.

Jay understood and spoke freely. "I think you should tell the driver you will direct him where to go. That will give us some time to calm down and think. At least we will be out of sight."

"OK!" Rosa quickly instructed the driver. She wanted to go further away from town and told him to go to Marina Hemingway near Barlovento, fifteen miles west of Havana. It was an active boating area for yachts arriving in Cuba. She didn't know for certain but there could be a waterfront alert out for them as well. She told Jay there was a harbormaster located there and it might be a good idea to find out if the harbor areas had also been alerted to watch for them. As they drove toward Marina Hemingway, Rosa asked Jay if there was anything in his luggage he couldn't live without.

"No! It doesn't matter now, my luggage is headed for Cancun, Mexico. To answer your question, I am assuming you might be concerned about me leaving something behind which could be traced. I don't know of anything left behind that could be traceable. The tour group is certainly a deadfall for us. If the tour group has already fingered us, those goons will most likely go back for more information. I have my passport, my tourist card, and my plane ticket. I guess my plane ticket will be useless now. That is where they will look first. If you have another thought lets hear it. Whatever you are thinking, let's do it. I am out of options."

"Good! I'm thinking we keep driving down highway 2.1.3 all the way to Mariel. It's about another forty miles. We can go find Uncle Julio and get him to take us out of here as soon as possible. We have to leave everything behind and never look back. I can't begin to imagine what might happen to us if we are caught. I'm sure Fuentes will have us locked up and throw away the key." She paused momentarily waiting for Jay to answer then interrupted. "Do you want to go to Mariel and take that chance? As I see it, we don't have a choice. Is that OK?"

"Are you kidding, of course it's OK. Can Uncle Julio get us safely out of Cuba?"

"If anybody can, he's the one!" Rosa comforted.

"Can he take us all the way to Key West?" Jay asked. "I'm not sure I can pull enough strings to get you into the U.S. but I assure you, I will do everything in my power to do that." Jay felt the full weight of her involvement directly on his shoulders and began to feel very badly about her status. "I'll replace anything you will lose if you don't go back."

"Hell, there is no question about that now. I can't go back!"

Rosa again instructed the driver to continue to Mariel. She leaned back to rest fully realizing this might be their last chance to get out of the country. Both were breathing heavily not certain what to expect next. Calming down was difficult. Many times she goaded the driver to hurry, "*Tener prisa, rapido!*"

This particular taxi wasn't the best transportation available. It was slow and used a lot of oil. The driver stopped for gas and Jay paid for the fill up. About half way to Mariel, the taxi completely overheated and came to a sudden stop. They hoped another taxi would come by. This area wasn't the place where taxis had regular fares. Not one taxi came by. Jay and Rosa successfully flagged down an old pick-up truck. When Jay flashed some U.S. dollars the truck driver was more than happy to accommodate the two. It was a small, old Japanese built truck. The seats were worn through from too many years of use, but the engine ran well.

The ride to Mariel was uncomfortable. They were stuffed three wide in a two-person seat. That didn't matter to either of them. It was too important to get there as soon as possible. The drive was taking too long and their fear escalated. The urgency in leaving the country before the ports closed was building. The necessity of finding Uncle Julio quickly was imperative. Being on the go since early morning and encountering all the problems, both were on a nervous high. They badly needed rest but leaving Cuba had to take priority.

Arriving in Mariel, Rosa excitedly directed the truck driver through each turn to the docks. When they got out of the vehicle, Jay paid the driver. Knowing transportation might still be needed, Jay wanted Rosa to ask the driver if he could wait a few minutes. At least until they had a chance to talk with Uncle Julio. Rosa relayed the message. The driver agreed to wait. They ran quickly toward Uncle Julio's boat. She called for him, but no answer. Rosa searched the boat for Uncle Julio. He wasn't on the boat. Rosa went back to the deck and surveyed the entire dock area. There were at least two dozen boats and each with a flurry of activity recovering from a day of fishing. But no Julio.

One of the nearby fishermen working on his boat told them Julio was in town but should be back any moment. They should wait. Knowing Julio would return, she released the truck driver. They walked onto the deck of the boat, found some chairs inside the wheelhouse, pulled them onto the deck and tried to wait patiently. Both were extremely nervous.

Rosa spoke first. "Tell me exactly what happened between you and Fuentes. Everything! Did you hurt him bad?"

Jay spoke freely and didn't leave out any detail. When he finished, he apologized. "That was the first time I have ever lost control of myself. I exploded and couldn't hold myself back. It was like twenty-eight years of hatred all came out at once. I wasn't thinking. I was just swinging and swinging and swinging, hard. I got even with that son-of-a-bitch and am glad I did." He paused. "I am so sorry I dragged you into this mess. Now I have ruined your life as well." He was shaking his head slowly back and forth and watching his feet, drowing in his own terrible disgust.

Rosa answered cheerfully, "I'm not sorry at all. I met you and I am glad and proud of that. We just have to leave as soon as we can." She mellowed slightly. "I wish you weren't married. I'm only sorry you are already taken. We could have a nice life together." She reached for his hand. Jay allowed the moment to continue and liked it more than he wanted to admit. He truly had feelings for Rosa. Now that she was going to the States, their separation might not be the last time he would see her.

The dust being stirred down the unpaved road by an oncoming vehicle, got their attention. Their first reaction was to hide. They immediately got up from the chairs and walked inside the wheel house not certain who was headed their way. Fortunately, it was Uncle Julio.

As soon as Julio saw Rosa he yelled at her in his own happy, outgoing style. *"Rosalito...mi sensational sobrina."* He ran toward his boat. They met on the gangplank and he gave her a big hug and swung her off her feet. Once again he was as happy as he could be seeing her. He went into a fever of fast-tongue Spanish that only Rosa could understand. Jay knew it was all good.

Rosa took Uncle Julio's hands in hers and became very serious. Jay knew she was telling Julio about their plight. Uncle Julio kept nodding his head up and down with every remark. The happy smile never left his face. He appeared more than eager to help. Jay was glad to see that Uncle Julio didn't object to anything Rosa had to say.

She turned to Jay. "He will need about seven hundred gallons of diesel fuel."

"That's OK. No problem. I'll pay for it. Does he think he can help us? When can he leave?"

Rosa turned toward Uncle Julio and spoke a few more words. He nodded his head in agreement. Jay instinctively knew Uncle Julio would do anything to help Rosa.

Julio spoke. *"Inmediatamente!"* Departure would take place immediately.

Uncle Julio began scurrying around to ready his boat. He walked to the next boat over and hired a deck hand to go along. The engine was started and allowed a few minutes to warm then the deck hand cast off the mooring lines. Uncle Julio eased his boat away from the dock and expertly moved it to the fuel pumps at the end of the dock.

Uncle Julio grabbed Rosa's hand to get her attention. He told her the fueling would take approximately thirty minutes and she and Jay should go into the ship's store and buy a few things to eat. She and Jay promptly left. Julio took on seven hundred gallons and filled his water tanks. Rosa and Jay returned with an armload of anything tasty they could find. Uncle Julio opened his log, set in the date and time. He ordered the deck hand to cast off the lines; he was moving away. Soon they were on their way outside the harbor.

Uncle Julio stopped at every boat along the docks and shouted something to the Captain of each boat. Each boat Captain responded with a loud...*Si!*

Jay wanted to know what that was all about. Rosa explained Uncle Julio solicited the help of each boat Captain. The boat Captains, Julio's long time friends, would follow them out of the harbor until they reached the three mile limit then they would screen Uncle Julio's boat by getting in the way of the fast boats should they appear. They could impede the chase.

Jay watched this unplanned but well orchestrated show of support. As they passed each boat along the docks the Captain would start his engines and pull out behind the *Caliente Mujer* as if marshalling for a parade. When they reached the mouth of the harbor there were nine boats trailing behind Uncle Julio, an impromptu flotilla.

Exiting the harbor Rosa and Jay cheered knowing they had escaped the possibility of confinement. Uncle Julio joined in and they all yelled in unison laughing and grinning at each other. A great sense of relief came over the two as the bow of the boat cut freely through the waters. Uncle Julio headed his boat due north seeking partial protection against being stopped by hurriedly reaching the three-mile limit and international waters. The trailing boats began a scatter pattern moving to the east of Julio's heading to stay between Julio and any fast boats that might come out of Marina Hemingway. Jay confirmed with Rosa, it was Uncle Julio and the *Caliente Mujer* which took the very first boat load of refugees out of Mariel to Key West. Four out of the nine Captains now following Julio used these same tactics for similar escapes in 1980. They knew what to do without being told. It was successful then and could be successful now sixteen years later.

Jay believed this show of effort was a great testament to the character and friendship of Uncle Julio. If nine boat Captains were willing to sacrifice themselves for Uncle Julio without asking any questions, they were without doubt the best friends in the world. Jay knew he didn't have any friends like these.

Uncle Julio was warned by one of his friends with radar that two returns were spotted coming out of Marina Hemingway area headed straight in their direction and were moving fast. Customs and law enforcement had fast moving power boats docked at Marina Hemingway which were used for drug intercepts. He couldn't be certain but they could be chasing the *Caliente Mujer*. Uncle Julio informed Rosa. She was upset by the information and told Jay. Both became distraught knowing they still might get stopped. The three-mile limit didn't matter when a crime or a security breach was being pursued. But with nine of Julio's friends screening and impeding the chase they just might escape.

Nightfall was nearing and soon it would be dark. Uncle Julio had an idea. Once out into the open sea and beyond the three-mile limit he would set the boat on a westerly course, straight into the last remnants of a beautiful sunset. If his friends weren't successful in stopping the chase he believed they still had a chance. He explained to Rosa, by taking a westerly course they would also be placing the powerboats directly on the stern. It would take longer and more fuel for the powerboats to close the distance.

Uncle Julio spoke to Rosa rather excitedly in Spanish. She grabbed Jay by the arm and pulled him out of the wheelhouse around the gunwales on the port side to the stern of the boat. As she looked off the stern into the dark distant horizon she told Jay what Uncle Julio planned. They had to watch for any signs of light off in the distance. The two power boats were about fifteen miles to the stern. The powerboats sat low in the water but had powerful forward searching spotlights. If she could see any light coming from that direction, the powerboats would be gaining on them. Then they might have to take a different action. Uncle Julio turned off his running lights and his cabin lights; anything to make them more difficult to locate. The nine boats in the screening flotilla were now out of sight.

Jay and Rosa watched through the darkness for about ten minutes when they started seeing lights to the stern. Rosa walked quickly to the wheelhouse to tell Uncle Julio while Jay stayed on 'watch'. She returned with some profound questions.

She passed them to Jay. "Uncle Julio wanted to know how serious we were about escaping. I told him we were very serious. He then wanted to know if we were serious enough to engage in a gunfight if we had to. I told him I was. How do you feel?" She waited for Jay's answer.

"You mean like a gun battle?"

"Exactly! That is exactly what I mean!"

"What is the alternative?" Jay wanted to know.

"Life in jail and they don't parole anyone!" She responded emphatically.

"Then hell yes. I am real serious. What does he want us to do?"

"He will open the arms vault and give us an M-16 and a twelve gage shotgun. If they get too close we might have to shoot our way out."

Jay was dumbfounded. He nodded slowly while considering the circumstances. Nothing had prepared him for this. Taking up arms against another person was unthinkable.

Then he thought about spending the rest of his life in a Cuban prison. The survivor instinct took over and with profound determination he reaffirmed to Rosa, "Yes...I'm ready to do it!" He turned to watch the lights on the horizon and could see they were getting even more discernable. No question, the powerboats were closing the gap.

"What about Julio? If we do any shooting he will never be able to return to Cuba either."

"He's with us. He said whatever we want is what he'll do."

Rosa and Jay returned to the wheelhouse to advise Uncle Julio of the latest. Uncle Julio gave them the key to the arms vault. They took out weapons. Rosa gave brief instructions to Jay on the M-16 and they returned to the stern to maintain a vigil for the fast boats.

The lights began to get bigger and bigger. The powerboats were closing. Rosa rushed into the wheelhouse to give Uncle Julio an update. He tried to calm her down by further explaining distance was on their side. The powerboats had two huge engines and fuel consumption reduced their distance of no return to a thirty-mile radius. His boat, the *Caliente Mujer*, was already twenty-five miles out of Mariel. That would place the powerboats beyond return range. He felt for certain the powerboats would be required to turn around soon. If the authorities watching, controlling, and patrolling Cuban waters didn't call off the chase, the captain of the boats certainly would. Rosa returned to the stern to tell Jay. The oncoming lights were very bright and a halo was visible around the glaring spotlight, indicating they were way too close.

Jay pulled back the bolt on the M-16 placing a round in the firing chamber. Rosa fiercely pulled back the pump handle on the shotgun and slammed a load of twelve gage double '00' buck shot forward. Both were ready for the consequences. They waited watching for the bow waves to become visible announcing the ultimate closeness. This would be the final moment of truth, now or never! They waited, holding their breath out of total fear. Neither wanted what might come next.

They watched the lights become extremely bright and knew the boats were within minutes of boarding. Suddenly the bright lights of both boats swung off to the left and continued in a 180-degree turn. Both held their breath and waited silently. Then the lights were turned off. They stared into the night as the two boats disappeared into the darkness. Both were emotionally drained and every muscle in their bodies was weak from stress. It was over. Rosa rushed forward to tell Uncle Julio while Jay continued his lookout in disbelief. As Uncle Julio had predicted the chase boats turned around and headed back to Marina Hemingway. Rosa returned to the stern. The relief she witnessed on Jay's face was textbook. His head dropped, he closed his eyes for a moment of silence and his mouth opened for more air. Rosa was equally relieved. Both were between shouting, jumping for joy and crying. They held onto each other like their execution had been stopped by a last minute reprieve.

Uncle Julio would have to sneak back into harbor and he better have a very good alibi when he returned. Julio had a trump card. It was all his friends back in Mariel. When he returned he knew they would meet him at sea and usher him in. He might get away with his odyssey. Without doubt he could be questioned thoroughly by Customs and someone from the Department of Security.

After five hours and fifty miles due west, the boat was placed on a northeasterly course for the Florida Keys. He told Rosa and Jay, "Maybe nine hours, we be in Florida!"

Jay knew his journey was coming to an end and the last scare put his feelings in turmoil. He took Rosa by the hand and walked out to the front deck to allow the night air and the salty spray to clear his mind. He was more than fond of Rosa and knew all this was coming to an end. He didn't like the idea of never seeing her again. Anytime he thought about it, he squeezed her hand. She knew what he was feeling. She was feeling the same way. They had endured a lot together.

Leaving Cuba might allow her to see Jay again. For that reason, she wasn't sorry. But to leave her beautiful and beloved country was more than she could take. Anytime she thought about leaving, tears welled up in her eyes. There was no comfort in thinking about the circumstances. Both blocked the inevitable from their minds.

They stood in the wind for nearly a full hour before moving back inside. There was something therapeutic about the sea and the salt spray. The quiet, undisturbed peacefulness of the sea had wondrous curing powers. Exactly that same driving force caused many people take up a life on the water. Rosa's Uncle Julio was one of those. His life was tied to the sea and the peacefulness it brought.

When they entered the wheelhouse, Uncle Julio told them both to go below and get some rest. He further advised that nothing would happen for at least the next eight hours. They gladly took his suggestion and went below to the crew quarters.

After seven hours of plying through the waters on a course of zero-two-zero degrees on autopilot, the single side band radio barked out a message.

"This is the United States Coast Guard, ship sailing the Florida Straits approximately twenty-eight miles south west of Florida Keys, identify yourself and your purpose."

Uncle Julio responded. "*Caliente Mujer*, Cuban registry, is twenty-seven miles south west of Florida Keys with four persons on board, two Cuban nationals and two American citizens. Estimate time of arrival in two hours. Two American citizens want to come ashore. We have no contraband. You are welcomed to board."

"Be advised, the U.S. Coast Guard vessel Point Largo will intercept in two hours. Maintain present course."

Uncle Julio acknowledged. He went below to awaken his two weary passengers and give them the news.

Rosa looked at Jay who was now the one who couldn't wake up. "We've made it. We should be on a Coast Guard vessel within two hours."

Jay stood up, still groggy. "Thank God! Two more hours and we've made it!" It was early morning and the sun wouldn't break the horizon for another hour. Rosa went into the galley to make coffee. She yelled at Uncle Julio. "Where's the coffee?"

He knew she wouldn't be able to find it. He came below to show its location. The autopilot was keeping the ship on course, so Uncle Julio stayed below to help finish making the coffee and to get the first cup for himself. Jay and Rosa poured themselves a cup and went topside. Feeling relieved from their all-day emotional roller coaster, they needed to be alone with each other.

Jay spoke. "What will you do now?"

"I don't know. I'll probably go to Virginia, maybe marry and have a house full of kids one day. What will you do?"

"I'll go back to Oklahoma and forever dream about you."

Rosa answered. "OK, I'll take that as a compliment! What will you really do. Do you think your trip was a real success?"

"I wish I knew. Right now my mind is totally bogged down. It went in total overload back at the airport. I have all sorts of thoughts. Did I truly kill Pardo?" Jay paused. "If I did, I didn't intend to! What will happen to Fuentes? Where will you be in the future? Will I ever see you again? All those kinds of thoughts are running through my small brain."

Jay looked away from Rosa then spoke in a cautious manner. "My wife's name is Penny. I can't wait to see her. She's a great person and I really do love her. Meeting you has really muddied those waters for me. I have never felt for anyone, other than my wife, the way I feel about you right now. It's a weird kind of fascinating magnetism, maybe even an infatuation. I don't know! How can anyone be in love with two women at the same time? You have constantly been on my mind and I don't want our relationship to end. You are so real and such a great person too!" Jay was sincere in his admission. There was a sense of sadness in his voice.

Rosa spoke up with an unexpected cheerfulness. "This was all part of the game. I got you through this, now you can go back, have a family and get your life back."

"I feel so sad. I think I have ruined your life. Because of me you have to leave Cuba. The country you love so much. I won't ever get over that. And Uncle Julio was willing to give up his boat and life for me. How can I ever repay either of you?"

"Don't worry about it. Life will be better for all of us."

Jay wanted more endearing words of affection, not sterile words without feelings. He tried in vain to search her mind. "How do you feel about me?"

Rosa was searching for an answer when they were interrupted by a ship off in the distance. There was a sweeping search light to the northeast on the distant horizon. Jay knew it was the Coast Guard vessel. His time with Rosa was truly coming to an end. The vessel came closer and closer. Jay could hear Uncle Julio trimming down the engines and becoming dead in the water. The Coast Guard vessel came along side and a loud speaker barked out, "Request permission to come aboard."

Uncle Julio flashed his lights granting them boarding approval. Soon a launch was in the water with six men on board, all with side arms. They came aboard and interviewed the two passengers. Jay had his passport and tourist card. Rosa had nothing.

The Lieutenant spoke to Julio. "We've been watching you ever since you left Mariel. Did you know you had two fast boats trying to catch you?"

Julio nodded. "Yes, I know! Maybe after us. Don't know. "

"Are you folks escaping or something?" The Lieutenant asked.

Purposely not waiting for an answer, the Coast Guard Lieutenant took charge of the interview. Since Rosa had no ID he asked her to write down her full name. She readily complied. He then used the ship's radio to talk with his mother ship. While on the radio he gave their names and what credentials they possessed. The information was passed along to the shore communications and operations shack. They in turn, passed it along to proper authorities. The boarding party inspected the ship for contraband. There was none.

It was more than twenty minutes before a return communication was received from shore-based operations. Jay was asked to provide a contact name and phone number. Rosa was also asked to give a contact name and a phone number.

Jay searched his mind for the name of the FBI Agent in Miami. The name eventually came to him. Jay asked them to contact FBI Agent Sam Bascom at the local number for the FBI. Jay knew his acceptance and approval would be forthcoming. He feared Rosa would be detained. Rosa gave them a memorized toll free number and asked them to call that number.

The shore based communications called both numbers to check for credential credibility. The FBI number had to be forwarded to Sam Bascom in his residence. He authorized entry approval for Emanuel J. Cobb. The toll free number Rosa gave the Lieutenant surprised everyone including Jay, when the query came back asking for her code name.

Rosa spoke, "Cobra. My code name is Cobra." The code name was passed to the toll free number in Langley, Virginia. Her approval was nearly instantaneous. Both were approved for entry. The CIA would send someone to bring her in.

Jay watched all the information passing back and forth and couldn't believe what he heard. Rosa was a government agent of some sort. He looked at her in disbelief. His bewilderment grew. He had a million questions he needed to ask. Circumstances made it impossible.

He watched as Rosa started saying her goodbyes to Uncle Julio. Since Jay was nearby, Rosa spoke in English so Jay could understand the conversation.

"This may be the last time I see you Uncle Julio. I may never come back to Cuba again. But I will try. Maybe my Dad and I can meet you half way some day and visit." She had tears of sadness in her eyes.

"OK. *Mi maravillosa sobrina.* I hope we can visit. Tell my brother I miss him." Julio had a few tears filling his eyes. His show of affection was real. The tears highlighted the affection he had for Rosa.

Their tears of sadness continued as they hugged each other. Uncle Julio nearly broke down. Rosa was crying as well. Uncle Julio told Rosa to give his little brother a big hug. After the goodbyes, Jay took a hand full of money and gave it all to Julio. He was more than grateful and he tried as best he could to let him know it.

Jay and Rosa turned away and boarded the launch for motoring to the Point Largo. They were both greeted by the Captain of the ship and sent below to the galley to await their arrival at the Key West Coast Guard Station.

After two and a half hours the Point Largo pulled along dockside in Key West. Both Jay and Rosa had to wait for a helicopter dispatched for their pick-up. While they were waiting on the dock, Jay again began to ask a myriad of questions. They were standing on the dock alone. He had the privacy to seriously probe Rosa for personal questions.

"Are you an agent of some sort?"

Rosa answered. "Yes, I worked in Havana undercover for the CIA. What you and I did blew the hell out of my cover. I know I'll be assigned to Langley for a while. Maybe after this recent encounter blows over I might stand a chance to be reassigned back to Cuba. My Mom and Dad live here in Miami. I'll stay with them for a while. I haven't seen them for nearly four years. They will be thrilled."

Rosa asked. "What will you do?"

Jay pulled the Indian Thunderbird medal from his pocket, held it up with the index finger of his left hand. "I am going to have a son, and I am going to place this around his neck and tell him all about his grandfather. My Dad's medal will also be the indisputable positive proof to Mom that my Dad is dead."

Jay reached inside his collar and displayed his own identical medal. "Then I am going to have a second son and place my medal on his neck and tell him all about the crying blood that I avenged in Cuba."

He looked at Rosa. She looked puzzled. Jay asked, "Didn't I tell you about my heritage?"

"I remember about the three interrogators you wanted to find. I don't remember about your heritage." She shrugged her shoulders.

"I am Cherokee Indian. Indian lore says that when family blood is spilled, it is crying blood. Then it is appropriate to seek revenge and it is the responsibility of the first born to avenge the crying blood.

"The U.S. Government claims it didn't know the names of those three Cuban interrogators. I found the names and I went for my family's revenge. These two medals prove it. When my Dad went to South East Asia, he had these two medals made, custom made for the two of us. He wore one and sent me mine. I still have the letter he wrote to me when he sent it. He asked me to be the man of the house and take care of my Mom. I have done that in every way I know how. That is why I went berserk when I saw Dad's medal around Fuentes' neck. I truly lost it. What I did, wasn't like me at all. I'm not a violent person. But that man jeering at me and taunting me with my Dad's medal, brought on a flood of hatred. I couldn't control myself!" Jay looked directly at Rosa for understanding. He needed her approval.

Rosa's eyes met Jay's. Her face signaled understanding. Verbalizing it was impossible. She had an overwhelming urge to go to Jay, grab him in her arms and never let go. It was an urge practicality had to overrule. Her trained, stoic, business like temperament came forth. She could only offer a glimmer of a sympathetic smile.

A helicopter from the U.S. Department of Customs approached, it set down on the dock beside the Point Largo. The downdraft from the copter sent sand and gravel flying in all directions. Both Rosa and Jay closed their eyes until the rotor generated hurricane subsided. Agent Sam Bascom stepped down from the doorway and greeted Jay and Rosa.

He looked at Rosa and asked, "Cobra?"

She nodded in the affirmative.

Bascom turned to Jay. "What the hell...were you doing in Cuba? I got some reports about you arriving in Cuba and couldn't believe it. How the hell did you get there?" Agent Bascom was rather chilling in his questions. "Now...am I going to get more reports about what went on down there? Things I should know about?"

Jay answered, "I don't know what you might hear." He looked at Rosa as he spoke and offered a wry grin. She smiled back and shrugged her shoulders knowing the results of their escapades would soon be general knowledge in all the Miami newspapers.

Agent Bascom was ordered from CIA Headquarters in Langley, Virginia, to bring in Cobra. He motioned for Rosa to board the helicopter. Agent Bascom and Rosa had a quiet but brief conversation once she was settled in the copter. The Custom's Officer looked over Jay's passport, his tourist card and then motioned for him to get on board too. This was official government business and normally civilians were not permitted to ride in government aircraft without signing waivers. Under the circumstances, even though Jay Cobb was a civilian, the requirement to sign a waiver was overlooked. The copter lifted off for Miami with everyone on board.

Thirty-five minutes later the copter landed at the Opalocka Airport on the Custom's heliport. Jay exited first and helped Rosa out of the copter. Agent Bascom pointed out his car to Rosa. Because the two shared this yet to be revealed ordeal, Agent Bascom told them to take as much time as they needed to say their goodbyes.

They stared at each other, one waiting for the other to make a move. Jay wanted Rosa to reach out for him in a final embrace. Rosa also wanted a final embrace but thought better of it. They continued to stare at each other. Time stood still.

Finally, Rosa reached out her right hand as if wanting to shake his hand. Her eyes bored holes into his. A troubled, reluctant glint of a smile formed on her face.

Jay didn't understand the reason for a handshake but offered his in return. He smiled back at Rosa and waited for something to happen.

She took his hand in hers, shook his hand and said, "Jay, this is where we part!" She turned quickly and walked toward Agent Bascom's vehicle.

Jay stood motionless for a moment in total disbelief. Then he ran after her. He spun her around by an arm. He couldn't let her leave without something more. Whether she liked it or not, he wasn't going to allow her to leave without a proper goodbye. He put his arms around her and kissed her hard on the mouth.

Rosa responded to his show of affection and spoke, "Whew...that's what I wanted and I'm glad you took the initiative. I wasn't sure I should." She stared into Jay's very soul through his eyes and liked what they were telling her.

Rosa was still wearing the wrap-around skirt with the pockets. She put her hands into her pockets and spoke again. "Let's take a walk. I need to tell you the truth." She moved across the macadam surface with her head down. She appeared to be watching her feet take each step one at a time. Her mind was churning fast. Jay followed at her side.

"Jay!" She turned to face him. "Now that we are safely back in the States, I'm going to tell you some things you don't know! First off, Agent Bascom has just informed me that Benitez Aguillar has disappeared. He probably left the U.S. thanks to you! Secondly, remember those two men you dealt with in Customs when you first arrived. The taller and older one was Carlos Rodriquez. He is undercover in Cuba for the CIA also. He has been there longer than I have. He was sent there specifically to find out if any American POWs were sent to Cuba from North Vietnam. He has been through forty-seven of the ninety-eight prisons in Cuba and hasn't found any indications that American POWs are in Cuban prisons. When you feel a need to gripe about your government not caring, you should think twice before you speak." Rosa paused and moved a pebble around with her foot, deep in thought. Then she looked up at Jay.

"You were never in a threatened position. Carlos picked you up first then handed you off to me. What we did, you and I, was a bigger thing than you could ever imagine. When we took on Fuentez, then we both became hunted fugitives.

"This effort, it too was dubbed 'The Cuban Project'. In CIA Headquarters, the Cuban Desk devised a plan, approved by the Congressional Intelligence Committee, to force some changes in the prison system in Cuba; to move it away from its known inhumane treatment. The two men most involved in maintaining such harsh treatment were Fuentes and Pardo. We needed to get them removed if we were to push their system toward better treatment of inmates. You were our catalyst for action. A man in the DIA picked you out three months ago. Both Fuentes and Pardo were known to be Hanoi interrogators. It was decided we would help you along. You showed up too quickly and Carlos didn't know you were coming. Luckily, he was able to pick you up anyway and passed you to me."

Jay was shocked at Rosa's revelations. He could not believe what he was hearing. As she spoke he was shaking his head, not condemning not judging.

"We had to be very careful not to reveal ourselves in the process. It didn't work with me. When Pardo died I knew that was the end of it for me. I knew I had to get out of the country fast. Carlos told me I had no choice." She paused slightly. "Remember that newspaper article about Pardo?" Jay nodded his head. "You asked about how did Miami get the news so fast? That article was a plant. We did it to stir up concern and to get the ball rolling. And now that Fuentes has met some personally damaging impairments, there will be another article in the Miami papers. An article like Pardo's placing the blame on ex-prisoners who underwent bad treatment in the prison system." Rosa looked up at the sky before continuing.

"The Cuban Minister of the Interior is a woman. We believe she will relieve Fuentes of his position as soon as the press release is published. That is if Castro will allow it. That should help the system to get rid of the bad apples. Don't be surprised when you read about this in the papers. Your name will never appear, nor will mine. So when you go home, you shouldn't let anyone know where you were. Let that be a secret. OK?" She offered a warm smile.

"Another point you should be aware of. If Fuentes is not relieved of his position, he could come after you. Not personally come after you but send someone after you. There are others like Benitez Aguillar here in Miami who would take on the task to track you down. Don't let this scare you. Chances of it happening are minute. Just be aware. If you should feel suspicious about anything, call Agent Bascom in Miami." Rosa watched Jay intently. She couldn't take her eyes off him. This man had captured her heart. Bringing herself to reality was now a test of her character.

Jay answered. "You mean all the things which happened were half way planned to happen? What about you and me? Was that planned also? Were you toying with my emotions?" Jay wanted answers.

"No! Anything between you and me was real. It was what I wanted. You could have been my reward. But you were too good." She laughed. "I am glad you were faithful to your wife. That makes you an even better catch." She paused, her mind swirling and awash with hesitation. "Our friendship will live forever in my memory and hopefully in yours also! We both have to move on!" She tilted her head offering a smile. "Please feel free to look me up some day. You are a good man Jay Cobb." She turned and walked toward the waiting vehicle.

"Wait a minute. If you are going to be in Miami, after I buy some clothes why don't I take you out to a nice restaurant for dinner?"

"No Jay. It needs to stop here. But call me some day. OK?"

Jay sadly watched as Rosa turned and walked away. She wanted to be strong for Jay's sake. Rosa never looked back holding her head high in the wind, her hair flowing in the breeze. She opened the front door to Bascom's vehicle and before entering shouted across the rooftop at Jay. "Give Penny and Marcie my best regards." She closed the door and Bascom drove off.

Jay took a final look as they drove away. His eyes were clouded. He took a large breath to clear his head and stood motionless until the vehicle was out of sight. His search was over! Then he realized what Rosa said as she departed and thought, how did she know my Mom's name?